HANDY-VOLUME SERIES.

No. VII.

GERMAN TALES.

BY

BERTHOLD AUERBACH.

GERMAN TALES.

BY

BERTHOLD AUERBACH.

WITH AN INTRODUCTION

BY

CHARLES C. SHACKFORD.

BOSTON:
ROBERTS BROTHERS.
1869.

Entered according to Act of Congress, in the year 1869, by
ROBERTS BROTHERS,
In the Clerk's Office of the District Court of the United States, for the District of Massachusetts.

CAMBRIDGE:
PRESS OF JOHN WILSON AND SON.

CONTENTS.

	PAGE
CHRISTIAN GELLERT'S LAST CHRISTMAS	9
THE STEP-MOTHER	45
BENIGNA	165
RUDOLPH AND ELIZABETH	205
ERDMUTHA	273

INTRODUCTION.

BY C. C. SHACKFORD.

ERTHOLD AUERBACH was born at Nordstetten, a village in the Würtemberg part of the Black Forest, on the 28th of February, 1812. And it is interesting, as throwing light upon the manner in which some of the most seemingly casual observations in his writings are the result of his own personal experience, to recur to Eric's story, in "Villa Eden," of a friend of his, born on the 28th of February, who found it so troublesome to be continually told: "How fortunate that you were not born on the 29th, for then you would have had only one birthday every four years."

His parents were Jewish, and his early studies were in the Jewish Theology, at Hechingen and Carlsruhe; but he went afterwards to Stuttgardt, where he remained until 1832. He then studied at Tübingen, Munich, and Heidelberg.

His first essay in literature, which he himself does not call a book, was "The Jewish Nation and its Recent Literature." It was published in 1836;

"Spinoza," in 1837; "Poet and Merchant," in 1839. In 1842, he wrote a biography of Spinoza, to accompany a translation of his collected works. Up to this time, he seems to have been occupied with a line of study and thought connected more particularly with his Jewish descent; but, in 1842, he published a work entitled "Educated Citizens: a book for the Thinking Middle Classes." He also wrote, this year, "Rudolph and Elizabeth" and "What is Happiness?"

He now entered upon an entirely different career as an author, by a happy inspiration devoting himself to tales of German life, which at once gave him, not only a German, but a European, reputation. They were at once translated into the various languages of Northern Europe, and placed him in the front rank of writers of fiction. In 1845–6, he published the "Gevattersmann," or "Godfather," a sort of "Poor Richard's Almanac," which was, after a few years, superseded by his "Volkskalender," or "People's Almanac," that has been annually published up to the present time. In 1856 appeared "Barfüssle," or "Little Barefoot," and then "Joseph in the Snow," and "Edelweiss." These were followed by "On the Heights" and "The Country House on the Rhine." Besides these books, he has written "A Diary in Vienna, from Latour to Windischgrätz," containing an account of his revolutionary experiences; and he has also contributed several valuable critical papers on literature and art to the periodicals and newspapers.

Few authors can show a more worthy record of an industrious life and a fertile genius. Each book marks a change in the experience of the writer, a steady growth in ability to master his intellectual materials, and a higher and broader view of literary art. He wields, as he advances, a more facile pen, and his genius takes up the crude substances of life and nature, moulding them at his will according to its own universal laws. He is no longer a Jew or a German, but an interpreter of universal human experience.

In the preface to an edition of his collected works, written in 1863, Auerbach says: "On a mild day of autumn, like this to-day, twenty-six years ago, I wrote the preface to my first book, 'Spinoza.' I little imagined then what a path I should pursue, led on by the course of events and the impulse of creating. I now send forth an enlarged edition of my works, as a friendly greeting to the old friends and a welcome to the new. Whenever a new friendship is formed between two who have long followed their own separate life-paths, until familiarity and similarity of taste have united them, it is necessary to impart what lies behind their first meeting."

And this is not an inappropriate preface to this collection of tales. Those who have made an acquaintance with Auerbach's larger and more mature works will be glad to see these earlier studies for his masterpieces, as we may call them. They are sketches in which the germs of his later productions may be clearly traced. Only one of them comes, strictly speaking, among his "Village Tales," and this has not before been translated into English.

The "Village Tales" are taken, Auerbach himself informs us, from the families of his own native village. The first series are comparatively uninteresting, except as lasting pictures of manners and phases of provincial life which are fast disappearing, and will soon be found only in the books wherein they have been portrayed. In collecting and translating the tales for this volume, it was thought better to give such a variety as would be characteristic of Auerbach's genius in different directions, rather than to repeat the "everlasting peasant," by taking them from the earliest village stories.

Of "Christian Gellert," it has been said by Whittier: "It is full of beauty and of pathos. I have never been able to read it with dry eyes." To many others besides the revered poet, in his solitary musings, there will come a tone of cheerful encouragement and an exhortation to trust in those real, even if unseen, spiritual forces which abide in every higher thought, every generous expression, every sincere purpose for human good.

The novelist has given a life-like portrait of Gellert, who, born in 1715, and dying in 1769, is a prominent name in early German literature. Gervinus, in his history of German Literature, dwells upon the personal peculiarities of the man, entering as they did into the general character of his writings and making a part of their influence in the national literature; subject to moods of depression, introspective, dissatisfied with his own spiritual traits, he reminds us of Cowper, who, with his pious experiences, his fears, and his self-condemnations, tortured himself, but enriched our lyric poetry. Gervinus says of Gellert, "that he was continually longing after a stronger *dose* of devotional feelings." "He blushed bashfully at praise, but felt gratified at receiving it." He trembled from a mingled feeling of pain and pleasure on hearing an ode which had been written in his eulogy, after a false report of his death had been spread. This ode closed by saying, "earth weeps, but heaven is glad." He was a personal friend to the students, and his lectures were thronged, not only by them, but by the military, the nobility, and the citizens. He was consulted in spiritual matters like a father-confessor, and exercised a deep influence over students and a large circle of women.

The "Step-mother" is full of a deep and subtle knowledge of character, and is pervaded by a quiet spirit of wisdom, showing, better than could be done by many long essays, how moral influence can be exerted with effect, how disastrous are all concealments, and how short-sighted are all worldly wisdoms.

"Benigna" has been translated from the "Volks Kalender" for 1869, and, short as it is, presents such a picture as Auerbach alone succeeds in giving. The real end of life is shown without moralizing, and highest truths are taught without being directly proclaimed.

The tale of "Rudolph and Elizabeth," Auerbach calls "an idyl of cultivated life." It was written before the "Village Tales," which are idyls of peasant life, and the author himself gives this account of it: "On the Rhine, in 1841, soon after the translation of Spinoza's collected works, I undertook to treat individual problems of speculative ethics in so-called philosophical novels. They were to be made up, not so much of events and actual conflicts in life, as of conversations and the unfolding of definite subjects of thought."

This method, which Auerbach wholly dropped in his village stories, he has resumed in some degree in his latest and most complete work, "The Country House on the Rhine." There the two characteristics of story-telling and philosophic speculation are fused together more perfectly than in any other recent German writer of fiction, even if an entire commingling of the two into one higher form has not been effected.

Lessing says that the whole secret of novel writing is, "Good stories, well told." But as civilization becomes more complex, and life more intense and varied, a good story includes something more than a simple peasant's life, however well it may be told, and something more than a series of extraordinary catastrophes, however graphically and naturally they may be described. To tell a story well is something else than to depict external events, paint minutely costumes and scenery, and dash the canvas with high colors and grotesque forms. The novelist must interest by depicting those characters who are moved by the interests of the time. He must not so much discuss abstract questions, as place the problems before us in living forms and with a concrete existence.

In another of his early prefaces, Auerbach writes: "It is nineteen years since I left thee, my native village. The silent attraction of childhood's love has now drawn my spirit back to thee, and, with indescribable emotions, I call up again the tones that have long since died away. Before my window rolls the mighty Rhine, that main artery of Germany; a gleam of light, like a ribbon of silver, streams along the farther shore, and the waves ripple tremulously in the moon-beams. The waters of the Neckar, which rustle by my birthplace, have been joyfully received into the bosom of the great river and are borne by it onward to the sea. So may these pictures of German life, which I send out into the fatherland, mingle like a rivulet out of my native hills in the great stream of German life."

The pioneer in this field of simple peasant life was Immermann, whose "Münchhausen" is referred to by Auerbach in the story of "Rudolph and Elizabeth." This vein became exhausted, but in it was embodied only one side of Auerbach's genius. A French critic, St. Renè Taillandier, in 1857, wrote of him: "The author of 'Village Stories' will have a success as great as that which attended his early efforts, only in undertaking great problems, and depicting the vices or the virtues of the real society of his times." Fortunately, he has advanced in this path.

The "Volks Kalender" tales are marked by all the characteristics of his genius, and deserve to be more widely known. They are of essential human interest, and are graphic representations, sometimes pathetic and sometimes humorous, of our common humanity in a great variety of forms.

"Erdmutha" is one of the author's most effective later series of German tales. The readers of Auerbach will meet here in the heroine a type of character with which they are already somewhat familiar, but which has traits of its own that make it interesting and attractive.

No one can rise from the reading of these stories

without a deeper insight into the spiritual laws that interpenetrate all human life, and those subtle influences of character and temperament which are continually operating within and around us. They are sketches that are elsewhere filled out with more completeness, but they are valuable in themselves, and valuable helps to the full understanding of Auerbach's genius as a portrayer of human nature and human character.

It is perhaps proper to state that all the tales comprised in this volume are now published in this country for the first time.

CHRISTIAN GELLERT.

CHRISTIAN GELLERT.

HREE o'clock had just struck from the tower of St. Nicholas, Leipzig, on the afternoon of Dec. 22d, 1768, when a man, wrapped in a loose overcoat, came out of the door of the University. His countenance was exceedingly gentle, and on his features cheerfulness still lingered, for he had been gazing upon a hundred cheerful faces; after him thronged a troop of students, who, holding back, allowed him to precede them: the passengers in the streets saluted him, and some students, who pressed forwards and hurried past him homewards, saluted him quite reverentially. He returned their salutations with a surprised and almost deprecatory air, and yet he knew, and could not conceal from himself, that he was one of the best beloved, not only in the good city of Leipzig, but in all lands far and wide.

It was Christian Fürchtegott Gellert, the Poet of Fables, Hymns, and Lays, who was just leaving his college.

When we read his Lectures upon Morals, which were not printed until after his death, we obtain but a very incomplete idea of the great power with which they came immediately from Gellert's mouth. Indeed, it was his voice and the touching manner in which he delivered his Lectures, that made so deep an impression upon his hearers; and Rabener was right when once he wrote to a friend, that "the philanthropic voice" of Gellert belonged to his words.

Above all, however, it was the amiable and pure personal character of Gellert, which vividly and edifyingly impressed young hearts. Gellert was himself the best example of pure moral teaching; and the best which a teacher can give his pupils is faith in the victorious might, and the stability of the eternal moral laws. His lessons were for the Life, for his life in itself was a lesson. Many a victory over the troubles of life, over temptations of every kind, aye, many an elevation to nobility of thought, and to purity of action, had its origin in that lecture-hall, at the feet of Gellert.

It was as though Gellert felt that it was the last time he would deliver these Lectures; that those words so often and so impressively uttered would be heard no more from his mouth; and there was a peculiar sadness, yet a peculiar strength, in all he said that day.

He had this day earnestly recommended Modesty and Humility; and it appeared almost offensive to him, that people as he went should tempt him in regard to these very virtues; for continually he heard men whisper, "That is Gellert!"

What is fame, and what is honor? A cloak of many colors, without warmth, without protection: and now, as he walked along, his heart literally froze in his bosom, as he confessed to himself that he had as yet done nothing, nothing which could give him a feeling of real satisfaction. Men honored him and loved him: but what was all that worth? His innermost heart could not be satisfied with that; in his own estimation he deserved no meed of praise; and where, where was there any evidence of that higher and purer life which he would fain bring about! Then, again, the Spirit would comfort him and say,—"Much seed is lost, much falls in stony places, and much on good ground and brings forth seven fold."

His inmost soul heard not the consolation, for his body was weak and sore burdened from his youth up, and in his latter days yet more than ever: and there are conditions of the body in which the most elevating words, and the cheeriest notes of joy, strike dull and heavy on the soul. It is one of the bitterest experiences of life to discover how little one man can really be to another. How joyous is that youthful freshness which can believe that, by a thought transferred to another's heart, we can induce him to become another being, to live according to what he must acknowledge true, to throw aside his previous delusions, and return to the right path!

The youngsters go their way! Do your words follow after? Whither are they going? What are now their thoughts? What manner of life will be theirs? "My heart yearns after them, but cannot be with them: oh, how happy were those messengers of the Spirit, who cried aloud to youth or manhood the words of the Spirit, that they must leave their former ways, and thenceforth change to other beings! Pardon me, O God! that I would fain be like them; I am weak and vile, and yet, methinks, there must be words as yet unheard, unknown—oh! where are they, those words which at once lay hold upon the soul?"

With such heavy thoughts went Gellert away from his

college-gate to Rosenthal. There was but one small pathway cleared, but the passers cheerfully made way for him, and walked in the snow that they might leave him the pathway unimpeded: but he felt sad, and "as if each tree had somewhat to cast at him." Like all men really pure, and cleaving to the good with all their might, Gellert was not only far from contenting himself with work already done: he also, in his anxiety to be doing, almost forgot that he had ever done any thing, and thus he was, in the best sense of the word, modest; he began with each fresh day his course of action afresh, as if he now for the first time had any thing to accomplish. And yet he might have been happy, in the reflection how brightly beamed his teaching for ever, though his own life was often clouded. For as the sun which glows on summer days, still lives as concentrated warmth in wine, and somewhere on some winter night warms up a human heart, so is the sunshine in that man's life whose vocation it is to impart to others the conceptions of his own mind. Nay, there is here far more; for the refreshing draught here offered is not diminished, though thousands drink thereof.

Twilight had set in when Gellert returned home to his dwelling, which had for its sign a "Schwarz Brett" or "black board." His old servant, Sauer by name, took off his overcoat: and his amanuensis, Gödike, asked whether the Professor had any commands; being answered in the negative, Gödike retired, and Sauer lighted the lamp upon the study-table. "Some letters have arrived," said he, as he pointed to several upon the table: Gellert inclined his head, and Sauer retired also. Outside, however, he stood awhile with Gödike, and both spoke sorrowfully of the fact that the Professor was evidently again suffering severely. "There is a melancholy," said Gödike, "and it is the most usual, in which the inward depression easily changes to displeasure against every one, and the household of the melancholic suffers thereby intolerably; for the displeasure turns against them, — no one does any thing properly, nothing is in its place. How very different is Gellert's melancholy! Not a soul suffers from it but himself, against himself alone his gloomy thoughts turn, and towards every other creature he is always kind, amiable, and obliging: he bites his lips; but when he speaks to any one, he is wholly good, forbearing, and self-forgetful."

Whilst they were talking together, Gellert was sitting in his room, and had lighted a pipe to dispel the agitation which he would experience in opening his letters; and while smoking, he could read them much more comfortably. He reproached himself for smoking, which was said to be injurious to his health, but he could not quite give up the "horrible practice," as he called it.

He first examined the addresses and seals of the letters which had arrived, then quietly opened and read them. A fitful smile passed over his features; there were letters from well known friends, full of love and admiration, but from strangers also, who, in all kinds of heart-distress, took counsel of him. He read the letters full of friendly applause, first hastily, that he might have the right of reading them again, and that he might not know all at once; and when he had read a friend's letter for the second time, he sprang from his seat and cried, "Thank God! thank God! that I am so fortunate as to have such friends!" To his inwardly diffident nature, these helps were a real requirement; they served to cheer him, and only those who did not know him called his joy at the reception of praise.—conceit; it was, on the contrary, the truest modesty. How often did he sit there, and all that he had taught and written, all that he had ever been to men in word and deed, faded, vanished, and died away, and he appeared to himself but a useless servant of the world. His friends he answered immediately; and as his inward melancholy vanished, and the philanthropy, nay, the sprightliness of his soul beamed forth, when he was among men and looked in a living face, so was it also with his letters. When he bethought him of the friends to whom he was writing, he not only acquired tranquillity, that virtue for which his whole life long he strove; but his loving nature received new life, and only by slight intimations did he betray the heaviness and dejection which weighed upon his soul. He was, in the full sense of the word, "philanthropic," in the sight of good men; and in thoughts for their welfare, there was for him a real happiness, and a joyous animation.

When, however, he had done writing, and felt lonely again, the gloomy spirits came back: he had seated himself, wishing to raise his thoughts for composing a sacred song; but he was ill at ease, and had no power to express that inward, firm, and self-rejoicing might of faith which lived in him. Again and again the scoffers and freethinkers rose up before his thoughts: he must refute their objections, and not until that was done did he become himself.

It is a hard position, when a creative spirit cannot forget the adversaries which on all sides oppose him in the world: they come unsummoned to the room and will not be expelled; they peer over the shoulder, and tug at the hand which fain would write; they turn images upside down, and distort the thoughts; and here and there, from ceiling and wall, they grin, and scoff, and oppose: and what was just gushing as an aspiration from the soul, is converted to a confused absurdity.

At such a time, the spirit, courageous and self-dependent, must take refuge in itself and show a firm front to a world of foes.

A strong nature boldly hurls his inkstand at the Devil's head; goes to battle with his opponents with words both written and spoken; and keeps his own individuality free from the perplexities with which opponents disturb all that has been previously done, and make the soul unsteadfast and unnerved for what is to come.

Gellert was no battling, defiant nature, which relies upon itself; he did not hurl his opponents down and go his way; he would convince them, and so they were always ready to encounter him. And as the applause of his friends rejoiced him, so the opposition of his enemies could sink him in deep dejection. Besides, he had always been weakly; he had, as he himself complained, in addition to frequent coughs, and a pain in his loins, a continual gnawing and pressure in the centre of his chest, which accompanied him from his first rising in the morning until he slept at night.

Thus he sat for a while, in deep dejection: and, as often before, his only wish was, that God would give him grace whereby when his hour was come, he might die piously and tranquilly.

It was past midnight when he sought his bed and extinguished his light.

AND the buckets at the well go up and go down.

About the same hour, in Duben Forest, the rustic Christopher was rising from his bed. As with steel and flint he scattered sparks upon the tinder, in kindling himself a light, his wife, awaking, cried:

"Why that heavy sigh?"

"Ah! life is a burden: I'm the most harassed mortal in the world. The pettiest office-clerk may now be abed in peace, and needn't break off his sleep, while I must go out and brave wind and weather."

"Be content," replied his wife: "why, I dreamt you had actually been made magistrate, and wore something on your head like a king's crown."

"Oh! you women; as though what you see isn't enough, you like to chatter about what you dream."

"Light the lamp, too," said his wife, "and I'll get up and make you a nice porridge."

The peasant, putting a candle in his lantern, went to the stable; and after he had given some fodder to the horses, he seated himself upon the manger. With his hands squeezed between his knees and his head bent down, he reflected over and over again what a wretched existence he had of it. "Why," thought he, "are so many men so well-off, so comfortable, whilst you must be always toiling? What care I if envy be not a virtue?—and yet I'm not envious, I don't grudge others being well-off, only I should like to be well-off too: oh, for a quiet, easy life! Am I not worse off than a horse? He gets his fodder at the proper time, and takes no care about it. Why did my father make my brother a minister? He gets his salary without any trouble, sits in a warm room, has no care in the world; and I must slave, and torment myself."

Strange to say, his very next thought, that he would like to be made local magistrate, he would in no wise confess to himself.

He sat still a long while; then he went back again to the sitting-room, past the kitchen, where the fire was burning cheerily. He seated himself at the table and waited for his morning-porridge. On the table lay an open book; his children had been reading it the previous evening: involuntarily taking it up, he began to read. Suddenly he started, rubbed his eyes, and then read again. How comes this verse here just at this moment? He kept his hand upon the book, and so easily had he caught the words, that he repeated them to himself softly with his lips, and nodded several times, as much as to say: "That's true!" And he said aloud: "It's all there together: short and sweet!" and he was still staring at it, when his wife brought in the smoking porridge. Taking off his cap, he folded his hands and said aloud: —

"Accept God's gifts with resignation,
Content to lack what thou hast not:
In every lot there's consolation;
There's trouble, too, in every lot!"

The wife looked at her husband with amazement. What a strange expression was upon his face! And as he sat down and began to eat, she said: "What is the meaning of that grace? What has come to you? Where did you find it?"

"It is the best of all graces, the very best, — real God's word. Yes, and all your-life you've never made such nice porridge before. You must have put something special in it!"

"I don't know what you mean. Stop! There's the book

lying there — ah! that's it — and it's by Gellert, of Leipzig."

"What! Gellert, of Leipzig! Men with ideas like that don't live now; there may have been such, a thousand years ago, in holy lands, not among us; those are the words of a saint of old."

"And I tell you they are by Gellert, of Leipzig, of whom your brother has told us; in fact, he was his tutor, and haven't you heard how pious and good he is?"

"I wouldn't have believed that such men still lived, and so near us, too, as Leipzig."

"Well, but those who lived a thousand years ago were also once living creatures: and over Leipzig is just the same heaven, and the same sun shines, and the same God rules, as over all other cities."

"Oh! yes, my brother has an apt pupil in you!"

"Well, and why not? I've treasured up all he told us of Professor Gellert."

"Professor!"

"Yes, Professor!"

"A man with such a proud, new-fangled title couldn't write any thing like that!"

"He didn't give himself the title, and he is poor enough withal! and how hard it has fared with him! Even from childhood he has been well acquainted with poverty: his father was a poor minister in Haynichen, with thirteen children; and Gellert, when quite a little fellow, was obliged to be a copying office-clerk: who can tell whether he didn't then contract that physical weakness of his? And now, that he's an old man, things will never go better with him; he has often no wood, and must be pinched with cold. It is with him, perhaps, as with that student of whom your brother has told us, who is as poor as a rat, and yet must read ; and so in winter he lies in bed with an empty stomach, until day is far advanced ; and he has his book before him, and first he takes out one hand to hold his book, and then, when that is numb with cold, the other. Ah! tongue cannot tell how poorly the man must live; and yet your brother has told me, if he has but a few pounds, he doesn't think at all of himself; he always looks out for one still poorer than he is, and then gives all away: and he's always engaged in aiding and assisting others. Oh! dear, and yet he is so poor ! May be at this moment he is hungry and cold; and he is said to be in ill-health, besides."

"Wife, I would willingly do the man a good turn if I could. If, now, he had some land, I would plough, and sow, and reap, and carry, and thresh by the week together for him. I should like to pay him attention in such a way that he might know there was at least one who cared for him. But his profession is one in which I can't be of any use to him."

"Well, just seek him out and speak with him once; you are going to-day, you know, with your wood to Leipzig. Seek him out and thank him ; that sort of thing does such a man's heart good. Anybody can see him."

"Yes, yes; I should like much to see him, and hold out to him my hand, — but not empty: I wish I had something!"

"Speak to your brother, and get him to give you a note to him."

"No, no; say nothing to my brother; but it might be possible for me to meet him in the street. Give me my Sunday coat; it will come to no harm under my cloak."

When his wife brought him the coat, she said: — "If, now, Gellert had a wife, or a household of his own, one might send him something; but your brother says he is a bachelor, and lives quite alone."

Christopher had never before so cheerily harnessed his horses and put them to his wood-laden wagon; for a long while he had not given his hand so gayly to his wife at parting as to-day. Now he started with his heavily-laden vehicle through the village; the wheels creaked and crackled in the snow. At the parsonage he stopped, and looked away yonder where his brother was still sleeping; he thought he would wake him and tell him his intention: but suddenly he whipped up his horses, and continued his route. He wouldn't yet bind himself to his intention — perchance it was but a passing thought; he doesn't own that to himself, but he says to himself that he will surprise his brother with the news of what he has done; and then his thoughts wandered away to the good man still sleeping yonder in the city; and he hummed the verse to himself in an old familiar tune.

Wonderfully in life do effects manifest themselves, of which we have no trace. Gellert, too, heard in his dreams a singing; he knew not what it was, but it rang so consolingly, so joyously! . . . Christopher drove on, and he felt as though a bandage had been taken from his eyes; he reflected what a nice house, what a bonny wife and rosy children he had, and how warm the cloak which he had thrown over him was, and how well off were both man and beast; and through the still night he drove along, and beside him sat a spirit; but not an illusion of the brain, such as in olden time men conjured up to their terror; a good spirit sat beside him — beside the woodman who, his whole life long, had never believed that any thing could have power over him but what had hands and feet.

It is said, that on troublous nights, evil spirits settle upon the necks of men, and belabor them so that they gasp and sweat for very terror; quite another sort which it was to-day sat by the woodman: and his heart was warm, and its beating quick.

In ancient times, men also carried loads of wood through the night, that heretics might be burned thereon: these men thought they were doing a good deed in helping to execute justice; and who can say how painful it was to their hearts, when they were forced to think: To-morrow, on this wood which now you carry, will shriek, and crackle, and gasp, a human being like yourself? Who can tell what black spirits settled on the necks of those who bore the wood to make the funeral-pile? How very different was it to-day with our woodman Christopher!

And earlier still, in ancient times, men brought wood to the temple, whereon they offered victims in the honor of God; and, according to their notions, they did a good deed: for when words can no longer suffice to express the fervency of the heart, it gladly offers what it prizes, what it dearly loves, as a proof of its devotion, of the earnestness of its intent.

How differently went Christopher from the Duben Forest, upon his way! He knew not whether he were intending to bring a purer offering than men had brought in by-gone ages; but his heart grew warm within him.

It was day as he arrived before the gates of Leipzig. Here there met him a funeral-procession; behind the bier the scholars of St. Thomas, in long black cloaks, were chanting. Christopher stopped, and raised his hat.

Whom were they burying? Supposing it were Gellert! Yes, surely he thought, it is he: and how gladly, said he to himself, would you now have done him a kindness, — aye, even given him your wood? Yes, indeed, you would and now he is dead, and you cannot give him any help!

As soon as the train had passed, Christopher asked who was being buried. It was a simple burgher, it was not Gellert; and in the deep breath which Christopher drew lay a double signification: on the one hand, was joy that Gellert was not dead; on the other, a still small voice whispered to him that he had now really promised to give him the wood: ah! but whom had he promised? — himself: and it is easy to argue with one's own conscience.

Superstition babbles of conjuring-spells, by which, without the co-operation of the patient, the evil spirit can be summarily ejected. It would be convenient if one had that power, but, in truth, it is not so: it is long ere the evil desire and the evil habit are removed from the soul into which they have nestled; and the will, for a long while in bondage, must co-operate, if a releasing spell from without is to set the prisoner free. One can only be guided, but himself must move his feet.

As Christopher now looked about him, he found that he had stopped close by an inn; he drove his load a little aside, went into the parlor, and drank a glass of warmed beer. There was already a goodly company, and not far from Christopher sat a husbandman with his son, a student here, who was telling him how there had been lately quite a stir. Professor Gellert had been ill, and riding a well-trained horse had been recommended for his health. Now Prince Henry of Prussia, during the Seven Years' War, at the occupation of Leipzig, had sent him a piebald, that had died a short time ago; and the Elector, hearing of it, had sent Gellert from Dresden another — a chestnut — with golden bridle, blue velvet saddle, and gold-embroidered housings. Half the city had assembled when the groom, a man with iron-gray hair, brought the horse; and for several days it was to be seen at the stable; but Gellert dared not mount it, it was so young and high-spirited. The rustic now asked his son, whether the Professor did not make money enough to procure a horse of his own, to which the son answered, — "Certainly not. His salary is but 125 dollars, and his further gains are inconsiderable. His Lectures on Morals he gives publicly, *i. e.*, gratis, and he has hundreds of hearers; and, therefore, at his other lectures, which must be paid for, he has so many the fewer. To be sure, he has now and then presents from grand patrons; but no one gives him, once and for all, enough to live upon, and to have all over with a single acknowledgment."

Our friend Christopher started as he heard this; he had quite made up his mind to take Gellert the wood: but he had yet to do it. How easy were virtue, if will and deed were the same thing! if performance could immediately succeed to the moment of burning enthusiasm! But one must make way over obstacles; over those that outwardly lie in one's path, and over those that are hidden deep in the heart; and negligence has a thousand very cunning advocates.

How many go forth, prompted by good intentions, but let little hindrances turn them from their way — entirely from their way of life! In front of the house Christopher met other woodmen whom he knew, and — "You are stirring betimes!" "Prices are good to-day!" "But little comes to the market now!" was the cry from all sides. Christopher wanted to say that all that didn't concern him, but he was ashamed to confess what his design was, and an inward voice told him he must not lie. Without answering he joined the rest, and wended his way to the market; and on the road he thought, — "There are Peter, and Godfrey, and John, who have seven times your means, and not one of them, I'm sure, would think of doing any thing of this kind; why will you be the kind-hearted fool? Stay! what matters it what others do or leave undone? Every man shall answer for himself. Yes, but go to market — it is better it should be so; yes, certainly, much better: sell your wood — who knows? perhaps he doesn't want it — and take him the proceeds, or at least the greater portion. But is the wood still yours? You have, properly speaking, already given it away; it has only not been taken from your keeping." . . .

There are people who cannot give; they can only let a thing be taken either by the hand of chance, or by urgency and entreaty. Christopher had such fast hold of possession, that it was only after sore wrestling that he let go; and yet his heart was kind, at least to-day it was so disposed, but the tempter whispered, — "It is not easy to find so good-natured a fellow as you. How readily would you have given, had the man been in want, and your good intention must go for the deed." Still, on the other hand, there was something in him which made opposition, — an echo from those hours, when, in the still night, he was driving hither, — and it burned in him like sacred fire, and it said, "You must now accomplish what you intended. Certainly no one knows of it, and you are responsible to no one; but you know of it yourself, and

One above you knows, and how shall you be justified?" And he said to himself, "I'll stand by this: look, it is just nine; if no one ask the price of your wood until ten o'clock, until the stroke of ten, — until it has done striking, I mean; if no one ask, then the wood belongs to Professor Gellert: but if a buyer come, then it is a sign that you need not — should not give it away. There, that's all settled. But how? what means this? Can you make your good deed dependent on such a chance as this? No, no; I don't mean it. But yet — yet — only for a joke, I'll try it."

Temptation kept him turning as it were in a circle, and still he stood with an apparently quiet heart by his wagon in the market. The people who heard him muttering in this way to himself looked at him with wonder, and passed by him to another wagon, as though he had not been there. It struck nine. Can you wait patiently another hour? Christopher lighted his pipe, and looked calmly on, while this and that load was driven off. It struck the quarter, half-hour, three-quarters. Christopher now put his pipe in his pocket; it had long been cold, and his hands were almost frozen; all his blood had rushed to his heart. Now it struck the full hour, stroke after stroke. At first he counted; then he fancied he had lost a stroke and miscalculated. Either voluntarily or involuntarily, he said to himself, when it had finished striking, "You're wrong; it is nine, not ten." He turned round that he might not see the dial, and thus he stood for some time, with his hands upon the wagon-rack, gazing at the wood. He knew not how long he had been thus standing, when some one tapped him on the shoulder, and said, "How much for the load of wood?"

Christopher turned round: there was an odd look of irresolution in his eyes as he said: "Eh? eh? what time is it?"

"Half-past ten."

"Then the wood is now no longer mine—at least to sell:" and, collecting himself, he became suddenly warm, and with firm hand turned his horses round, and begged the woodmen who accompanied him to point him out the way to the house with the "Schwarz Brett," Dr. Junius's. There he delivered a full load: at each log he took out of the wagon, he smiled oddly. The wood-measurer measured the wood carefully, turning each log and placing it exactly, that there might not be a crevice anywhere.

"Why are you so over-particular to-day, pray?" asked Christopher, and he received for answer:

"Professor Gellert must have a fair load; every shaving kept back from him were a sin."

Christopher laughed aloud, and the wood-measurer looked at him with amazement; for such particularity generally provoked a quarrel. Christopher had still some logs over: these he kept by him on the wagon. At this moment the servant Sauer came up, and asked to whom the wood belonged.

"To Professor Gellert," answered Christopher.

"The man's mad! it isn't true. Professor Gellert has not bought any wood; it is my business to look after that."

"He has not bought it, and yet it is his!" cried Christopher.

Sauer was on the point of giving the mad peasant a hearty scolding, raising his voice so much the louder, as it was striking eleven by St. Nicholas. At this moment, however, he became suddenly mute; for yonder from the University there came, with tired gait, a man of a noble countenance: at every step he made, on this side and on that, off came the hats and the caps of the passers-by, and Sauer simply called out, "There comes the Professor himself."

What a peculiar expression passed over Christopher's face! He looked at the new-comer, and so earnest was his gaze, that Gellert, who always walked with his head bowed, suddenly looked up. Christopher said: "Mr. Gellert, I am glad to see you still alive."

"I thank you," said Gellert, and made as though he would pass on; but Christopher stepped up closer to him, and, stretching out his hand to him, said: "I have taken the liberty — I should like — will you give me your hand, Mr. Gellert?"

Gellert drew his long thin hand out of his muff and placed it in the hard oaken-like hand of the peasant; and at this moment, when the peasant's hand lay in the scholar's palm, as one felt the other's pressure in actual living grasp, there took place, though the mortal actors in the scene were all unconscious of it, a renewal of that healthy life which alone can make a people one.

How long had the learned world, wrapped up in itself, separated from the fellow-men around, thought in Latin, felt as foreigners, and lived buried in contemplation of by-gone worlds! From the time of Gellert commences the ever-increasing unity of good-fellowship throughout all classes of life, kept up by mutual giving and receiving. As the scholar — as the solitary poet endeavors to work upon others by lays that quicken, and songs that incite, so he in his turn is a debtor to his age, and the lonely thinking and writing become the property of all; but the effects are not seen in a moment; for higher than the most highly gifted spirit of any single man is the spirit of a nation. With the pressure which Gellert and the peasant exchanged commenced a mighty change in universal life, which never more can cease to act.

"Permit me to enter your room?" said Christopher, and Gellert nodded assent. He was so courteous that he motioned to the peasant to enter first; however, Sauer went close after him: he thought it must be a madman; he must protect his master; the man looked just as if he were drunk. Gellert, with his amanuensis, Gödike, followed them.

Gellert, however, felt that the man must be actuated by pure motives: he bade the others retire, and took Christopher alone into his study; and, as he clasped his left with his own right hand, he asked: "Well, my good friend, what is your business?"

"Eh? oh! nothing — I've only brought you a load of wood there — a fair, full load; however, I'll give you the few logs which I have in my wagon, as well."

"My good man, my servant Sauer looks after buying my wood."

"It is no question of buying. No, my dear sir, I give it to you."

"Give it to me? Why me particularly?"

"Oh! sir, you do not know at all what good you do, what good you have done me; and my wife was right: why should there not be really pious men in our day too? Surely the sun still shines as he shone thousands of years ago; all is now the same as then; and the God of old is still living."

"Certainly, certainly; I am glad to see you so pious."

"Ah! believe me, dear sir, I am not always so pious; and that I am so disposed to-day, is owing to you. We have no more confessionals now, but I can confess to you: and you have taken a heavier load from my heart than a wagon-load of wood. Oh! sir, I am not what I was. In my early days I was a high-spirited, merry lad, and out in the field, and in-doors in the inn and the spinning-room, there was none who could sing against me; but that is long past. What has a man on whose head the grave-blossoms are growing," and he pointed to his gray head, "to do with all that trash? And besides, the Seven Years' War has put a stop to all our singing. But last night, in the midst of the fearful cold, I sang a lay set expressly for me — all old tunes go to it: and it seemed to me as though I saw a sign-post which pointed I know not whither — or, nay, I do know whither." And now the peasant related how discontented and unhappy in mind he had been, and how the words in the lay had all at once raised his spirits and accompanied him upon the journey, like a good fellow who talks to one cheerfully.

At this part of the peasant's tale, Gellert folded his hands in silence, and the peasant concluded: "How I always envied others, I cannot now think why; but you I do envy, sir: I should like to be as you."

And Gellert answered: "I thank God, and rejoice greatly that my writings have been of service to you. Think not so well of me. Would God I were really the good man I appear in your eyes! I am far from being such as I should, such as I would fain be. I write my books for my own improvement also, to show myself as well as others what manner of men we should be."

Laughing, the peasant replied: "You put me in mind of the story my poor mother used to tell of the old minister; he stood up once in the pulpit and said: 'My dear friends, I speak not only for you, but for myself also; I, too, have need of it.'"

Christopher laughed outrageously when he had finished, and Gellert smiled, and said: "Yes, whoever in the darkness lighteth another with a lamp, lighteth himself also; and the light is not part of ourselves,—it is put into our hands by Him who hath appointed the suns their courses."

The peasant stood speechless, and looked upon the ground: there was something within him which took away the power of looking up; he was only conscious that it ill became him to laugh so loudly just now, when he told the story of the old minister.

A longer pause ensued, and Gellert seemed to be lost in reflection upon this reference to a minister's work, for he said half to himself: "Oh! how would it fulfil my dearest wish to be a village-pastor! To move about among my people, and really be one with them; the friend of their souls my whole life long, never to lose them out of my sight! Yonder goes one whom I have led into the right way; there another, with whom I still wrestle, but whom I shall assuredly save; and in them all the teaching lives which God proclaims by me. Did I not think that I should be acting against my duty, I would this moment choose a country life for the remnant of my days. When I look from my window over the country, I have before me the broad sky, of which we citizens know but little, a scene entirely new; there I stand and lose myself for half-an-hour in gazing and in thinking. Yes, good friend, envy no man in the rank of scholars. Look at me; I am almost always ill; and what a burden is a sickly body! How strong, on the contrary, are you! I am never happier than when, without being remarked, I can watch a dinner-table thronged by hungry men and maids. Even if these folks be not generally so happy as their superiors, at table they are certainly happier."

"Yes, sir; we relish our eating and drinking. And, lately, when felling and sorting that wood below, I was more than usually lively; it seems as though I had a notion I was to do some good with it."

"And must I permit you to make me a present?" asked Gellert, resting his chin upon his left hand.

The peasant answered, "It is not worth talking about."

"Nay, it might be well worth talking about; but I accept your present. It is pride not to be ready to accept a gift. Is not all we have a gift from God? And what one man gives another, he gives, as is most appropriately said, for God's sake. Were I your minister, I should be pleased to accept a present from you. You see, good friend, we men have no occasion to thank each other. You have given me nothing of yours, and I have given you nothing of mine. That the trees grow in the forest is none of your doing, it is the work of the Creator and Preserver of the world; and the soil is not yours; and the sun and the rain are not yours; they all are the works of His hand; and if, perchance, I have some healthy thoughts rising up in my soul, which benefit my fellow-men, it is none of mine, it is His doing. The word is not mine, and the spirit is not mine; and I am but an instrument in His hand. Therefore one man needs not to utter words of thanks to his fellow, if every one would but acknowledge who it really is that gives."

The peasant looked up in astonishment. Gellert remarked it, and said: "Understand me aright. I thank you from my heart; you have done a kind action. But that the trees grow is none of yours, and it is none of mine that thoughts arise in me; every one simply tills his field, and tends his woodland, and the honest, assiduous toil he gives thereto is his virtue. That you felled, loaded, and brought the wood, and wish no recompense for your labor, is very thankworthy. My wood was more easily felled; but those still nights which I and all of my calling pass in heavy thought — who can tell what toil there is in them? There is in the world an adjustment which no one sees, and which but seldom discovers itself; and this and that shift thither and hither, and the scales of the balance become even, and then ceases all distinction between 'mine' and 'thine,' and in the still forest rings an axe for me, and in the silent night my spirit thinks and my pen writes for you."

The peasant passed both his hands over his temples, and his look was as though he said to himself, "Where are you? Are you still in the world? Is it a mortal man who speaks to you? Are you in Leipzig, in that populous city where men jostle one another for gain and bare existence?"

Below might be heard the creaking of the saw as the wood was being sundered: and now the near-horse neighs, and Christopher is in the world again. "It may injure the horse to stand so long in the cold; and no money for the wood! but perhaps a sick horse to take home into the bargain; that would be too much," he thought.

"Yes, yes, Mr. Professor," said he — he had his hat under his arm, and was rubbing his hands — "yes, I am delighted with what I have done; and I value the lesson, believe me, more than ten loads of wood: and never shall I forget you to my dying day. And though I see you are not so poor as I had imagined, still I don't regret it. Oh! no, certainly not at all."

"Eh! did you think me so very poor, then?"

"Yes, miserably poor."

"I have always been poor, but God has never suffered me to be a single day without necessaries. I have in the world much happiness which I have not deserved, and much unhappiness I have not, which perchance I have deserved. I have found much favor with both high and low, for which I cannot sufficiently thank God. And now tell me, cannot I give you something, or obtain something for you? You are local magistrate, I presume?"

"Why so?"

"You look like it: you might be."

Christopher had taken his hat into his hands, and was crumpling it up now; he half closed his eyes, and with a sly inquiring glance, he peered at Gellert. Suddenly, however, the expression of his face changed, and the muscles quivered, as he said: "Sir, what a man are you! How you can dive into the recesses of one's heart! I have really pined night and day, and been cross with the whole world, because I could not be magistrate, and you, sir, you have actually helped to overcome that in me. Oh! sir, as soon as I read that verse in your book, I had an idea, and now I see still more plainly that you must be a man of God, who can pluck the heart from one's bosom, and turn it round and round. I had thought I could never have another moment's happiness, if my neighbor, Hans Gottlieb should be magistrate: and with that verse of yours, it has been with me as when one calms the blood with a magic spell."

"Well, my good friend, I am rejoiced to hear it: believe me, every one has in himself alone a whole host to govern. What can so strongly urge men to wish to govern others? What can it profit you to be local magistrate, when to accomplish your object you must perhaps do something wrong? What were the fame, not only of a village, but even of the whole world, if you could have no self-respect? Let it suffice for you to perform your daily duties with uprightness; let your joys be centred in your wife and children, and you will be happy. What need you more? Think not that honor and station would make you happy. Rejoice, and again I say, rejoice: 'a contented spirit is a continual feast.' I often whisper this to myself when I feel disposed to give way to dejection: and although misery be not our fault, yet lack of endurance and of patience in misery is undoubtedly our fault."

"I would my wife were here too, that she also might hear this; I grudge myself the hearing of it all alone; I cannot remember it all properly, and yet I should like to tell it to her word for word. Who would have thought, that, by standing upon a load of wood, one could get a peep into heaven!"

Gellert in silence bowed his head; and afterwards he said: "Yes, rejoice in your deed, as I do in your gift. Your wood is sacrificial-wood. In olden time — and it was right in principle, because man could not yet offer prayer and thanks in spirit — it was a custom and ordinance to bring something from one's possessions, as a proof of devotion: this was a sacrifice. And the more important the gift to be given, or the request to be granted, the more costly was the sacrifice. Our God will have no victims; but whatsoever you do unto one of the least of His, you do unto Him. Such are our sacrifices. My dear friend, from my heart I thank you; for you have done me a kindness, in that you have given me a real, undeniable proof, that my words have penetrated your heart, and that I do not live on for nothing: and treasure it up in your heart, that you have caused real joy to one who is often, very often, weighed down with heaviness and sorrow. You have not only kindled bright tapers upon my Christmas-tree, but the tree itself burns, gives light, and warms: the bush burns, and is not consumed, which is an image of the presence of the Holy Spirit, and its admonition to trust in the Most High in this wilderness of life, in mourning and in woe. Oh! my dear friend, I have been nigh unto death. What a solemn, quaking stride is the stride into eternity! What a difference between ideas of death in the days of health, and on the brink of the grave! And how shall I show myself worthy of longer life? By learning better to die. And, mark, when I sit here in solitude pursuing my thoughts, keeping some and driving away others, then I can think, that in distant valleys, upon distant mountains, there are living men who carry my thoughts within their hearts; and for them I live, and they are near and dear to me, till one day we shall meet where there is no more parting, no more separation. Peasant and scholar, let us abide as we are. Give me your hand — farewell!"

And once again, the soft and the hard hand were clasped together, and Christopher really trembled as Gellert laid his hand upon his shoulder. They shook hands, and therewith something touched the heart of each more impressively, more completely, than ever words could touch it. Christopher got down stairs without knowing how: below, he threw down the extra logs of wood, which he had kept back, with a clatter from the wagon, and then drove briskly from the city. Not till he arrived at Lindenthal, did he allow himself and his horses rest or food. He had driven away empty: he had nothing on his wagon, nothing in his purse; and yet who can tell what treasures he took home; and who can tell what inextinguishable fire he left behind him yonder, by that lonely scholar!

Gellert, who usually dined at his brother's, to-day had dinner brought into his own room, remained quite alone, and did not go out again: he had experienced quite enough excitement, and society he had in his own thoughts. Oh! to find that there are open, susceptible hearts, is a blessing to him that writes in solitude, and is as wondrous to him as though he dipped his pen in streams of sunshine, and as if all he wrote were Light. The rain-drop which falls from the cloud cannot tell upon what plant it drops: there is a quickening power in it, but for what? And a thought which finds expression from a human heart; an action, nay, a whole life is like the rain-drop falling from the cloud: the whole period of a life endures no longer than the rain-drop needs for falling. And as for knowing where your life is continued, how your work proceeds, you cannot attain to that.

And in the night all was still around: nothing was astir; the whole earth was simple rest, as Gellert sat in his room by his lonely lamp; his hand lay upon an open book, and his eyes were fixed upon the empty air; and on a sudden came once more upon him that melancholy gloom, which so easily resumes its place after more than usual excitement.

It is as though the soul, suddenly elevated above all, must still remember the heaviness it but now experienced, though that expresses itself as tears of joy in the eye.

In Gellert, however, this melancholy had a more peculiar phase: a sort of timidity had rooted itself in him, connected with his weak chest, and that secret gnawing pain in his head; it was a fearfulness which his manner of life only tended to increase. Surrounded though he was by nothing but love and admiration in the world, he could not divest himself of the fear that all which is most horrible and terrible would burst suddenly upon him: and so he gazed fixedly before him. He passed his hand over his face, and with an effort concentrated his looks and thoughts upon surrounding objects, saying to himself almost aloud: "How comforting is light! Were there no light from without to illumine objects for us, we should perish in gloom, in the shadows of night. And Light is a gentle friend that watches by us, and, when we are sunk in sorrow, points out to us that the world is still here, that it calls and beckons us, and requires of us duty and cheerfulness. 'You must not be lost in self,' it says; 'see! the world is still here:' and a friend beside us is as a light which illumines surrounding objects; we cannot forget them, we must see them and mingle with them. How hard is life, and how little I accomplish! I would fain awaken the whole world to goodness and to love; but my voice is weak, my strength is insufficient: how insignificant is all I do!"

And now he rose up and strode across the room; and he stood at the hearth where the fire was burning, made of wood given to him that very day, and his thoughts reverted to the man who had given it. Why had he not asked his name; and where he came from? Perchance he might have been able in thought to follow him all the way, as he drove home; and now . . . but yet 'tis more, 'tis better as it is: it is not an individual, it is not So-and-so, who has shown his gratitude, but all the world by the mouth of one. "The kindnesses I receive," he thought, "are indeed trials; but yet I ought to accept them with thanks. I will try henceforth to be a benefactor to others as others are to me, without display, and with grateful thanks to God, our highest benefactor: this will I do, and search no further for the why and for the wherefore." And once more a voice spoke within him, and he stood erect, and raised his arms on high. "Who knows," he thought, "whether at this moment I have not been in this or that place, to this or that man, a brother, a friend, a comforter, a saviour; and from house to house, may be, my spirit travels, awakening, enlivening, refreshing — yonder in the attic, where burns a solitary light; and afar in some village a mother is sitting by her child, and hearing him repeat the thoughts I have arranged in verse; and peradventure some solitary old man, who is waiting for death, is now sitting by his fireside, and his lips are uttering my words."

"And yonder in the church, the choir is chanting a hymn of yours; could you have written this hymn without its vigor in your heart? Oh! no, it *must* be there." And with trembling he thought: "There is nothing so small as to have no place in the government of God: should you not then believe that He suffered this day's incident to happen for your joy? Oh! were it so, what happiness were yours! A heart renewed." . . . He moved to the window, looked up to heaven, and prayed inwardly: "My soul is with my brothers and my sisters: nay, it is with thee, my God, and in humility I acknowledge how richly thou hast blessed me. And if, in the kingdom of the world to come, a soul should cry to me: 'Thou didst guide and cheer me on to happiness eternal!' all hail! my friend, my benefactor, my glory in the presence of God. . . . In these thoughts let me die, and pardon me my weakness and my sins!"

"And the evening and morning were the first day."

At early morning, Gellert was sitting at his table, and reading according to his invariable custom, first of all in the Bible. He never left the Bible open — he always shut it with a peaceful, devotional air, after he had read therein: there was something grateful as well as reverential in his manner of closing the volume; the holy words should not lie uncovered.

To-day, however, the Bible was lying open when he rose. His eye fell upon the History of the Creation, and at the words, "And the evening and the morning were the first day," he leaned back his head against the arm-chair, and kept his hand upon the book, as though he would grasp with his hand also the lofty thought, how Night and Day were divided.

For a long while he sat thus, and he was wondrously bright in spirit, and a soft reminiscence dawned upon him; of a bright day in childhood, when he had been so happy, and in Haynichen, his native place, had gone out with his father for a walk. An inward warmth roused his heart to quicker pulsation; and suddenly he started, and looked about him: he had been humming a tune.

Up from the street came the busy sound of day: at other times how insufferable he had found it! and now how joyous it seemed that men should bestir themselves, and turn to all sorts of occupations! There was a sound of crumbling snow: and how nice to have a house and a blaze upon the hearth! "And the evening and the morning were the first day!" And man getteth himself a light in the darkness: but how long, O man! could you make it endure? What could you do with your artificial light, if God did not cause his sun to shine? Without it grows no grass, no corn. On the hand lying upon the book there fell a bright sunbeam. How soon, at other times, would Gellert have drawn the defensive curtain! Now he watches the little motes that play about in the sunbeam.

The servant brought coffee, and the amanuensis, Gödike, asked if there were any thing to do. Generally, Gellert scarce lifted his head from his books, hastily acknowledging the attention and reading on in silence; to-day, he motioned to Gödike to stay, and said to Sauer, "Another cup: Mr. Gödike will take coffee with me. God has given me a day of rejoicing." Sauer brought the cup, and Gellert said: "Yes, God has given me a day of rejoicing, and what I am most thankful for is, that He has granted me strength to thank Him with all my heart: not so entirely, however, as I should like."

"Thank God, Mr. Professor, that you are once more in health, and cheerful: and permit me, Mr. Professor, to tell you that I was myself also ill a short time ago, and I then learnt a lesson which I shall never forget. Who is most grateful? The convalescent. He learns to love God and his beautiful world anew; he is grateful for every thing, and delighted with every thing. What a flavor has his first cup of coffee! How he enjoys his first walk outside the house, outside the gate! The houses, the trees, all give us greeting: all is again in us full of health and joy!" So said Gödike, and Gellert rejoined:—

"You are a good creature, and have just spoken good words. Certainly, the convalescent is the most grateful. We are, however, for the most part, sick in spirit, and have not strength to recover: and a sickly, stricken spirit is the heaviest pain."

Long time the two sat quietly together: it struck eight. Gellert started up, and cried irritably: "There, now, you have allowed me to forget that I must be on my way to the University."

"The vacation has begun: Mr. Professor has no lecture to-day."

"No lecture to-day? Ah! and I believe to-day is just the time when I could have told my young friends something that would have benefited them for their whole lives."

There was a shuffling of many feet outside the door: the door opened, and several boys from St. Thomas' School-choir advanced and sang to Gellert some of his own hymns; and as they chanted the verse—

> "And haply there—oh! grant it, Heaven!
> Some blessed saint will greet me too;
> 'All hail! all hail! to you was given
> To save my life and soul, to you!'
> Oh God! my God! what joy to be
> The winner of a soul to thee!"

Gellert wept aloud, folded his hands, and raised his eyes to heaven.

A happier Christmas than that of 1768 had Gellert

never seen; and it was his last. Scarcely a year after, on the 13th of December, 1769, Gellert died a pious, tranquil death, such as he had ever coveted.

As the long train which followed his bier moved to the church-yard of St. John's, Leipzig, a peasant with his wife and children in holiday-clothes entered among the last. It was Christopher with his family. The whole way he had been silent: and whilst his wife wept passionately at the pastor's touching address, it was only by the working of his features that Christopher showed how deeply moved he was.

But on the way home he said: "I am glad I did him a kindness in his lifetime; it would now be too late."

The summer after, when he built a new house, he had this verse placed upon it as an inscription: —

"Accept God's gifts with resignation,
  Content to lack what thou hast not:
In every lot there's consolation;
  There's trouble, too, in every lot."

THE STEP-MOTHER.

THE STEP-MOTHER,

A TALE.

TWO NATURES TOGETHER AND IN ONE.

ULL harmless as the dove, and wise as the serpent, were the Baker-at-the-Steps and his wife; *i. e.* he was wise, and she was harmless; and he was so wise that he sometimes actually ordered himself according to her harmlessness. For instance, when he was going to set about any thing after his tricksy fashion, he often informed himself what straightforwardness and simplicity would think about it; and he hadn't far to go for his information, he had only to ask his wife. He then either followed her advice because straightforwardness was the wisest, or he took his measures so that the claims of straightforwardness were at the same time included in his arrangement. So that people said, the Baker-at-the-Steps was incomprehensible; sometimes his plans were like a field full of mouse-holes, and sometimes all was as open and free from guile as if he had no idea what cunning meant. And he passed for seven times as cunning as he was, for of course people didn't know how cleverly he could employ the honest simplicity of his wife. The Baker-at-the-Steps was well to do; people, however, gave him out to be rich; and, strange to say, as men become good or bad because they are so considered, so it happens also that men become rich because they are so considered, particularly when they can take advantage of this opinion of the world, as the Baker-at-the-Steps could. While he was not in the least arrogant towards small folks, he was very dignified towards great. However, there were not many of the latter sort. Even the owner of the paper-mill, the richest and therefore the greatest man in the neighborhood, and whose son was a district magistrate — even the old paper-mill owner was treated courteously by the Baker-at-the-Steps, not because he considered him a great man, but because he considered him a little one. Of course, there was no need to tell him so to his face, and so the saying went abroad, that both towards high and low there was not a more courteous man than the Baker-at-the-Steps. "When I was market-boy," was his expression for many years; then, however, it changed to, "When I was fruit-measurer." The Baker-at-the-Steps had filled both offices, before he had made himself Baker-at-the-Steps, and the town had made him Town-councillor. He liked telling the story how, when he was a lad of sixteen, and as strong as a sapling, he had come into the town, and had helped in the corn-market to load and unload the sacks, and carry them to and fro, and how glad he had been to receive two kreuzers for the carriage of six sacks. Then he liked to tack on to that how he had become sworn fruit-measurer, how at last the old Steps-baker had had him enrolled as apprentice, and how he had got on by degrees from a beggar-boy to something.

It must be acknowledged, such frequent relations did

him good; you could see it in his contented tone, and in the whole manner in which he described the details.

It was not only a feeling of satisfaction at repose after past labors, it was also thankfulness for the course of his destiny, united with a proud self-complacency. And besides, it was wise for him to talk so. By himself telling what he had been, and what he had become, he gained respect; had he been silent and let it ooze out through others, there would have been no lack of malicious and envious insinuations. As often as he mentioned in this place or that how matters had gone with him in his distress, the small folks were grateful to him for placing himself on an equality with them, and the great folks praised his modesty, and were glad to be able to show him by their favor how high he had advanced.

For they, the great men, put themselves on an equality with him.

The Administrator of Finance often called for him on his stroll from the town to the ale-house; aye, sometimes he sat with the Baker-at-the-Steps, or looked out of the window, as he smoked a pipe with him, and was glad to have it appear what high honor was reflected upon the house thereby. Still you couldn't find a more comfortable house than that of the Baker-at-the-Steps. Be it remarked in passing, it was built on the stone staircase called "the Steps," which led from the upper town to the lower, if you didn't want to go the carriage-way to the Crown and Post-Office. The house of the Baker-at-the-Steps was what people call a thoroughfare-house; the staircase which led to the sitting-room served also for a public way. In the sitting-room there was always an air of comfort; the smell of fresh bread made it almost nutritious to stop there, and the countenance of the mistress of the house looked as though it had "May God bless it" always inscribed upon it.

They say that in famine-times a loaf of bread of the same weight has not the same nourishment as in a plentiful year. It may be, perhaps, that the nourishing matter therein is less developed; still, there is something besides which cannot be weighed and measured, and this is the universal blessing which works the miracle of satisfying with a little. So it was with every one who bought a loaf of the Bakeress-at-the-Steps; it was as though, by the manner in which she handed it over and nodded at the same time, she made a peculiar blessing rest upon it, so that it was much more nourishing than other bread from other people. She was economical also for other people. When So-and-So, or So-and-So, wanted new-baked bread, she would not give it; and if she were much pressed, she said inwardly, "God forgive my sins!" and protested aloud, "I have only stale, and you will see that it is more nourishing." To a woman who insisted with all her might upon having new bread, she called out once, "We only bake yesterday's!" and this witticism caused much laughing in the town.

From her seat by the little sash-window, the Bakeress-at-the-Steps obtained a knowledge of the world, which continually made her more and more amiable, good-natured, and gentle. However, she had already a good foundation to build upon, for she was the daughter of the model-teacher Straubenmüller, a noble and high-souled being, who, exactly because he entered so warmly and so heartily into every thing, was doomed to an early death. It sounds strange perhaps, but the title "model-teacher" is no ironical appellation, but a real, expressed title in ——.

A primary school had been erected in the town with numerous classes, and the appellation "model-school" had been given to it. Although, generally speaking, it was not noted for the production of model-men, the daughter of the model-teacher was worthy of her father and his calling. It was no slight matter in her favor, that she married the fruit-measurer, and without any pride lived quite happily with him. She let people talk as they pleased about a girl, so well brought up and so cultivated, marrying a man who was hardly above a day-laborer. She understood his manliness; and it was just this esteem of his wife that helped the Baker that was to be in all his undertakings; and he remained thankful to her for it all his days, though, after his peculiar fashion, he expressed it thus: "Yes, my wife is the slyest of the sly; she purchased me on spec: she calculated well, too, for she knew that in a few years I should rise in price and be worth treble." She was always silent and modest withal. The Baker often called her his house-clock; "it hangs on the wall, goes on quietly, doesn't tell everybody what happens, but when you look at it, tells you what o'clock it is."

The Bakeress, however, knew what o'clock had struck among others also. How many people of all grades came to her, and stopped a shorter or longer time before her window! She attended many on their path through life; particularly on servant-maids she kept a watchful eye. It appeared as though she could read their faces; and many an observation, which she dropped casually in their hearing, saved one girl or another from error. She bound people to her by giving them some commission which was to be executed in passing; half the town was thus in her service, and confided in her without reserve. They had conferred favors upon her, and so were willing enough to ask her help and counsel. She was the secret hirer of servants, and could find out very cleverly what this girl or that was good for; and yet — it was quite wonderful — she tolerated no loitering when they came to fetch bread; in a moment down came the window, and said: "The conversation is over." And the gold cap-fringe on the back of her head, which alone was now visible through the pane, seemed almost to say, "Speech is silver; silence is gold."

Till within a few years the Bakeress had had nothing but happiness and joy in her household. Her only daughter was married to the oil-mill owner in the valley, and lived in peace and comfort, and her only son was host of the Crown in the little town, just in the corner of the market-place, where every vehicle that comes from the mountain is obliged to pull up and take off the drag. That was not unprofitable for mine host's business, and her son's wealth and prosperity were multiplied. It was seldom, however, that the Bakeress came to the Crown, and it was always made a festival when she did: on these occasions she never went into the bar, but sat in the back-parlor with her daughter-in-law and the two children, and took it very kindly, though protesting against it, that they made stronger coffee than usual for Grandmother. The Baker's wife preferred being at home; and when, as was always the case, she went nicely dressed to the Crown, the fruit-women who vended their goods on the other side of the street looked knowingly at one another, and every face grew brighter to which she nodded a greeting. For about two years, however, the Baker's wife had been often sad, for the hostess of the Crown, who was her niece too, was dead; and her niece's eldest child, named Ernestine, then seven years old, had been taken by her grand-parents to live with them. The father had kept his son, a child of two years, with him, and the Baker's wife had given up to her son, as housekeeper, a relation who had lived with her twenty years.

While the wife continually sorrowed for her niece's death, the husband's sole thought and endeavor was how to help his son to another wife, and indeed such a one as would enhance the lustre of the family; so that, as the Baker always desired, a new wing might be added to the Crown, and the Bear, the Lamb, the Horse, and the Eagle, *i.e.*, the inn so called, be ruined. A niece of the paper-mill owner seemed the most suitable match, and he himself had once alluded to the subject, and it was not for nothing that, instead of joining the company at the Post, he went so often of an evening to the Crown; but neither mine host of the Crown nor his mother entertained the idea, when the Baker spoke of it. Mine host of the Crown didn't mean to marry again; he wouldn't make his children step-children.

It is a common saying, that married folks in course of time become alike; it was not the case here. The Baker was lank, overgrown, and sharp-boned — every thing seemed to turn to bone in him; his upper lip showed no red, whilst the under was rather protruding; all his features were sharply defined: his wife, on the contrary, was round, plump, and comfortable. But, in spite of their outward and inward differences, they lived peaceably together, and with careful scrutiny you might discover many points of similarity between them. The Baker's back-room, throughout the neighborhood, went by the name of the Baker's-office, for the Baker was what is called a lawyer by nature, and he made a profitable practice by this talent; there was seldom an action in the whole district, which had not first come before his judgment-seat; and every one quoted a saying of his that might have come from his wife also: "Rather tell me what your opponent says." It was natural, as every attorney has experienced over and over again, for a client to state the case to him in such a way that nothing in the world could be clearer than that he was in the right, and that there could be any doubt and dispute about the matter was utterly incomprehensible.

At such times the Baker often said to the applicant: "What use is it, you rascal, deceiving me? Just tell me what your opponent has to bring forward, and I can advise you better; put yourself for once in the other man's position, and then see what you can and what you cannot demand."

That was certainly rather hard. There are but few men — and even these few very seldom — who can treat themselves as utter strangers and examine themselves with another's eye, which is comprehended in that grand saying: — "Know thyself;" knock at your own door; call for once upon yourself as though you were a stranger. What a strange request that is! First, you must believe that you do not know yourself, for not till then can you know yourself. From the lawsuits and their discussions at the Baker's, therefore, proceeded often something more than the mere settlement of 'meum' and 'tuum.' The renunciation of a claim often became the giving up of an opinion. The Baker thus became also often the peace-maker, and he bore at such times an odd sort of sceptre — nothing more or less than a fly-flapper, which he handled so dexterously that he could flank off a fly from the rim of a glass without upsetting the glass; and this requires no ordinary skill. When, then, a dogmatical, stubborn litigator was for pursuing a right to the last tittle, and scorned all compromise, the Baker often said: — "Look you; you can't flank off every fly, you must let some escape." And he had the satisfaction of arranging many a dispute ere it came before the legal tribunal.

The Baker had also a snuff-box, with which he did much execution; it was really a playing-box, although it performed no music. The snuff therein was always fresh, but the Baker took no snuff himself; he only used his box for the purpose of gaining, thereby, all manner of lucky pauses for himself and others. When he bestowed a few taps upon it with his right-hand forefinger, then opened the box, and played awhile with a pinch, as he held the box quietly in his left hand, and let the pinch drop through the thumb and finger of his right, it seemed as if he gained outwardly what he required inwardly, — rest on the one side, and telling deliberation on the other; and when, gradually bringing the pinch towards his nose, at last, as if suddenly recollecting himself, he threw away the particles, and briskly addressed his visitor, the whole of this was clever shamming on purpose to get time for deliberation, and gain an advantage. At times, too, he succeeded in cooling a heated antagonist by quietly holding out to him the open box: indeed, this was often a means of reconciling refractory adversaries. No one, not even his own wife, knew how useful that snuff-box was.

People often told the Baker that he ought to get licensed to keep an inn, and his house would be one of the most frequented in the neighborhood; but on that point he was perfectly agreed with his wife, that it couldn't be. She maintained, for instance, that she couldn't become a hostess; she would then no longer have any house of her own, and she felt as if she would as soon live in the street. Now, every one who entered her parlor was obliged to greet her courteously; but if she kept an inn, she would be obliged to come forward and be polite, even though she were not so inclined. The Baker, although he did not go so far or so deep for his reasons, was quite of the same mind as his wife. He desired simply to be no obstacle to his son, and he discovered a clever means of becoming actually useful to him. While it was an agreeable thing in itself to the Baker to have a son a landlord in the town, a species of publicity, so to speak, in which one is still at home, — one can go into the inn, and yet be at home, can demand attendance as a guest, and deference as a relation, — he availed himself of the fact to still further profit. He had, both in summer and in winter, his regular hours at which he was to be found at the Crown; and when any one inquired for him, he was told, "He is at the Crown at such and such a time;" and he gave public audiences there, and when it was desired, private too, in a particular little room. The wine-sale at the Crown seldom lost any thing at the conclusion of bargains; and plenty of Johannisberg was drunk on occasions of peaceable reconciliations. Yes: a considerable portion of his own business — for he drove an improving fruit trade near the bakery — did the Baker transfer to the Crown, which not only brought his son all manner of profitable trade, but also made him more attentive to his father's business, for which he would otherwise never have properly fitted himself; for mine host of the Crown had inherited somewhat of the quiet, tender nature of his mother, or, as the Baker called it, — "of the stay-at-home model-teacher."

Mine host of the Crown had been a year at the Seminary, but his father knew better than to leave him to a "beggar's livelihood," as he called it; and it was a harsh speech which the son never forgot, when his father said school-teachers were the step-children of the world. A story, too, of mine host of the Crown had got abroad, which vexed him much. Once, when he wanted to buy a considerable quantity of horse-hair, he used the expression horses' hairs; and malicious people made up a whole story about it. They told how that mine host of the Crown had asked a peasant, — "Have you any horses?" "Why?" "I should like to purchase their hairs." This story was, of course, readily listened to, and it was of no use for mine host to protest; many an errand-boy thought himself mighty grand as he asked: "Will you buy any horses' hairs?"

That was all forgotten long ago, but a real awkwardness in mixing with the world, and severe struggles to overcome this, gave mine host enough to do. He had, so to speak, a High Dutch style of thought, and too keen a sensibility. In buying and selling he could not practise deceit; on the contrary, he was easily over-reached, and every piece of dishonesty, nay, even every piece of rudeness, always surprised him afresh. His father often said to him: "You are only fit for your mother's counter, and not for the world out here. You are one of the people who walk about in the world so lost in their own thoughts, that every dog which barks unexpectedly makes their hearts leap to their mouths! Keep your eyes open, and you'll find that many dogs are muzzled, many only bark and don't bite; and, should one come to biting, you're strong enough, you can defend yourself."

Because mine host readily and honestly confessed his own failings, the Baker only considered him still weaker and more in need of guidance than he really was; for sharp, anti-penitential natures consider those who frankly acknowledge their faults, weak and contemptible. Thus mine host was prompted to dependence upon his father, both through filial affection and mistrust of his own powers. The Baker, on his part, wished to make his son more self-reliant, especially as, since his wife's death, he had been quite lost, and readily allowed himself to be directed in the smallest matters. His father hurried him from business to business, on purpose to divert his mind; yet was at the same time, particularly gentle. When the son himself complained that he had done this or that awkwardly, his father consoled him, and argued him out of it. He labored with all his might to strengthen his son, that he might qualify him for the great plans which he had in view.

It was autumn when his father, one evening, after all the guests had gone, said to his son: "You must be off early to-morrow to the Brisgau, and take care to have lentils, and beans, and hemp; you can then look about you leisurely for flax and clover-seed, and Indian corn."

The son would have made objections, but his father had already thought of these, and easily overruled them. He took upon himself to look after the inn, as he always did; and next morning, long before day, mine host of the Crown stood, while his horses were being put into the wagon, by the bedside of his little son, and tears stood in his eyes: when the little fellow had his nightcap on, he was so like her who was dead. . . .

The fresh morning breeze soon cleared mine host's thoughts; and as the sun rose, and stood flashing in the heaven, with the earth so refreshingly laden with fruits, and his two horses stepping so bravely along the road, mine host felt all at once quite light at heart. He reproached himself for always relapsing into soft-heartedness; and considered his father right in denying him the quality of manly confidence. It should be otherwise. As if he were therewith taking himself in hand, he gathered up his horses' reins, and, with a crack of his whip, drove on. The world is even yet fresh, and, even at the worst, it is of no use to give way, whatever the day may bring forth; and his children are just beginning their walk of life, and stand in need of a strong-minded father.

He smiled quietly as he thought his boy was just getting up, and soon his little sister would come to take him to Grandmother. It seemed wonderful to him that he should stay so much at home; he seemed to himself strange, lonely, and dissevered, while the horses were drawing him far away into the world. He looked hard as children met him who were going with their school-bags to school, for it struck him how he had once himself wanted to devote himself to teaching. He would, at this moment, have been sitting yonder, very likely, waiting for the children; and now he was driving along with a pair of splendid horses. He nodded to the teacher, who was looking out of the window, and the teacher took off his cap; he thought, no doubt, an acquaintance was greeting him—perhaps even some one high in office. "Yes, father shall not say any more—'You're not fit for a life in the world, where one wrestles with another, in buying and selling, for the advantage.'" That's the character, certainly, of the old host of the Crown; but here is a new, a different one, who will show the world what he can do, and that it is not for nothing he is the son of that man who has the reputation of being the cleverest man in his neighborhood, and is so too. . . .

"What's in your wagon?"

"Wheat."

"Sold?"

"No."

"How much a sack?"

"The market-price."

"Good: we shall meet again in the town."

Such was the laconic conversation which mine host of the Crown, pulling up his horses, carried on with a peasant, who was driving a heavy load towards the town; and now he "tchick'd" with his tongue, the horses stepped out, and he drove quickly off. The peasant looked wonderingly after that man, so impudently bold, and the light which he was just about applying to his pipe he dropped beside him, so that he sprang up and searched a while to see that he hadn't set his cart on fire. Still, as he went along, he frequently shook his head after the man who had acted just as though he would say, "Who cares for the world?"

The clouds in the heaven are not more fleeting and changeful than the thoughts of men, especially of those who carry something heavy at their hearts and battle with it, at one time rising above it, at another sinking beneath it. Night and day alternate in their spirits, the one melting imperceptibly and gradually into the other; and, without being able to discern when the change has taken place, on a sudden it is night, and on a sudden it is day.

The host of the Crown, who had set out to drive a profitable bargain, was thus at one time yielding, and immediately afterwards grasping; impenetrable, and then self-conscious. He bought, in fact, about a hundred sacks of wheat, and he hadn't come out at all to buy wheat; but his father should see that he could trade on his own account, and that should become manifest more and more.

A DIFFICULT CUSTOMER.

N the Brisgau there was a report that there was nothing more to be done in pulse — Mr. Goldstumpf of Freiburg had bought it all up: and mine host of the Crown was now so daring, that he drove straight to Freiburg, to see whether he couldn't rid Mr. Goldstumpf of some of his booty. That was certainly a very bold venture. Nobody had ever yet gained an advantage over Goldstumpf, except when Mr. Goldstumpf sucked out thereby a still greater one for himself. To get on smoothly with him, it was always the most advisable to trade with money in the one hand, and goods in the other; for in any other case you never failed to get entangled, what with oral and written agreements, in a lawsuit, unless you would allow yourself directly to be overreached. The Baker had a lawsuit pending with him from the past year. Goldstumpf's proper name was Fridolin Stumpf: he had acquired the addition to his name, because he was one of the richest men in the country, and liked to boast of it. Besides, however, he had the name Suwarrow; for he wore large riding-boots, which reached to the knee, hung with a tassel in front, and people called them "Suwarrows." He dressed after the mode which prevailed at the commencement of our century; and particularly noticeable was his double neckerchief, a white, and a black one over it, so that the white one looked like the edge of a collar. There were many people, however, who would willingly have tied his neckerchief considerably tighter for him, or rather would have liked somebody else to do it. He had been keeper of a small beer-house in the town: in the war-time, however, he had suddenly grown to great estate; it was said that he had been a French spy, and certainly he went in and out among the foreigners as though he was one of them; and soon he received large orders for the supply of the armies — oats, meat, and shoes, whereby he made considerable gains; of course, not always in the honestest manner. Still he obtained his most considerable property from the sequestration of the convents, receiving their goods as spoils of war, according to the phraseology at that time.

We must not omit to mention that the memory of these antecedents would have passed away, had not Goldstumpf, by his harsh, relentless way of taking possession, drawn public attention upon himself. He had mortgages upon many houses in the town, and was always talking of removing to Switzerland; but by degrees more houses fell into his hands, which he could not get rid of, and he treated his tenants with extreme severity. Still, he set his mind upon once more becoming respected in the town. He wouldn't be driven away, and he would not remove until he regained his reputation. But in that he did not succeed, and now he remained there for fun. He wanted to break people's hearts by showing them how well he got on, and how he was always getting richer. He succeeded in that, but himself and his family were none the happier.

He was always accompanied by a great dog, a brute well suited to his master: for he was often at night beset by men whom he had reduced to misery; and soon indeed his dog was his only companion. It was commonly reported that in an important family-suit he had perjured himself. The story then went on to say, that his wife could not bear the idea of his taking the oath; and as he did take it, and his wife soon after drowned herself at the upper mill in the Dreisam, it was plain that, broken-hearted at his perjury, she had put an end to herself. After he lived with his three children, two sons and one daughter, alone.

By and by Goldstumpf once more made acquaintances, who drank with him and joined in all kinds of conversation. They were partly parasites, and partly people to whom it is indifferent how and with whom they pass their time. Very often Goldstumpf felt that he was only respected by those people who must be indifferent to him or contemptible; and that those shunned him whose respect alone, openly showed, could be of any use to him. But, as happens in higher and lower situations, he forgot all that, and congratulated himself that people paid him reverence. Suppose he knew that they only shammed their admiration, what of that? That they even gave themselves the trouble to sham, was sufficient evidence of his power.

'Tis a hard saying, "The sin of the father is visited upon the children," and it really is hard, but it rests with the children to decide how this visitation is to be accomplished. The trampling under foot of the moral laws which they have before their eyes can plunge them into still deeper ruin, make them still more wicked, or the contrary: they take the evil to heart; it is a hard chastisement, but straightforward acknowledgment and an unbending will give release from the very heaviest. It is always painful to sever one's self from the source of one's being, or to labor for its purification; and yet that is a penalty which is not wanting even in the best of conditions.

The eldest son of Goldstumpf had played such loose and dangerous pranks, that his father had taken him secretly to the Rhine, put him on board a vessel, and sent him to America. The second son had caused his father trouble of another description, by marrying a young neighbor of no family, who was so poor that he had been obliged to buy her wedding-dress. It was not until after a long trial before the judges, that Goldstumpf gave up to his son his maternal inheritance; and, as if for aggravation's sake towards the father, the young man's warehouse was always patronized by the whole town, and people in every possible manner distinguished the young merchant and his wife, as modest as she was pretty. Fourteen years had now passed since the father had exchanged a word with his son; and as for his daughter-in-law and granddaughter, he had scarcely ever had a glimpse of them.

Now he lived alone with his only daughter in a large house in Gau Street, which had formerly been part of a convent, and his daughter was as quiet and retired as though she had actually been in a convent. Many persons pretended that Goldstumpf was not so rich as he appeared: he had too many occupations; and it is a true proverb, though too little known, "Callings various, gains precarious."

It could not be clearly ascertained how matters stood

with him, and what people at any rate wished for him was once expressed by a picture which suddenly became circulated upon the snuff-boxes. There was written beneath it, "Suwarrow's end," and Goldstumpf was depicted thereon to the life, sitting upon his dog. He immediately bought up all he could get hold of; but it was of no use, for there were already several secured, and soon they reappeared in greater numbers, and then he did what he might have done at first,—laughed at the malicious trick, which was soon forgotten.

Much of what was known about Goldstumpf, embellished with all kinds of fabulous additions, now came into mine host's head as he drove to Freiburg. But when he from Zähringen looked upon the taper spire of the Cathedral, there flashed across his mind a recollection of an old chum living there. Yonder, not far from the magnificent building, dwells Gessler, who worked two years with the Baker-at-the-Steps as journeyman; he settled here as a master-baker. How rejoiced he will be at the rencounter! "He will no doubt have accommodation for you and the horses," thought mine host.

The master-baker by the Cathedral was easily found: he lived by the Exchange, just where you get a full view of the Cathedral with its three large and many small spires. As mine host drove up, it was just eight by the sun-dial, and it struck by the Cathedral-clock; and as mine host of the Crown drove up to his house and stopped, the baker came to the house-porch. He looked tall and broad, and the clean shirt, which neither coat nor waistcoat concealed, appeared by contrast with his red braces still more brilliant. For some time he did not recognize mine host of the Crown, and then, throwing up his hands, he cried: "God bless me! is it you? Yes; it is mine host of the Crown, and no one else in the world is more welcome than you:—that is glorious, that is good!"

"What is the matter? what do you mean? I never saw you in such a state before in my life!" said mine host of the Crown to his chum, whose face beamed joy; "one would hardly know you, you are so changed."

"Yes, just consider, this very minute I have seen for the first time in the world mine own child. It is but a few minutes since my wife brought me a boy, a fine fellow, and I had scarcely seen him, when I heard you drive up, and I ran out."

"Yes, yes, you look like it: the glance with which a man looks for the first time on his first child is still upon your countenance. Oh, that is a happiness which never recurs: no, never! Is all safe; all well?"

"All as right as can be," the midwife says.

"Go in-doors," said mine host of the Crown, and gathering up the reins of his horses again, he prepared to mount; "go in and keep quiet: that is the most requisite now. I had intended staying with you, but now that cannot be; I will put up yonder at the 'Genius,' and come again towards evening. I mean to stop a few days here; I have business to transact."

"No, no, you mustn't go; I will put up your horses at my neighbor's, and there is plenty of room for you at my house. You shall be the first to sleep in our spare bed, and I cannot tell you how glad I am that you have come. Look you; I am so devoted to you, so——"

The young, strong man could say no more from inward emotion, and mine host of the Crown said: "I cannot help thinking myself it a good sign, that I should arrive just at this moment."

The baker recovering his speech continued: "Therefore you must remain with me, — I must have some one with me; I have already sent word to my mother at Kirchzart. Oh that she were already come! I can't expect her yet; my nag is ill, and I have sent for another, and it will be a long while before my mother comes. It all happened so suddenly. An hour before, my wife had been drinking coffee with me. Have you any feeling in you? Come in; it is all ready here, or soon will be."

"No, I will go to Kirchzart and bring your mother. Send some one with me to point her out, should I meet her on the way. There, your journeyman can sit by my side."

"No, no: why send away my journeyman and you with him? why! I shall be still more alone!" retorted the baker; and mine host of the Crown was obliged to allow the journeyman to drive away with his team, and himself went with his old chum into the parlor, and saw him give the first poor boy who came to buy bread, two large loaves, and two coffee-rolls, as they call them, of puff paste, and shake his head at the money he offered. Then the Cathedral-baker ran round into the parlor, took hold of various things, and didn't know what he wanted; he counted the prongs on the upright grate at the oven, on which they placed the boards with the allowance of paste — he counted both as if he didn't know how many there were; and soon, as though some one had suddenly ordered him, he put a large basket of rolls from the table on to the stand, and then from the stand on to the table again. Nothing would do but mine host of the Crown must himself see the young mother and the recent arrival. Mine host complied reluctantly and cautiously, brought his chum back again into the parlor, and bade him now reflect quietly upon his happiness, and not disturb the mother and child.

The young master-baker said he was as tired as though he had run to-day up and down the mountain, and yet he couldn't sit quietly on his chair, and was always listening at the bed-chamber; and when the purchasers came with their kreuzers and groschen and knocked at the window, he signed to them to be quiet, and as often as a poor man came he would take no money for his bread. Mine host of the Crown tried to hinder him, by warning him that he ought to wait awhile before he did this; for if he did so to-day, he would have in an hour's time all the beggars in the town before his window, and his wife and child would have no rest, of which they were now so much in need.

The two friends sat quietly together, and with peculiar shyness the Freiburger asked at last after mine host's business. He made answer with equal reserve: for it is the strange part of business intercourse, that, especially among such as follow the same trade and pursue the same calling, they observe a sort of understood caution. One holds it not right to question the other more closely, and the other considers himself not bound to give explicit answers.

Soon the Freiburger's mother came, and brought a little grandchild with her, a boy of four years, whom she could not suffer to be away from her. The Freiburger now committed every thing to his mother, and dressed himself properly, for he would not go to the market except properly dressed.

It was time for the two friends to be at the corn-market.

"I don't know how it is," said the Freiburger as they

walked, "I feel as if the world were all changed: I have a boy at home, and all seems so strange to me, and I should like so much to tell everybody! Tell me, what do you want to buy, that we may not oppose one another?"

"I want to buy and sell. I should like to get pulse, and I have wheat to get rid of should the price suit me."

"And I want to buy wheat."

"You can ascertain what is the current price."

Mine host of the Crown felt himself in particularly good humor to-day — he had found a friend in happiness and comfort, not to omit that he had evidently made a favorable purchase; and with a satisfaction he had never yet known, he took here and there from the open sacks a handful of corn, weighed it carefully in his hand, and hurried away again to the throng.

Mine host of the Crown transferred to his friend what he had purchased on the road, and he even succeeded so far that his loss and gain were as nearly as possibly equal. This self-won advantage gave mine host still more confidence. He was bold enough to go straight to Goldstumpf's house. It was a long while before he could open the great gate; and when he got inside, he saw heavy padlocks upon the iron doors. Goldstumpf was away.

"When will he be back?" asked mine host of an old servant he saw in the entrance-hall. She went into the parlor, and mine host heard a clear maiden's voice answer from within: "My father will be away eight or ten days."

The voice interested mine host amazingly; and when the old servant came back, he said: "Is that the daughter of the house of whom you inquired?"

"Yes, certainly."

"Cannot I go in and speak with her?"

"No, why? what do you want?" said the voice from within.

"I only wished to ask where your father is, and whether I could not perhaps find him out. I have my own conveyance with me!"

An odd laugh resounded within, which had reference no doubt to the last remark, by which mine host wished to make it appear, that he was not the sort of man to be kept waiting before the door like a beggar. And with the laugh came an answer again from within: "My father is in Lenzkirch."

"Very well; I will go to him."

"Stay, you can take something for him with you. There are his fur-gloves which he has forgotten;" and the door was slightly opened, and from the aperture a pair of gloves, trimmed with foxes' fur, was held out to mine host; but he saw nothing of the holder. With a laugh he said through the aperture: "Suppose now I were to run off with the gloves!" and softly and quite close by him the answer came: "Then is your voice deceitful, for you have the voice of an honest man." Mine host could not help laughing aloud, and his laugh was echoed from within.

He left the house, and stood awhile in silence before it; it was as if he had come from an enchanted castle, so wonder-smitten was he: but he had the gloves trimmed with foxes' fur in his hand, and all wonder was at an end.

Next morning mine host set off again, and promised to return after a few days. He had told his friend nothing of what had happened to him.

In Lenzkirch he found Goldstumpf directly, for he drove

all kinds of trade with the watchmakers: in fact, there was nothing by which money was to be made to which he did not turn his hand. He passed a good deal of his time, too, at the inn, and was talkative and affable; he liked particularly to tell stories of the war-times. He had the credit of understanding how to dress up and spin his stories excellently. Altogether, if you could overlook the fact that Goldstumpf loved nothing but himself and money, you might have called him a really pleasant and agreeable man; and so he was too, as long as it was a mere question of conversation. He was quite a different person, however, as soon as he came to business; then his clumsy powerful frame appeared almost agile, his broad head, deep-set between his shoulders, became erect, and the powerful, brawny hand, with its large signet-ring, appeared to every opponent irresistibly inclined to clutch.

Mine host of the Crown had wavered much upon the road as to whether he should tell Goldstumpf that he had come on his account or not. In the latter case he must belie the gloves, and in fact it was the most prudent course to abide by the simple truth. Mine host had some of his mother's nature herein, that he felt himself shaky whenever an action was to be founded upon untruth or deceit; he felt himself strong, firm, and knowing, only when he went straightforwardly to work, and on this occasion it was a considerable advantage to him. Goldstumpf liked very much to make out that he was known and sought out far and wide; and when mine host of the Crown, who was tall and substantial-looking, said in the coffee-room that he had undertaken a long journey to transact some business with him, he smiled quietly, tapped his Suwarrow boot with his riding-whip according to his custom, and with his other hand stroked his dog's head; then he cast his eye over the whole room where the business people and others sat, that they might carry away the fame of him as a man in much request. Goldstumpf seemed to hold mine host in peculiar favor, but it was really ostentation which made him drive with the stranger to a country house in the neighborhood which belonged to him, and made him explain to him generally the extent of his transactions.

"So you are from Rottweil?" was his first question to mine host; and this being answered in the affirmative, he continued: "Then you know the Baker-at-the-steps?"

"Of course, quite well."

"And he will learn to know me pretty well, too: I am at law with him, and the case will soon be decided."

Mine host didn't feel bound to say at once that he was the Baker's son; he thought he would put it off to a favorable opportunity, but, strange to say, this opportunity never came; and mine host of the Crown, who had intended to deal quite openly with Goldstumpf, had already a concealment from him, and was growing gradually so accustomed to it that it did not disturb him.

It is a sad truth that evil natures corrupt those who come in contact with them. The falsehood even, with which one faces such and such a person in not giving him plainly to understand what opinion one has of him, breeds a confusion in the soul; and it often happens that while one is inwardly fearful of letting out the expression of his real opinion, he attempts all kinds of apologies for errors, and paints in particularly strong colors all that makes the good points conspicuous. And thus the inward contempt is changed, as it were necessarily, to an outward expression of esteem. The honest man feels he is playing false, but cannot help himself, and is conscious that virtue has gone out of him. The inward horror for wrong is often accompanied with an indefinite feeling of anger at having partially yielded to it, and at having now lost that right which in the first place was voluntarily resigned.

This was the case with mine host of the Crown, when he perceived that he must have given Goldstumpf to believe that he respected him highly; whereas, exactly the contrary was the fact. When with him, he was, as it were, stupefied and intoxicated; as soon, however, as he had time for reflection with himself alone, he was inwardly ill at ease. Every day he made up his mind to go, and yet could not: it was a strange magic circle, in which he had become confined. Goldstumpf managed, under various pretexts, to take mine host about with him for several days, and mine host hoped in consequence of this familiarity to be able to conclude a clever bargain, which would be followed by many others. When at last they returned to Freiburg, Goldstumpf demanded such unusually high prices, that mine host was obliged to go away empty: in fact, Goldstumpf had found out from mine host how buying and selling went in other quarters, he had had a pleasant fellow-traveller for many days, and now he might go home empty, and Goldstumpf laughed in his sleeve.

GODFATHERS AND GODMOTHERS.

MINE host of the Crown returned in ill-humor to his friend, whom he found this time quite crest-fallen, although his wife was now pretty well, and was sitting in the large arm-chair. "What is the matter? what is the matter with you?" said mine host.

"Why, the baby has brought me a second baby and imbittered my life," said the Cathedral-baker.

"I should like to know how?" said the wife, with a voice trembling with passion.

"There, mine host of the Crown shall decide," cried the Cathedral-Baker.

"Nothing of the kind; settle it alone with your wife. I will know nothing about it," answered mine host.

"Nay, you may as well hear," said the wife, with a suddenly tranquil, clear tone. "I wanted a dear friend of mine for godmother for my child; and because he doesn't want her, he says I imbitter his life."

"I will have nothing to do with the family," cried the baker passionately, "or with anybody belonging to the house: I am one of the youngest burghers in the town, and I can't alter what all the guild and myself into the bargain couldn't. No single creature will have any thing to do with them; and you only do it out of aggravation. Why, people will say I'm leagued with them, and I shall lose all my credit."

"Ah! who is it, pray," asked mine host, "whom you want for godmother?"

"The best soul in the world," answered the wife; "goodness itself, the truest of hearts! How can she help it, if her father is not respected?"

"Eh! who is it then?"

"Goldstumpf's daughter."

"Indeed!" said mine host, with slow enunciation: and the baker broke in with, "There, you see! he is a stranger, far away from Freiburg, and yet see how astonished he is, how he changes color at the idea of asking a man to give his first child such a godmother. I won't say any thing against her: she may be an angel for all I know, only she is Goldstumpf's daughter:—who will stand godfather with her? Nobody? not a beggar in the streets."

"Oho! don't be so vehement. If the christening were to be to-morrow, I could tell you of a godfather."

"A proper godfather, no doubt!"

"I don't know—do you consider me proper?"

"What! you?" said the baker in amazement.

"Yes, I will stand godfather."

The baker for joy clapped mine host upon the back so heartily that he writhed again; but by way of recompense, the happy father added, "Yes, it is so; you have some of your mother in you! Wife, haven't I often and often said, the Bakeress-at-the-Steps is the best of women as far as bread is baked? And you, host, are not quite so good, but you have a bit of her! Now, it's settled; the christening is to-morrow, and you must stop here: we have your promise, and you can't back out. I'll go straight and ask Goldstumpf's daughter to be godmother."

"Goldstumpf's daughter?" said his mother.

"When mine host of the Crown will stand with her, I can have no objection. Mother, bring my Sunday coat and my hat, and then I'll call on my way home at the minister's, and the butcher down there has just killed a calf; I'll order a piece of him for roasting. Our bake-oven is heated; in an hour the joint might be put in, or even to-morrow early. So, God bless you!" and away he ran, and wife, mother, and friend looked smilingly after him.

The young mother now informed mine host of the Crown what an honest, noble-hearted creature Goldstumpf's daughter was: she was certainly, on her father's account, shunned by the world, but reconciled herself to it more and more, and indeed she was as wise as she was good. Mine host of the Crown paid great attention as she proceeded to say, "Could you hear any thing better than what she once said to me? 'Come,' said she, 'do you know what is the greatest misfortune? To make too many claims. There sits an unhappy object, and waits and hopes, and demands of those who are well off to render some assistance, but in vain: those who are well off take no thought thereof. Then, and not till then, you feel how forsaken you are, and you could be spiteful against the world, but still it is unjust.' Yes, mine host, I feel proud that she is my friend, and she has often laughed at me for being jealous of your mother."

"Of my mother?"

"Yes, understand me rightly, however. My husband, whatever happens, always says, 'The Bakeress-at-the-Steps does so-and-so: ah! there's not another woman in the world like her; and her house-keeping is so good, and one never sees how it is kept in order, one doesn't hear the mill rattle.' I put every day, as long as the season lasts, my fresh bouquet of flowers on the board with the new-bread: but then it is always, 'The Bakeress-at-the-Steps is much prettier, and with her the flowers last for a week as fresh as when they were gathered.' God forgive me, one would really suppose she was a witch!"

Mine host laughed, and she continued, "Yes, I laugh now myself, when he cries up his old mistress; but that I can do so, is owing to Thaddea."

"Thaddea is her name?"

"Yes; why?"

"It is a pretty name. Tell me how she assisted you."

"By all means. 'Susan,' said she, 'congratulate yourself that your husband knows such an excellent woman. Don't depreciate her; you hurt him and yourself too. There is nothing better, no truer happiness, than to know some one whom you respect from the bottom of your heart;' and—pardon my vanity—since then my husband has said once or twice, 'You will be a real Bakeress-at-the-Steps.' That is my highest praise! But when you come again in the summer, you must bring your mother with you."

"That cannot be; my mother scarcely ever leaves the house, much less the town—and then it is so far."

"Thaddea, too, would very much like to see her once. My husband says she is something like her; for when she is once here, he is polite to her and pleased with her. No one could look in her face and be spiteful. She looks so . . ."

"Well, how does she look?"

"You know Goldstumpf?"

"Yes."

"Very well. A student who was staying with us made a very good remark one day. 'You know,' said he, 'there are mirrors in one side of which you look quite natural, and in the other swelled up to the size of a bull's head; such a resemblance is there between Goldstumpf and Thaddea. It is the same countenance, but how different?'"

Mine host of the Crown couldn't help laughing aloud. He sat still for some time; then went round into the town to purchase a christening present for the young mother and the child. Whilst mine host was in the town, Thaddea arrived; and by her appearance you would say that the comparison of the student, though malicious, was appropriate. The young mother had much to tell her of the tall and gentleman-like man who would stand godfather with her. She said, she had never believed before in the praise her husband bestowed upon the Bakeress-at-the-Steps; the son showed what the mother must be. She talked herself by degrees into extravagant praises of mine host of the Crown. Thaddea listened quietly, and said little. When at length she wished to depart, the baker's wife detained her, saying she must see the gentleman with whom she would stand sponsor the next day. When, however, it struck nine by the Cathedral-clock, and mine host had not yet made his appearance, Thaddea went away.

On the morrow, Thaddea and mine host of the Crown cast expressive looks at one another, and quickly withdrew their eyes again, as they saw on their return home with what new delight the mother clapsed her child.

The father held out to her her child, and eyes and arms were stretched forth to receive him, and first tremblingly, and then with fresh, happy delight, the mother embraced her child. Her child had been into the world, separated from her, received into the fellowship of men and baptized, and now it was once more with her: and as a mother in her child embraces her own life, which hath severed itself from her, and which now she can clasp in her arms, so was it here when the child was for the first time restored to his mother. That happy glance, when the mother for the first time saw and clasped her child, was here renewed under higher auspices, unmixed with pain: and with a smile of self-complacent satisfaction the mother gave her breast to the little one restored.

Thaddea couldn't help giving the little boy whom grandmother had brought with her a hearty kiss.

All now went joyously at the Cathedral-baker's. At last they sat down to the christening dinner. Mine host of the Crown sat next to Thaddea, whose speech and actions were very modest and pleasing, but betrayed at the same time some shyness; for she felt that a kindness was being shown her when she was invited to cheerful society, and still she felt very grateful that she had been chosen for the honor of sponsorship.

Mine host of the Crown elicited that Goldstumpf had set off early in the morning for Kenzingen: he immediately conjectured that he would at once forestall the hemp-market, of which he had imprudently given him information, but he said nothing about that: in fact, he didn't mention that he had had any transaction with him. He gazed upon Thaddea with a quiet smile: he had already spoken once with her without seeing her; and if it were possible to picture a person from a voice, she was just what he would have fancied. She was near the end of her twenties, and that comparison of the student struck him, more and more, as very appropriate. In Thaddea's manner of speaking, it was easy to see that she had not been accustomed to society; conversation was difficult to her, and she had none of those meaningless observations which are only used to show attention or prevent the conversation from dropping. What she said was to the point and natural, and sometimes she simply inclined her head.

It was even plain that it was not only when she was speaking or being spoken to that she was conversing.

The baker's mother indiscreetly introduced the topic, whether Thaddea's father were yet reconciled with his son who had married the poor seamstress. An attempt was made quickly to divert the conversation, but Thaddea said, "The world will not believe it, but it is the case. My father, too, is sorry for his fourteen long years of misery; but he cannot retract, and I know no way of settling it, unless something extraordinary should happen. My heart is ready to break when I meet my brother and his wife and children, and yet cannot speak to them."

"I can easily imagine that," interrupted the baker.

"No, you cannot imagine it; whoever has not experienced something of the kind himself, can never know what it is: yonder they go, and I have kind words to say to them, and they to me, and we cannot speak to one another. It must be like the feeling of one left for dead, who hears the world around him where he lies, and yet can make no sign."

"Ah! let us now talk of other matters," said the baker's wife, who, after the manner of the more sanguine sort of women, liked to make herself and others believe, that a thing is forgotten as soon as it is concealed and put aside; and she continued,—"If I were in your place, Thaddea, I know what I would do: I should drive out with my father about the country, and not squat at home; you never will change your position."

"I am not at all anxious," said Thaddea.

"Nay, that is not what I meant," returned the baker's wife; "you might if you would."

"But I've no wish." The conversation thus once diverted, did not return again to the old channel.

Mine host of the Crown amused himself with the little boy whom his grandmother had brought with her, and teased him with all kinds of boyish pranks.

"You are a genuine godfather," said Thaddea; "you seem to be fond of children—that is a proof of a kind heart."

"With me, not particularly: I have just such a boy of my own at home, and he has, God help him! no mother living."

Thaddea's eye dilated, and over her countenance passed a strange fleeting expression, which the young mother alone noticed; it might be that Thaddea's face changed in that way, because the young mother looked so piercingly and strangely in her eyes. Thaddea meanwhile took up something from the table, and holding out to mine host of the Crown a pretty sugared cake, she said: "Give this to your boy with my love;" and quickly added hesitatingly, "I may send him something; you know we stood sponsors together."

"The father gets a pair of fur gloves, and the son a cake. You give queer presents," said mine host. To the astonishment of everybody, Thaddea in particular, he told how he had already spoken to her, as if she had been in an enchanted castle, and she had given him a true-token. There was now much laughing, and every thing, even the most natural word, was made to serve for a new joke. The whole company became so merry, the excuses which Thaddea offered being all turned to subjects for fresh raillery, and there being nothing but laughter and uproar in the room, the grandmother took the convalescent to her room again, for fear she should suffer. Thaddea would have borne her company, but mine host of the Crown set on the little stranger, bidding him "hold her fast, and not let her go!" And Thaddea was obliged to remain in the room, and the raillery was renewed; but it soon changed to a different strain, for mine host of the Crown stood at the window with Thaddea, and talked with her on all kinds of topics. She was particularly affected when he said: "When I am away from home, and see children, I cannot tell you how it touches my heart. In earlier years I couldn't bear little children, and my wife was quite right when she said to me once: 'There you see again, we women are better than you men; you only like children when you have them of your own, but as for us, we can be quite happy, even with strange children. I could romp and play with them, and watch them and tend them the livelong day; but you men, when you have children, are tired of them in half an hour.' Oh! she was a clever, good creature! Yes, too good."

A pause ensued, and at last Thaddea said: "It seems to me, that people in your part of the world are much more enlightened than they are here. When I hear you talk in this way, I fancy you must have studied."

"I must take the praise, intended for my neighbors, to myself. I have studied, or rather I might be said to have studied. I was a year at the Seminary."

"And why, sir,"—Thaddea suddenly said, "Sir,"—"why did you give it up?"

"I am an only son, that is, I have only a sister, and my father was quite right; but when we know one another a little better, you will see that there is still a bit of the teacher in me."

"And in me too; had my father allowed it, I should have been a teacher."

"Then we have much in common. You are also an only daughter. If it were not for that wicked proverb!"

"Which?"

> "Ladies, beware of an only son:
> Let an only daughter be wooed and won!"

Twilight had set in: mine host of the Crown could not see what a flush spread over Thaddea's face; he only heard her breathing become more hurried, and after awhile she said: "I didn't know the proverb. But, good heaven! there is eight o'clock striking; I must go home."

"Nay, stay a little longer. Who knows how long it may be ere we meet again?"

They both stood without speaking while eight o'clock was clashed with mighty strokes from the Cathedral-tower. When it had finished striking, mine host of the Crown asked: "How old are you?"

"Thirty," answered Thaddea, as if the strange question and open answer were a matter of course; and mine host of the Crown continued: "I should like to fancy to myself all that has passed with you during the years in which this clock has announced the hours."

"It is good," answered Thaddea, "that much should pass away and be no more, like the striking of a clock."

Again they were both silent for a longer time, and then mine host of the Crown said: "I am going back home to-morrow as early as possible. But perhaps I may return."

Again a longer pause, till Thaddea said: "What is your son's name?"

"Magnus."

"Well, kiss Magnus for me; and when you come again, I will send him something better."

"I take you at your word."

It had become late, and the old servant came with a lantern to fetch Thaddea home.

"Now you will give me a hand instead of a glove, will you not?" said mine host

"Ah! think no more of that; good night, Mr. Godfather."

"Good night, Miss Godmother! God bless you; and preserve a kind remembrance of me!"

Thaddea moved away, and the baker's people were much astonished when mine host of the Crown sent for his horses, put them to, and, in spite of every objection, drove away home through the darkness.

CONFESSIONS.

"GOD bless me! is all well?" asked the Baker-at-the-Steps of his son, as he pulled up at the Crown. "All right, all right," said his son, as he descended. "How are the children?"

"Quite well: but how much have you bought, and at what price? Have you samples with you, or are the goods coming after you directly?" With such questions did the Baker-at-the-Steps overwhelm his son; but he hurried on before, and not until he had kissed his boy did he say: "I only bought a hundred sacks of wheat, father, which I resold: I have come empty."

"Then you should do as Schmul of Vieringen did."

"What did he do, pray?"

"On coming home from business, just as you have done, he entered the house backwards; — 'Why, Schmul,' says his wife, 'what is the matter?' Says he: 'I have done no business, I am ashamed of myself, and can't bear to show my face.'"

"I have had something else to do, though," answered mine host peevishly.

The old Baker-at-the-Steps was irritable, but he had himself to a great extent under control, and he only asked: —

"Why, pray, do you look so joyous? Just put the boy down; he has been able to walk alone a long while. Come, Magnus," said he sharply to the child, "get down and go into the kitchen; I have something to say to your father."

"No, no, let the child remain, I have brought him something; there, Magnus, there is a cake for you. Hey! it's broken; never mind, eat it: somebody sent it you who is very fond of you. Where is Ernestine? Go to grandmother and fetch her; or no, stop there, and say I will follow directly."

With these words mine host of the Crown put the boy outside the door, and said to his father: "Father, I think I have found a wife."

"Has she any money?"

"Rather too much, I believe."

"Well, all your superfluous cash you can pay over to me."

Mine host of the Crown walked restlessly up and down the room, stretched, and shook himself, and looked about him like a stranger. He examined every piece of furniture in the parlor, as if chair, table, and cupboard were meditating some treachery.

Every traveller brings home with him a wrong notion of the time of day; it is neither morning nor mid-day with him, as with those who have stayed at home: he has seen so many strange places, and has been among so many strange people, his head is so full of the world without, that he cannot properly accommodate himself to those who have remained in the old beaten path, and the usual course of things.

The Baker-at-the-Steps, a good judge of human nature,

in which capacity he had of course his first experience in himself, for many years had adopted a strange custom, which, however, was serviceable to him. Immediately after his arrival from a long journey, he lay down for an hour; and it was one of his best natural gifts, that he could sleep when he wished. Thus he was always wakeful and active. When, therefore, directly after his return home, he had had his nap, and then roused himself again, he showed rare energy and powers of speedy organization. He was at once quite at home again, and free from all that uneasiness, which, like a strange atmosphere, still clings to the traveller.

He tried to induce his son to adopt this method, but mine host of the Crown could not be prevailed upon; he couldn't sit stlll a minute; his father had prescribed him three pinches of snuff, which he had taken, and yet he could give no coherent account. Now he stood at the window, looked through the panes, and said: "We will go to my mother, to my child."

"You don't budge from here: have you no more to tell me?"

"Yes!"

"Well, what is it? Out with it!"

"Father, I say, if I am to marry, I will marry her, her only."

"Indeed! where does she come from?"

"Freiburg."

"A large town — that isn't well; she will not suit our little place." And taking a pinch, the Baker continued: — "I was with the father of the present Post-master of Schramberg, when he went a wooing at Darmstadt. The girl asked mine host of the Angel, 'whether Laudenbach were paved?' 'Oh, yes,' said I, 'if you jump from one stone to the other,' winked to mine host of the Angel, and left the room. He soon came after me, and we got to our inn, had the horses put to, and away we went like wildfire; and that was quite right. It will never do to take a girl from a large town. I tell you they would like the streets new paved, after their own fashion, and the houses fresh built: and when wind and rain come, they act as if in their own part of the country it were perpetual sunshine. If you will follow my advice, you will not take one from a large town, they are full of pretension; at the best you set before them they make a face, as a dog does when you hold a glass of wine to his muzzle."

"Nay, she is modest and humble — too humble."

"Indeed! There will be some difficulty, perhaps?"

"I can't say exactly."

"Come, tell me who she is."

Mine host of the Crown told his tale, with some reservations certainly. The Baker-at-the-Steps took a fresh pinch, and in the manner in which he took his snuff lurked an inexpressible satisfaction, and he said: —

"Ah! you take after the model-teacher's family; they always act as though they couldn't count five, and are all the while as cunning as they can be. That was very sly of you, not to buy Goldstumpf's beans and peas; you mean to have the vegetables and a good piece of meat into the bargain."

"Father, do not make jokes of that sort; you know I can't bear it," said mine host, and his face grew red as fire. "I can't tell you how I feel — I would not have believed that I could ever feel so again: if any one had told me so then — then . . ."

And the strong man wept and sobbed aloud.

The Baker let him weep on; he knew that these outpourings of the heart were good and necessary. He sat still upon his chair and took no snuff, but only held the open box to his nose.

"Come to your mother," he said at last, and mine host of the Crown went with his father to the paternal house.

When mine host of the Crown saw his little daughter here, he took her up, put his arm round her neck, kissed her, and would scarcely allow her to leave him again. But soon after the first kisses were over, the Baker's wife sent her little grand-daughter away to the parlor, and said to her son: —

"Raymond, that does not please me. Why should you kiss the child almost to death? I cannot bear the present fashion of fondling and kissing children in that way. I could count upon my fingers the number of times my poor father kissed me, and yet he loved me as much as ever father loved a child, and I him as much as ever child loved a father. Don't do that again, Raymond: it is not proper."

"Ah! mother there is a reason for it."

"Eh? How so?"

"O mother, I cannot say what I feel to-day, as I look upon my children: it is certainly for their good; yet I feel as though I were taking away what they have a right to expect . . . at my hands . . . from me . . . nay, I am taking nothing from them, I am going to give them — yes, I . . . I am going to give them a mother."

At the last words, the Baker's wife started up, then she seated herself again hastily with a deep sigh, and said: —

"Oh! you men, you men! What you men are, passes

belief! Ah, me! when a young mother dies, her babe should be buried with her in the grave; the best it had in the world is gone, and the worst of all may come — a step-mother. Oh! how often have I seen in these cases every pretension, and every claim, made to that which is highest and holiest of all — a mother's love: and in a moment it is falsified, and its sweetness gone! Yes, you have consoled me, have reconciled me. I should not complain so bitterly that she is dead; I weep not because she is dead, for what is death? I weep because something else is coming, which is far worse, far worse than death, a thousand times harder. Yes, yes, too truly does the old proverb say: — 'When a man marries a second time, the altar weeps.'"

The Baker's wife burst into tears, and that was unusual with her, for she liked to control her emotions: as she had but now rebuked her son's passionate kissing of his child, so in her own case she could not tolerate this passionate outburst.

Fortunately, there was a tap at the window: she had to serve bread, and after that she recovered her former self-possession.

Mine host of the Crown, who had omitted many circumstances in his story to his father, now told his mother how it had all come to pass, and she shook her head deprecatingly, as he mentioned how his mother's fame, spread by the Cathedral-baker, had been of the greatest assistance to him in winning the damsel's kindly feelings. He thanked his mother for being such a blessing to him, but she repeatedly waved her hand in a deprecating manner.

Meanwhile, the farther he proceeded in his story, the

more steadfast and penetrating grew her gaze, and at last she said: —

"Well, if it must be, I believe you have made the best choice. A young woman who has a hard lot to bear, who is shy and timid, and takes refuge in the silence of her own thoughts, is a step-child of the world. She might have become soured, quarrelsome, and have a spite against the whole world; because she and hers were of no repute, the whole world must be good for nothing, and every thing seem full of hypocrisy and deceit. I know one so venomous, she suffers not a bird to pass, without plucking a few feathers —"

"Nay, mother, she is not so; she has a noble spirit, a compassionate soul."

"Well, well; she is a step-child also, and such a step-child of the world may make a good step-mother, who knows what want of love is, who will be content to find happiness in quiet, and in doing good; who will also be content with a quiet wedding, and will not wish for much music and bustle, and for you to act as though you were just of age, and in the world for the first time. If she be such, as I fancy . . . but bless me! who can tell? Who can tell how a little experience alters first impressions? But one thing pleases me much, that she said nothing kind or encouraging to *you*, but only sent your child a present; if that is only an earnest of her intentions, she may make you a heaven upon earth. There is nothing harder in the world, than to be a second mother."

"Your mother is right," said the Baker, roguishly, "there is a proof again, that we men are better than the women. There are more kind step-fathers than step-mothers."

"That is easily explained. A father sees but little of his child till it is grown up; he has much less to do with it; but a mother must tend her child at all times, and a woman till she is forty years of age is still half a child herself, and can be a child's friend and foe. But on that subject we have not now to speak. I should certainly have been better pleased had you chosen one without money — she would have been grateful . . . but who knows? . . . Above all, bethink you, you do not marry for yourself; you marry for your children. As for Ernestine, she remains with us, of course; she knows how much we make of her — rather too much: her grandfather encourages her in her stubbornness and self-will; but I know how to manage her. I believe still, that she will be a good girl some day; but I cannot expect of a stranger that she should understand such a child's management. It cannot do Magnus any harm, even if he should get a little roughly handled; a boy must learn to put up with it, and it is a good apprenticeship for life. Ernestine, however, is once for all ours; on that score she shall not be overburdened. But why did she not send Ernestine something?"

Luckily, a visitor arrived at this moment, so that mine host of the Crown was not forced to answer the last question.

Now, after that mine host of the Crown had spoken out so confidingly and precisely to his mother, an apprehension came over him that he had imposed upon himself, that he had deceived himself — certainly, it was quite plain, he had in a manner deceived Thaddea. He now recounted to his father on the road to the mill, how he had spoken to Thaddea of only one child, and had not at all mentioned the other, and how she must believe that he had but one child.

"Then," said the Baker, "I have it. I wanted a clew to this sudden determination of a young woman to give hopes to a widower with two children."

"You are right, father; so I must not dissemble, and we shall see what will come of it."

"I can tell you at once; nothing will come of it."

"That will grieve me; but not so much as to see my children all my life treated like strangers, without any love; that would daily wring my heart."

"How you talk! I believe from all you have told me, that the girl would treat Ernestine, too, with kindness.

"I believe so, too."

"But Goldstumpf will not give her to you; and in his position no more would I. Look you, one child is no child; on the contrary, a good girl would think it only a pretty plaything; she will have a doll, with which to play. But two children are indeed children, many children a houseful of children. So what think you?"

"What?"

"Why, you must really have but one child. Ernestine is no longer yours; we will not give her up; she must be ours."

"Aye, but can I disown my child?"

"You need not do that—certainly not eventually—there is no doubt of that. Trust me, when you go and say, 'I have forgotten one thing; I have a little daughter of nine years of age;' what do you suppose she will think of you? 'It can't be helped now. What a pretty father,' she will think, 'that says not a syllable about his child.'"

"Ah! that is exactly proof for me; therefore it is just good for nothing. I should not have the heart to disown my child; it is doubly wicked, a crime against my child, and a crime against her whom I would make my wife. No, no; that must not be; so let us say no more about it."

"And I tell you it is the best way; Ernestine is ours."

"But it cannot remain concealed from Thaddea; and when she ultimately discovers it, what will she think of me?"

"Better than now, for now you are a simpleton. Have I not told you a thousand times that I know better than you how men get on in the world? Now follow my advice. It is skilfully knitted, and I will soon tie the knot tight: leave it to me. Be thankful that you have me still at your elbow."

"But my mother, what will she say when she hears of it?"

"She will not know of it just yet."

"And how am I to behave to my child when she meets me, when she calls me, when I call to her? Nay, father, it must not be. How happy have I been, and now . . . but it shall not, must not be!"

"Your mother said a sensible thing to you," answered the Baker: "a girl who marries a widower must not ask music at her wedding; but as for you, you are asking music already."

"I? O God, no!"

"Yes, yes. I was once young as well as you; things are then as bright as bright can be, when you have seen her who is to be your own; but that comes but once in life, never again. The sun rises but once in a day, and every church has but one consecration, as my father-in-law's proverb hath it. You must now marry with deliberation, and not ask for every thing to be playing joy-bells in your heart."

"Nay, without that I will not marry."

"You ought to have been a school-master, I declare; you are of the model-teacher's kidney. What need have you to tell me all that? Keep it for yourself and your bride. And as for Ernestine, take matters more easily. For the present, you cannot introduce Ernestine; but take things more easily. You take every thing too much to heart."

The Baker broke off: he was sufficiently clever to know that the tree is not felled at a single blow; but the work is to all intents and purposes done when once the soil, in which the roots rest, has been cleared away all round. Mine host of the Crown could not but reflect that there was much reason in what his father said. He certainly did take things too much to heart; he must own it himself. However, it should be otherwise. Certainly, in the present instance it was quite in place to take things more seriously, and he smiled as he thought of a beautiful scheme. His father had said himself that he needn't tell him every thing. So be it! His father should work away in his clever fashion to bring things to rights, and for himself he would tell Thaddea at his very first opportunity the whole truth.

Very well, he would take things more easily.

The Baker for several days said no more on the subject; he let his arguments silently gather strength within his son, and he smiled grimly one day, when mine host of the Crown said to his mother, "Do you see, mother, how I follow your advice? I am quite sedate and free from over-fondness towards Ernestine, and I will remain so. It is better to be a little roughly handled in childhood; you take things more easily in after-life."

The Baker smiled grimly; he knew what this speech foreboded; and in the evening he innocently asked his son, when they should start for Freiburg.

"To-morrow, if you like, or even to-day," answered mine host.

But Ernestine had accidentally surprised her grandfather and father, as they were talking of her being disowned; something took place in the heart of the child, but did not outwardly show itself. Her grandfather had in the presence of the child, in spite of all her grandmother's endeavors to prevent it, often remarked how helpless, and easily biassed, and overreached mine host of the Crown was. He had, after his fashion, often done so with coarse jokes; and when his wife represented to him in strong colors the impropriety, he said, "I can't help speaking out to you; before the world, of course I shield him as much as possible." These words, however, had pierced the soul of the child; and now when she saw herself disowned, this discovery, combined with what she had heard before mentioned—often with ridicule—awakened in her a singularly stubborn resolve.

There are matters in which there is no sign of acidity apparent; it is only when a new matter is introduced and unites itself with the acid ingredient, that it becomes evident. So, too, with dispositions; suddenly the results of bitter impressions show themselves at the addition of a new fact with which they unite. In the morning, while her grandmother was still asleep, Ernestine hastily rose, dressed herself quite alone; and when at the first glimmer of day her father and grandfather started for the market-town, there stood Ernestine on the hill behind the trees, looked fixedly after them awhile, and then hurried forwards. She afterwards confessed, that, though not quite clear about it, she too had meant to plod to Freiburg, and there to rush into the presence of all, and cry: "I also am your child!" She ran on and on, and wept and sobbed as she went.

Accidentally the miller's man was coming down the footpath with his asses all laden with corn-sacks; he saw Ernestine, and called out to her; and as the child gave vague answers, without any further questioning he seated her comfortably upon one of his asses, and brought her back to the town. The gate-keeper's children were already at play here, and Ernestine, whose thoughts were thus turned towards her brother, could no longer be detained; she sprang from the saddle and rushed into the town home to her brother. As long as her father and grandfather were away, Ernestine would not suffer her little brother out of her sight; and,—where the people got the rumor from, there is no saying,—but she was continually being asked when her new mother was coming. And Ernestine was quite proud when she heard people say, there was no need for her father to marry again, for that she would soon be grown up, and even now could take a mother's care of her little brother. And the old servant often told the children the Story of the Juniper-tree; how a wicked step-mother killed her step-child; and how the little sister buried her little brother's bones under a juniper-tree, and the little brother became a bird, and sang so wondrously, and how he wore a large mill-stone round his neck, which he dropped down from the tree upon the wicked step-mother, and ground her to powder. . . .

THE TRIP A-WOOING.

ERY silently, father and son drove on for some time; the latter was sad at heart; he would willingly have turned back again, but dared not show his weakness to his father. At last he confessed he had perhaps said too much; he had not yet been nearly explicit enough with Thaddea to be sure of her answer, and with Goldstumpf not a word had been said upon the subject.

"I don't know what to think," answered the Baker; "you are not a bit like a man who already has a household and two children. You act just like a raw young lad, so timidly and awkwardly. It would seem to me too, as if we were getting into the fog, but now we are once on the road we must go on till we get into a clearer atmosphere. Don't try to settle beforehand what and how every thing is to be; we must regulate our trade by the market."

Mine host seemed to himself spellbound and shackled, as it were, by his father; and the latter was cunning enough to keep his own particular plan a secret.

Now that his son had of his own accord turned his thoughts to a second marriage, that fact must be kept steadily before his eyes: and though nothing should come of the present venture, it was not difficult to involve him in another, for which the Baker already intended to provide.

Mine host of the Crown's thoughts had outstripped the wheels, quickly as they rolled along; he was by Thaddea's side and telling her all — when he was suddenly made aware that he was still sitting in the wagon, and that his father was asking him all manner of questions, while a strange world was all around him.

When at length he arrived again at our baker's house in the Cathedral-close, and the young baker bade his old master heartily welcome, the Baker-at-the-Steps said: "It is quite proper to call me 'master' still; but it is better, more respectful to yourself I mean, to call me now only Mr. Deputy."

"Oh! very well, Mr. Deputy," said the baker.

Whilst the Baker-at-the-Steps sat with the young wife, and inquired more particularly about Thaddea, and lastly said point blank why he had come, mine host of the Crown was walking up and down the town full of uneasiness. He was now a stranger there, where he would be soon perhaps at home, and in these very streets Thaddea had for so many years passed to and fro, had been a child and grown a woman, had known nothing of him, and he nothing of her, and now they would both of them soon have no more thoughts, or joys, or sorrows, but what they would share in common.

Perhaps here or there went one who knew her, and with whom he might have spoken of her; but he was not sure, and could not inquire. He went through King-street, and stood a long time at the Brisachs-gate, and examined the dazzling picture of St. Martin with his sword dividing his cloak for the naked beggar. He was lost in contemplation of the picture, and then again he fancied he could trace thereon Thaddea's eyes, which must have rested upon it so many, many times.

Mine host of the Crown had strolled up to the Castle-hill, and from here he looked out far around upon the refreshing prospect, away yonder to the town and the valley of the Rhine all along to the Vosges. And here in the neighborhood, how winsome is all! The mountains unite the coolness of the forest and the luscious joyousness of the vine — and every growth is so thriving, so plenteous!

Nature uttered no sound; and all that gave warning of men and their thoughts and their labors, was the chime of clocks, yonder from the city, and the bugle-call of the signal-men, away off in the forest, as they practised their counter-signs: for in those days the third world-wide power, the factory-bell, was not heard therein.

The scent of the autumn-fading leaves, the distant hum of the busy town, all roused in mine host of the Crown a remembrance which had not yet grown old: how he had once before on such an evening gone up from the house to the mountain: and he could not comprehend how the trees should still be standing, the carriages still rolling along the streets, and the drovers still singing by the side of their grazing herds, and hallooing to each other, and cracking their whips. There is the teeming world: and there, in the heart of it, is death; for yonder, down beneath, lay ——

But away! Reminiscences may rise; but they cannot bring life back again; and just now there must be something different. But can it be possible that spring is coming back again, and you are rejoicing in it?

As if flying from himself, he hurried down from the Castle-hill. A light, evening autumn-breeze had already risen. At Carthusian-street, mine host of the Crown suddenly stood still at a garden hedge; behind it appeared a well-kept garden, with a pretty summer-house. He remained rooted to the spot: it seemed as if he recognized a voice, which said: — "Yes, Joseph, go now: go through the next garden, that father may know nothing about it. Oh, God! a time must come when we shall no more meet in secret, stealthily as to-day. Go quickly, go; I am so frightened."

There was the sound of a man stealing swiftly away; and mine host of the Crown trembled: it was Thaddea who had spoken. He wished, pierced as he was to the very heart, to slip away, but Thaddea just at this moment turned round and recognized him. She gazed vacantly at him, and only passed her hand once over her forehead, as though recovering from a dream. At last, mine host of the Crown managed to utter the words: "Good evening, Miss Godmother."

She was wonderfully composed, and said: "Ah! is it you? Nothing but miracles are happening to-day: it is scarcely five minutes since I was speaking of you."

"Of me?"

"Yes, my brother was just here: the brother of whom I told you; with whom my father cannot bear me to speak."

"So that was your brother then? Forgive me!"

"What should I forgive?"

"No, no. I don't know what I am talking about. May I come in?"

Thaddea made no answer; and without farther questioning mine host opened the gate, and walked into the garden. He stood by Thaddea's side not far from an apple-tree, whose heavy, rosy-cheeked fruit pulled the branches almost down to the ground. Mine host took an apple in his hand, but did not pluck it, and said: "So you were speaking of me? That is well. I, too, have spoken much of you, but I have still more to say to you; you must know all I mean; and my father has now come with me, and we are now staying here, and it is God's dispensation that I was destined thus to meet you beforehand. How did I gaze at every one I met in the whole town, and would fain have asked—'Can you not tell me where I can see my fellow-sponsor, if it be but for a few minutes?' And now here I am, and still I know not what to say, and you have not yet once given me your hand in token of welcome."

She held out her hand at this, and it trembled: mine host of the Crown continued:—

"I am now no longer a young man; I have already seen much sorrow, and it becomes me not to be any longer thus, and yet I know not how it is . . . oh that some one would speak for me! I cannot say myself, that . . . that none can say any ill of me—oh! if my mother were but here!"

"You are a pretty tall child for a mother's darling; it can speak for itself, it can," said Thaddea, playfully; but mine host did not look at all playful, and she continued:—"You are happy in still having a mother!"

"Yes, and such a mother! I am her son, and it might be put down as vanity on my part; but the whole town, the whole neighborhood is witness that she is uprightness itself, and none can know as I do how sincerely she speaks good of all men, and does good to all men, of which they know nothing. She who is no more, she knew it too; how many thousand times have we spoken of it! and when we spoke of it, we felt as though we were coming from the church. Still my mother can laugh and be merry; and so once could I, and could again: oh! I could wish for nothing more delightful than to see you sitting by my mother, and both of you gazing in each other's eyes. Look at me now — I know no longer what I am saying."

"Yes, yes," said she; "I thought you loved your parents thus, and what a happiness it is still to have a mother — and such a mother! The Cathedral-baker has told me much of her."

"'Tis kind of him, but he cannot know her so well as her own son."

"Certainly," said Thaddea; "what one's parents are, no stranger can know. My father — why should I not say so? — is, I well know, looked upon with an evil eye by many; but still I know he has a tender heart, and is only ashamed to let the world perceive it; and you will honor and respect my father too."

"Assuredly!" said mine host; "and I love you twice as much for saying so, and shall ever keep it in mind."

For a long while they said not another word; and during the pause two apples fell from the tree, and both stooped after them; mine host raised them, gave Thaddea one, and kept the other himself. Thaddea received the apple as a matter of course, and as she gazed upon its rosy cheeks, she said: —

"How is your little son?"

"Quite well. And what I have to say besides . . ."

Mine host of the Crown could say no more, for the little boy from Kirchzart, who was staying at the Cathedral-baker's, ran suddenly into the garden, and said: "Miss Thaddea, you must come to my aunt directly; she has something particular to tell you — this moment."

"May I not accompany you?" said mine host.

"No!" was the answer; but in the tone in which it was spoken, notwithstanding the decided negative, there was something so cordial that mine host assented cheerfully.

"I had so much to say to you," stammered he; but the maiden expressed to him with a look that he should say no more before the boy. She quickly drew her shawl round her, motioned to mine host to leave the garden, and hurried with the boy with swift steps away.

Mine host moved a few strides after her, then stopped; there were many emotions within him, but above all rose the thought, "Why did you not tell her all at once? Oh! had you but done so! Then there had been no more deception, no further gulf between you!" He was so disheartened that he sat down on a heap of stones upon the road, and it pained him deeply that what he had hitherto concealed, must now, perforce, remained concealed. He himself appeared like a rejected, disowned child; and now he felt as if his child were sitting by him, and involuntarily he clutched with his hand at his side.

No, it should not be.

Quickly he rose up and went to the town; he knew where Thaddea was to be found, and he could tell her even now: now it did not seem to be deception.

AN UNEXPECTED MEETING.

HILST mine host of the Crown was on the Castle-hill and in the garden, the Baker-at-the-Steps had found out quite enough from the wife of his former apprentice, and this time he found the straightforward way to be not only the best, but also the shortest. He learned that Goldstumpf drank his evening glass at the hotel called the "Wild Man," in Salt Street, and he went to him at once. He found him alone at a table. "With your permission," said he, and sat down opposite. Goldstumpf laid his hand on his huge dog's head, nodded, and looked wonderingly at the stranger; or was it really the Baker-at-the-Steps? "Aha! he is coming to make a compromise. Good: whoever is the first to come a-begging, has found out that he is in the wrong, and must also pay for it."

Goldstumpf lifted his glass to his mouth, but did not drink. He was of all things careful of health: his favorite saying was well-known; "I have, thank God, nothing to reproach myself with; I have denied myself nothing in my life." He felt that he was now in a triumphant, joyous state of mind, and under these circumstances a glass of wine does no good: he must first let every thing return to a state of rest; then the flavor is better. He still kept sharply watching the Baker over the rim of his glass, but the latter said: —

"Oh yes, it is I, in the flesh. To-day we can drink peaceably together, and to-morrow appear together before the Court."

Goldstumpf felt quite sure the rascal gave his case up for lost, and that was the only meaning of his fair words; but he resolved not to return them, and said: "I'm not to be trifled with, friend; you will find out to-morrow whom you have to deal with."

"You do me honor by be-'friend'-ing me; come, let us clink glasses upon it," said the Baker, and clinked his glass against Goldstumpf's; but the latter never stirred his: "There," said the Baker, "we can talk more easily upon 'friend'-ly terms. Are you vexed, now, about that lawsuit? Why, I thought I was doing you a kindness: you know you are never happy unless you have at least a dozen actions going: and, besides, I wanted to try what chance a man would have in a race with you; and to be outrun by you is no disgrace."

Goldstumpf smirked, and, stroking his dog's head, said to him: "We two never make a mistake, do we, Turk?"

And the Baker likewise turning to the dog, said: "You're a Turk, and your master's a pagan. Yes, you're well suited, you're not to be caught alive: now, don't bite me, I'll not do any thing to you. You're a match for men, and your master for something else ——."

Goldstumpf laughed. Now the game was won.

The Baker was quite sure, if he could only get a hearing, there was nothing which he could not arrange. "Look you now," said he; "there are roads so narrow you wouldn't believe that two vehicles could avoid a collision there, and pass one another—particularly when they're full—yet they do. But how? One pulls up; then the other can get by. You drive on, you drive on! and I'll pull up."

"You're no fool," said Goldstumpf, and nodded to the Baker, and the latter easily passed on to considering the lawsuit dropped. He spoke in raptures of the large business connection of his opponent, and took occasion to hint that he must have also no lack of profitable transactions: but what was it all in comparison with the old war-times, when such large slices of luck were to be had! Goldstumpf became more and more pleased as the Baker recounted some of those well-known master-strokes which he had displayed in his commissariat dealings at that time, and particularly how, once upon a time, in Villingen, at head-quarters, he delivered forty yearling-calves instead of four hundred oxen.

Goldstumpf laughed, and soon, of his own accord, began to tell him one of his cunning tricks; and the Baker edged nearer and nearer, and soon they were nudging and whispering to each other, and then laughing aloud, and Goldstumpf clinked of his own free will with the Baker, as the latter showed him some dodges in corn-meting, and how a corn-measurer might be the first corn-merchant without anybody knowing any thing about it for years. The two became continually more familiar, and although they still for some time longer be-'friend'-ed each other, they once more drank together, and clinked in token of brotherhood. Just as the Baker was putting down his glass, he looked out of the window and said: "Why, what is all this? There—yes, there goes my son!"

He rapped upon the window-glass. and mine host of the Crown felt a shudder run through him, as he suddenly looked up and saw his father's and Goldstumpf's eyes directed down towards him; and both signed to him. Mine host went in. He could not, for the life of him, comprehend how every thing should succeed so rapidly: yonder Thaddea was now sitting with the Cathedral-baker's wife, and here was his father already on such good terms with the man he dreaded. Mine host had nearly dropped from sheer terror, for a monster sprang suddenly upon him; the dog, who knew him from the Lenzkirch journey, had welcomed him after his fashion, as though he considered it only proper behavior towards his master's friend, and indeed his bounden duty.

"Heyday! Are you the son of that fellow there? Of that rogue? and yet can be so honest? I wouldn't have believed it. House here! a bottle of Margrave!" cried Goldstumpf.

The trio sat familiarly together, and mine host of the Crown was full of trembling within as he heard his substance made a subject of boast by his father, and when the latter put pointedly and prominently forward the fact, that he had but one child, who inherited an independent property on the mother's side.

Until late in the night they sat together, and Goldstumpf became jollier and jollier, asserting that he liked the Baker because he was a rogue, and one of the old sort; and that he liked mine host of the Crown too, because he withal still appeared an honest fellow. It was so nowadays; the children were now much more particular than their fathers had been: he found it even in his own children, particularly in his daughter.

Mine host of the Crown trembled as he mentioned her, but the Baker said calmly: "Oh! you have a daughter too? Is she married yet?"

"No; she won't have any one."

Mine host of the Crown kicked his father under the table; he did not know what his son meant, and now merely asked Goldstumpf whether he would be at home next morning, and whether he might call upon him.

"No," said he; "I must go to Kirchzart to load oats."

At length they separated. On the way home, the Baker said to his son: "The business is as good as done. Don't you see I was right? I sounded Goldstumpf, and he said directly, that a girl who had a home of her own, and didn't mean to be nothing more or less than a married nursery-maid, must be foolish to marry a widower with several children. So at present he must not know any thing about Ernestine."

"But Thaddea must know it before we are engaged: I will not yield that point on any condition; that I am determined upon."

"Very well, I will undertake that: but, mind, you must not say a word on the subject."

"Why?"

"I have my reasons. That is sufficient for the present."

The father and son went together to the Cathedral-baker's, and there it was arranged that the Cathedral-baker's wife should ask Goldstumpf to take her with him to Kirchzart—of course, only to induce Thaddea to go too; and then, as if accidentally, mine host of the Crown and Goldstumpf's son should meet them there.

At night mine host of the Crown wished to have a long talk with his father, but the latter was soon sleeping the sleep of the just. But mine host of the Crown started up often in the night, and fancied he heard the voice of his little daughter, so mournful, so complaining. He counted each quarter, as it struck from the Cathedral-tower and the other clocks that chimed beside, and between whiles pined for his old schoolmastering, which often allowed him to see that the chimes of the Cathedral rang out the quarters always in quint and terce to the key-note of the full hour. For the first time for a long, long while, he was weeping in the early morning as the day dawned.

He looked pale, and it was not until the Cathedral-baker's wife said that she and Thaddea were going to Kirchzart, that his cheeks were tinged with red again. He took the Cathedral-baker's wife aside, and told her how he hoped, by God's blessing, Thaddea would be a good mother to *both* his children. They had *both* good hearts; though Ernestine had been a little spoilt by her grandparents: she would remain with her grandparents. They were *both* good children. He repeated the word "both" over and over again, that the Cathedral-baker's wife also might not forget to impart this to Thaddea. He did not exactly lay any charge upon her, but he was quite sure she would not forget it, and he felt an inward triumph at having forestalled his father and behaved honorably.

The Cathedral-baker's wife appeared to understand it all.

She had packed some provision in a hamper to take to Kirchzart, because they would not be prepared there for so many guests; and with an air of great certainty, she said: "That is the betrothal-feast."

The sun was already warm before they could start, for

the Cathedral-baker's wife must take her baby; and Goldstumpf drove up to the house to take them. The Baker-at-the-Steps went out to greet him, but mine host of the Crown did not show himself; he only stole a glance as the Cathedral-baker's wife gave her baby into Thaddea's arms, and saw how the latter laid it on her bosom and kissed it; he heard her beg her friend to allow her to keep it in her arms; and now away rolled the vehicle.

Before her departure, the Cathedral-baker's wife had also imparted to mine host of the Crown that Thaddea had said how nice it would be should her brother find his way to Kirchzart; and the Cathedral-baker's wife had told her, as a secret, that it was mine host of the Crown's design to invite him. Thaddea had thereupon been quite overjoyed: mine host should, therefore, make no delay, but execute his plans at once: he should go straight to her brother and tell him what they were about. How cunning the world had become all at once! and how cleverly the Cathedral-baker's wife had devised something in his favor! Why is it, pray, that things so seldom go straightforward in the world?

Mine host of the Crown was inclined to tell his father what orders he had received, but he gave up the idea: he had a feeling that there are things which cold-blooded deliberation dissuades from, as surely as simple impulse insists on trying at all hazards. He had, first of all, a feeling of joy that he could be of service to Thaddea; secondly, he said to himself: "By God's blessing, he will be your brother-in-law, and then you will have shown him already how you feel towards him, and altogether — the matter is in good hands."

Without, therefore, saying any thing about it to his

father, he went to his future brother-in-law, and was not a little astonished when the latter told him that Thaddea had already spoken of him, and even the very evening before had ventured to summon him into the garden.

As to his going, as if by accident, to Kirchzart, with his wife and one child, he would not hear of it. But at the repeated pressure of mine host, he said: "At all events, my wife and child shall stay at home. I cannot subject them to the chance of my father insulting them or turning them out of doors; do you think I can?"

"I'm sure I cannot tell."

"But I can—and so, to please my sister and to please you, for I tell you honestly I like you, I will ride over alone. Whatever treatment I meet with, I can bear it from my father: he is, and always will be, my father."

"I thank you from the bottom of my heart; I don't know—I feel all at once so certain—I think all must be well; indeed, I cannot bring myself to believe that there should be men in the world living at variance with each other."

"Yes, yes, my sister was quite right."

"In what?"

"That I must not tell you; but she rightly divined your character; and now I tell you—she is my sister, and I should not sing her praises—I tell you, you must have done some good in the world to be allowed to win her for your wife; God does not give a man such a wife without a reason."

With his heart swelling high, mine host returned from the brother's. He had found another being worthy of his admiration, whom he should one day call brother. Oh! what deep springs lie concealed! and oh! these hours, when the magic wand reveals them to quicken and refresh!

Soon mine host of the Crown himself put his horses to, but the Baker-at-the-Steps drove: they were obliged to make a considerable détour to arrive, not by the Freiburg, but the opposite side, that the meeting might appear all the more accidental. There was nothing against which mine host of the Crown could raise his voice; he was obliged to acquiesce in all; and this détour, which took them hither and thither, for nothing in the world but deception's sake, caused him the most heartfelt pain.

The Cathedral-baker's wife was right, the provisions she took with her served for the betrothal-feast.

Immediately after his arrival, the Baker-at-the-Steps had hurried to Thaddea, and spoken to her in a low, earnest tone: then he came with an air of triumph to his son, and said: "The chief point is settled and clearly understood, and I have told her all: so much for that. Now I will go to Goldstumpf; he is at the oats-lading."

The Baker-at-the-Steps found Goldstumpf directly at the Corn Exchange, and the fat rogue leered as the Baker-at-the-Steps now showed him how to mete so as to bring more or less, according to inclination, to the measure. Then the Baker took him aside and told him straightforwardly what was going on. Goldstumpf at first would hear nothing said about it; then the Baker said: "You see your daughter is of age: don't a second time cause a child to marry against your inclination. Cry whoa! before the horses stop of themselves. Look you, there are drivers who, when they are ascending a hill, don't trouble their heads to think when they ought to rest their horses; and when they stop of themselves, whoa! cries the driver, and puts a stone under the wheel. It is too late then. Had he done so sooner, he would have been entitled to gratitude, and the horses would have done their work all the better afterwards. You have still time; take my advice and cry whoa! otherwise, the horses will stop of themselves."

"I have no objection; in fact, I never had any objection," answered Goldstumpf; "but I must tell you honestly, you're mistaken."

"I? how?"

"I'm not so rich as you think; my daughter will not have half so much as you imagine."

"I'll imagine a little, then; but you must leave me at perfect liberty to believe you or not, you honest, honest father-in-law, you poverty-stricken rascal! Your hand — it is a bargain."

They both held out their hands, and there was a mutual squeeze. Goldstumpf was man enough to hold his own against the Baker's hard, bony fist: the Baker did not succeed here in what gave him so much pleasure when he shook hands with any one; to wit, nearly breaking his fingers in two.

Goldstumpf had been taken by surprise, but he quickly made as though he had anticipated it all, and a smile, full of bitterness and sorrow, passed over his features as Thaddea came up to him hand in hand with her lover.

He felt a grudge against her for leaving him; he had never thought of it and never intended it, and it was with a peculiar huskiness of voice, and dimness of the eye, that he gave her his consent.

When they were about sitting down to table, a horseman came galloping up to the inn. Goldstumpf looked out, but bobbed down again as if he had been shot. The steps were mounted; the door opened; and with a cry of "Oh! my dear brother!" Thaddea flew to the new-comer, and fell upon his neck.

The Cathedral-baker's wife was sly enough to disguise the whole matter: she said aloud to mine host of the Crown: "That is your bride's brother;" and turning to the brother, she said: "That is the bridegroom and his father."

The brother and mine host looked at each other with surprise, and held out their hands.

How could the Cathedral-baker's wife, that simple body, be so sly as neither by voice nor look to betray any thing! She played her part so well indeed that Goldstumpf, as he saw the look of surprise on the part of the two men, really thought it the result of a first meeting.

"Well, I intend to begin!" said Goldstumpf; and without further notice of his son, he sat down at the table. He was particularly merry; and when glasses were clinked at the health of the wedding couple, he clinked with his son, as he said: "You here too!" and those were the first words he had spoken to him for thirteen years.

His son was so astounded at the question, that he could make no other answer than "Yes, father!" Beyond this, Goldstumpf acted just as though his son had not been there.

Mine host of the Crown made continual attempts to bring father and son together; but Goldstumpf always behaved as if there were nothing but empty air where his son was sitting.

When at length they were preparing for the drive home, the Baker-at-the-Steps took his son aside, and said: "Be on your guard, Raymond. I have tried to talk it out of your father-in-law; but still he may think again, that it was your contrivance that the brother should drop in, as if accidentally."

"Yes, father, it is so; and I am proud of bringing it about. I shall not give over until all is peace and happiness."

"Speak lower: and I tell you, you should give up: you can't level all hills, — you or your mother either: and I can tell you, you'll find you've lost the game altogether with Goldstumpf, if you do any thing further in the matter."

The presence of the brother was the outward and only cause of uneasiness which interrupted the harmony of the entertainment; for the inward, arising from the child that was ignored, was no longer experienced.

As Goldstumpf mounted to his seat, he said to all the others: "Good-by, pleasant journey;" but as for his son, he again behaved as though he were empty air.

It was a joyous drive home. They were obliged to be home while it was still daylight, on account of the child; and Thaddea had said: "I am glad the child was present at our betrothal: you know I shall soon have one of my own. If it were but as small as this! But still I will caress him and love him; and then he will be sure to love me. Is not Magnus our boy's name?"

"Yes!" Mine host could say no more.

The two fathers had driven on together; they were extremely merry; and Goldstumpf had tied a red ribbon on his whip-handle, and, in spite of the protests of all, given his dog a few sausages.

Mine host of the Crown drove the Cathedral-baker's

wife and Thaddea. The latter had again insisted upon holding the child in her arms, and in a low tone she sang the child a lullaby; and mine host made his horses go at a quiet pace over the smooth road, that he might hear her voice. She sang so charmingly! The evening sun was glowing red: from the Cathedral-tower chimed the bell for vespers, as Thaddea, lifting up the child to heaven, said: "Make me a kind and strong heart, O God! that I be no step-mother, but a mother indeed!"

"Amen!" said mine host and the Cathedral-baker's wife, as if with one mouth: and the three spoke not another word until their journey's end.

FORSAKEN.

URPASSINGLY happy as mine host of the Crown was, the idea of the concealment was still continually a burden to him: he had not spoken freely and openly with Thaddea upon every point; but as for Goldstumpf, it never occurred to him that he had also been deceived.

Mine host stood in the corn-market like one lost. As though it were the first time he had seen it, he watched the perpetual heaving up and down, the peculiar swing with which the sacks were loaded and unloaded, and how the countrymen, leaning with crossed arms on their sacks, drove their bargains. Twice, indeed, was he almost knocked down by the sack-carriers, who move out of the way for nobody: for, like a man in a dream, he was watching a little girl, who, in the midst of the noise and confusion, perched upon one of the heaps of sacks piled up all round the pillars, was calmly sleeping.

He searched for the Cathedral-baker; he was on the shelf beneath the grand staircase, calculating and paying away. He asked him whether his wife had said any thing to him about Ernestine.

The baker replied, smiling: "Oh! yes: and now make yourself quite happy: I really believe you don't know what a lucky man you are!"

Mine host of the Crown, of course, could not tell that his father had already taken his precautions, and imposed silence upon all; and he was weak enough not to seek certainty at the fountain head.

The Baker-at-the-Steps was standing not far from the couple with Goldstumpf. They were rubbing barley in their hands, and were deliberating how they should now play each other's game; but the Baker-at-the-Steps took a peep on one side, and in the face of his son and his former apprentice he read what had been the subject of conversation. He smiled at his own thoughts.

The Baker-at-the-Steps hastened his return home: principally on account of the sale of the Postmastership in his own town, which was to take place the next day. Mine host of the Crown had but a few minutes for a parting interview with his betrothed: and the wedding was settled to take place in a few weeks. She gave him several presents for Magnus. Mine host was particularly pleased with a pair of muff-gloves which she had knitted herself; and she owned with a blush that, under any circumstances, she would have found an opportunity of sending them to the child.

It was on mine host's lips to ask whether she had nothing for Ernestine, but the question died away within him.

On the drive home there were all kinds of discussion, and the Baker-at-the-Steps said: "Trust me, I am an old, experienced man: no porridge is eaten so hot as it's cooked. Things, when they really come, are not so pretty and not so ugly as you picture them at a distance. That the old one will laugh at it, I am ready at once to take my sacred oath; and, as I said, I have devised a plan. We old folks will regularly adopt Ernestine: then it is really the plain truth which we have said. Now make yourself happy as you ought: I say, with the Cathedral-baker, you don't know at all what a lucky fellow you are."

And, in fact, mine host did become much more cheerful, and the Bakeress-at-the-Steps had every thing told her; and in the evening Ernestine had to take a quantity of bread to the houses of the poor. The grandmother had no notion that she was thereby fortunately removing from the father the look of the child, of whom he had himself told Thaddea nothing.

In the town and neighborhood there was much talk, when people heard of the engagement of mine host of the Crown with Goldstumpf's daughter: and when the Post-office inn was sold by auction, the Baker-at-the-Steps bought it, and obtained for his son the charge of the Post-office.

Mine host of the Crown had no idea that this had been planned in concert with his father-in-law; and it was not until now that Goldstumpf pointed out in the paper the engagement of his daughter "to Mr. Postmaster Burkhart, only son of Mr. Deputy Burkhart, of Rottweil."

It was now said in the town that the Baker-at-the-Steps would buy up half the place, and many fabulous accounts were given of the enormous riches of Goldstumpf. Meanwhile, his berth in the Post-office was in other ways agreeable to mine host of the Crown: he not only thus commenced a new sort of life in a new house, and so got rid of many old and sad remembrances; but his ingenuity in all descriptions of writing came by that means into request again. His mother made the most magnificent arrangements for her son, and the whole borough was in a commotion, when, in the month of November, two carriages, decorated with flowers, and with postilions merrily blowing their horns, drove into the town. In the first sat the new Postmaster with his wife, and Goldstumpf and the Baker-at-the-Steps in the second.

The Baker's wife had, no doubt, exerted herself too much in preparing for her son's arrival: she was now so unwell she was obliged to lie down. That was the only vexation amid the joyous emotions which the family and the whole town experienced. On the other hand, however, it was lucky; since they thus got over the difficulty about telling the whole truth immediately.

At their entry, when the postilions blew their horns, there was a general cheer: but one single child stood unnoticed aside, and her eyes dilated, and there was something savage in her expression, as she saw the woman alight who had robbed her of her father.

Little Magnus had been prettily dressed up in a neat postilion's suit; and the whole town had done nothing but talk of how the young wife had carried him in her arms up the steps, — and he was a pretty heavy weight.

"Where is Ernestine? why is she not here? She must see her mother!" said the Postmaster to his father, as he stood in the hall; and the latter answered: "Be quiet for a day or two longer, until Goldstumpf has gone: then we will tell her."

"Will tell her? Haven't you told her then?"

"Come, come; don't pretend you thought I had. I am quite pleased to see you so cunning for once, and trying to take me in."

"I! O God! you do me wrong. But let me go: not another minute will I bear this deception. Let me go."

"Eh? Will you give your wife no better reception than a quarrel on the spot with her father? As soon as Goldstumpf has turned his back, we will set matters to rights; rely upon it. Now show a little sense."

Mine host of the Crown was obliged to be pacified; and Thaddea who saw him so pale and almost every moment trembling, said: "I can easily conceive, dear husband, that such an entry is painful to you, after having once already . . . but an inward voice tells me that we shall be very, very happy; and it pleases me well to think I can be by your side. You are stronger than you imagine, and than your father likes to allow. If only you have some one near you, by whom your own good heart is well supported . . . and such will I be."

Mine host wept silently. But there were now fresh days of merry-making, for Goldstumpf rode, walked, and drove in great style everywhere about, and in the public room at the Post he felt himself quite at home, and Turk could already open the door. There Goldstumpf often used to say, he hoped soon to retire from business and settle down in those parts. He would then have the old Crown inn comfortably fitted up, — that is to say, fresh-built of free-stone from top to bottom, and the windows should have mirror-panes, that all the world might admire themselves therein.

In private the Bride said with tremulous voice to her husband: "Believe it not: my father will never move hither; he has long intended to leave Freiburg, but cannot: it vexes him too much when he can no longer vex the people by showing them how well he is doing. He cannot leave Freiburg."

"Be not uneasy," said the former host of the Crown,

now the Postmaster; "even should your father move hither, he will be loved and prized by me: I will honor and reverence him as is but right: of that be well assured. We have all our failings, and there is not one quite as he should be. Believe me, I am not so upright as you imagine, and I have need that others should have patience with me too."

"You are a good creature; that be assured I shall never forget," said Thaddea.

Goldstumpf took his departure, and the Postmaster accompanied him half the way, until they met his father-in-law's conveyance. The Baker-at-the-Steps had wished to undertake the task, meanwhile, of telling the young wife the plain truth. Mine host of the Crown, however, had said: "No, neither you nor I: tell my mother all, and she shall do it: when she is our help, all goes well."

The Baker-at-the-Steps could not, or would not, acknowledge that his son considered him unworthy to tell the whole truth now, for he answered: "Bravo! you are wise. I must honestly say, to see you so wise rejoices me as much as if I were so myself, and still more. Yes, yes, the good a father possesses in his son, is better than if he had it in himself."

It was well the Postmaster was not at home at the revelation to his mother, for the bitter cry, which she ceased not night and day, would have lacerated his heart. She invoked her who was dead, she invoked all good angels, and conjured them to let her take no part in this fearful sin: she was so beside herself that indeed there was some fear for her life; and Thaddea, who would have nursed her mother-in-law in her sudden illness, was not permitted to do so. A little maid, a child of nine years of age, cried after her: "She will not see you on any account; you . . ."

Thaddea seemed to herself quite lost for the two days during which her husband was away; and had she not had Magnus with her, she would have pined away for very sorrow. She felt an uneasiness, a strangeness, which she could not explain to herself.

In the afternoon of the day when the Postmaster was without fail to return, she dressed herself gayly and intended to go to meet him; afterwards, she changed her mind and stayed at home. She had no notion of exposing in the public street the tenderness of her reception. However, she would not have found her husband, for the Baker-at-the-Steps, now that his wife was out of danger, went to meet his son: he made him alight outside the town and walk with him to the court-house. What he had hitherto deferred, he would now accomplish; he would adopt Ernestine.

UNDER THE ROLLING WHEEL.

VERY afternoon as it struck half-past two, came in the fast coach from Schaffhausen, and the guard blew a merry note, and then little Magnus always appeared, and he was allowed to sit upon the saddle-horse, which was unharnessed, and went panting and weary, of his own accord, to the stable.

To-day was the first clear winter-day. The ground was frozen hard. To-day Ernestine had earnestly beckoned her brother, and little Magnus was just springing across the street to her as the horses came by: there was no time to pull up, and with a cry of "My Magnus! my brother!" Ernestine flew to the child. He had been thrown down, but she laia no hold on him; she sprang to the bridle of one horse, and, though lifted high up from her feet, she forced him back. The young wife, who had looked out from the window, rushed down and hurried to Magnus, whose forehead was bleeding. In a moment a crowd was collected, and they were obliged to tear Ernestine away, who was clinging to the horse's bridle with unconscious convulsiveness. The mother now raised her bleeding child, and with a cry of sorrow shrieked: "Alas! my poor dear child!"

"No! he is not yours, he is mine: he is my brother, he does not belong to you," sobbed Ernestine.

The mother grew ashy pale as she looked upon the child, who clung to her and almost tore her clothes from her body. She dragged the child with her into the house. There she at once washed little Magnus's wounds: he had, fortunately, only the skin of his forehead grazed, and his left eyebrow torn; he soon opened his eyes, and a surgeon who was luckily passing came in, and pronounced the wounds not at all dangerous.

"What does that child — Ernestine I think her name is — mean?" asked the wife of the old servant.

"Why, she is yours as well as Magnus: she is his little sister: but, for God's sake, do not say I revealed it."

"That is exactly what the child herself cried out. Oh, Heaven! how I have been treated!"

The wife pressed her white lips together; she needed all her energies to keep her from sinking to the ground.

The Baker-at-the-Steps had been sent for, but he was nowhere to be found; and yet he had not told any one that he was going into the country.

Of course he could not be found, for he was at the Court-house with the Registrar, in the back room.

That there might be a portion of truth in what they told Thaddea, and also because Ernestine was so beloved by her grandfather and grandmother that they could not bear to part with her, it was determined that she should really no longer be the Postmaster's daughter. Her grandparents were to adopt her regularly as their child, and settle upon her a full child's portion. It was a hard trial for the Postmaster to consent to it, but he saw no other escape, and they were for that purpose, in the office and the Baker-at-the-Steps was having an adoption-certificate drawn up.

Just as the Registrar called in his two clerks and bade them sign their names as witnesses, the elder said to the Postmaster:

"Your little boy, Magnus, has fallen under one of the horses, the town surgeon is at your house, and the physician has been sent for."

The Postmaster hurried away; his father could not overtake him.

Must he lose one child because he had disowned the other? "Yes," thought he, "I have sinned. Oh that I alone might expiate my sin without bringing pain on those I love! Oh! Magnus, my poor child, what have you done that you should die!"

The people in the street signed to him to make haste, and many shouted to him, and yet the Postmaster felt as though his knees must give way; and could it be so far from the office to the post? He felt as though he must thrust away the houses with his hand that he might shorten the road. At last he arrived at his house. A crowd of people was assembled there, who opened to let him pass; he stood upon the steps, and could neither draw a breath nor raise a foot, as the old servant shouted from an upper window:

"Come up, sir. Magnus has already asked for you, and it is nothing to signify."

He succeeded in mounting the steps, and when, on opening the door, he cried: "Wife! for God's sake—our child!" his wife drew herself up, looked as though she would speak but could not find utterance, and then sank lifeless upon the ground at the feet of Ernestine, who stood by her: her sudden fall brought the child to the ground also, but she quickly recovered herself.

"She knows all now; Ernestine herself revealed it," said the old servant to her master; and he felt as though he were in the fiery eddies of hell: yonder his bleeding son, here his discarded daughter, and there his wife lifeless—it might be, dead. He covered his face with both his hands: his hair stood on end.

The surgeon soon brought his wife to her senses again; and he and the servant carried her to her bed-chamber, and laid her upon her bed. When the Postmaster touched her, she shrank as from a lightning-flash, and repulsed him with a motion of her head. The Postmaster hastened into the other room to Magnus, whilst Ernestine clung to his knees. "How much life is thine? how long hast thou been in the world? and what use hast thou made of it?" said a voice in the Postmaster's soul; and after he had quieted the two children, he went in to his wife: she looked fixedly at him with open, tearless eyes, in silence. He took her hand; she suffered it, but did not return the pressure, and he said: "Thaddea, show me that you have not lost all faith in me; you shall see it will all be well again. I have deserved a heavy chastisement, and God has dealt graciously with me. Oh! be kind also; you were so ever!"

"Go to the children; leave me now alone," said his wife; then she buried her head in the pillows, and sobbed deeply.

"Yes, sleep awhile," said the Postmaster, as he went out softly closing the door.

Then, alone, Thaddea suddenly darted up and gazed

wildly round her. "Betrayed! deceived! and by him!" she muttered and her whole body heaved with mighty passion; but she sank back again, and found relief in tears; and seldom in a woman's heart has a harder battle been fought than now Thaddea waged.

ADMITTED AND ACQUITTED.

NSEEN, meanwhile, the Baker-at-the-Steps had also come into the room and heard every thing. He was at first so deeply shocked that he was forced to sit down. Soon, however, he attempted to turn the matter into ridicule, that it might be taken more easily.

"Father, this comes of artful contrivances; however, I will make you no reproaches: God grant that the reproaches I deserve may be forgiven me too." Thus the Postmaster spoke to his father, and the latter, without answering, bade a servant go immediately to his wife and tell her to come as quickly as she could—at that very moment. Turning to his son, he continued:

"Now, I'll tell you how it will be: the two women will forthwith make an alliance, and abuse us, and paint us as black as ever they can lay the color on: that's wholesome, it acts like purging, and then all is clear. Your wife will, at first sight of your mother, weep and complain, and pour out all her heart: do not disturb her; let her say what she will; let her spend her wrath: when the wrath has been spent, a quiet dinner and a quiet night's rest once more—and the next day, all is sunshine. And what now looks as if it could never be got over, will be cooled down by even-song. Catherine, bring up a bottle of red wine: I must have a glass of something; I feel queer all over: and you have a glass too; a good glass of wine inside you, like a fresh nag, helps you to top the hill better."

When the Baker's wife, in her usual neat attire, walked into the room and saw the two men over their wine, she looked not a little astonished thereat: however, she said, perhaps from invariable habit, "God bless it!" and turning to the children, she said, "Be quiet, Magnus, I have already heard it is nothing to signify; and, Ernestine, do not hang upon me so, you are now not mine only; God be praised, that is over." She would have separated the girl from her when she entered the bed-chamber, but the child would not leave her, and she said: "Well, for my part I think perhaps it is better: come with me, but you must be good and well-behaved:" and the two men looked after her without saying a word, as she vanished with Ernestine behind the chamber-door.

What would not the Baker-at-the-Steps have given, could he but have heard what was going on in there! but not a syllable could he catch. In the bed-chamber, however, the Baker's wife said: "Thaddea, dear, you must be destined for favor and happiness, because your lot has been so hard. Soon each will come and say, 'I am guiltless!' I say not so; I am guilty: I should not have suffered it for a single moment: and you must have remarked, dear, that there was something strange with me. I could not help it. Oh God! what creatures we are! I am not so kind to you as I should be, because an injustice has been committed through you, or properly speaking against you, or in plain terms by us. Oh! my dear girl, I pray you pardon me, do not now as I did; be not angry with the guiltless cause of an injustice. Be kind to this child. Come, give your hand to your mother. Come here, Ernestine, still nearer."

Thaddea put her arm round the child's neck and kissed her; but the child tore herself away with a look of evident aversion, and her grandmother quietly removed her into the next room; then she sat a long while in silence beside the wife, whose hand she clasped with her right hand, while she placed her left upon her burning brow.

And as now the hands of the mother for the first time thus caressed her daughter-in-law, her words also became proportionately tender and warm: she had, for the first time, called her "dear," and opened her whole heart to her. Strange must have been Thaddea's feelings, for she said, as she carried her mother's hand to her lips: "Thank God! he has given me once more a mother. I feel it; and I can henceforth be a mother to two. Why was there any doubt of it?"

The Baker's wife now spoke so earnestly, so warmly, concealing nothing which was wrong, but also laying particular emphasis upon all that was good, that Thaddea said once more: "Ah! my husband was right; I had thought it was excessive filial affection when he sounded your praises so highly, as though you were more than mortal: now I myself see that it is really so. Oh, why did he do me and himself that wrong? Never would I have believed he could be so false, so deceitful! Where is he now? Ah! I know how heavy his heart must now be; for he has done grievous wrong, and the knowledge of that is the hardest burden a good man can bear. And he is a good man still—yes, still. He has but to come to me, and I will help him bear his burden: I am strong.

I will get up: it is all over now: I will go to him myself."

"It wanted but this to show me how good you are at heart. That now, in the very moment when you have been outraged—that at this very moment you should only think how hard a burden he has to bear, and should be willing to stand by him and help him to bear it, is more, love, than I shall ever forget: and there is One who forgets nothing; He will reward you for it in this world and in the next."

With these words the Baker's wife opened the door, and said aloud: "My son, you are to come in!" and that in a tone which told of entire happiness: and now she went out into the sitting-room and sat down opposite her husband, and drank a sip of the wine which stood before him, and said:

"A happier hour I have never had all my life long, and shall never have again. Oh! there is nothing more beautiful than an upright heart, and our son is the luckiest man the whole world over."

The Baker-at-the-Steps did not understand what was meant, and his wife did not give herself the trouble to enlighten him further.

Meanwhile, the Postmaster was standing in his wife's presence: she held out to him her hand, and said: "Forgive me, that I shrank just now so rudely from your touch. I could not help it; it was an insurmountable feeling. But weep not now: you have done more violence to your own feelings than to mine: yes, you have grieved your own heart, and belied it towards your child, your wife, and the whole world. Why had you no confidence in me? Did you not then believe that it would be a happiness to me to befriend yet another child? And what feelings have you roused in the child! Perhaps it may never be in my power to conquer them; but you shall see I will not be wanting; and God will help me."

The son in the bed-chamber was not much less astonished than the father in the sitting-room; and he seemed lost, as he wondered whether it could be his wife—his sore-afflicted, deceived, and slighted wife—who thus spoke. He could not but tell her how it had all happened; and she smiled. When he persisted in taking all blame to himself, and would have left his father out of the scene altogether, she only said:

"Tell me honestly: is it not simple pride of man which makes you unwilling to appear before me as though you had suffered yourself to be ruled by your father? Is it not simply for that that you wish to leave him out of the scene?"

"You are certainly a real father confessor," said the Postmaster; "I am not quite sure it is not so: and be it as it may, if he did mislead me, it is my fault that I suffered myself to be misled: and even if it were not so, he is my father, I have younger shoulders than he, and you are my wife; and do you not love me still? Then I can better bear the blame; but pray pardon him too."

"Willingly, from my heart. It is easy to pardon those who are really blameless and good; we must pardon the others also."

"Father, you can come in too," cried the Postmaster cheerily.

"Nay, I can now go out," said Thaddea: and she went with her husband into the sitting-room.

The Baker-at-the-Steps offered her his glass, and said: "Have a glass of wine, daughter-in-law!"

Holding the glass she said, "Your good health," and took a sip.

The Baker-at-the-Steps, smiling triumphantly at his son, now said: "Yes, dear daughter-in-law, we did not deceive you so very much after all: I have adopted Ernestine before the Court, and formally: she is ours, not yours: not yours, Sir Postmaster, nor your wife's, do you understand? But I am well aware it is, on that account, not the less pretty of you, dear daughter, to take every thing so well; there are daughters-in-law who would scratch a man's eyes out for it. Now, it is right that you should know all; still the principal matter remains as it was; Ernestine is ours, and shall remain with us."

"Nay, she is mine, my child! And the child's place is with her father, her brother, her mother; with her who should and will be her mother, I mean:" and her voice grew firm, as she continued: "On that subject not another word. From this hour Ernestine shall remain with us, and be our child. You need not be afraid, Ernestine: you shall go and see your grandparents as often as you please: but here is your home, and here are your parents. Say you not so, grandmother? You will pack up her things and send them here to-day?"

"Leave her at least to-day with us, or as long as you have Magnus to attend to."

"No, not an hour longer shall the child be away from her natural home. Say no more: all shall be forgotten and forgiven: but on that point I will not hear another word."

"She has no right to demand the child, and I shall not give her up," said the Baker-at-the-Steps, turning half to his wife and half to Thaddea.

"I have no right? But my husband has, and his rights are mine."

"I will make a compromise," interrupted the Baker-at-the-Steps: "leave us the child for another year: a year from to-day, if God grant us life, I will bring the child to you."

Thaddea was for awhile undecided; suddenly she turned her head, and said: "I cannot suffer myself to be misled; I see quite plainly, the child must in this way be spoilt and ruined."

"Yes, she is spoilt already," said her husband, and his father laughed in his face.

"I will keep the child!" said Thaddea once more with decision; "and you shall have her again: but she must leave me in love."

The two men and the grandmother looked at Thaddea with amazement. Her whole manner showed a decision which inspired inevitable respect: the two strongest characteristics of her being, humility and firmness, appeared to-day in the most vivid light.

Ernestine remained at home.

Thaddea, to prevent anticipation, had expressed an intention of herself informing her father of the state of the case. The Baker-at-the-Steps had begged her so to put the case as though she had known all previously; and he tried jestingly to convince her she *had* known all before, that she might find the lie easier. But Thaddea would be no party to deceit; and she had a powerful supporter in her mother-in-law.

For a long while there came no answer from Goldstumpf.

One day the whole house was full of joy, although of short duration. Thaddea's brother, on his way from Switzerland, was travelling down-country, but could only wait while the horses were changed. Thaddea could only just shake him by the hand; but he promised to stay longer on his return.

"Have you any news of my father?" said she.

"Oh dear, no! but there is something the matter with him: he is said to be more wild and furious than ever."

Thaddea trembled, as she thought what a fearful scene her father would make again.

The day after her brother had been there for a moment, when the whole family was sitting quietly together, the door opened—and who entered? Why—Turk, Goldstumpf's huge dog. How comes he here? He knows how to open the door.

"My father is coming! Peace, for God's sake!" cried Thaddea.

They looked out of the window, and, surely enough, there was Goldstumpf getting down from a chaise, which no one had heard drive up. In a loud voice he gave the coachman orders to drive to the Lamb, and he would follow immediately. And now he came in; and all the hands which had been outstretched to him became rigid; so wild, so furious was Goldstumpf's look.

"I haven't much to say," he began: "I have heard how you have deceived me and my child: and those are your honest people! those are your kind-hearted people! And what do folks say of me? What care I? Come with me, Thaddea, this moment:—just as you stand there shall you leave this house. You must not live another second with people who have treated you thus: of myself I will say not a word. Come now: take nothing with you: what belongs to you I will recover by law. Come!"

"Father," said Thaddea, "this is my husband;" as she laid her hand upon Raymond's shoulder.

"And I'll tell you what names you deserve, you honest people! Or let conscience tell you! Come, Thaddea!"

"Nay, father!"

"You will not? Shall I curse you for ever?"

"Father, you cannot."

"If it were true,—and it is not,—if all were true that people say of me," cried Goldstumpf, "it would be child's play to what that fellow, and that, and the whole hypocritical family have done!"

Hitherto no one had spoken except Thaddea and Goldstumpf; but now the Baker-at-the-Steps said: "You're quite right, Stumpf: I told that fellow it would come to this; but what do they care for us old ones? Nothing any longer, nothing at all. Because they can read and write better than we can, we are to be of no sort of account. You see now, Raymond, what a piece of work you have made."

Goldstumpf gazed at the Baker with not less astonishment than did the others. He, the prime originator, now washing his hands of the whole! What could it mean?

"With you, too, I have nothing to say," said Goldstumpf. "Thaddea, I ask you once more: will you go with me this moment? No? Very well! Then I must go alone; and you shall hear from me."

"I will go with you," said the Baker-at-the-Steps; and linked his arm in Goldstumpf's.

The two women and his son looked after him in amazement; and they could still see through the window how Goldstumpf tried to shake the Baker off, but the latter would not relinquish his hold; and, positively, he brought him back from the road to the Lamb, and now they were going in the direction of the Baker's house.

The old Baker-at-the-Steps kept repeating as they went, "You are quite right; I agree with all you say; you can say whatever you please: only go with me, and don't oblige yourself to make the matter public, and then find you can't reverse it."

"That is just what I want. I want not to be able to reverse it."

"Very well; you can manage that just as well in an hour's time."

The Baker succeeded in dragging him, exasperated to the highest degree, into his house; and there they sat in the "Baker's chambers:" and Goldstumpf was himself perplexed that he was so completely justified by his adversary. His hatred and his fury were by that means already partially subdued; but it appeared that it was not fury alone which prompted him: it repented him altogether that he had given his daughter away; he felt alone and forsaken. Now was the best opportunity of winning back his daughter for ever. He wanted once more the property Thaddea had inherited from her mother: and Thaddea herself, when once she was divorced, could not leave him again, must tend him patiently her whole life long, and have no further wishes for herself. The Baker-at-the-Steps was clever enough to worm from him these secret motives; and now he said something to him, —it was not true, but a lie more or less mattered little now,—he gave him to understand that if his daughter came to live with him, he would not have her only.

Goldstumpf gave his dog, who had been rubbing himself against him, a kick; and the Baker nodded at the dog, and his glance seemed to say: "Soho! the shot has spent itself upon you: now all will be well." But aloud he said: "Look here! you are just like an unskilful rider who has lost his reins: he grabs after them like this, you see, without thinking how, at each duck of his head, he pricks his bridleless horse with the spurs in his boots." The Baker-at-the-Steps sat down, rider-wise, upon a chair, and illustrated his proposition with much cleverness. It was enough to make one laugh, but Goldstumpf was not equal to laughing yet.

"Well, I was mistaken in you," said the Baker.

"How so?" snarled Goldstumpf.

"I should have thought you would laugh enough to split your sides at the addition you receive; or properly speaking, not you; it doesn't concern you at all, of course."

Goldstumpf bit his lips, and threw himself back in the arm-chair and closed his eyes. Now the Baker-at-the-Steps wished to induce him to try his approved method, to go to bed just for an hour: then all would get comfortably settled and put to rights. Goldstumpf laughed aloud at this proposition, and now a further step was made towards victory. Only let the adversary once laugh, and passion and fury are at an end. Goldstumpf, struggling hard against it, shouted: "The devil take you for making me laugh! I won't laugh! I—ha! ha! ha! I'll knock you down if you make me laugh any more."

But the Baker began to sing him a child's lullaby, and that in so laughable and absurdly impudent a manner, that Goldstumpf once more was forced to laugh. As, however, he raised his fist again, and actually smashed a chair, the Baker-at-the-Steps changed his tune; and, with really masterly skill, he abused, in the character of Goldstumpf, with the very raciest terms, both the Baker-at-the-Steps, that good-for-nothing sack carrier, and the Postmaster, that hypocritical, beggarly schoolmaster, and the whole world in the same fashion. And then he cursed that he couldn't take his child with him; and then he swore nevertheless he would take her.

Goldstumpf struck his strong fist upon the table, and roared: "Anyhow I am not going to be made a fool of. I know who I am; and you'll not catch me with chaff."

The Baker-at-the-Steps was helpless; his artifices were all in vain. In his embarrassment he seized a cap belonging to his wife, which lay upon the bench. She had thrown it off in a hurry, and put on another. And now, as he held in his hand his wife's cap, it was as though he learnt to mould his thoughts after hers, and to arrange things after her fashion, for he said:

"Look you here! You've a hard lot in the world! Don't take what I say in bad part: you are without a single real friend to be a check upon you; you associate with people who are indifferent to you, or else must flatter you because they live by you. What your position is with reference to your children, you know yourself but too well. Having once chosen the headstrong path, you imagine you will lose caste, and people will point the finger at you if you turn to the right or left. You persuade yourself it is strong-minded, you show a master-spirit by not giving way an inch. But do you know whom you harm most by that? Yourself. You have still a void at your heart. Now don't fly into a passion, but hear me out," continued the Baker-at-the-Steps, as he slowly twisted a ribbon of the cap round the forefinger of his left hand. "Tell me now honestly, is it worth while, for a trumpery world's opinion, to spurn from you the best that you might have, only that everybody may say: — 'Yes, Stumpf is a strong-minded man, a man of iron'? And what does the world give you in exchange? What you can buy, not a jot more! But if you would for once be forgiving and gentle; believe me, that is a draught which no landlord can pour out for you. Try but once the taste of it, and the more you drink, the more you will thirst for it: try it but once, it will do you good. Let the sardonic devils show their teeth and grin! After a day they will envy you, and then the cry will be: 'We cannot bear to see him so happy!' Give me one grasp of the hand; open your fist. Come, try it for once!"

The Baker spoke now with a voice full of emotion; and his words seemed to loosen Goldstumpf's inward determination, as well as his clenched fist. But still, as Goldstumpf now gave him his hand, he tried to squeeze his until he should roar again. The Baker was not disinclined for it, and strong withal; and so they strove with one another, and each squeezed the other's hand so vigorously, that it seemed as if they must mutually crush the bones; at last the Baker cunningly cried out: "I've found my master!" And now Goldstumpf laughed almost pleasantly.

Whilst the two men were sitting together, and the Baker-at-the-Steps was watching Goldstumpf like a wild beast, the Postmaster, with his mother and wife, was canvassing his father's strange conduct. The Baker's wife knew her husband exactly; for she said: "He was right, and he is wise; it is better he should lay all upon you, you still remain the son-in-law; and if he is quite free of blame, there is still one of us there to speak with

Thaddea's father, and arrange matters before they go too far."

And so indeed it came to pass. In an hour's time Goldstumpf came back with the Baker, after they had been to the office and seen the certificate of adoption.

Thaddea would have embraced her father, but he put her aside. He spoke little, and only said: "I don't care, I can't alter it." He had also, however, ordered his chaise to the house immediately, and announced his intention of going away; and, without a single shake of the hand, he departed. But strangely enough, he did not take the road homewards to the high land, but down-country.

A change had taken place in Goldstumpf, such as only a storm could produce. Even while he raged, he could not in secret divest himself of the impression which had been made upon him, by the fact, that Thaddea had, under the influence of invincible love, taken to her bosom a strange child — a child they would have kept from her. An inward voice said to him: "Wherefore with thy violence dost thou make thyself a step-father to thine own children?" When then the Baker-at-the-Steps, after all his droll talking, repeated as it were all his own thoughts aloud, he bit his lips almost through. And now at his departure, he was not yet resolved whither to go: and yet it seemed to him all at once so dreary to go home. He stood by the chaise, and felt that it was all one whither he went: he had really a warm attachment nowhere, and suddenly he cried to the driver: "Turn round! drive down-country!" He threw himself back in the chaise, as if purposeless — as if overcome by a strange spell; he was resolved now to efface all differences; he did not own to himself, and much less to any one else, that peace would do him good, and he required it; he flattered himself he was playing the part of a magnanimity which is gracious toward a spoilt, weak, and good-for-nothing world.

So he went in search of his son, and after a few days he drove up with him to the Post, and Thaddea was full of joy and happiness, but Goldstumpf kept saying: "The world is altogether deceitful; why should I imbitter my life by holding fast to one thing? I am the only really honest man I know;" and with this consoling reflection he departed, in company with his son.

OBSTRUCTED.

VEN in actions, of which one cannot believe it possible that there can be any misunderstanding, by keeping one's ears open, and observing the words and looks with which people criticise them, one finds a distortion and a misconception which could not have been imagined.

Thaddea's cleaving to her child, for instance; could that well be called any thing beyond a sort of self-willed sense of duty? And yet, from house to house the story went, that inborn devilry, unwarrantable love of rule, and desire of oppression, such as could only have been inherited from Goldstumpf, had suggested Thaddea's course of action. She grudged the poor child its kind education at the house of its grandparents: and, alas! it must be owned, that, while here and there a man was found to undertake Thaddea's defence, it was principally the women who condemned her.

Even Thaddea herself had suddenly become faint-hearted; for it often happens, when under an inspired impulse, amid a storm of emotions, a self-sacrifice has been undertaken, there arise afterwards doubts of its practicability, mistrust of individual strength, and perhaps even the reflection, that such a sacrifice is useless, and to no purpose.

Thaddea saw in everybody's glance something chilling; she did not feel sure whether it were on Ernestine's account; she fancied she was, from her life at home, too mistrustful — too suspicious of mankind. And still, as she could not but notice that there was some inexplicable obstacle between her and mankind, she attributed it to the character which her father bore, and which, painted in still blacker colors, had found its way here too. What pained her most was, that even the Baker's wife, who had adhered so closely to her, now, when the exciting moments were over, behaved towards her with some stiffness. She had often enough experienced in life, that she would never meet with unadulterated good-will, but would first have to clear away the hindrances of prejudice; and now she had saddled herself with a heavy hindrance. But Thaddea soon got over her sorrow, and was once more the quiet, self-relying nature. She conquered every doubt, every desire to look for approbation, or to listen for applause. She was one of those natures who dare to trust themselves; to believe that what they desire with all their souls is also right, and that there is need only of time to make it appear plainly before their own and others' eyes.

In Ernestine, she had a model to work upon in her endeavor to conquer the evil opinion of the world. She treated Ernestine with never-varying equanimity: and the latter often looked askance at her, and wondered what it could mean. And as with Ernestine, so she behaved herself towards all her new circle — relations and strangers. She had self-possession and firmness enough not to live even in the matter of men's love from hand to mouth, so to speak. She did not belong to those who wish to be loved at first sight, who have a smile ever ready — who, in the visits which they pay and receive, are evidently more or less always thinking; "As soon as your back is turned, they will say: 'Ah! but what a splendid woman! so clever, so kind, so handsome, &c. &c.'" Thaddea could wait for things to come about naturally. Sincere humility, as well as sincere self-confidence, were so blended in her as to constitute a peculiar character. She met every one with composure, but was not abashed before all when the hand, which was offered spiritually as well as bodily, was either not grasped, or not in the way she expected.

Besides, she could now so much the more easily dispense with the world in that she had a husband, who, with unaffected zeal, lived only to please her; and she had a child, to whom she could hourly dedicate all her love, and who soon clung to her with an earnestness that cheered her heart.

Little Magnus, who was full four years old, could scarcely speak at all, and that so inarticulately, and after such a peculiar style of word-mimicry, that it was only by habit and faithful attention thereto, that anybody could understand him. This circumstance the child was aware of, from the fact that his father was often obliged to say, "Wife, what is he saying now? what does he mean?" And his wife could explain clearly what the child was prattling; and when she explained it, the boy looked up in her face with a happy, thankful expression. Without laboring for that single object, Thaddea, by her way of managing the boy, won still more the heart of her husband. Day after day she had some new circumstance to tell him, from which it appeared how quick and good-natured the boy was, and all that he wanted was careful and attentive training.

No words of love for himself, however tender, would have warmed the father's heart so much, as these evidences of love for his boy; and the child appeared to him made over anew; indeed, it seemed as though hitherto he had never been washed and neatly clad: even in his every-day morning dress, he always looked now decked out for Sunday. The more the Postmaster felt cheered at heart to see how his wife managed the boy, and how he clung to her with tender love, the more painful was it to him to see Ernestine's stubborn, obdurate manner. She did with rigorous punctuality what she was ordered, but nothing more.

Nothing came spontaneously from the child — not a word of love, or of hatred; and her father was almost inclined to doubt whether there were a single emotion of heart in the child to be awakened. He was often on the point, in a moment of violent anger, of chastising her. He saw how she met his wife's truly motherly care with a bitter scowl; and the "Thank you," that she was forced by necessity to utter, was so bitterly snarled out, that it sounded almost like a curse.

Thaddea, however, was wise enough to pacify her husband, saying: "Trust to me, I will win the child's heart; but it is not to be taken by storm. Nothing was ever, in my ideas, more vexatious, than for hitherto unknown relations and friends to come into a house, and say to children: 'Do you hear, I am your uncle, your aunt, your cousin John, or your cousin Mary; so you must love me.'

A child's notions of the relationships of life are confined to habit, services, and confiding association. I observe that Ernestine fears me no longer, and I can tell you, I am glad I did not allow myself to be diverted from my purpose of keeping her with us: now is the time for winning her love — now or never."

CHASTISEMENT AND LOVE.

EEPER than the visible wound upon little Magnus's forehead was one invisible, and that was in the heart of Ernestine.

It was difficult to explain, and so it was considered almost a miracle, that Magnus, since his accident, was particularly brightened; and, what was most remarkable, that difficulty of speech he had formerly experienced, in some unaccountable manner, he lost so quickly and replaced by rapidity, that you would have thought he was a wholly different child. Ernestine, on the contrary, had gone back, and always moved about as though she had been, the moment before, knocked down. The whole family laid siege to Thaddea; she might as well allow the child, at least for a time, to return to her grandparents: she could, of course, at a later period, have her back again; but Thaddea insisted, that if she did not labor now without intermission to overcome the child's natural aversion and win her love, it would be lost to her for ever, and there would remain something deep-seated in her, of which no one could predict the consequences. Only to the Baker's wife she owned in secret that she would have no objection to transfer the child, at a later period, once more to her grandparents; but not until she had learnt to live at home in perfect love with her and her father.

Thaddea was a wise and good mother; she was not, as is so often the case, simply fond or cross, kissing or scolding, imperturbable or irritable: she had a quiet, measured, and unchangeable gravity which wins, not soon, but all the more certainly; and with such an undeviating character, every, even the slightest mark of affection, becomes a significant expression. If she had but once stroked little Magnus's head, it was more than all your passionate, ecstatic outbursts of love; and it was just this which delighted the Baker's wife so much in her daughter-in-law; and she was never tired of singing her praises: so that the Baker-at-the-Steps, whenever he saw his wife in earnest conversation with a friend, used to say: "You've been preaching about Thaddea again, I know: she's always your text."

The Baker-at-the-Steps, meanwhile, had sundry grudges against his daughter-in-law. He took particular interest in the Post-office; not only on account of its general atmosphere of business, but principally on account of the mails. He was activity itself, when he was present as the letters were sorted, and liked to peer into the letters, scanning addresses and seals with peculiar gusto: but soon the Postmaster put a stop to it. And the Baker-at-the-Steps believed, perhaps not without justice, that it was at the instance of his daughter-in-law when the Postmaster said in a decided tone: "It is contrary to my duty, father, and I cannot allow it!"

Besides, the Baker-at-the-Steps found the propriety and dignity which Thaddea, without being proud, always preserved, extremely irksome. There was nothing more disagreeable to him than a uniform behavior, demanding true respect: whether it were that the habits of his past life, and his life generally, rebelled, or because his pride revolted, as he felt that he was wanting in every thing which could effect the same in him. He would fain have changed subdued dignity into a noisy familiarity. He only felt quite happy and comfortable in his shirt-sleeves. To his wife he lamented that Thaddea, though she didn't exactly insist upon it, behaved in such a manner, and kept a body in such order, that he felt inclined to put on his Sunday coat when he went to see her. He tried all his never-failing jokes to bring Thaddea to his way of thinking, but he had no success; and between father-in-law and daughter-in-law — a relationship which generally awakens once more some of the gallantry of youthful days towards woman — there was a life of estrangement.

The Baker-at-the-Steps paid Thaddea all reverence, of course, because she was so rich, and yet behaved so modestly to everybody; however, he gave her also to understand that he considered her pertinacity, in keeping his grand-daughter, as nothing but a particular kind of pride and obstinacy.

Thaddea found it hard to bear this misconstruction, but she had sufficient power over herself to go straightforward on her way, without looking to the right or left; and the triumph of perfect uprightness is this, under the burden of misconstruction nevertheless to persevere, sure of itself, and sure that the ultimate result will overcome ill-will: and this way of sorrow is more easily trodden, when there is the cheering sound of good report from without, and of this her mother-in-law gave full measure.

Hitherto Thaddea had displayed not the slightest fondness for Ernestine, but managed her with carefulness and determination. She superintended, too, her school work; and she bestowed peculiar attention on her writing. Whilst the Postmaster felt exceeding pleasure in his child's reading so plainly, rapidly, and expressively, Thaddea kept most attentive watch upon her good writing; and this is universally the case with mothers in considering their children's school instruction: and do women lay so much stress upon beautiful writing, because it is something visible to the eye, something connected with beauty, which is actually tangible? The Baker's wife, whose happy understanding with her daughter-in-law increased more and more, suffered her to go on just in her own fashion, and only pointed out to her the obstacles in her way. She once said to her daughter-in-law: "I will tell you when Ernestine will be really your child: when you have once given her a hearty box on the ear. Until you do so, you feel, without being aware of it, that you are strange to her, and so dare not chastise her; and that she is strange to you, because she does not provoke you, as a child of your own would; for one's own child is provoking just because it is dear. You want the child to feel at home in its parents' house; but by treating it half as a fine young miss, and putting no hard work upon it, you make it from that moment a complete stranger in its own home. The child fancies, because it is not even once made miserable, it is not at home. God knows, you are about the first step-mother who has been obliged to be told so."

"It may be: I will try," said Thaddea: "and be sure, on the first opportunity, I will chastise her."

"Stay," said the Baker's wife, "you are not yet quite

perfect. Do you know which is the best box on the ear?"

"No!"

"That which is given without prologue or epilogue — without threat or warning. Smack! once — one sound cuff, and not a word besides — that does most good, both to the giver and receiver, that lasts for ever. Ask your husband: I gave him, twice in my life, a box on the ear without speaking a word, and he has never forgotten it. But to confine both yourself and child to civil phrases, sooner or later spoils the parents as well as the child."

It would not have been in the child's nature to remain so long hardened against its mother, had it not keenly watched its grandfather's discontent, and had not strangers labored to incite it. When they met Ernestine in the street, they pitied the child for being obliged to go about in such or such a dress — one day too warm, another too cold. "Ah!" said they, "it is very hard not to have your own mother:" and, "Doesn't your step-mother leave you to sleep all alone? What a shame! such a forsaken child, all alone. Do you get enough to eat, dear? Only tell me, and I will gladly give you something. Ah! if your own mother had dreamt of this!"

Thus was Ernestine continually stopped when she went along the streets, and her inward opposition was provoked afresh. An additional reason, to be sure, was, that Thaddea found fault with, and corrected many things in the behavior of the child which her grandparents had been more indulgent to, or had not censured at all.

There are many people who are very thankful to hear good advice, and cannot protest sufficiently how much good it does them, and how glad they are to be told of this or that by those who mean them well. But it is only a firm, upright heart, which can break off its habits of life, especially when it believes that it has been acting with the best intentions, and that it only rested with others to avail themselves thereof.

It flashed all at once like a sudden revelation upon Thaddea, as she sat and thought in silence, that you must be kind to a child without expecting any return. "Ah ! yes," thought she, "I see in my husband what natural parental love is : he would give them the very best morsel from his own mouth, aye, the last he had upon his table, though it was what he fancied most. Can that be the love only of natural parents, and cannot I also attain to it ? I can towards Magnus be even more, for he is more confiding. Should reward be looked to in such a thing as this ? It must, it must be that one can take the place of the actual mother: to that end surely we are fellow-creatures — to that end we have the power of thought — to that end we can form rules for guidance in our brain ; and my mother-in-law is right, the child is too much a stranger to me."

Thenceforth, Thaddea kept Ernestine to all kinds of household duties. She often sent her on errands hither and thither; she demanded all kinds of services from her. The Postmaster shook his head in silence, but the child was pleased thereby, inasmuch as for a child there is nothing more pleasurable than to be able to show its importance ; a real consciousness that itself too has some power and can accomplish something, a real feeling of delight in its own consequence, which becomes an idea of its indispensability, is most beneficial to a child. Thus Ernestine was happy and cheerful in all these duties, until compassionate people complained more and more that she was obliged to be her step-mother's Cinderella, who, of course, in secret, belabored and thumped her ; and the child had such spirit, that she would tell no tales of her horrid step-mother. Why, you could scarcely get a word out of her ; but everybody knew what was the reason she was so shy of answering when any one questioned her. When, therefore, Ernestine told them that she slept alone in the dark, that she washed and dressed herself, compassionate women clasped their hands above their heads in horror. Thus was the child again continually estranged from her mother, who devoted herself to her with all her might. Thaddea now would often feel a doubt, whether her toil would meet with success ; but the confidence which she had once expressed to her husband, and which he had clung to, now returned again, as it were, from him to her. The Postmaster was as happy as in the days of his full youth : for your softer sort of people have, with many disadvantages, this one advantage over the hard and firm, that there is in them an inexhaustible power of rejuvenescence, just because every thing moves them more ; or, properly speaking, because they continue in a constant state of youthful growth.

The Postmaster, though he certainly could not be acquitted of weakness, gained at Thaddea's side daily in manly firmness. He had hitherto lived only in a humdrum fashion, he needed not to exert himself to here and there preserve appreciation and love. Now that he wished to show Thaddea he could act firmly and decidedly, he gained visibly in manly confidence.

Thaddea had only on one single occasion entered upon the subject, while her husband made frequent mention of the past and comparisons between the melancholy he had suffered and the exceeding joy he now experienced at finding every thing so bright and fair and happy: and in the midst of his delight he was always reproaching himself for days gone by.

"I have often noticed," she then said, "you are just the reverse of me: I cannot work in a room, cannot be easy, nay, cannot sleep a wink, unless every thing about me is properly arranged in its place: you on the contrary can, and it has its advantage."

"You are always right, and find some good in every thing."

"Then we must both learn from each other; you will become more orderly, and I no more so over-careful, as though some one were standing behind and drilling me. I am always pleased to see the postilions harnessing the horses so quickly; yet they do it with the greatest deliberation, with slow movements: that is better than restless hurry; and yet they are always ready in time."

The house of the Postmaster would now have been perfectly blest, had the child allowed herself at last to be won and the memory of the past been wiped out.

It was towards the end of March: days spring-bright had already paid a visit: but now, deep snow was lying again on the ground, and people found themselves once more in winter; but it could not last long. The mother was telling her children that the starlings had already come, and gone again; where they now sojourned none could tell: and the children listened wonderingly.

Ernestine sat by her mother's side; she was learning to sew. There was need of much patience with her, for the child was averse to this work.

Thaddea was sitting at her wheel and spinning: little

Magnus was playing with his wooden bricks behind the table. The mother rose and left the room, to superintend some household business: when she came in again, the flax was pulled to pieces, and the wheel in disorder.

"That is your doing," said the mother, sternly; "come here, Ernestine — here, quite close. See what work you have made: do you see what great trouble I have to put all in order again? I tell you for the last time — I tell you, you shall be whipt if you do not leave the spinning-wheel alone. Now, sit down and go on with your sewing; move your stool this way — to my left side — that I may be able to see how you manage."

She did so. And now nothing was to be heard but the low whirr of the spinning-wheel, as it went softly round; and Thaddea for a long while did not look at the child, that she might have time to recover herself.

What passes in a child's soul who can tell? The expressions and sensations of children are often of themselves a marvel. They have silent thoughts, never formed into words; they have decisions often springing up within them, which none would believe had they not had experience thereof themselves.

Never before had Thaddea spoken so sternly to the child as to-day; never before had the child seen such an expression upon her face; her eye so steadily, so piercingly fixed upon her; and now, doubtless, there was a peculiar heaving and tossing in the childish bosom: she pressed nearer to her mother than she had ever pressed before. Was it fear or love that prompted her?

Thaddea was conscious of the approach; and, lifting her hand from her spinning-cotton, laid it briskly upon the child's head, and said no more than "Be a good girl!"

Then once more was heard for a while nothing but the whizzing of the wheel; and two hearts went beating side by side, but none boded how they would find accord.

The sun of early spring shone warmly through the window; Thaddea rose and moved the pots of flowers, which she had brought with her from home, within reach of the sunbeams. A peculiar good-will stole over Thaddea; for there are moments in which we participate in the spirit of universal life. How must the warm light refresh the little plants, as they receive, for the first time here, the welcome sun; they grew far away from here, but the sun can find them everywhere. Thaddea for an instant folded her hands; for, in such moments of concentration and fixed attention upon familiar objects, it seems as though the most familiar suddenly brought a lesson before the eyes. Nurtured in sunshine! And love is the sunshine of the human heart! Poor child of man, on whose tender years of life there is no love to shine!

Thaddea felt she must find some means, as she had brought the plants into the sunshine, of bringing the child also into a position to perceive the love which she devoted to it. She turned herself towards the child, and brighter sunbeam never gleamed than the light that now shone in her eyes. The child, probably, felt this look without seeing it; for it shrank within itself, but moved no further, and did not look away.

And yet Ernestine's obstinacy was not yet subdued.

Her mother once more left the room; and as she suddenly opened the door and came in, the child was standing again at the spinning-wheel. With rapid step Thaddea approached, lifted her hand, and smote the child's cheek that it burned again — once!

She said not a single word. She seated the child once more on the stool hard by her, gave her her work in her hand, without adding any warning. Now the wheel went flying round, and now the cotton dropped : but faster than the wheel revolved the thoughts in Thaddea's heart. It had come at last: she had chastised the child, and the child sat by her side and sobbed; and for a while both again were silent.

Whoever pays attention to children will very frequently find, that even the best managed do not like obeying a prohibition implicitly and unconditionally. This sudden curtailing of their own will by the limiting power of a stranger's, clashes too much with the self-conceited, nay, honorable feelings, which are stirring even in a child. Forbid him to touch any thing; he will abstain only by slow and gradual steps, and will like to touch it just once more, that he may seem to obey the command of his own free will. At the same time, even when a child has been justly chastised, there abides in the mind of the chastiser a certain displeasure against himself; and nothing is more dangerous than, under the influence of such feelings, to immediately console the child, and promise him something nice on a future day, or even give it him at once. Thaddea allowed Ernestine to exhaust her tears, gladly as she would have dried them for her. Not until some time had elapsed, and Ernestine had become quite composed, did she say: "If you are a good girl, you shall, next winter, have a spinning-wheel of your own, and I will teach you to spin."

"Yes, and mother keeps her promise," cried wise Master Magnus from behind the table, and Thaddea smiled happily at this childlike confidence: for she had taken care that promises should never be made to the children, which were not kept.

Again all was silent in the room. Thaddea felt Ernestine nestling closer and closer to her, nay, she thought she saw the child kiss her dress, and now the child's head really sank upon her lap. She softly moved the wheel with her right foot, and the child rested against her left side and fell asleep: and now it was breathing heavily, and Thaddea gazed down upon the child and in her soul there was music like the burden of the old song, —

"What is softer than eider-down?
A mother's lap.
What is sweeter than honey-comb?
A mother's breast."

And her glance grew yet more earnest; and now the child opened her eyes, and a glance met them — aye! a true mother's glance; and none could have said which was the first, as one bent down and one sprang up, and, "My child!" "My mother!" was all they said, and a bright sunbeam darted obliquely through the panes, and mother and child were clasped in a close embrace.

But Thaddea did not long give way to such caressing; she liked to put her feelings of love into some practical form, and the Bakeress-at-the-Steps was not far from right, when she said of her, "You see goodness in all she does, but you cannot say, it is just there! Her goodness is like the butter which is baked in the bread: it is everywhere!" Thaddea soon took Ernestine on her lap and taught her to spin; and when her father came in and was astonished to see them thus, Ernestine cried out to him with cheerful tones, "Father, mother has promised that next winter I shall have a wheel of my own, and mother keeps her promises." And, indeed, Thaddea did keep her promise; Ernestine became her child.

Goldstumpf has been dead some time. The Baker-at-the-Steps hadn't much good to say of him after his death, for what he left was so insignificant, it was hardly worth saying any thing about; and besides, in his last years, Goldstumpf had displayed sincere piety, so that the Baker-at-the-Steps used to say of him: "Yes, yes; that is just it — the good years he kept to himself, and the bad ones he gave to God."

It was, however, no little matter for the Baker-at-the-Steps that he did not make Thaddea feel how Goldstumpf had deceived him: he didn't own to himself that he had also practised deceit against the dead, and he maintained that Thaddea was the one who smoothed away all difficulties.

Ernestine is now married to the model-teacher at Neustadt. The old Baker-at-the-Steps danced with his wife at his grandchild's wedding, and at supper was very merry, saying, it certainly couldn't be helped, teaching was hereditary in his family. Folks call Ernestine, too, the handsome teacher; now, however, it is only in her daughters that you can see how handsome she once was, though not one of her daughters can compare with her in height: they have all rather the short figure of the model-teacher, who is a son of the merchant Mr. Stumpf of Freiburg. The handsome teacher has now, however, a new style of beauty with her gray locks; and a peculiar glance, a peculiar brightness spreads over her features when, with her thrilling voice (she used to sing treble), she asserts that, alas! among a hundred step-mothers, there is scarcely one good, real mother to be found, who will give a child what it most needs: the spiritual mother-milk, which is truly love. And when she relates how she reached the highest happiness, how at first she had been stubborn, and disowned, and then with all the more joy entered her heaven on earth, and how Thaddea had ever remained the same to her, even when she had children of her own: at such times, she makes all who hear her happy too, for to hear of the good deeds of one strong heart—this gives strength to all other hearts.

BENIGNA.

BENIGNA.

CHAPTER I.

THE PROUD BEAUTY.

IT was Whit-Sunday. The grain was waving in the far-spreading fields, and the wild rose blossoming in the hedge.

In the narrow foot-path which led through the rye-field a young man and a maiden met. They stopped. They were both almost a head taller than the tall stalks, and both were handsome. The youth had broad shoulders, and was powerfully built; the girl, who carried her broad-brimmed coarse straw hat on her arm, had a clear rosy complexion, and on her forehead waved heavy flaxen locks; her roguish bright blue eyes, form, and countenance were all so charming, it was a pleasure to look at her.

The maiden nodded and smiled; the young man hesitatingly held out his hand. "Good morning, George! What's the matter?" said the maiden. "This is my Patron Saint's day, and you haven't got even a kind word for me?"

"Your Saint's day? Yes: your birthday does, indeed, come at the most beautiful time in the year; but even roses have thorns."

"What's the matter now?"

"You've deeply hurt my mother's feelings.

"Oh, pooh!" said the maiden, with a scornful laugh.

Her beautiful teeth shone, her eyes glistened; and besides the dimples in her cheeks, over her whole countenance were little smiling ripples, as if a hundred eyes were opened at once.

"Don't treat the affair so lightly," said the youth; "perhaps you are not aware of what you have done?"

The maiden shrugged her shoulders.

"Then I will tell you once more," continued the youth. "Yesterday you went down to our smithy to deliver your work, and when the agent said, 'Show it to the old woman,' you replied, 'Pooh! pooh! I should like to keep a goodly distance away from such a creature;' and you said many other wicked things contemptuously and angrily. Didn't you see that it was my mother? only say no.'

"No!"

"But when she called out to you, 'I hope you will be made fun of in your old age,' did you see then it was my mother? More's the pity, she has grown old; and, while carrying coal, she can't make the same appearance she used to when going to the dance. But when you recognized her, why didn't you go back and say, 'Forgive me, I didn't know it was you.'"

"I didn't wish to do that."

"And anger has very naturally caused her to say things against you. But what did you do then? You told the inspector he ought to give her a pinch of snuff, for you would like to see once how such a scarecrow would sneeze; and then you burst out laughing."

"Now I have had enough," replied the maiden; "I shall laugh where I please, when I please, and at what I please. Get out of the path, or I shall be obliged to trample down the grain."

George stepped aside, and Benigna went by him.

He was looking down, when suddenly, as if some one had called him, he looked up. Benigna was on her way through the cornfields. He followed her until he came out of the high grain where the path turns, and then in the meadow near the tall hazel-bush he stopped: here they had first confessed their love. He thought she would at least turn round again and call out to him, "Don't be offended with me."

But she kept on without looking back; and he thought he saw on her face a smile which said, "I know that you are watching me, and would like to run after me, for I am the beautiful Benigna." She was indeed beautiful, — more beautiful than can be adequately described, — and she knew it too; for the men could not refrain from always telling her of it by their looks, if not in words. Everybody smiled on Benigna, and she laughed at everybody. Wherever she came, whether to old or young, rich or poor, there came happiness; she had only to show herself in order to bring some good to each one: for what is there better than youthful strength and beauty? "It seems as if you could inhale fragrance from her face as from a rose," the old host of the "Lamb" used to say, who died at Easter.

But Benigna seldom showed herself: she was industrious at her work. She was an embroiderer.

The factories in neighboring Switzerland, and also in that country, furnished to the villages engraved patterns of curtains, pocket-handkerchiefs, &c.; but the work which Benigna did always had something more than the engraved patterns: something of her peculiar beauty seemed to have been interwoven with it.

Benigna, who had long ago lost her parents, lived with

an old aunt; and as she had such an independent bearing and such a natural air of authority that every one did homage to her, she never met with opposition. She had often been advised to go to the city, as she could make her fortune there; but she had no desire to do that: to be the belle of the village, and shine as the rightful queen in a dance or on a sleighing party, was enough for her. Besides, since the last church festival in the fall, there had been a settled engagement between her and the blacksmith George, who was the only one really suited to her in form and manly beauty. George was the only son of an old widow, who, although bent and feeble, was not afraid of hard work; she assisted in the blacksmith's shop, and the form bent over with age, otherwise not agreeable, clothed in rags and covered with coal-dust, had provoked from Benigna the ridicule we have just mentioned.

It never occurred to her that any one could feel hurt at being mortified; she herself was so heedless of flattery, that she threw every thing to the winds, and lived in the present moment. But the mother of George had, from the beginning, been opposed to the engagement. She would continually fill her son's ears with complaints, that, in marrying a beautiful woman, he would bring on himself the greatest misery, as seventy times every day it would be remarked how beautiful she was: he would find it out one of these days; whenever he went anywhere with his wife, he would not keep from anger and distrust, for it would be a constant vexation to him to have everybody paying attention to her. She was all very well now, and nobody could say any harm of her farther than that she looked upon every one as a fool; but who could answer for it, that she would never be any thing worse?

Very naturally, George paid no regard to these peevish remarks; although, in every thing else, he treated his mother with the greatest respect.

But now his mother had been ridiculed, and she begged him with uplifted hands not for her sake, — although she had a perfect right to ask it, — but for his own, to give up Benigna.

"A person who does not respect her elders will never respect her husband," she repeatedly urged. "Only think, you might do something which did not please her, or you might be sick; then she would quit you at once, and not trouble herself about you."

George tried to appease his mother, but in vain.

In the evening, he remained at home longer than usual; he still thought Benigna would come with a kind word for his mother. He resolved not to go to her, not to look at her, until she, of her own accord, asked pardon: that was the least she could do.

But after waiting a long time in vain, he thought perhaps she might not wish to come alone; she would wait until he came with her to his mother.

The old Bridget was well aware what was going on within her son, and endeavored to strengthen him, saying that he would get over it in a few days, and then he would be rid of the whole thing.

George stood at the garden hedge, humming gently to himself this song: —

> "In summer, in summer, in summer,
> That is the fairest sight;
> Then the roses bloom in the garden,
> And soldiers march to fight!"

Then just as his mother came home, he started off as it

he had neglected something important, and must attend to it immediately. He approached Benigna, who received him with a smile. She knew he couldn't be separated from her a single day; and when he commenced again about his mother's mortification, she begged him to leave the stupid old story alone; and she so charmed him, that he was again perfectly happy.

For several days his mother went about very sad, and without saying a word. George did every thing in his power to persuade Benigna to go to his mother and beg her pardon in a few words; but Benigna declared that she would never do it.

"But suppose I should leave you?"

"That you are just as little likely to do as I am to ask her pardon."

And she was right.

But George couldn't endure his mother's silent resentment, and so he forced himself to a deception in which he felt justified. One day he told his mother that Benigna begged a thousand pardons, only she could not come to her; that she was of a very peculiar temperament; if his mother would only go to her, she would see how good Benigna was. He told Benigna how kindly his mother felt towards her. Benigna nodded. Old Bridget went and said to Benigna, who was sitting at her embroidering frame: "I forgive you, and you must forgive me, too, for wishing you to be laughed at some day as you laughed at me! We ought neither of us to have done so."

"Yes, yes, it's all right," replied Benigna, and she bit off the thread in order to put it in the needle; but when Bridget offered her her hand, she stitched on very industriously.

"You are beautiful: every one must acknowledge that," said Bridget. "May I tell you something?"

"Why not?"

"Look, I have never been beautiful, but I can imagine how it would seem."

"Well, how is it?"

"It must be delightful, very. But if you are always thinking about it, then I don't believe it is good for you; for you imagine every one must treat you differently because you are so beautiful."

The old woman talked very feelingly with Benigna, who concluded with, —

"Yes, yes, I will take care."

But as soon as Bridget had gone, she placed herself before her looking-glass, — she had procured one of pretty good size, — and she smiled as she looked in, and was exceedingly well pleased with herself.

Autumn came; George and Benigna were published in church. When old Bridget was congratulated, coming out of church, she silently nodded her thanks; and yet she had only a suspicion, she was not sure, that Benigna had insisted on George's sending his mother to her sister's, who lived at a little hamlet a few miles off; but George had explained, with deep feeling, that he would never do that; he wouldn't leave his mother until death took her from him; and he couldn't send her to his aunt's, for they had such a disorderly house there, it would kill her. At last Benigna gave in; but she said, in a roguish tone, "Do you know why I consent?"

"Because you like me, and have also a kind heart."

"I like you, but I can't bear having people always talking about their kind hearts; I consented, because it is the first time you have been wise enough not to threaten to leave me : for that you can't do."

The wedding was celebrated, and a handsomer couple than George and Benigna never stood before the altar of the village church. Every one was joyful; only mother Bridget's melancholy mood experienced no change.

At the wedding repast she had no relish for any thing; and, later, when they were dancing, she sat in a corner eating a piece of bread which she took out of her pocket.

CHAPTER II.

HANDSOME IS THAT HANDSOME DOES.

EORGE had now the most beautiful wife anywhere about; he had always been one of the best and jolliest workmen in the blacksmith's shop; but now he seemed to have new strength. As he stood with naked arm, swinging his great hammer, and the huge fire kindled by the bellows blazed up behind him, he took out the glowing iron and hammered it again and again on the anvil,— singing, and keeping time with his companions, while they swung the powerful hammers; it was a greater pleasure to see George than all the others.

But at home there was a sullen atmosphere. The mother complained to her son that Benigna never thanked her for any thing she did for her, and yet she worked like a servant, yes, like two; but Benigna allowed herself to be waited on as if it ought to be so. George tried to comfort her, saying that Benigna was an embroiderer, and could not attend to the house duties, as then she would be unfitted for the finer work; but his mother maintained that Benigna might just once say: "That is right, mother!" or, "You have done that well!" She even affirmed that Benigna still had an aversion to her. "I'm afraid, I'm afraid," mourned the mother, "your wife won't be gentle and kind until there comes to her a great misfortune; and a misfortune which comes upon her comes also on you."

Benigna, on the other hand, was continually complaining of her mother; so George had many heavy trials. He respected his mother, and loved his wife beyond measure. But now a bitterness, sharper than ever, had taken possession of Benigna; and it mortified George above every thing, that, when they went on a visit, or to any amusement, or to the "Leider-tafel" the workmen got up among themselves, Benigna would not on any account permit his mother to go with them; and, when she was in the presence of men, she not only accepted their homage, but even contrived that they must offer it to her. When George called her to account for it, she said his mother provoked her into doing it; and then when she wept over his hard-heartedness, he was inconsolable, and begged her pardon, beseeching her to be kind and cheerful.

So a year passed. The mother complained, and Benigna complained; but George had patience with both, thinking things would go better when there was once a child in the house.

For the first time George was terror-struck with his wife when she said she wished no children: a woman kept her beauty better when she had none.

All day long George wandered about as if lost; and at the shop his stroke always came too soon or too late to be in time with the regular stroke of his fellow-workmen.

His mother, noticing his absent-mindedness — Benigna didn't trouble herself about it — told him she would try moving to her sister's, but he must say nothing about her going away to his wife; for if she should come back again she would be obliged to humble herself anew, and it would be so much the worse for her.

George promised; and, while his mother was away, laughter and merriment prevailed in the house: Benigna exercised all her fascination on her husband, only he was frightened once when she said, "You see we should get along well enough if your mother wasn't here."

"You mean if she were not living here, but at her sister's?"

"Of course, of course," said Benigna, quickly; and she tried to look very pleasant.

For the first time the beautiful countenance of his wife seemed to George distorted, and yet—he could not tell why he did it, but he did it—he disclosed to her his mother's intention not to return; and then her countenance assumed so joyful an expression he could not carry to his mouth the cup of coffee she had given him, as if her wicked look had poisoned it. But he forced himself to it; and while they were still at breakfast his mother came in.

George received her kindly, and was doubly kind, inasmuch as he felt guilty of having betrayed her.

He made a sign to his wife not to say any thing about it, and went off to the blacksmith's shop.

When Benigna was alone with her mother, who was drinking her coffee, she said, "Mother, you will take your goat with you too."

"My goat? why?"

"You would do well to take all your things, and live in future with your sister."

Mother Bridget looked her full in the face, put down the cup, left the room, and went to her chamber; Benigna took no notice of her until noon : she found her on the bed crying and wringing her hands. Benigna gave her very few words, saying only that she must come to her meal, as she would send her nothing.

While Benigna was sitting at the table with the little girl she had taken for help, she saw her mother leading the goat, going away from the house with tottering steps.

"Shan't I call her ?" asked the girl.

"No, she will come of her own accord."

The mother wanted to go to the blacksmith's shop and complain to her son, because he had betrayed her to his wife ; but she sat down on the hill and talked to her goat, telling her she was blessed in not having a daughter-in-law ; then she prayed to God that she might die there, rather than make her son's married life unhappy. She waited until George came, and was led by him back into the house, and went to the table with them as if nothing had happened.

Weeks and months went by. All was quiet in George's home, but he often told his wife that his mother seemed to him to be failing all the time ; Benigna shrugged her shoulders.

"I'm afraid she won't live long," said George.

"It's the rule that old people should die," coldly replied Benigna.

"Wife !" exclaimed George, "don't be so wicked."

"I'm not at all wicked. I only hope I shall die before I am old and wizzled : to be in the world and take no pleasure in yourself, and have nobody take pleasure in you, it would be better not to be here at all."

"I don't blame you for such speeches, because you never knew your mother," replied George.

"You ought to put yourself at my embroidering frame, and I ought to be a blacksmith; I believe you're a tailor, and no blacksmith," concluded Benigna.

At last mother Bridget could keep up no longer, and lay sick in bed.

One day she called George to her, and asked him to tell her truly whether Benigna had ever commissioned him to beg her pardon. He confessed that she never had. "Then it's well," said his mother. "Now it's all right."

After that she could not be brought to utter a word.

George told his wife that her former ill-treatment still weighed on his mother's mind, and she ought to make up now for her past neglect. But Benigna laughed at him for bringing up such an old story; with her usual wanton thoughtlessness, she tried to persuade him not to take so to heart the course of nature: for old people were better off when they were dead.

George told her if she kept on talking in that way, she would succeed in driving him from her out into the world. Benigna laughed at him, saying,—

"And when you have got as far as the Haselberg, you'll come back: you can never live away from me."

George sent for his mother's sister; and her son and sister were with her when she died. She scarcely spoke in her last days, and George closed her eyes.

He went into his wife's room, and told her all was over. She turned and looked out the window, then turning back to him and stroking his face with her soft hand, she said, "You have grown ten years older in the last few days. Stand up straight, for I will have no such old husband."

One word reminded George of what his mother once

said: "Would his wife, who now cared so much for him, love and nurse him when he was old and feeble?"

He suppressed the evil thoughts, and said, "Now just do one thing for me, — you were not able while she was alive to take from her soul what you thoughtlessly did, — now, for my sake, go up and beg pardon of the dead, and look at her face, peaceful as an angel!"

"I'm not going up; I will look on no corpse; I can't look at a corpse; no one shall see me when I am dead."

George might urge and entreat as much he pleased, Benigna would not enter the chamber of death. All night George sat by his mother's body, and the thought that he would only wait until she was buried, then he would leave his wife, almost drove him to distraction; and with the feeling that he must leave her, was mingled the thought of her beauty, and how happy he had been, and could be again.

The bells were tolling. Mother Bridget was being carried to the grave. George was standing in the sitting-room with the relations. Benigna had put on a mourning cap, and now — he could not himself tell why — he turned, saw Benigna looking in the glass, and it seemed to him as if she nodded to herself with a satisfied air, — for the mourning was becoming to her.

He clenched his fists, and it seemed to him as if he must annihilate two persons there, — the one in the looking-glass, and the living one, — and then his heart contracted with bitter anguish that he should have such thoughts at such a time, and he certainly must have seen wrongly; how could any human being be thinking of a beautiful appearance at such a time? Then he heard Benigna say to her aunt, "Just put a pin in there, so that the crape will not entirely cover my forehead."

With a convulsive spasm, George fell senseless to the floor. They raised him up, and two men were obliged to support him, so that he could follow his mother to the grave.

When Benigna said to him, "George, how you appear! be a man, compose yourself," it seemed to him as if all the hammers in the blacksmith's shop had suddenly struck him on the head: this voice sounded so shrill and harsh. He walked behind his mother's body, and before him, in the air, danced the beautiful face of his wife: her beauty haunted him continually. It was hateful to him, and he would never take any more joy in it. He tried to fix his thoughts only on his mother's death; but in the very midst of the thoughts was mingled the beautiful picture, and he saw it double, — saw it in the glass, and living.

They returned from the funeral. George sat at the table and eat with his wife, his aunt, and other relations, but without once looking at his wife, and his nerves quivered whenever he heard her voice.

Night came, he went into his mother's room and sat there on the bed with his face between his hands. Benigna came in with a light.

"Put out the light!" he cried.

"Why?"

"I don't want to see you; I cannot see you. Put out the light!"

"Don't be so foolish;" and Benigna tried to comfort him. "Now you shall see how happily we will live together, we two alone."

"We two alone? With you alone? The dead stands between us!" cried George, going up to her; and he snatched the light out of her hand, and threw it on the floor so that it went out. "You're not bound to me, nor I to you any longer."

"I think you are crazy," replied Benigna.

"I could be; hasn't the death of my mother changed you too? I have often reproached myself for having wronged her; will nothing change you?"

"I don't know how I ought to change; I am satisfied with myself as I am, and have pleased you and everybody else."

"Very well, remain so; but I have sense enough still to know I can live with you no longer. I must go away from you; you can admire your beauty alone in the glass, and can let other people tell you how beautiful you are: you are a snake in my eyes. I am going to leave you."

"You are going to leave me? Do you know any one more beautiful out in the world?"

"Beautiful! beautiful! Is beauty, then, every thing?"

"To be rich is fine too; but that, alas! I am not. Come, come, be sensible, and go into the sitting-room with me."

"Never with you. I am going out into the wide world."

"Then I'll say adieu, and wish you a pleasant journey!"

With these words, Benigna left the chamber, and went out into the sitting-room.

After awhile she saw her husband leave the house with a walking-stick in his hand; he stood still a moment where the foot-path entered the road. She wanted once to call him back, but she said to herself that she had done enough, and would lose all her respect if she was more yielding. The lingerer heard the window raised, and saw a bright light stream from it on the path before him, but he stepped over it into the dark night.

Benigna sat alone, talking to the light. "He'll soon come back again when he has got rid of some of his notions in the open air."

Hour after hour went by; George did not return. Suddenly she began to feel timid in the house from which a dead body had that day been carried, and now her husband had left it.

She went to her aunt's, where she had formerly lived; but when she got there, seeing there was no light, she went back, thinking it was better she shouldn't betray herself: no one should know that the beautiful Benigna's husband ever left her an hour. On the way, it occurred to her how he had loved her and still loved. How could he leave her?

She hurried back to the house; he must certainly have returned by this time, and would be anxious at her absence. She went in, — no one was there. She did not want to go to bed; she would wait until he came. But the oil had been spilled when the lamp fell, and the light went out, and she sat in the dark until morning came. The day came, — but no George.

She looked in the glass, and was amazed at the strange, neglected face which it reflected; with new courage, she washed and dressed herself, and went to work. But she fell asleep over her embroidery-frame, and was awakened by a visit from her aunt. One of George's journeymen, also, came to ask if he was going to be idle much longer: work was so hurried now. Benigna told him her husband had gone away on family business, but would return that evening, or early in the morning. Evening came, morning came, and no sign of George. Weeks and months went by. Benigna never showed herself in the village.

She worked all day, and at night wept, — wept incessantly. In the village, there were all sorts of reports concerning the disappearance of George.

But as year after year passed, he was scarcely thought of, and Benigna could hardly be recognized, she was so changed. She, the beauty, once so much admired, was now rarely seen. The ill-treatment of George's mother was much talked about and exaggerated; but when it was known Benigna was growing blind, compassion was again felt for her.

Benigna became blind, and the aunt employed, as a means of begging, this sorry-looking form, which was now bent and wasted away. She led her into the neighboring villages, representing her as an object of compassion, — a woman deserted by her husband: once very beautiful, and now wretched and helpless. Benigna heard this patiently, without uttering a word. Thus ten years and more passed by. The aunt died, and Benigna was now doubly forsaken.

CHAPTER III.

BEAUTY SOLD CHEAP.

T was mid-winter. The snow crunched under the feet of the men going towards the Rathhaus.

The groups of people wandering about the street were continually increasing, and they were heard to say to one another:

"That's a fine joke!"

"Perhaps so, but I don't like it."

"To sell at public auction a forsaken old blind woman!"

"She's a burden to the public."

"And it will cost us a pretty penny."

Such was the talk here and there.

The village was one of the poorer sort; it had only a little arable land, and this was for the most part in the possession of three farmers.

The inhabitants consisted principally of stone-cutters, charcoal burners, and blacksmiths. Down in the valley could be heard the pounding and hammering of the great factory; and a broad column of smoke ascended from the rocky cliffs covered with snow, into the clear sky.

A man in shabby clothes, who was followed by a scolding woman, came from a little house standing by itself on the hill-side at a distance from the street, and joined the group.

"Korbhans, will you take Benigna into your house?" he was asked.

"I would; my wife doesn't want to."

While he was speaking, a little girl about seven years old came running up, and said, "Uncle, aunt will burn the house down if you bring Benigna home!"

"Now you must certainly do it," urged the others; "you must show yourself master."

Korbhans went somewhat timidly with the rest of them. They reached the Rathhaus. There were many people here, who, until the proceedings began, were smoking their pipes at the entrance. At last, the parish official came and summoned the assembly into the large council-chamber.

The common council sat at the table, and not far off, cowering down in a corner, sat a female form enveloped in all sorts of rags, that hung down in tatters: her chin was resting on her hands which grasped a crutch.

"Come, let us proceed to business," began the mayor. "There sits Benigna. The parish is poor, and let him not undertake to support a forsaken widow"—here the cowering form groaned—"who is not willing to take, as part pay, the blessing of God in addition to the small sum the parish can pay. And it would be a very good thing if your wives had come with you, for it will depend upon the wife, chiefly, how she is treated."

A sum was named, which the parish would pay for the yearly support of the blind woman; but no one said a word when the question was put whether any one would take her for a less sum, for every one who wanted to have any thing to do with the matter very naturally wanted the highest pay.

"I will take her for the sum proposed," cried Hans, the basket-maker.

"And I," "and I," was heard from different quarters.

"Who spoke first?" asked the blind woman of a little girl standing near her, who was the school-master's daughter.

"Korbhans," replied the maiden. "For God's sake, I hope he won't get you: his wife is worse than a fiery dragon."

The blind woman dropped her crutch, and the little girl picked it up and gave it to her again. Then there was rapid bidding here and there, so the school-master's daughter did not have time to tell the blind woman the name of each bidder.

At last only one voice was heard, and the parish-clerk cried:

"Going, going,"—he made a long pause,—"Gone!" he cried, and struck with his hammer on the table.

"Who has me?" asked the old woman.

"Korbhans," was her answer.

"Come here, Hans, give me your hand; I knew your mother and your wife's mother well."

The councilmen were all astonished at hearing Benigna speak so suddenly.

One of the farmers, with a huge nose, thinking he ought to say something, thus exhorted her,—

"Yes, Benigna, only don't come to us with complaints! Now you are provided for; and have patience, the parish will do more for you when it can. And be grateful!" he concluded, stretching out his nose to the other councilmen, as if they ought to bear witness to his skill in speaking.

"Come with me now," said Hans. "Where's your bed?"

"At the school-master's," answered Benigna, "and a little trunk too."

The maiden accompanied the old woman part of the way, but when they reached the slope of the hill, which the children had worn smooth in coasting, Benigna couldn't go any farther on the slippery surface.

"Put your arms round my neck," said Hans, stooping down, "and I will carry you up the hill on my back."

He carried Benigna into the house on his back. The children made merry over the funny sight, but the school-master's daughter told them there was nothing to laugh at. "It was kind of Hans," she said.

On the way, he said to Benigna:

"My wife is a little bit of a scold, don't trouble yourself about that: when she has scolded enough, she stops of her own accord; and if any thing is the matter, just tell me, I will take care of you the rest of your days."

Hans had a conviction, which many in the village shared, that Benigna had treasure concealed somewhere; it was not pure kind-heartedness which made him so benevolent to Benigna: he hoped to coax it out of her by winning her confidence.

"Yes, yes," said the old woman on his back, "I will reward you well."

Hans smiled to himself, thinking: that means, then, that she has some treasure.

He carried Benigna into his sitting-room. No one was there but the little girl, who called out angrily, "Phew! now we have got the old witch, sure enough!"

Hans placed Benigna on the bench; her crutch fell

down, and the child snatched it up quickly, saying, "That I will put in the fire, then you can't stir from your place, and can't touch me, you old witch."

The child ran out in the kitchen and threw the crutch into the open fire, but Hans quickly rescued it.

His wife was standing by the fire, and said:

"You can take care of her, I do not want to have any thing to do with her."

"You will be kind to her. At least go in and tell her that you mean to treat her badly."

"Do you think I can't do that?"

She went into the sitting-room and said: "It is known of old what sort of a person Benigna is: she might have beguiled Hans in all sorts of ways, but she herself wasn't the fool to take care of an old, blind hag."

At last, she asked Benigna why she had not put an end to herself.

"Because I must live longer in order to grow better; and you too!"

The wife left the room, and Benigna sat alone. She heard nothing but the rattling of the shovel in the large stove; it seemed as if the wife wished to vent her indignation on the stove; and a voice from the kitchen called out, "All the children laugh at me, because I must lead the blind witch. But I will not, a single step."

The child came into the sitting-room, complaining that it had frozen its hands while sliding.

"Then don't go right to the stove," said Benigna.

"So you are there, are you?" cried the child. "You are smart not to know when it's dark."

"Is it dark already?" asked Benigna.

"Yes, indeed."

Benigna sent word by the child, that she might perhaps help to prepare supper: she could peel potatoes and cut bread.

The child went out, and was heard laughing outside. When she came back, Benigna asked her to tell her how the furniture was placed in the room, so that she might not stumble against it.

The child explained every thing; but when Benigna wanted to leave the room, she put an overturned chair in the way, so that she stumbled over it, and fell down; then she left the room laughing, and Benigna sat down again on the bench.

Hans had handed Benigna over to his wife and gone to the inn, with the consoling thought, that she must be kind to her when she saw that the thing couldn't be altered.

After awhile he came back, bringing Benigna's bed. It was put in the attic, where the child slept. Benigna asked the child if she had a good bed too, but she was perverse, and told her that it was none of her business; Benigna, however, felt of the wretched little bed and noticed how poorly it was covered; then she took some covering from her own bed and put it on the child, who doubled up her fists in wrath against the witch, but put up with the liberality, and soon went to sleep.

The child called out "mother!" in her sleep, and Benigna shuddered. She had never been called mother, nor had she wished to be called so.

She sighed in the quiet night, and asked, in the cold, wintry air, how long she must live in darkness and misery before death would release her.

While Benigna was lying awake in the attic, Hans was

talking with his wife, and he asked her to treat Benigna well; it was as good as certain, she must have treasure buried near the tall hazel-bush, as she used to be led there so often by old Margaret, who was dead; and if she was treated kindly, she would tell her benefactors where the treasure was, and make them rich.

His wife replied, if Benigna had any treasure, she would not have allowed herself to be sold at auction; but Hans maintained she had done it intentionally, she had always been peculiar; and he had it from his sister, to whom the dead aunt had imparted it, that Benigna had some secret or other. The wife at last allowed herself to be persuaded, and it was evident also to her that Benigna had some concealed treasure, for formerly she had earned a great deal, and latterly begged a good deal.

CHAPTER IV.

THE HIDDEN TREASURE.

AY dawned. The wife came, and helped Benigna down stairs into the sitting-room. Benigna nodded, things were already looking brighter: ill-nature had not lasted over night.

But the child would not eat out of the same plate with Benigna. Hans wanted to punish her, but Benigna entreated him not to do it, saying that she had had enough. "Now eat alone," said she, turning to the child. "Isn't your name Babi? I had a little sister of that name, who died young."

The child was frightened at this good-nature, and looked grimly at Benigna, for even she was beginning to have a better feeling; and the first stirring in this young but already hardened soul, was anger against the better emotion.

Benigna knew this was a forsaken child, who was considered a nuisance by every one; her mother, a sister of Hans's wife, was a servant in the capital.

Benigna could spin well, and she spun from morning till night. Hans and his wife nodded contentedly. Benigna was no trouble, she nearly paid her board by her spinning; so the parish allowance was almost clear gain.

This agreement was the first for a long time between this couple, as formerly there was only quarrelling and disputing; there had always been poverty in the house, and the proverb says, "That the horses kick at the empty crib."

Hans, who, especially in winter, had very little to do, hung round gossiping here and there, and his wife thought, by scolding him, to keep him at home and at work; but it worked just the other way. At first they had avoided violent quarrels before Benigna; but she said, one day: "My husband is out in the world, perhaps he is dead. Oh, how wrong it is that you, as long as you are together, should not live happily!" After saying that and more still, in her presence there was a certain degree of restraint.

Hans still had a work-bench in the house, at which he had formerly carved a great variety of wooden implements, especially ladles and spindles. It was now put into use again; and as he sat at it working, he often talked with Benigna, who was spinning.

His wife, too, went about more contented, and often she even brought a cup of coffee to Benigna out of the regular time, which, to be sure, was only roasted carrots, but it served very well as a beverage. But the greatest change was in the child. Benigna often asked her to do this or that for her: at first, it was done reluctantly, but afterwards it seemed to be a pleasure to be able to help others, and gradually became a feeling of spontaneous benevolence.

Babi came of herself, and asked to do this or that for Benigna, to lead her here and there; and the child felt that here was a person, for the first time, who appreciated her kindness and attention. Benigna heard the child recite the lessons which she had at school; she understood especially how to reckon well, and had also good old proverbs in her head, and songs in abundance. The school-master came and told them that little Babi was getting to be his best scholar.

So the winter passed more quickly and pleasantly than any one had for a long time. In the spring, when the willows were full of sap, Benigna learned the art of braiding baskets. She took to it easily, and with her nimble fingers she could soon braid neat little baskets ; indeed, the patterns for embroidering which she had in her head helped embellish them, so that they found a ready sale.

Now Hans's wife wanted to be continually praising the good fortune which had brought Benigna into the house ; but Hans held off, for they must not make it known, otherwise she would not show them the buried treasure, and the sooner they had that so much the better. He and his wife often alluded to the secret treasure ; Benigna smiled at it, and, in smiling, her face assumed a singular expression. She was wise enough not to deny the secret treasure, for she knew that that made the people she lived with much more tractable.

In the harvest-time she kept the child gathering ears of corn, and she went with her into the forest to pick up wood. Hans often led her to the Haselberg, for he kept hoping she would show him the place where the treasure was buried, but she never got so far as that ; he could, however, put the heaviest load on the wheelbarrow, she would go behind and push so hard, that Hans, going before, did not have to pull at all.

So, in the summer, the corn and wood were gathered, and there was a supply of every thing in the house as never before. But the best of it was, there was a peace in the house that formerly had never been known, which nourished and warmed still more than the bread and the fire. The ears which Babi had gathered, Benigna threshed by themselves in the shed, and the child became more and more attentive and industrious.

When the news came that her mother was dead, Benigna comforted her all day long; finally she said:

"You can do me a kindness."

"How? Am I to go anywhere for you?"

"No, call me mother after this. Will you?"

"Yes, indeed; mother!"

For the first time Benigna kissed little Babi, and from this time was called by her, mother.

And it was now the seventh year that Benigna had lived in the house of the basket-maker.

CHAPTER V.

THE CRY ANSWERED.

T was almost time for mowing.

There came up the street a tall and handsome man, with snow-white hair, carrying on his back a heavy bundle of scythes. Not far from Hans's house he set down his bundle against the garden-wall, laid out the scythes, and made them ring. They sounded well, and the man said, in a foreign dialect, to some men returning home from the field in the mid-day heat, that they were real steel scythes; he showed them the mark of a manufactory in Leoben. He received for answer, if he would remain here over night, by this evening or to-morrow morning, being Sunday, he would be able to dispose of his wares. The people passed on: the man stood leaning on the fence looking at it strangely with his one eye, the other was covered with a black shade. Then he heard the sound of a solitary flail in Hans's house.

There is nothing more melancholy than to hear a solitary thresher, — unless it is to be one's self the solitary thresher, — for the keeping time with the stroke enlivens and cheers the labor of persons working together; but the solitary thresher must voluntarily put forth his strength anew at every raising of his flail.

A barefooted maiden about thirteen years old, with a rosy brown face and bright eyes, came up the street with a bundle of gleaned ears, and turned aside into the foot-path leading up to the house. The stranger called out to her and asked :

"Who is threshing there alone ?"

"A forsaken old blind woman," replied the maiden.

"What's her name ?"

"Benigna."

The child went up the hill with her bundle of ears, and the stranger gathered together his scythes : they rang of themselves, for his hand trembled.

After he had packed up all his scythes, he went up the path to the little house.

Benigna stepped out of the shed, and cried out into the empty air :

"Who called me ?"

The stranger stood still and held his breath. Then Benigna, receiving no answer, went back into the shed and began threshing again.

The stranger turned, took his bundle on his back and went towards the village ; he returned to the "Lamb" inn, and asked if he could obtain a night's lodging ; but he did not open his scythes again to-day ; he had a pint of beer before him, but the flies drank more of it than he did.

When it was evening he left the village, and went through the fields as far as the hazel slope. There he sat until dark. He came back into the village, sold the inn-keeper two scythes, and was told that he might have disposed of many if he had been there after work-hours.

At bedtime, the man wandered out of the village again,

and, sitting behind the hedge on the road by Hans's house, he heard Benigna say to Babi :

" I'm not going to church in the morning, but you must all go and leave me at home ; to-morrow, I must be alone and think alone."

A thrill passed through the stranger when he heard that.

" Are there many stars in the sky ? " asked Benigna, after a long time.

" Yes, indeed, many millions ! Oh, mother, if I could only make you see ! "

Hans called out of the window, that Benigna and Babi ought to go to sleep : it was very late.

The house door opened and shut ; the stranger sat on the slope of the hill until midnight sounded from the church-steeple ; then he went back into the village and sought his lodging-place.

It was a bright, clear morning. The stranger made good profits before church, for it had become known that he had the best scythes for sale, and sold them cheap.

He often cast strange glances from his one eye at the men who were buying of him, and started when he heard this name and that.

The bells rung, and the people went to church ; the stranger, too, went in.

He waited at the door until everybody passed by him.

When the bells stopped, the organ sounded in the church and the singing began ; he went slowly to the church-yard, and stood for a long time by a grave, the cross of which had sunk into the ground.

Then, turning, he went quickly towards Hans's house.

He saw Benigna sitting on a bench in front of the

house. Her hands were folded, and she was praying to herself in low tones. Now unfolding her hands, and stretching out her arms, she cried:

"Oh, George, if I only knew whether you were alive or dead! And is it possible that you will give to me no token? Do you ever think of me now? I have suffered more than any one else in the world, and have deserved it more than any one else. Oh, if I could only say to you, 'Forgive me!' When I come to you in heaven and ask your forgiveness, do not send me away from you; I have hell here already, and I can only pray to God that he will not thrust you also into hell, for you too have certainly suffered enough, and you did right; but you were hard, — no, not hard, you were right. George, forgive me, forgive me, in heaven and on earth!"

The stranger could contain himself no longer: he started forward, saying:

"Benigna, here I am, lying at your feet; forgive me, as I forgive you. Benigna, do you not know me, — not even my voice?"

The old woman, at first motionless, now got up, and passed her hand over his face; but when she felt the black shade she drew back, exclaiming, "Oh, George, it is you, your voice; but what is that?"

"A spark burned my eye; you are blind, but I can still see you. Come with me: come, before they get home from church. Once I left you, now you leave every thing! Come, we cannot talk here, and I have so much to tell you."

"If I could only weep," moaned Benigna.

George continued urging her to leave the house.

She started up, exclaiming:

"Yes, I will go with you. I will take your hand, my prayer is heard. Do with me what you will: thrust me down the precipice; throw me into the water; do what you please, I will go with you wherever you take me."

They sat down together, and could not speak a word.

Benigna raised her husband's rough hand to her mouth.

Now they heard indications that church was over.

"Come, we will be off before the other people come," urged George.

While the bells were ringing, they went along the road into a foot-path, and then up the height among the hazel-bushes.

CHAPTER VI.

THE TREASURE DUG UP.

" HAVE brought you to the place which, for thirty years, waking and sleeping, has been before my eyes. Now don't you speak, only let me explain," began George. "What you did was frightful enough, but what I did was the most frightful thing in the world. You mocked old age, and now, old yourself, you have been obliged to endure mockery a million times worse."

Benigna groaned. "No, that's not what I meant to say," said George, consolingly, stroking her face with his left hand. "I have taken revenge, but revenge is the bitterest thing in the world: there are no scales in which one can weigh it. I have dragged through the whole world, wandering even into Turkey, and from there back to Poland and Russia, and then over the sea and back. I have worked until my joints were stiff, and yet took no rest. For ten years now I have been in Styria; then when, four months ago, a spark flew into my eye, I recalled every thing, and thought I should go crazy: it burned into my head and heart, and I thought I should die; the one thing always before me was myself as I struck the light out of your hand, and strode away down the road, while the light streamed out of the window. Enough! I swore then, that when I should be well, I would go and find you, pardon you, and do what good I could for you the rest of my life. I must still wear the shade, but my eye is uninjured: yet it was useful in keeping the people from recognizing me. If I could only make you see once more! Well, I am now here, and the few years we have yet to live we will make easier to each other; every thing must be forgotten; it must be so, that it may be well with us on the earth. You will go with me now, and we will live together; will you not?"

Benigna, with a passionate embrace, threw her arms around his neck.

"We'll not go back into the village; we don't want to take leave of, or thank any one, no one need know what has become of us: in the worst that can come, we can only help each other. I will leave my scythes, and you leave what you have. I have money enough with me; I have saved up a little property, and have work and a good employer, in Styria: there we will live together until death separates us."

Benigna consented to go with George wherever he should take her. She only lamented leaving in such a secret and ungrateful manner the people who had been so kind to her; and mourned especially that Babi, whom she had brought up as her own child, would be thrust out into the world again, to be a vagabond and liable to be misled.

Finally, George consented to go to Hans's house. Hardly had they agreed upon that when they heard voices, and these words: "There she is, and the scythe-dealer is with her."

Hans, his wife, and Babi, who were looking for Benigna, came to the hazel-grove; and they could not restrain their astonishment when they heard who the scythe-dealer was. They willingly consented to Babi's request that she might go with Benigna.

At last, after they had recovered from their amazement and become composed, Hans asked: "Now tell me honestly, Benigna, have you already dug up the treasure which you had buried?"

"I have never had any," replied Benigna.

"But you have left us one," said the wife; "we are now, God be praised, in peace and prosperity."

They all returned to the village, or, more properly, to Hans's house, which was the last one in the village, so that they need be seen by no one, for George insisted on that.

But he thought of something better: Babi must get the mayor; and, under promise of secrecy that he would be silent until they were gone, George handed over to him a handsome sum, to be given back to the parish for the money pàid out for the support of his wife.

"That's just!" cried Benigna; "that's right! You have been all your life a proud and honorable man! That's just!"

"This, too," said George: "but every debt is now paid off and squared."

"That is better still," rejoined Benigna.

When it was dark, George took his scythes, and, while thousands of stars were shining in the heavens, went with Benigna and Babi down the valley, past the quiet blacksmith's shop, and on as far as the beautiful land of Styria.

Not a great distance from the pretty town of Leoben, on the Mur, at the edge of the wood beyond the meadow, there stands a small cottage. There, on a bench in front of the house, sits an old blind woman with a beautiful maiden; in the evening George comes up from the forge, and gives his hand to Benigna and the daughter.

After many and terrible tribulations, George and Benigna now led a happy life, and are in the enjoyment of it even to the present day.

RUDOLPH AND ELIZABETH.

AN IDYL OF CULTIVATED LIFE.

RUDOLPH AND ELIZABETH.

CHAPTER I.

THE FIRST MEETING.

"WHERE is the street *St. Mary on the Capitol?*" asked a young man, in a travelling suit, of a good-humored, full-faced native Cologne woman, whose head was covered with a small, loose cap, and whose smoothly parted hair was rolled up in a mass behind.

"You go through that gate, and then take the right-hand turn."

Rudolph expressed his thanks, and, passing through the Byzantine gateway, found the desired street.

This was in the early part of September, 1841, whose summer-like warmth seemed to make up for the rainy days of the three special summer months. A hot noon-day stillness pervaded the street, on one side of which there was a row of trees.

Rudolph remained still for a while, in order to recover himself. He regarded with particular interest the whole surroundings, for here his friend Charles passed and re-passed, in joy and sorrow; and all was consecrated, for on all the eye of his friend had rested. Rudolph experienced an unwonted excitement of his whole inner being:

his pulse beat quickly, his cheeks glowed, and it seemed as if he were raised into a new atmosphere.

It was more than the seeing again the dearest friend of his youth would naturally awaken, and yet what else could it be? Placing his hands together, as if he were holding between them the hand of his friend, he said to himself:

"Blessed if you find him again what he was once, and, if he is different, love shall still remain the same."

He found the number of the house, and, entering it, saw the name of his friend — Charles Meurer, Doctor of Laws — upon a door, at which he knocked. No one opened it; he knocked at all the doors, but they remained closed. He walked impatiently up and down the entry, hearing nothing but the sound of his own footsteps, and deliberating what he should first do, in the city where he was an entire stranger. "Fate does not desire, and it is not well to indulge in, such youthful excitement in our manly years; this tempest of feeling must subside," he said to himself.

He stood leaning against the door-post, engaged in deep thought. Just as he was going away, turning almost involuntarily, and knocking at the nearest door, he heard the rustling of a dress and hurried steps; a bolt was shot back, and the door opened, when there stood before him a girl of rare beauty, blushing almost to the very eyes. Rudolph stood there as if a thunder-bolt had fallen, and the maiden gazed at him with surprise, as she held the kerchief, fluttering upon her partially covered neck with one hand, and a book in the other. They stood thus speechless for a moment, until Rudolph, collecting himself, asked:

"Does not Frau Meurer live here?"

"Yes: she is out."

"And Dr. Meurer?"

"My brother has gone to the Board of Trade, but may be in at any moment."

"Are you his sister? That is pleasant," said Rudolph, hurriedly. "I am his friend; and, with your permission, I will wait for him," he added, entering.

The startled maiden looked shyly down to the floor, her hand still holding the latch; as the catch snapped in the lock, she gave a nervous start, but raised her eyes and fixed them with inquiring perplexity upon the man, whose countenance wore an expression of gentle excitement and trustworthy sincerity. Unconsciously, the girl assented with a nod.

Rudolph, wearied by his journey, and feeling weak after his excitement, sat down on a chair; and the maiden, laying her book down upon the work-table, took a seat in the recess of the window.

"You live in a street with a widely known historic name," began Rudolph. "St. Mary on the Capitol is suggestive of the two greatest periods in the history of the world."

"But we live back of St. Mary on the Capitol," said the maiden, getting up in her confusion and sitting down again.

The felicitousness of this simple reply made Rudolph's countenance light up more brightly. A pause occurred, and the girl, taking up the embroidery upon which she had been working, tried to thread her needle, but her hand trembled. Pressing together her lips, she drew a long breath, and then placed the silk thread in the open book, which she laid upon the window shelf.

"I have interrupted your reading," said Rudolph; "may I take the liberty of asking whom I have pushed aside?"

As if she could not help it, the girl gave the book to Rudolph, and then looked out of the window in embarrassment.

"Ah! 'Münchhausen,' by Immermann: a very fine book!" He opened at the place where the thread was put, and found it was where Lisbeth and the Huntsman are shut up alone in the church, and, with God's holy sun beaming on them, pledge each other at the altar. Rudolph could not utter a word, and it seemed to him a strange coincidence, a favorable indication, placed as he was here alone with a maiden whose first glance had thrilled his inmost soul. How gladly would he have embraced her, and said: "Lisbeth! my Lisbeth!" but he restrained himself, looked upon the book without seeing the words, while many forms were present to his imagination, and he himself was one of them; his breathing became deep, and the girl silently looked towards the window. Two persons, who had never before seen each other, sat here without speaking; but a third, who was dead, hovered over them like a glorifying sun, and the rootlets of their being became entwined together.

It was a peculiar association of ideas that led Rudolph now to say: "Immermann's death must have awakened here, too, the deepest sorrow."

"Yes; but it is terrible how soon a name dies out: a few days, a few weeks after a death, the bitter loss is spoken of, and then the world must interest itself in something else, and the name of the man who occupied such a place in its regard is no longer mentioned; at every opportunity, the names of the good ought to be spoken, and their memory extolled."

"I once had this idea," said Rudolph: "each city, each province, each nation, ought every year to recount its sacred history, and a service be held for the commemoration of all its good and great souls. The oratorios, which are almost everywhere brought out each year, and which constitute a sort of universal divine service, would give the grandest framework for such a celebration."

"Well, why don't you carry out this idea? it would be truly magnificent!"

"It can't be carried out, because the police in church and state would wrest the word to glorify their own particular stars; how few names would be mentioned, and those frequently not the best! And besides, it is not necessary. What is the object of holding fast by by-gone names? Monuments need not stand in isolation in the open air, but should be the pillars of a grand edifice, with no other claim than as contributing to its support and ornament. We should not be called upon to complain of the decline of piety, if the old gravestones were used in the construction of the new sanctuary; the inscriptions upon them should be honored, but their fixed solidity should be employed to subserve the uses of the new structure. And if time effaces a name, what does it matter? If the thought, the feeling, the life of a great spirit has gone into the mind and soul of those who lived with him, and lived after him, then he lives for all time: each bosom that heaves through him, each heart that is made strong by his influence, praises him, though it names not, or does not even know, his name. Just as we need not expressly praise God and the goodness of nature every time we experience enjoyment; the enjoyment itself and the blissful reception are the best expressions of our grateful remembrance, in the real acceptation of the word."

"You seem to have the same views as my brother."

"We found each other in love and youthful friendship, and were first made aware, by blessed experience, how our hearts beat in harmony, like two voices which are different, but yet blend together as one."

"Men are situated more freely and favorably for cultivating friendships, for they are out in the great world, and can make an independent selection; we girls are more dependent upon chance and conventional arrangements, which circumscribe us within a limited circle."

"You are right in that remark, and you will not charge me with upholding the superiority of men, if I maintain that friendship is almost an exclusively manly virtue."

"Virtue? I cannot grant that, for we have also the capacity, but it is not brought out and cultivated."

"You are a strict sentinel, and let nothing contraband pass," said Rudolph, joyously smiling; "but I use virtue here merely in the sense of an unfolded capacity. History, in ancient times, tells us only of friendships between men."

"Simply because men wrote the histories."

"And very right, probably, that they should, as they make the history; the old Greeks were consistent, and, regardless of the claims of women, had no actresses, men taking the female parts."

"I don't see how I have reached this point," said the girl, blushing deeply; "I did not desire to claim a different position for girls: I only meant that we could be friends as well as men."

"But in a wholly different way from men. Just consider

that it is for the most part chance and propinquity, which produce friendships in girls, — a happening to live in the same neighborhood, a certain equality of conditions, a similar position, and especially a long-standing relation between the parents and the families, are the occasion of their origin. The girl must soon receive her friend into the house, and here are more parental interferences and restrictions than with the boy, who ranges out of doors, through field and wood, with his companions. With a girl, grace of manner and propriety of deportment are the chief objects of education; with a boy, knowledge and strength. It is hardly possible for a girl to mingle with those in a higher position than her own, while a boy, as it were, carries his diploma of rank and condition in his satchel. For example, the girl generally has her sister for her most intimate friend, while the brothers seldom sustain this relation to each other! In the period of enthusiastic feeling, friendship between girls is like that between boys, resting upon the same indescribable and unconscious impulse. The girl becomes now the head of a family, in the fulfilment of her destiny; and although she is differently situated, she retains almost the same connections as before; but the man becomes freed by marriage from previously existing family ties. A wife, after marriage, becomes a different personality, while a husband remains, in external respects, the same; a man's friendships sometimes endure after marriage, but a woman's almost never. The friendship of men is based upon more universal interests and participation in affairs; that of women is only personal, and with the change of personality and its interests ceases, and the confiding intercourse comes to an end. The endlessly frequent correspondence between two girlish friends almost always drops when one of them becomes a wife."

"But I have a married friend with whom I have kept up a constant correspondence, with the exception of a brief interval."

"Is she happy?"

"I am sorry to say she is not."

"That only confirms my view. Only when the new state is attended with dissatisfaction, is there a full return and a fast clinging to the confidential utterances of earlier life."

The girl's countenance suddenly grew pale, not so much on account of this expression, as from becoming aware how she was discussing, with a stranger, some of the deepest experiences of the soul, although only in a general way; and notwithstanding the stranger was her brother's friend, it was wonderful, and inexplicable, how they had advanced so far. These thoughts were the work of scarcely more than an instant, when suddenly the door was opened.

"Is it you, dear mother?" said the girl, going to meet the person who entered.

"Elizabeth," said the latter, as she looked with surprise at Rudolph, who was deeply moved when he heard her name,—it was really Lisbeth. Quickly composing himself, he said, bowing to the mother,—

"I hope that your son has already made you acquainted with my name: I am the gymnasium-teacher, Braun, from ———, in Westphalia."

Elizabeth looked with astonishment at Rudolph, for she had formed a very different idea of him from the descriptions of her brother.

"You are heartily welcome," said the mother: "we have often spoken of you; but I have disturbed you in the midst of your earnest discussion with Elizabeth. May I ask what it was about?"

Elizabeth looked apprehensively at Rudolph, involuntarily raised her hand, as if in a deprecating manner, and then cast down her eyes to the floor. Rudolph thought that this was a hint to him, and said, in a careless way that surprised himself:

"We were speaking of life at the University, and the relations of friendship there formed, — what charm they had for ingenuous natures."

Rudolph was well pleased with this adroit turn, for he thought he perceived a smile on Elizabeth's countenance. In this silent consciousness that they possessed a secret together, there was a powerful tie binding them to each other, and cementing quickly a most interior union.

"Yes," said the mother, "Elizabeth has often envied Karl because he was a student, while she could not be one." She inquired now in regard to the maid-servant, and whether she had gone for Karl.

"No, I have given her permission to go with her sister to the railway station."

The mother shook her head, and Elizabeth, taking her hat and shawl, carried them into an adjoining room, and did not appear again.

The mother now entered into conversation with Rudolph concerning his journey, and whether he had ever been in Cologne before, &c.; she was surprised to find that she had to ask him sometimes the same question over two and three times, before Rudolph seemed to comprehend her meaning. His thoughts were, evidently, elsewhere. But Frau Meurer, a sensible and cordial person, now asked him whether his parents were still living. This is a friendly question which immediately knocks at the inmost chamber of the heart, and we feel, when it is asked, the summons of a loving spirit bidding us welcome: we are no longer alone, no longer strangers, and all our beloved ones are gathered with us into a new home of the heart.

Rudolph now spoke, with the deepest emotion, of his absence from home when his father died, of his fond mother and loving brothers and sisters, who were still living.

Karl now came in.

"Fridolin! old chum!" cried Karl; and the friends closed in a long embrace.

"Well," said Karl, clasping once more the waist of his friend, "you are of respectable size; philosophy has not yet abstracted all the flesh from your bones; there's a fair show of the positive about you, but this broken horse-shoe here, these outrageous whiskers: I'll make you doff them."

"You are the old shaver still. You ought to have been barber-general, and had a whole army to shave, instead of a few clients."

Karl soon took his friend to his own room, for they must see each other alone. They sat there together smoking, and the friendly talk blended together as did the clouds of smoke from their cigars. They began with personal matters, but soon rose to the highest questions of the age, imparting to each other the results of their inquiring glances into the movements of the time: for this is the characteristic and the dignity of our era, chide it as we may for being egoistic, that our best aspiration and effort are devoted to the promotion of the general welfare. But much as the friends had to say to each other, the mutual exchange of experience and thought was connected, as is usually the case, with what was nearest and of most immediate interest. Rudolph gave an account of the excellent persons he had become acquainted with during his journey.

"Rarely have I passed a single night away from my native place without gaining some new acquaintance. The spirit of our Fatherland seems to me to be unfolded in blooming freshness, an infinite deal of knowledge and activity scattered on every side, and a holy revelation trembling on all lips. There was a plain elderly merchant from Mannheim, the city which is as prosy and regular as a rationalistic church, wholly without any poetry and any history. I tell you, that man possessed a historic consciousness of our position, which it was really cheering to contemplate. There was also a commercial traveller, generally a most intolerable set. I soon recognized the Jew in him, but he was also a man who had a noble and genial comprehension of human relations and affairs. I see in every man who comes into near proximity to me, or whom I attract, an ambassador of the universal spirit, which reveals itself as the spirit of the age through a thousand tongues. One must go out among men, in order to gain courage and zeal for the fresh life of joyous activity now dawning upon us. I thank God and Destiny, that my soul has remained open to hear, everywhere, the voice of this Holy Spirit, and I will retain the consciousness of this susceptibility, notwithstanding I have now entered upon the years of benumbing manhood."

"You will hear the echo everywhere, because you awaken it," said Karl, clasping his friend's hand; "it is a good thing, especially, that the age with its powers won from nature sends men on journeys, for they are truly themselves when freed from the ordinary routine of daily life. Come across these persons in their offices, their warehouses, their workshops, and they would regard with amazement your transcendental demands. You have the good fortune to hit upon the talismanic word that sets free their souls; you give utterance to your best ideas and sentiments, lovingly and disinterestedly, and even those persons whose ruling principle is vanity, look upon it in the first place as a tribute of high regard to them that they should be selected as the recipients, and they feel highly honored and flattered, and consider it very fine, that they are supposed capable of understanding them; they are favorably disposed to you in the first place from vanity, and, afterwards, from the good feelings that you have aroused within them."

"Yes, it is exactly so," said Rudolph; "if we are the best we can be towards others, they are, in turn, the best they can be towards us. This exerts a mutually elevating and purifying influence; all external considerations are kept in the background, and the soul itself is manifested. If I draw near to people whom I have never before seen, whose existence I have never heard of, they are breathing with me the same vital air, upon them gleams the same sunlight as upon me, they are a part of my world and I am a part of theirs, we meet each other, and become a part of each other's conscious being; then I feel the call and the desire to become the joy-giving and joy-receiving partner of their existence, so that we may clasp each other's hands, and rejoice that life enfolds us in its embrace. It is stupid and unnatural to be shyly and proudly locked up in one's self; we are placed here in God's world, like the flowers of the field, whose fragrance and beauty are for the eye and sense of all living beings whose eye and sense are open."

"And this universal love," said Karl, smiling, "is for most people what a violet is for the cow: she wants nothing of fragrance and color, she merely wants to fill her stomach. Men recognize the profitable alone, and not the loving. I used to desire to benefit everybody; I wanted to refresh and gladden them and myself by friendly and noble interchange of favors; but I have since perceived that people do not desire this, and do not appreciate this, and I have withheld my love, and let them 'gang their own gait,' and there's an end of it."

"And have you not become much poorer thereby? You cannot be everywhere and with every one so happy and gladsome, and the world becomes to you morose and shrivelled. I have, like you, outlived many illusions; but what does it matter? This is the triumph of consciousness, that we do not allow our innermost real-self to be broken in pieces by the world and stolen from us, that we make no concession in our essential being."

"But, for once, you must make one concession to the world," said Karl, rising; and, as in life, what is significant and what is purely external and superficial are placed in juxtaposition without the least disturbance, so was it here. Rudolph must immediately sit down and allow himself to be divested of his light whiskers, "the broken horse-shoe." He was really improved by the operation,—the delicate and finely cut features of his face appearing in bolder relief.

"Come, let us now go," Karl then said; for after any mental excitement he was always restless, and eager for some bodily exertion. He often complained of himself, that only by a rapid walk or a sharp ride could his superfluous energies expend themselves.

The friends left the room.

"Elizabeth," cried Karl. She came, and looked at Rudolph with surprise, for he seemed now again a stranger.

"Elizabeth," said Karl, "let a bed be prepared in my chamber; Rudolph will stay with us." The latter bowed without speaking, and the friends went away from the house.

They sauntered, arm in arm, through the lively streets of the old city whose splendor and historic greatness are everywhere visible, and which, to-day, is rising into fresh importance; they went together, as in their youthful days, neither saying let us go this way or that: they went as having but one soul and one body.

Karl met several friends, who gave him a cordial recognition; but he introduced Rudolph to no one, saying, "I want to have you, in the first place, all to myself, and then you are to receive from me bran-new people."

They proceeded to the landing, where they soon saw themselves mingling with the crowds of moving life. Karl knew his friend's fondness for mixing in the bustle of popular excitement, and letting the tumultuous whirl pass before his contemplative gaze; then innumerable thoughts fluttered before him, like genii of all sorts; and he often followed out one thought, while looking upon this changing diversity to its strictest and remotest consequence:

seeing nothing of all the whirl, and having his mind, like the magnetic needle in the storm, immovably fixed to the one pole.

The friends often stood still without speaking, yet retaining hold of each other's arm. This is the silent blessedness of a friendly affinity, that each can be wrapped in the other's thoughts without the mediation of speech.

They went up the river, along its bank, until they had left behind them the bustling crowd, and the Siebengebirge were seen clad in a violet and golden robe ; the sun was setting, and the friends stood for a long time gazing at the glowing splendor.

"To-morrow," said Karl, "we will take a trip together up the Rhine."

"And your mother too?"

"And sister," added Karl.

While the friends were mingling thus in the busy life outside, Elizabeth was occupied in getting the best linen out of the chest, and making up the bed.

CHAPTER II.

THE EVENING CONVERSATION.

THE little circle sat cosily around the centre-table, lighted by an astral-lamp. They were calm and cheerful in themselves, and happy in each other. The beautiful evening and the wine were praised, and so too was the meat; for there is nothing more evident, than that where kindly, loving people are, every thing is good and beautiful.

"Were you born in Westphalia?" asked the mother, of Rudolph, among other questions.

"No, I am an East-Prussian."

"Long live brave East-Prussia, which has solved the four questions!" cried Karl.

The glasses rang loud, as they drank this toast.

"It is magnificent," said Rudolph, "that the German nation is beginning to put off its provincialism, its cantonal spirit, as the Swiss term it; this has been so finely manifested in this instance. North and South, East and West, we are all one, — all must acknowledge the concerns of each province, of each State, to be those of the one united Fatherland."

"Our ecclesiastical differences, the Cologne entanglements, as they are called," said Karl, "are a terrible hindrance to a compact, political unity: the first and most essential requisite is by this means divided and rent in pieces; for if Germany were one ecclesiastically, there would be far better success."

"Very true," replied Rudolph; "but Germany has another vocation than that merely of political freedom; just because it is ecclesiastically divided, and this division again is mixed up with geographical and state boundaries, just for this reason does it manifest its special calling to be the acknowledgment and the realization of mental freedom, and of a pure, universal humanity; this becomes its peculiar, historical, and appropriate work. The German sincerity of belief, its religious and political faith, will attain a higher result through philosophic science, which pervades every sphere; sameness is not the highest, but freedom of differences, of individualities, in their purely personal and their social manifestations. This is of far higher value than the old tolerance, or sufferance, which is temporary and changing."

"Tolerance changeable?" asked the mother; "why so?"

"Because tolerance proceeds from mood, or rather from feeling; people let one another go on in their own way, because they are disposed to be yielding, and pardon the erroneous and limited views, as they always consider them to be. But if the feeling changes, then, as we have had clearly shown, the old opinion breaks out afresh, and in glaring colors; the only sure basis is a pervading knowledge and acknowledgment. Mere peaceful acquiescence, humane indulgence, is far inferior to conviction and knowledge, which become love: the former allows varieties of opinion to prevail, so far as there is something universally expedient perceived in doing it, but the peculiar differences are regarded still as erroneous, or sinful; but the latter learns to justify, and to love the individual, with all his peculiar opinions."

The mother shrugged her shoulders slightly, and it was not easily perceptible whether she was unable to follow the thought, or whether she wanted to divert the conversation from what she considered an unsuitable subject. As she said nothing, Rudolph continued:

"Harmony is the result of knowledge, and of the perfect development of individual tendencies; it is the very essence of harmony that all the instruments and voices shall not be in unison, but shall have an accordant sound, each part maintaining its own peculiar tone, and preserving its own purity of note; and by virtue of this separate purity, through the inmost related nature of the different parts, in free and independent action, the combined whole is produced. As I view it, this is the higher German freedom, and the real harmony."

Elizabeth looked with beaming eyes at Rudolph, and every feature intent with interest; at his closing observation she nodded involuntarily, and when he asked her if she "accorded" with him, she felt herself exalted and honored by this question, uttered as it was in a tone very different from one of mere gallantry. After a little hesitation, while she was considering whether it would not be wrong to withhold the application she had in mind, she replied:

"Is it not a confirmation of your view, that we Germans are the only nation who have a popular music consisting of four-part songs?"

She was glad that she had spoken the words; for it was

strange that she should now feel so diffident and shy, when she had already conversed with Rudolph to-day so freely and without embarrassment, in the unusual circumstances in which they had been placed together. His thoughts now seemed to her so deep that her feeling of respect made her timid; but Rudolph was charmed to find that his remark was so intelligently appreciated by her. Karl now engaged in the conversation, saying:

"And the clatter of the wheels of the locomotive makes the instrumental accompaniment to your vocal harmony. Material interests! this is the sound heard on every side. Away with you, you philosophers! the Exchange is the peripatetic school of the new era; freedom must be based upon stocks, and pay a good dividend. Material interests are the talismanic words of the modern age: no one thinks of a disinterested love of liberty, much less of hazarding material well-being in its behalf. Since, once for all, it is settled that we are to become an industrial people, all beauty, all higher energies and nobler developments must succumb."

Another would, perhaps, out of regard for the ladies, have led the conversation to less serious topics; but Rudolph, out of a still higher regard for them, continued it in the same strain. He believed that we manifest a true respect for woman, when we seek to interest her, not merely in trifles and elegant frivolities, but when we discuss before her and with her the most serious matters; and he believed that this was necessary in order to rehabilitate the dignity of man in the eyes of woman, the loss of which was manifest in the misunderstood efforts now made for her emancipation. Following, therefore, the impulse of his heart as well as his conviction of what was best, he said, turning to Karl:

"I am surprised that you, too, are one of the political supernaturalists or idealists; you may laugh, but it is a fact. You think you are standing on the foundation of practical reality, and all the while you are up in an ethereal elevation of mist and cloud; you believe that you exalt the Ideal, the Divine, the Free, when you separate them from every material interest. But in regard to liberty; looking at that alone, see how in the history of all free nations and states, — Rome, Venice, Genoa, the Hanseatic towns, the Netherlands, England, — it has always had a rich material basis and a material lever. As God is in the world, so is freedom only in material well-being. Don't misunderstand me: material well-being is not liberty, but is its fitting body, and *it* is the soul. You cannot separate God and the World, Soul and Body, except in idea; you can never do it in reality: material well-being is very different from covetousness and lust of enjoyment. All things are liable to abuse, but this does not exclude their essential worth and their legitimate use. Every discerning man must rejoice, therefore, at the striving after material prosperity."

"I know," said Karl, smiling bitterly, "that it is the fashion now to proclaim to the world how great, strong, and happy we are; we call ourselves free, because we are allowed to say to an audacious neighbor, 'Thou shalt not steal;' but no bold word has any one to speak against the long-standing thefts and frauds which more immediately concern us. I know that you will probably reckon me as one of the antiquated liberals of the year 1830, and stow me away in the lumber-room of a past era; I acknowledge that here and there matters were carried to an extreme in representing all existing conditions as monstrous and barbarous, and thinking to spur up the nation by these bitter accusations; but now the whole manner of speaking is reversed, and people flatter and pamper and ogle, and form a mutual assurance and admiration society, until at last we come to believe that we are very well off. It is a wonderful age: lambs and wolves pasture together, philosophers and industrialists draw peacefully in the same harness. I don't belong to this contented crowd; what is good has been called forth by the spirit of the age in the very teeth of what these gentlemen themselves have sought to accomplish."

Karl expatiated yet further in this tone, and herein there was revealed a radical difference of opinion between the two friends: Karl was one of those who take for their starting point the actual, the immediate, the nearest, and call for this with vehemence; while Rudolph, fixing his regard upon the universal and its unfoldings, held fast to the conquering thought and the Idea. The conversation seemed to be diverging too far, and Rudolph brought it back again to the point, saying:

"Just for this reason, that, as you say, the spirit of the age rules over matter and establishes the good in spite of the efforts of all these gentlemen, for this very reason the striving after material well-being has nothing dangerous for the victory of the Idea. Material well-being is health; and freedom, as Börne has already said, is simply health."

Karl, also, made an effort to set matters right; taking up his glass of wine, he said:

"In drinking, there is both spiritual and material well-being. Join me, we will drink to your prosperity."

Elizabeth spilled some wine in touching Rudolph's glass.

"Elizabeth," said Karl, "wishes to symbolize hereby, that in all well-being the cup must run over."

He rose, seated himself at the piano, and sang a Polish song in a spirited voice, but a little too powerful. He then urged Elizabeth to sing, and when she declined, urged her more and more pressingly. At last she began, with trembling voice, the sweet, popular song of the lower Rhine,

"In summer, in summer, in summer, that is the fairest time."

"I cannot, I cannot," cried she, after the first notes, covering her face with both her hands.

"Elizabeth," said Karl, "was a perfect musical prodigy when she was a child from six to seven years of age; she soon learned music, and could tell at once what note the house-bell sounded when it rang."

"For entire days," said the mother, "she intoned every thing she said, after a way of her own.

"Must I be present while you are giving a personal description of me?" asked Elizabeth. Rudolph turned the conversation, in accordance with what seemed to be her wish, by diverting it towards himself.

"It is astonishing," he said, "what droll peculiarities children oftentimes have. I loved nothing better, when a child, than the pompous funeral processions, which I always was present at without the least notion of their serious meaning; it is very noteworthy that children can form no conception of death. My mother has told me that once, when I troubled her, she said to me, 'Rudolph, if you are not good I shall die.'—'Mother,' replied I, with unconcern, 'hey, but there wouldn't be any splendid funeral like a soldier's.'"

As they spoke of the mysterious origin of our spiritual

existence, the floodgates of deepest feeling seemed to open, and the stream of conversation to swell with more and more inspiring themes. Something had been said concerning the religious consciousness, and Elizabeth, in a very low breath, uttered the words :

" The love I had in childhood to our Saviour is indescribable. Ah ! so divinely good, he took upon himself all the sufferings of the world ; I wanted to imitate him. I thought to myself, that there must be a certain amount of sorrow and wretchedness in the world ; and when I saw any one unhappy I longed to take his unhappiness, and joyfully did take sorrow upon myself, for it seemed to me then as if others were delivered from it as long as I was suffering." Her eyes glistened, and Rudolph drank in their bright rays. All discussion ceased with this unfolding of the deeper sentiments ; and, after a pause, he replied :

" I was not so tender-hearted as you were, Fräulein Meurer ; in my childhood, I looked at moral questions from a wholly opposite point of view. I was always taught that the highest was to subdue our nature : but I was rather an unruly subject. When, for instance, I was in church, and all was so silent during the prayers that nothing was heard but the ticking of the clock in the lofty tower, I would often say to myself, 'Hey, you are a real good fellow ! you might now shout, or fling your hymn-book through a window-pane, and isn't it being real good not to do it ?' "

Without any special intention or effort on their part, the conversation gradually became limited to Rudolph and Elizabeth ; Karl played variations to a modern opera theme, while his mother, resting against the back of the chair, turned over for him the leaves. Rudolph and Elizabeth were seated a little distance from them. How fluent they had been while mother and brother were listening, and now, as they sat near each other, comparatively alone, they were speechless. They had gone back to the days of their childhood, and had unfolded to each other the strangely significant trifles of their early life, which might be regarded, however, only in a general way. But there is a pleasing charm in the feeling that one gains a deeper knowledge of himself from these general considerations, and that a ready and sympathizing ear is given to these unfoldings, so intimately related with the individual self. This feeling is based upon the greater or less degree of consciousness that we are received by another in our individual personality, and not in those general traits and characteristics which we possess in common with all other human beings.

Thus the two sat together, listening to the echoes of childhood as they died away softly in each other's soul, not without awakening, however, a secret magic charm in the present. They were most likely engaged in the same train of thought, when Rudolph said, in a low tone :

" Were you satisfied with the reply I gave your mother, when she inquired about the subject of our conversation ? "

Elizabeth cast a glance of perplexity towards her mother, and then, looking down, said :

" But if you put on an expression of sincerity, you thereby tell an untruth."

Rudolph defended this experience, that so frequently and necessarily occurs in intercourse with the world ; he spoke at length, and on a variety of themes, relating some of the events of his journey : what he said was almost a matter of indifference to him, for the words were an excuse for him to fix his eyes upon her face and to draw her look towards himself. If they could have looked at each other thus, without talking, Rudolph would have liked to be wholly silent.

The mother, meanwhile, going into Karl's chamber, placed a book upon the table by Rudolph's bed, after putting a blue paper-mark at a particular passage. Returning to the parlor, she stationed herself again behind her son's chair, who, in the ardor of his playing, kept his body in energetic movement in every direction. She placed her hand gently upon his head, and he immediately stopped.

It was late before they separated for the night; and the two friends chatted a long time together after they were in bed and the light had been put out. There is a cosy and pleasant intimacy in the interchange of words from unseen lips of friends; for then many things are openly spoken which would not find utterance in the light. There are very many who are unable, in the most intimate intercourse with friends, to say the word "dear;" and most persons can write the warmest expressions of affection, but cannot utter them in words. But the mysteries of the soul's inner shrine are unveiled in the darkness of night, and find, then, expression in words: then, speech is thinking aloud.

Rudolph unfolded to his friend his own feeling of happiness at their meeting again, and at finding each other so faithful and constant in their attachment; he disclosed his feeling of exaltation in breathing the pure and fresh atmosphere of his friend's home; he gave himself up to the most unrestrained enthusiasm, and expressed even a desire now to die in this ethereal delight, for no higher joy could await him.

Karl, half asleep, replied in such a way as merely to show that he was still awake, and listening; and when Rudolph, thinking that he had expressed himself too strongly in saying that he could imagine no higher joy, endeavored to set himself right, he received no reply from his friend, who was fast asleep.

But there was such an excitement in Rudolph, that he fancied he heard the circulation of the blood in his veins. He recalled all the events of the day: this was not the way to get repose; but he deluded himself, if he imagined that he wanted to go to sleep. With closed eyes he surveyed the past, which became transfigured and glorified, and his imagination kindled, until at last he stood by the bedside of the sleeping Elizabeth, and pressed a silent kiss upon her closed eyes. Then he recoiled, as if he had committed a crime, and sought to gain control over his thoughts, but without success. He struck a light, thinking that he would recover himself on actually beholding the shape and form of the things that surrounded him.

Rudolph had the peculiarity, in common with many speculative thinkers, of making psychological experiments with himself; when the personal interests and commotions of life disturbed him, he often endeavored to raise himself to universal ideas, and general truths. He would then take his Hegel, or some one of the great ancient authors, and like godlike forms from the serene heavens, fixed and immovable, stood here in holy repose the great thoughts of the world; here was nothing to fasten to itself the flitting and temporary thoughts of the passing existence; and if he succeeded in raising himself thus above himself, his soul became peaceful and serene.

This individual peculiarity of Rudolph was only an enhancement of what appertains to the whole class of scholars, bookish men, learned men, or whatever else they may be termed, who feel poor and cold, if for several days, or even a whole day, nothing is contemplated but the visible forms of actual life, and nothing is heard but the sound of words whose echoes die away in the ear ; they take refuge then in the written world, and find there a peaceful resting-place.

Rudolph looked round for a book, and he was pleasantly surprised to find one on the table before him. It was Schleiermacher's "Sermons on the Christian Household," in which he found a mark of blue paper at the following passage: "As in the old myths angels often came down to men and presented themselves as guests, in order to prepare and strengthen them for heaven, so do we feel that in this natural order of things we are to be to one another angels of God, and for this end the strength of the Spirit is bestowed upon us. And as, in that olden time, the angels of the Lord appeared to his chosen ones, not only in the hour of solitary prayer and of painful sacrifice, but also while they rested under a fig-tree, ready to receive friendly visitants, so are we to console, teach, and elevate one another, not only in the solemn hours of devotion or of mourning, but also in the lighter moments of happy rest and joy. And how often we can do this without changing the key-note, which belongs to such a state, into one of sadness or gloom! Where you awaken by the joyfulness and confidence of your own heart the corresponding feelings in another's breast; where, by a fitting word, you save from a wrong sentiment or a mistaken opinion; where, by an easy and happy turn, you keep the jest from passing the bounds where it would become sinful, add to the common enjoyment without detracting from the higher worth of life, and keep alive a noble spiritual aspiration, — in all these cases, you are manifest as an angel of God. And these occasions must be frequent in the Christian's blessed life! Let us free ourselves more and more from the oppressive, and for the most part the useless fetters with which we have bound ourselves in our social life, so that those who belong to each other, by oneness of the Spirit which possesses them and by the love which animates their souls, may live more joyously together after all that is alien and disturbing has been put far away: then shall we be blessed in our common, social existence, as were those patriarchs of old; then will appear to each one, as he needs it, a consoling or warning messenger of God; then, unlike those in the ancient narrative, whose vaster strivings were interrupted by the Lord's confounding their language and scattering them over the earth, will a free, helpful intercourse be more and more spread abroad, beginning with the smaller domestic circle of individuals, and with whatsoever is united together in a beautiful, spiritual understanding and harmony. Using the same signs and speaking the same language, all will unite their energies for the accomplishment of the same end; and all, coming and going, giving and receiving, in friendly interchange, shall meet in the cheerful and yet significant moments of life as angels of the Lord. Amen."

"Amen!" said Rudolph, as if responding in low tones to an uttered prayer. He involuntarily kissed the open book, put out the light, and laid his head upon the pillow. He busied himself with thinking who could have placed the book there ; but soon he dismissed all his conjectures, and dwelt upon the tender, beautiful, essentially human, view of the Christian and truly human preacher, until he fell asleep. Strange ! His dreams had nothing to do with aught that had to-day so exclusively possessed his soul ; but his deceased father, of whom he had thought but once during the day, now was walking with him in his dream before the gates of his native city. It was a touching, almost a sad, sight, when the wearied father, whose day's labor as a letter-carrier was a toilsome, continual round on foot, allowing himself no rest at evening, would take his Rudolph by the hand, and enjoy alone with his dear son a wide circuit beyond the limits of the city.

CHAPTER III.

THE CATHEDRAL.

"T is singular that your sister's name is Lisbeth," said Rudolph to his friend, the next morning. The latter replied:

"I see nothing singular in that; but this is peculiar, that she will not allow herself to be called by any pet name, nor her name to be shortened: we must always use the four syllables in full. We would like to call her Lizzy or Betty, or even Bettine, and now you call her by the common name Lisbeth."

"The name is both an original German and Hebrew one," said Rudolph, in an off-hand way. "It is called Eliseba in the Old Testament."

"You haven't forgotten all your theology yet," said Karl, with a laugh. "Tell me now, Fridolin, you pious fellow, are you still as strict a moralist as you were when you were a theological student?" Karl added to this a direct question, to which Rudolph said in reply:

"You know what gave me support and confidence when I was studying theology. I must confess that I was dogmatically, or ecclesiastically, an unbeliever, and found the justification of my vocation only in moral purity, and in lending no ear to the slippery sophisms of a worldly morality; this justified me in becoming a moral preacher to a parish. And when I was induced, from internal and external considerations, to give up my theological career, I said to myself: "This shall be no license for me to fall in with the compliances of worldly life; I owe it to my own self-respect to remain faithful. Karl, in spite of the allurements of passion, I have been so."

Rudolph and Karl went to the cathedral, and Elizabeth with them.

Every one must have noticed that, on any lengthened journey, or a prolonged stay at a hotel or watering-place, after a deeply interesting and friendly interview of an evening, the next morning the participants seem nearer and more confiding to one another than they were even on parting the evening before. Each has withdrawn into his own individual life, and the recollection of the other has impressed itself pleasantly upon the soul as it slept, and they meet each other with fresh animation as old acquaintances.

So was it with Rudolph and Elizabeth, who regarded each other with a deeper feeling of interest. Rudolph admired her easy and firm gait, her erect carriage, resolute and self-possessed, which made her slender form appear taller in the graceful freedom of her movement. But Rudolph disliked the fashionable hat, which entirely concealed the beautiful shape of her head, whose comely roundness, set off by the smoothly parted hair, had not escaped his notice.

"You ought to walk to the cathedral," said he to Elizabeth, "with merely a veil on your head; that would be covering enough for you."

"Ha! you have an eye, then, for the fashions? That is nice. But however great a philosopher you may be, you cannot estimate the amount of courage it requires to slight the fashion."

Crossing the square, they suddenly stood facing the cathedral. No one spoke; Elizabeth glanced quietly at Rudolph, and his face seemed illuminated. After awhile, taking her hand, he said:

"Faith could do this! faith could remove mountains, unsettle them from their foundation, and fix them again fast; for faith is love, which eternally conquers all things."

He kept hold of Elizabeth's hand, and neither of them seemed aware that they were standing in the public street; they only felt that it ought to be and must be so.

They went into the cathedral, where mass was being performed in a side chapel, on account of some inside repairs. The organ tones, like sounds just dying away in the distance, had a peculiar and magical effect.

"I always seem so great, and yet so small, when I stroll beneath this sacred forest of pillars which our forefathers have planted. How little is a human form compared with this building, and yet how little is this gigantic structure in comparison with the work of Nature itself!"

Here and there, persons were kneeling in prayer before some altar, and uttering, in low tones, their heart-felt petitions, undisturbed by aught that was going on around them. Rudolph said to Karl:

"It has a sort of typical significance, that the devout Catholic does not suffer himself to be diverted and distracted by the noisy and unsympathizing movements of the children of the world; he allows himself and his church to be made an object of observation; he lets himself be speculated upon in every way, and he is not annoyed. So stands catholicism, with the waves of the world's history roaring around it, immovable and firm, in the midst of the free speculations of philosophy. The wave that sweeps along, the thought that mounts upwards on its wing, vainly imagines that it has crushed it: many a bold eagle of thought has become exhausted by its lofty flight, and, with crippled wing, dropped down from its sunward path motionless upon the rock beneath! Catholicism is the positive religion; it is the strictest logical development of belief."

And Rudolph now deduced this conclusion, that one must either become a Catholic or a Pantheist. Elizabeth did not seem to follow this course of thought, and asked Rudolph, after a pause:

"Are you not, then, a Catholic?"

"No," he answered very decidedly; although he felt no little trepidation afterwards, being well aware how important this might be to him personally. "But," he immediately said to himself, "her good-will" — he did not venture to call it love — "cannot and ought not to be at all affected thereby. It is not a blind, inexplicable attraction that has opened our souls to each other, but a knowledge of the character; it is not as children of any visible church, but as human beings, conscious of belonging to the church invisible, that we have found each other in its holy aisles of thought."

Rudolph would have liked to discover in Elizabeth's countenance what effect this new disclosure had produced upon her, but he could not, for they were now standing just before the cathedral-picture, that magnificent treasure of old German painting. In the midst of the church they had wandered away into general considerations; and there seemed to be a sort of difference, a feeling of estrangement, awakened in them, which they did not want to increase by any further discussion.

They at last went up the stairs without speaking, to the tower of the cathedral, and here, in this wide-spread, sunny view, they felt a new breathing of life. The mists had vanished, and the river, the plain, the city, and the distant mountains, looking now so near, were bathed in the fresh morning light.

After they had drunk in long enough the inspiration of this grand prospect, Karl began to explain to his friend the building in its present state and its contemplated completion; but he could not refrain from bringing in his heretical opinions, — heretical, inasmuch as they differed from the general opinion; and he closed by saying:

"This structure ought not to be completed; it ought to be kept just as it is. In what consists the peculiar beauty of a Gothic building? In its age, and not in the fact that it is absolutely beautiful. The superhuman, like the Faust of Goethe, ought not to be finished, for the imagination has its widest field when it is said 'the conclusion is wanting;' and thus the unfinished building is more thoroughly historic than the completed."

Karl, who was so opposed to material tendencies, to be consistent, ought to have rejoiced in this devotion of the age to a holy relic of the past; but it is very rare to find a principle consistently carried out in all its applications. Rudolph, however, did not address his remarks to this weak point, but replied:

"In this very thing consists the worth of our time, that knowledge and historic and æsthetic considerations labor for the completion of what was begun in devout faith. When the building has been completed by us, there will be cemented together in it the stones which both faith and free thought have laid; and it will be a monument of the spirit of national unity, and the spirit of the age, brought into harmonious reconciliation."

Karl expressed the fear that the enthusiasm for this national structure, got up according to order by the rulers, would prove a sort of child's rattle to divert attention from serious questions and sufferings, and that the community would be satisfied with having erected a monument to the idea of national unity before having carried it out to its practical realization.

Rudolph replied, with extraordinary vehemence, that we ought to take delight in every external expression of the idea of national unity. Karl was silent.

During all this time Elizabeth had remained silent, and had frequently gone apart from them. Accustomed though she was to a certain freedom of mind, this readiness of Rudolph to kindle up so easily on every occasion, and fire off his whole broadside of philosophy, troubled her somewhat.

As they were making the descent, Elizabeth took her brother aside, and whispered something in his ear; but he said aloud:

"No, no, you must go with us to the exhibition of paintings."

Rudolph was standing some steps below; looking up to Elizabeth with an expression of sadness, he asked:

"Why do you not wish to accompany us?"

Elizabeth was greatly touched by the question, and answered:

"I am going with you."

After making the rounds of the cathedral, they went

together to the Gürzenich,* or the Company's Hall, that scene of former splendid festivities, where last year (1841) the fourth centennial Jubilee was celebrated. Now there was on all sides the silent harmony of colors, and they strolled among the pictures without speaking, as if it was enough for the eye to converse with the paintings that addressed their speech to it.

Elizabeth was more particularly attracted by the landscapes, the masterpieces of which she was familiar with and quickly recognized, whilst Rudolph and Karl felt a stronger predilection for the historical and the illustrative pictures.

They stopped a long while in front of a large painting representing Rebecca and Isaac, having for its subject the passage in Genesis, chap. xxiv., verses 61–65. Rebecca, in rather a loose dress, is dismounting from a camel, while Isaac, deeply moved, is holding the reins in his hands: in the background, beautiful slave girls are seated on camels, and a brilliant coloring is thrown over the whole piece.

"The treatment is not sufficiently biblical," said Karl: "it seems to me as if they must be Bedouins; yet it is noticeable how we require a peculiarly ideal representation of the life of biblical peasants and shepherds, because these stories are idealized by us from early youth, and yet there is nothing but the patriarchal condition, sensuously speaking."

"Sensibly," suggested Rudolph; he then added:

"Our painters, however, might conceive in the same

---

* A building named from the man who gave the ground on which it is erected. It was finished in 1474, and contains a spacious hall, where the Diet formerly met, and banquets were given to the emperors.

way our life as it is poetically and practically unfolded;" and, turning to Elizabeth, he said, in a very low tone:

"I should like that some artist would paint the scene of Lisbeth and the huntsman: that would be grand! In the background, at a distance from both and unperceived by them, the clergyman spreading out his hands in benediction towards the pair kneeling in the foreground before the altar, while the glorious sun also shed down its blessing!"

Elizabeth listened with closed eyes.

"I think," resumed Karl, "that the painter has made a very good choice of the moment: Rebecca is turning her eyes away, and Isaac looks at her fondly; they have already exchanged glances of love, but the man is bold, and continues to look fixedly, but Rebecca turns her eye modestly aside, though she dismounts in order to go to him."

Rudolph, involuntarily turning towards Elizabeth, fixed upon her an ardent gaze; her look was also turned aside.

They went into another room, Elizabeth followed in silence, troubled with the fear of exposing herself in such a state of excitement to the look of other people; it seemed to her that they must read her inmost soul in her face. But they had other things to think of.

They strolled a long time round through the halls, and rejoiced at the pleasing creations to which the long peace and the favor of the time had furnished such ample scope.

Last of all, Rudolph and Karl were gladdened at seeing the well-executed busts of their teachers, Hegel and Gans.

The hours had flown by without their being aware of it, and it was now noon.

"I am always powerfully affected at the sight of paintings," said Elizabeth, as they breathed freely again in the street; "it is almost impossible properly to take in a single work of art, in one hour, to which the artist has devoted months and years. But here is a vast collection of pictures."

"It is always so," replied Rudolph, "with all the productions of genius; whenever we enter into them, we enter into the perception of their creator at the moment of their origination. Take a poem, for instance; you read it in half a day, while the poet required months, perhaps, for its elaboration. But this time was needed merely for elaboration; its genesis was the work of a moment. All the poetic forms, with their life and their destiny, arise in the poet's mind at one magic stroke, and the free activity of thought unfettered by any material substance works with an instantaneous rapidity, for which we have no standard of measurement, and almost no conception. Whenever we re-create in ourselves the completed work of art, we go through the same process of that immeasurable swiftness of the earliest conception. You have heard the saying, I think it is by Racine: 'The tragedy is finished, it has only to be put into verse;' so, with the painter, the real production of a picture is the work of a single moment, and the forms spring into existence which afterwards are externally embodied in color, in light and shade. If we succeed in transporting ourselves into that first creative moment, we take up that work wholly into ourselves, and we re-create it as quickly, as purely, and as immaterially."

"But you will not maintain that it is not very wearisome," answered Elizabeth, smiling. "Could you read an entire volume of poems, with a great variety of mental states and situations, at a single stretch? And yet it is only a single human life which is there disclosed." Elizabeth could not finish, and Rudolph could not re-state more fully his idea, for Karl said:

"And I always have a good appetite after coming from the exhibition. Laugh, if you will, but after any mental excitement, especially when I have taken part in a musical entertainment or looked long at paintings, I feel a very commonplace appetite."

He was urgent to have dinner at once.

CHAPTER IV.

THE RHINE.

N the afternoon, the whole party repaired to the steamboat, to make a trip up the Rhine to lovely Nonnenwerth. Rudolph was unexpectedly active and handy in looking after the trifling luggage of the ladies, in procuring them seats, and in other like services; he took an unusual pleasure in these little acts of assistance, for nothing is so refreshing to a heart whose interest is awakened, as to be able to remove a trifling annoyance, even if it be an external one, from the object of affection, although commonplace gallantry has caused this to degenerate into empty politeness.

The boat was uncommonly crowded, and Rudolph had taken a seat opposite the ladies, where they could overlook the various movements on shore.

When the boat turned, the sun shone directly in Elizabeth's face, and Rudolph immediately stood up; it was with a peculiar feeling that, for some time, he protected her with his shadow.

While they were passing along through an unattractive portion of the way, they engaged in conversation on a great variety of subjects; and now Karl, who had been talking with an acquaintance he had found, came up hastily, and seizing Rudolph's arm, said:

"Come, listen to this fine story; here one can see how every thing becomes mythical. They are contending what sort of a footstool, in a historical point of view, was given to the French Thiers by the resident of a German capital; seven footstools set up a claim. One asserts that it was upholstered, another that it was plain wood, a third that it was cast-iron, and a fourth that it was a three-legged stool, citing in proof the Pythia and all the witches; do come!"

Rudolph stepped up to the group of seven inhabitants of Cologne, each of whom was standing upon a stool, and with the keen wit that belongs to the people, was successively contending for the genuineness of his own claim. The umpire, a huge, powerful man, who was proceeding to his country seat, finally dismissed all the claimants, deciding that it was not a footstool after all, but only a foot-kick.

The affair was dismissed with a general hurrah, and then settled with some bottles of wine.

"One should travel," said Rudolph, on returning to the ladies, "in order to lose all confidence in physiognomy."

"I place great trust in the physiognomy of the hand," said the mother; "that is to say, through it real true-heartedness makes itself felt."

Rudolph smilingly extended his hand. "You are good-hearted," said she, returning the pressure of his hand.

"I think," said Elizabeth, "that most people appear inferior to what they really are."

Rudolph was greatly pleased at this charitable view of Elizabeth's, and agreed with it entirely. He added:

"And this is especially applicable to us Germans; a Spaniard, an Italian, even a Frenchman, with black hair, large eyebrows over dark eyes, and with a lively play of the muscles, makes a greater external show of mental activity than a blond, blue-eyed, quiet German face, and yet we Germans are the most intellectual."

The mother rejoined: "What proceeds from temperament or emotional excitement is very easily mistaken for the expression of inward spiritual affection."

The conversation was continued at great length, spiced with a great variety of anecdotes, and diverted to other subjects; Elizabeth was more fluent than yesterday, and every embarrassment seemed removed from her soul.

The boat stopped at Bonn, and a great crowd of country people, for the most part women, disembarked. They had a sort of nun-like look in their usual dress, with white kerchiefs tied under the chin, the long ends coming down to the shoulders.

Rudolph learned, in answer to his question, that they were on a pilgrimage to a sacred shrine. He drew his hand across his forehead with a sigh, and then it seemed to him a clever stroke of irony that the steamboats of the nineteenth century should aid the pilgrims along in their journey; a quiet smile hovered about his lips.

They came at last to that "paradise" of the lower Rhine, the Siebengebirge, or seven mountains; and who can depict in words the magic charm of this jewel, changing with varied hues in the reflection of the sunlight?

Our travellers went on shore at Nonnenwerth, whose spacious nunnery is turned into an agreeable inn. It is only when standing quietly on this peaceful island, that one can take into the soul all the beautiful grandeur of this scene, where the Rhine has gathered, as in one grand *finale*, all the strength and glory of its beauties, before it goes demurely and soberly to end its course in the ocean; for here, as if by a secret agreement with nature, the mountains and their lovely valleys almost cease on both sides of the river.

To the right is the bold Drachenfels, the jewel in that girdle of many peaks; and to the left, on the tufted rocks, the lovely Rolandseck, from whose open vaulted arch comes the legend of the love-swayed hero Roland. The friends wandered until late at night through the shaded walks of the island, and into spots where they could have an unobstructed view.

It was Saturday evening, and in all directions, far and near, the church bells were ringing, pealing forth a welcome to the coming Sunday, like some mighty organ under the far-spreading dome of heaven.

The tones one after another died away, and at last a single bell was heard tolling afar, like the voice of a lost child seeking its home; and then all was still under the peaceful shades of night.

The men walked together in silence, and the women also, side by side, their feet treading upon the earth, but their spirits raised by a holy power above all worlds: they were united in one feeling of the Infinite, their souls only a ray of the eternal light, in which they recognized themselves and the all wherein they were imbosomed.

Rudolph and Karl, who had been unaffected by the lofty cathedral, here felt themselves freed, as it were, from all earthly gravitation, and exalted into the higher all-enfolding sphere.

But however high one may be borne upward in this

devotional spirit, where he loses himself in the universal and divine, it is but for a short interval of time when measured by an earthly standard.

Thus the friends walked speechless side by side, long after they had recovered their ordinary tone of feeling.

It was a cloudless, starry night, with no changing moonlight shimmering on the earth, and the mountains stood there as if in silent awe, while the river with its lapping waves, unheard by day, glided by as if giving forth in gentle murmurs its feeling of inner peace.

Many may, perhaps, sympathize with Rudolph in the peculiar feeling excited by the consciousness of thus being shut up with persons who are dear to them on an island: shut up because one cannot freely change his abode. It seemed a delightful thing to him, to be removed in this way from the familiar mainland and set down upon an island with friends; and as he gave expression to this feeling, Elizabeth's eyes, as she looked at him, shone like the stars above. But Karl said, pointing to the bright windows of the cloister-building:

"I find it delightful that comfort has there fixed itself in the very midst of the beauties of nature."

"And I do, too," added Eric. "Comfort, abundance, riches, do not disturb the poetic, the pure joy in nature; they may even exalt it in many respects. It is a great mistake to suppose, as many are inclined to do in our age, and as has been embodied in literature, that expression of the age, that, inasmuch as we have given up the meagre pastoral, there is a universal and inordinate desire for an aristocratic enjoyment, and there can be no happiness except on carpets and in the midst of silk tapestry and hangings. Comfort, wealth, is pleasant; but the want of it ought not to disturb in the least the joy of existence."

"A good beefsteak and a bottle of wine would not disturb me in the least at this present," said Karl, laughing.

They went into the dining room, which was filled by strangers from different countries, among whom the egotistic, silent Englishmen were prominently conspicuous. Rudolph, also, met here an acquaintance from his own native city, an advocate, with his two daughters; and although he had always entertained a high regard and affection for him, it required a great effort to spend now a few moments with him in friendly chat. This direct interposition of his old environment disturbed him, he could not tell why.

When the good man remarked to Rudolph, with a smile, that he seemed entirely changed, the latter blushed deeply, and thought the remark was extremely impertinent. He had forgotten that his whiskers had been shaved off, and fancied that every one could read in his countenance the emotions of his soul. It vexed him that the world would let nothing germinate and grow silently in its own way; and this apparition from the old home seemed, moreover, to convey to him a sort of admonition. He returned to his friends silent and absent-minded. No one except Elizabeth seemed to notice the change in his mood, but she cast several times stolen glances towards the advocate and his daughters.

Karl, meanwhile, had become so enlivened by "comfort," that he engrossed the whole talk, and the rich fountain of his merry wit bubbled up unceasingly. Genuine humor, the overflowing of a joyous temperament, needs no great object, in fact no object at all, in order to manifest itself; a comical gesture, a wink of the eye, is sufficient to make others join in the mad whirl of merriment. Karl made use of two empty egg-shells as an occasion for a host of droll thoughts and suggestions; they represented two most exalted Mæcenases of art and science, who were rivals for the acquisition of antique relics.

Rudolph took particular pleasure in Elizabeth's musical and hearty laugh, for in the laugh there was an unconscious manifestation of that natural grace which does not overstep the boundary line of delicacy and refinement, even in the most unrestrained and impulsive outbursts.

They were in the merriest vein after all the guests had retired to their rooms, when Karl sprang up, and seated himself at the piano. Elizabeth must make no opposition to singing to-day, and she sang, first, with an unexpectedly droll *naïveté*, the song of little Hans, beginning: "No, I will not longer bear," &c., and then the "Alpine Horn" of Proch, with such freedom and ease, in such freshness and fulness of tone, that one could not but feel that her whole soul entered into it; and this feeling of heart-felt delight was shared by those who listened.

"How does the song please you?" she asked Rudolph.

"The melody is natural and beautiful, but the words are too silly and incongruously absurd; it seems to me as if it were patched together out of reminiscences from other songs, without any unifying sentiment. It is a pity that the beautiful melody should fare no better."

"Oh, no! no!" replied Elizabeth; "in a song the music is of far more account than the words. Those are the best songs which, without the music, say nothing, and with it every thing; then music has free and unlimited scope to express itself. The poems which can be declaimed are not real songs; but where a sentiment is expressed only faintly in words, music comes in and fills it out with a hundred-fold power."

Elizabeth continued the conversation with Rudolph in the same strain, seeking to convince him by several examples, and at last he acknowledged, with a thrill of pleasure, that the view he had previously entertained was in many respects a false one.

There was an indescribable feeling of satisfaction in the thought that his views had been corrected and filled out by a loved one; this is the most potent sway, this the noblest and surest understanding, as Rudolph experienced in the fullest degree.

Karl, who must have it all his own way to-day, now urged his mother to sing, and she finally, in a cultivated voice, but somewhat uneven, and showing marks of age, gave the lovely song of Jean Jacques Rousseau:

> " L'encens des fleurs enbaume cet asyle,
> Le lac est pur, l'air est fraiche et tranquille,
> Et la paix du soir se répand sur ces lieux;
> Oh ma patrie, oh mon bonheur,
> Toujours chérie, tu rempliras mon cœur!"

It is very pleasant to see the most fragrant blooms of past generations of culture flourishing in a living family, for there is something assured, natural, and unassuming in it, which does not often belong to a self-acquired cultivation. Rudolph was the son of plain commoners, and his father had been a letter-carrier; and although he held in the highest veneration and love the peaceful, paternal home, there was the absence in it of the higher intellectual and æsthetic influences, which are not always found, it is to be regretted, even in connection with position in society and a certain degree of pecuniary independence. It was for this reason that Rudolph was so deeply moved by this singing, as well as the whole atmosphere of cultivated refinement of the mother; and if any aristocracy is pardonable, it is assuredly only this one of inherited culture continued and freely carried on in the present generation.

After all had gone to bed, Rudolph went into Karl's chamber, and sat down at his bedside. They conversed for a long time about university life, that it was the only real centre of freedom in the life of to-day; they had never asked one another what was their parents' standing, or if they had, it had passed from their minds, and they were hardly aware of the fact that they belonged by birth to different religious confessions.

"Is your mother a Catholic, too?" inquired Rudolph.

"No, she is a Protestant."

"Then it was a marriage both by the ecclesiastical and the civil authorities?"

"Not at all; my parents were married by the civil, and not by the ecclesiastical, forms. But the world has never witnessed a more sacred union, or one more blessed by Heaven."

"Grand!" shouted Rudolph, who would have liked to add other inquiries; but even before his dearest friend he could not express his thoughts in words. He walked about the chamber with restless steps, and, stationing himself at last before the window, with his gaze fixed upon the star-crowned mountains, he asked:

"Why did you never tell me any thing about your sister when we were at Berlin?"

"Eight years ago she was a very insignificant little mouse. What was there to tell?"

"Has your sister ever loved any one?" asked Rudolph next.

Karl sat upright in bed, and said, as he looked at his friend:

"No; there are only two men worthy of her, and they are you and myself."

"No! no! no man is worthy of a maiden's first loving glances; no one, and we are not. Who brings to the maiden a life wholly pure and a heart never before touched?"

"O you great philosophizer!" said Karl, laughing.

"No, we will say no more about it." Karl was familiar, of old, with his friend's manner when he was strongly excited; he complied with his request, for he well knew that he would best smooth over any difference if he were left to himself. He thought that Rudolph would now go, but he continued standing a long time at the window without speaking.

"Good-night, Rudolph; take the light along when you go, so that you may not stumble in the dark," he said, smiling. Rudolph, taking the light, gave him his hand, and left the room.

Rudolph passed a night of troubled dreams; he could not remember them, but when he awoke, his cheeks were hot and his heart was beating violently.

CHAPTER V.

THE RUINS.

NE must abide with new friends under a strange roof, and stroll with them over mountains and valleys, if he would have a bond of fresh and free intercourse formed between his spirit and theirs, strengthened by a hundred-fold variety in the interchange of thought and feeling. He and they are on neutral ground, and in a single day a more intimate acquaintance is formed than in weeks and months of a regular routine of household life. This was proved to-day more clearly than ever by our friends.

After a walk on the island, they crossed the river, and ascended Rolandseck. It was a bright, peaceful Sunday morning, and the columns of smoke from the houses went up straight into the cloudless heavens. The sounds of the ringing bells hovered over the landscape glistening with dew, and it seemed as if the tones came from the very trees, fields, and mountains themselves.

The mother and daughter went forward, and Karl accompanied Rudolph. At the last house of the village of Rolandseck an old woman was sitting at the open kitchen window and weeping, while she was busy in peeling some potatoes. Karl inquired after the cause of her sorrow, and learned from her that she was the "best mother" — for so they call the grandmother on the lower Rhine — of the family, and her little grandchild, who had died early in the morning, was lying in the room overhead. She entreated the 'dear gentlemen' just to look at her John, who was only nine years old, and who had been, while he was living, an angel, so good and beautiful and loving: and now he looked just like the child of the mother of God.

"I have never looked upon a corpse," said Rudolph.

"What? go up with me now, just for a moment."

"No, no, not now."

"Yes, now, right away, you must; are you not ashamed of this faint-heartedness? Come!"

Rudolph knew the iron will of his friend, and followed him hesitatingly and reluctantly over the little open space before the clay-built cottage. They went in, and found the father lamenting his poverty, which would not allow him to pay for the costs of burial, as they had to bear the dead child to the church-yard of another village. The friends gave him what they thought sufficient for the interment.

"The gentlemen would like to see our dear John," said the grandmother, coming up to them.

"Yes, yes," said the father, going before them up a narrow rickety staircase that led to the attic. A fair blond boy was lying at length on some straw spread upon the floor, the hands folded over his breast, his cheeks still retaining their flush, and the hue of death visible only around the closed eyes. A lighted oil-lamp stood at the head of the child, and threw over the dark chamber only a few feeble rays. Karl went up to the corpse, and placed his hand over the mouth. Rudolph stood aside, dumb and motionless; not a word was spoken, and silently they descended the stairs.

"O God, O God!" said Rudolph, wringing his hands, as they went along the road; "this is death! Could one take in the thousand-fold interweavings of joy and grief, life and death, what a distracting thought it would be! Here, outside, all is gladness and life, the sun shines gloriously, the mountains, the stream, every thing, flooded with joyous life; and yonder a human being falls into the everlasting sleep! Karl, let us be glad, let us be happy and make others happy while we live; the night comes so soon, so soon! There has been a time when I thought that I could die joyfully, for the best of my life seemed to lie behind me; but now, now, I do not want to die yet, I want to live, for my life is just beginning."

The friends embraced and kissed each other, as if to confirm the fact that they were still living.

They agreed not to speak of this event to the ladies.

"We can and must get the better of it," said Karl.

"And," added Rudolph, "unless one is suffering affliction in common with others, it is necessary for him to overcome it by himself."

"It behooves a man," said Karl, "to conquer many things silently in his own breast."

"I am not of this opinion; but, come."

The two friends now ran a race up the hill, and rejoined the ladies in a more cheerful humor, for the active exertion of the physical powers is a potent specific for mental suffering.

Karl had joined his mother, and Rudolph accompanied Elizabeth. He spoke of their detention at the house of a family in affliction, and of the sadness of not being able to help our fellow-beings, much less to confer on them real joy.

"The most real joy," said Elizabeth, "is doing good."

"Doing good," replied Rudolph; "how beautiful and true the words! How few people, when they render assistance, have that noble longing to do good, — to confer happiness upon him whom they help! Barely to drag through life does not require a human being, but only an animal, or a plant, which has what is absolutely requisite for its needs; man gives a zest to life, and is thereby able to prolong his very existence."

"Very true; I understand what you mean. My mother frequently says, that we must not only give bread to the beggar, but butter too."

Rudolph heard these words with a quiet satisfaction. By a very natural association of ideas, he was now led to think of the selection of Schleiermacher's sermons placed by his bedside, and he put the direct question to Elizabeth, whether she had lately looked at the book. Her negative answer was given in such an unembarrassed tone, that Rudolph was certain that the mother had placed the book there.

They emerged from the wood upon the smooth, level path which leads to the ruins. Rudolph now felt almost entirely relieved of the painful depression which had weighed upon him, and soon recovered his youthful elasticity of spirit. In the course of a few hours, he could experience and unfold the most varied feelings in their utmost extent; many call this, using their own standard of time as a measure, light-mindedness or changeableness. It is in fact both, in a higher sense of the words. But who is there that can estimate aright by his own finite, individual standard, the infinite rapidity of thought?

They stood now on the summit, near the ruins, and surveyed the smiling landscape with delight: below, was the quiet island, embraced lovingly by the stream; beyond, was the chain of mountain-tops; and around on every side the villages. They called to mind, with grateful affection, the young and imaginative Freiligrath, through whose song the old legend lived anew, and the stones once more rose into walls. This trusty "Squire of Roland" has given again to the scene its fairest charm, — the view through the solitary arched window of the castle ruins. So powerful was the impression awakened by this prospect, that even an Englishman came up to Rudolph, and gave expression to his rapturous delight. Karl now pointed out to his friend the special features of the landscape, and enjoyed greatly his enthusiastic admiration.

"Fridolin," said he, "when I show this to you, and implant it in your soul, it seems as if I were making you a present of it all, in order that you might share it with me; and my joy of having this for my home is doubled; look, all this has been placed around my cradle by my home, the good god-parent."

Elizabeth looked in surprise at her brother, who seldom gave such unreserved expression to his feelings, while Rudolph replied:

"Do you remember the speech you used to make at the University when you became animated? Listen to it, ladies: 'Friend Fridolin, thou art my only friend, — I own a hundred castles in the Rheingau: they all shall be thine!'"

Rudolph declaimed this with such a comic pathos, that they burst into a laugh; then he continued:

"But you should yourself feel a fresh delight in this glorious beauty, and not merely take pleasure in my enjoyment of it. I couldn't bear that."

"You are right," said the mother; "it is always unpleasant to me, when any one reads a book aloud which he is already familiar with. It is better if there can be a like, or at least a similar, surprise; even if one cannot read so well and does not know so accurately the way, nor where the stumbling places are, nor where the sense and the author have made stops and dashes, yet the reader and the listener go along together."

"Dear mother, it is very different with a glorious view like this from what it is with a book," said Elizabeth; "a magnificent landscape is to me like a grand piece of music, which one must play and hear many times in order to understand and fully appreciate it as a whole, and in its various individual parts. A rich melody, a striking point, is readily seized, but the best is often that which does not at first make its way so easily."

The conversation was not continued. The friends sat where a perfect view could be enjoyed, and each seemed to be inwardly vexed that here, on this magnificent height, they should engage in such discussions; each would have liked, by a single word, to pour into the soul of the other the full stream of pure enjoyment in nature, and yet they had scarcely any thing more to utter than the usual exclamations, — splendid! heavenly!

Several hours later, we find our travellers on the other side of the river upon the Drachenfels.

As they were crossing in the boat, they sang the four-part Rhine song of Claudius. This song and that of "Prince Eugene" are perhaps the only songs in which all Germans of all the different provinces can join.

If one might offer a suggestion for another monument in this our monument-erecting age, it would be well to have near the Rhine a simple statue of Claudius, the "Wandsbecker Boten," in the vacant pillared temple on the Niederwald, whence the greater part of the wine-growing region of the Rhine can be overlooked. Karl gave expression to this thought, and Rudolph immediately went off into an impromptu enthusiastic speech on the uncovering of this projected statue; he expatiated on the exclusive credit due to the originator of the idea, who should receive his meed of praise as well as he who gave utterance to the claim, and he, moreover, who acknowledged its worth, &c.

Rudolph leaped and clambered among the ruins with all his youthful gymnastic dexterity, and, laying aside all the staid dignity of the professor, became the venturesome youth again, giving expression to his emotions of joy by shouting and singing from the lofty window of the half-ruined tower the name which filled his whole soul; and yet he had not the courage to express it with full and unreserved freedom. He made a pause between each syllable as he intoned the word, —

"E-li-za-beth!"

Elizabeth, happening to come near the dangerous place where he was perched, clasped her hands, calling out:

"Oh, God! Do come down, do, for my sake; it is dreadful to see you there;" and she closed her eyes to shut out the sight. The words "for my sake," and the tone, thrilled Rudolph; but his elevated position gave him boldness, so that he cried:

"I surrender; will you shake hands with me if I come down safely?"

"Oh, do come down!"

Rudolph was quickly by Elizabeth's side; he took her hand, which she did not withdraw, and held it long. As if they had held a silent conversation together, they seated themselves upon the grassy terrace before the tower, and gazed without speaking upon the scene, imbibing in full draughts the glorious fresh life all around them, and then, as if by some magical attraction, catching each other's glance, and seeing in this momentary gleam more than all the glory and brightness in the outward world.

At last Elizabeth said: "Would it not be possible to release ourselves from the consciousness of the relations we have to the buildings and the appliances of city life; in fact to be wholly freed of our self-consciousness, be dissolved into nature itself, and bloom in the flowers?"

"The Indian saints," replied Rudolph, smiling, "make some such attempt: they sink into the very centre of universal consciousness, losing themselves in the thought of the All, in the thought of God, and, fixed immovably to one place, they become trees wherein all free, personal, spiritual, and corporeal activity is dead, and their life in the All is that of a human plant. But when we live the mere life of nature, we degrade ourselves from the rank of men; and our life in human relations is far greater than any dissolving into, and absorption by, nature itself."

"You think I mean more than I really do, or I must have expressed myself imperfectly," remarked Elizabeth; "I simply mean this: it would seem to me to be the highest attainment if we could escape from ourselves into the simple life of nature outside of us, and allow the silent, blissful sympathies within us to have free sway and expression, without any thing of this reflection, and all this anxious consideration, which we experience only as human beings."

"No; with this absorption in nature, in the universal, we become passive creations, while, as men, we are to some extent creators also; the lyric, the spontaneous and most direct outburst of feeling, is not the highest, but the dramatic, wherein we create a new world, a human world. It is far higher for us to move freely and independently in the midst of a firmly established order of things, and take them up into ourselves, than to allow ourselves to be taken up into them."

Elizabeth did not think she was yet rightly understood, and therefore said:

"I will explain what I mean by an example: the highest music is not vocal music, or that which is attached to words, for then we are continually fettered down by the human thoughts, conceptions, and sentiments; but purely instrumental music is the highest, the infinite, and it may be termed the infinitely lyrical, where we are no longer restrained by human words and conceptions, but live freely and victoriously in the All. I am no longer conscious of any relation as sister, as daughter, for one lives in a sphere freed from all human limitations; and so also I think we might live in nature."

"I understand you clearly; but this instrumental music often becomes boundless, unsubstantial, vacuous, losing all real meaning and all healthy tone. This 'Bettinaizing,' as I might call it, is not superhuman, as you designate it, but, if the term may be allowed, sub-human. Every thing which has no sure, firm soil out of which it grows, but skips about like a will-o'-the-wisp in the blue ether, very readily changes from transcendental to nonsensical. We can apprehend in pure thought all things that surround us, and we ought so to grasp them; no words can embody and give us the fragrance of flowers and the brightness of the light. Through our human nature only do we apprehend all; and this human thought and human feeling, with all their sharpness and fixedness of outline, and all their limitations, are just as much nature as what is outside of us there, only it is a higher and freer nature. The firmly established, complete human being is nobler than all merely natural existence: we guide the ships and the stream on which they float, and stand over them in freedom. Is not this far nobler, that we take up into our consciousness what is outside of us yonder, and ourselves at the same time?"

"I thank you," said Elizabeth, rising after awhile, "for having made so many things clear to me; our Karl never enters into such conversations with me, but lets me keep all my mistaken notions."

They set out on the return home, and Rudolph accompanied Elizabeth. He took great pains to subject nature to spirit, and to humanize its influence, but he was also very apt to draw from it symbols and analogies; and so it now appeared symbolic that he had met with Elizabeth in the midsummer of her life, on the very boundary line which separates the blossom from the fruit. For as the fruit is the perfected blossom, so, in his view, knowledge was the matured condition of that original life-bloom, feeling. Many blossoms and many feelings must be wasted and fall to the ground, and only a few ripen into the fruit of knowledge.

On the first evening, Rudolph and Elizabeth had unfolded almost involuntarily to each other the history of their childhood, the mythical period of their lives, if we may call it so; now their lives had become so far a matter of common interest, that they went over together their earlier periods. This was the surest indication how deep this common life had struck root, and how many tendrils it had sent forth; for only to a friendship that we regard as established and irrevocable, do we venture, or do we feel inclined, to inquire into what makes its groundwork and its foundation. Rudolph pictured forth his wonderful excitement as he used to draw near his home, and how a magical charm seemed to hold him fast as he stood before the closed door. As he now asked what had at last caused the door to open, Elizabeth said:

"It is with the door of the house just as it is with my heart; when I am alone I shut the door, resolved to remain alone and let no one in, no matter who may come. But if any one knocks, I start up almost without thinking, and open the door; for I think that if I do not, some one will go away who is dear to me, and I am ashamed to ask beforehand in such a cold tone: 'Who's there?' And I do not want to keep still, and act a deceit. My mother has often said, when the door-bell rang at night: 'It is only some good-for-nothing fellow;' but very frequently it has been friends, who have been obliged to wait outside exposed to the wind and cold, or to go away without having entered the house."

"And is it the same with your heart?"

"Yes," said Elizabeth; and in her tone there was an elevation, a nobleness of soul, so that all the limits of ordinary reserve were overflowed. "Yes, I confess that I cannot do any differently; all resolves not to open it vanish, as soon as I hear a sound which penetrates within the sanctuary of the soul."

"That is excellent and noble in you."

"Not at all, it is no merit of mine; is it deserving any praise that I breathe?"

Thus they conversed together, without the least suspicion on their part that such inconsiderate expression of their feelings might be improper. Bright and clear, it stood before their conviction that they had become acquainted with each other's soul. Is it true that the mysterious, blissful sacredness of love ceases when it is thought of and acknowledged? To say that, would be the same as to say that one should and could merely believe in God, but not think of and acknowledge him. No, knowledge is God, and God is love; devotion and love, based in knowledge, are not merely overpowering, inflowing, momentary impressions, but permanent and steady influences; love does not hover over life as a supernatural revelation inapprehensible and unintelligible, miraculously poured out upon it like the Holy Spirit; but it is the abiding illumination of all the separate points which make up the circle of life, which is infinite and yet always bounded by its own circumference. Such were the thoughts that passed through Rudolph's mind, and he only gave expression, as it were, to the bare result, as he added:

"Literally, and in a higher than a literal sense, is it applicable to us, as the Scripture says: 'Seek, and ye shall find; knock, and it shall be opened unto you.'" He could and would say nothing further than this; for freely and undisguisedly as Elizabeth had unfolded herself to him, a thought, which he could not explain, withheld him from taking blissful possession of this beautiful life.

The sun began to set, sending forth its last glow over the earth as a farewell greeting. On the river bank were two hearts filled with emotion, and waiting in silence for the boat which should bear them to their home.

They went on board; and when it became dark, the ladies remained in the cabin. Rudolph went on deck, and begging Karl to leave him alone, he seated himself in a remote place in silent meditation.

It is a beautiful custom in the Church, when one period of life is drawing to a close and a new one is to be entered upon by marriage, to pass in review before God the whole past existence, and subject it to the purifying influence of religion. But Rudolph had stood for a long time outside of all ecclesiastical relations, and now upon this noisy steamboat's deck, beneath the glittering vault of heaven, he called up before his inmost consciousness the record of his whole life, of what he had thought and what he had done.

His youthful years, laughing and joyous, — that silent, happy time of early school-days, — came up before his view, when he first inhaled the fragrance of flowers from Hellas and Rome, knowing as yet nothing of "why and wherefore." Then came the troubled period when he was thrust out into a strange world, and must choose a vocation. The first string snapped, and pietistic zeal snatched from him his first youthful friend; then came the wild host of doubts and questionings. Who can measure the torments, awake and in dreams, which beset the solitary, inquiring spirit? He mingled in life, but he could not comprehend it, for Spirit, Law, God, had disappeared; and often in the silent night he rose and wandered about, until his head seemed to dash against an iron covering, and he sank down exhausted. Then came in silent and solemn train the spirit of knowledge, of philosophy, into his soul, and again a strong, friendly hand grasped his own, and life arose anew in a glorified form. He soon devoted himself to a calling for which his culture fitted him, but still there was a void in his life. Often did he stroll out towards the quiet village to visit a minister nearly related to him, and in many respects kindred in thought and feeling.

Here Rudolph suddenly stopped. Mary, the minister's daughter, arose before him in all the freshness and fulness of her youthful form; he often used to gaze upon her with quiet pleasure at her cheerful work, to take delight in what she said, the expression of a happy childlike soul; often did her image go with him as he returned home, and often did it come up before him in his lonely study. And when he went again in the direction of the village, it was this which first occurred to him, so that he confessed to himself that her presence, not less than the wise counsels of the father, was to him the attraction. She often sat at her work, listening to his conversations with her father, occasionally looking up and exhibiting by her looks that she was interested in them, even if she did not fully understand them. Never did Rudolph say one word to incline her thoughts and feelings towards himself, but he knew that she liked him; she cordially extended to him her hand when he came and when he went away, and had given him a beautiful token of remembrance on the last Christmas-eve.

By degrees, he had come to think of her as the companion of his future life; and, as he dwelt upon the thought, his pulse beat regularly, and it gave him a peaceful feeling of satisfaction to see her engaged in her household employments. Often he asked himself: "Is this love?" Then he would say to himself: "Your hypercritical spirit is capable of nothing else."

He suddenly rose, for now Elizabeth's image came before him, surrounded by all the attractive charms of her sincere and ardent soul: "No! no!" he said aloud to himself. With his hand upon his burning forehead, he paced up and down the deck, undergoing an extremity of mental anguish, as he sought to free himself from the charge of inconstancy. "Good Mary," said he, "we can never be happy together now. Did you forebode it, when, on taking leave of you, and promising to bring you back something from my journey, you answered coldly: 'I thank you,' while your father rejoined: 'Only bring back yourself?' I can never bring myself back again. Can I offer to Elizabeth a life whose inner germ has opened itself for another, although she did not know or imagine it? For a full and perfect, I offer a fragmentary, life." He stood for a long time motionless in thought.

"And yet, I must," said he again; "in the days of old, it was considered a symbol of the conquering majesty and miraculous power of love, for the lovers to pass through fire and water; but we have met on the burning heights and in the ocean depths of thought, and have passed through them. One spirit, one love, dwells in us, and what is still hidden and unmanifested, we will lovingly bear and sacredly respect. O bliss, to know each other! Thou art soul of my soul! Come, Elizabeth, through all the vicissitudes of life, each of us will carry this one thought: Thou art mine!"

For a long time Rudolph looked silent and peaceful into the dark, rushing river, until at last the twinkling of lights and the ringing of bells reminded him that they had reached Cologne. In the bustle that now ensued, he perceived Elizabeth, who asked him, with surprise, as he came up to her:

"But, where are you?"

"With you, and I hope we shall remain together."

He offered his arm to Elizabeth, and without waiting for the mother and Karl, he drew her out of the crowd. When they had reached a quiet street, he took her hand, and said, looking into her eyes:

"Elizabeth, may I call you Elizabeth?"

"Rudolph," replied she, in a whisper.

On the sacred threshold of her home, they sealed their love with the first kiss.

When Karl and the mother came home, Rudolph and Elizabeth came towards them, holding each other by the hand, and asked their consent to their union.

Karl embraced his friend with such violence that he was forced to cry out; but the mother kissed them on the forehead, saying: "God bless you, my children!"

Who can describe the happiness which this evening illuminated the house in the street "St. Mary on the Capitol?" We draw back, for at an intimate family celebration the eyes of strangers may be full of sympathy, but still they are strangers. Let him who has enjoyed and him who now enjoys the blessedness to call another being his, his own, let him recall the first hour of this full certainty of possession; and let him who has not experienced that bliss, question the thrilling beat of his own longing heart.

How happy was Rudolph's glance, as he walked out the next morning in the sunshine, arm in arm, with Elizabeth! It was a new life, without and within and around. All the passers-by seemed to them happy, and upon their countenances there was a beaming gladness; a poor boy offered them some flowers, which Rudolph took and presented to Elizabeth, giving in return a present of money to the youth.

They wandered farther and farther from the city, until they came to some gravestones, which were standing in silent and solemn rows; they entered the burial-ground, and Elizabeth led Rudolph to a stone, on which was the inscription:

"HERE RESTS FROM LIFE'S JOY, TROUBLE, AND TOIL, FRIEDRICH MEURER."

Those first flowers, which Elizabeth had received from Rudolph, she placed upon her father's grave; then they joined their hands as for eternity, and silently in devout prayer, side by side, they went away.

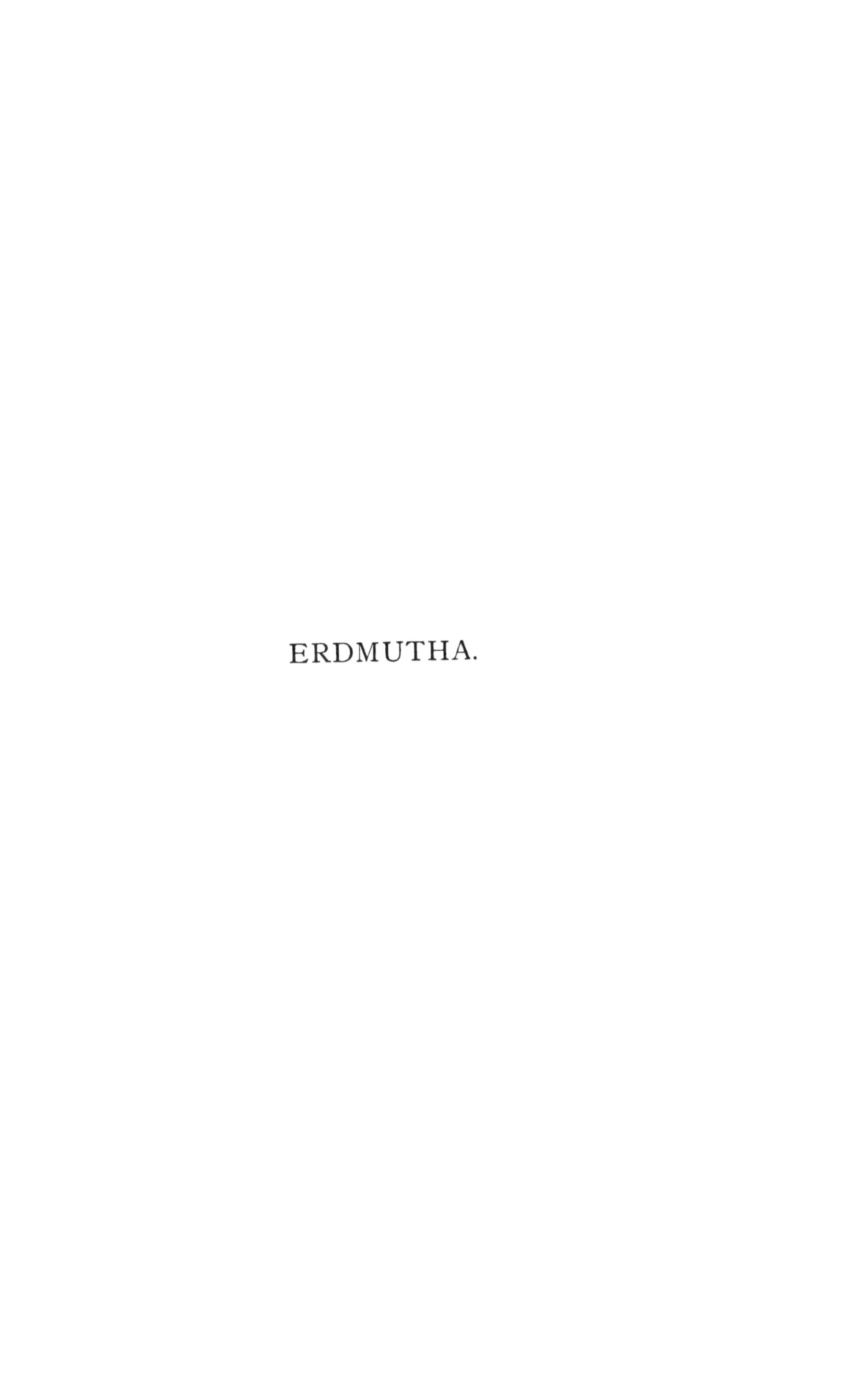

ERDMUTHA.

CHAPTER I.

GOTTFRIED OF HOLLMARINGEN.

"CYPRIAN bought the Sun inn at Leutershofen, to-day," announced the head servant of the Mayor Gottfried of Hollmaringen, as the latter was sitting at supper with his children and servants.

"Where did you hear that?" asked the mayor.

"I've been at the wine sale. The folks are having a jolly time there, still sitting together, I don't doubt."

"What did he pay?"

"Seven thousand florins for house and land, and two hundred additional for the wife. Very reasonable, everybody says."

Nothing more was said at table. After the son, the two daughters, and the servants had left the room, the mayor's wife began: "Don't be too much put out that your brother-in-law hasn't said any thing to you about his plans."

"He hasn't been my brother-in-law for a long while. The child's dead, and my sponsorship is over."

"Your sister's child is still alive."

"Well, well, that's nothing to the purpose; but I'll show him who I am. If I'm not his brother-in-law, I'm still

Gottfried of Hollmaringen, and he shall have reason enough for saying that I never let any thing be got out of my hands; that I hold on like a vice, now I've got the vice of the law to back me. He shall not take the property that comes to my niece from her mother away to a new place with him; to-morrow morning I'll slide a bolt on him."

While Gottfried was still speaking, a carriage with noisy inmates rolled up the street. Gottfried put his head out of the little window, and, in spite of the darkness, recognized the horses and heard the loud voices of Cyprian and his boon companions, who drove up the village and stopped before a large house, where, with bursts of noisy laughter, they called for lanterns; when these came, with other twinkling lights, the uproar was renewed, and sounded doubly loud through the quiet of the sleeping village.

"You're as drunk as a fool! No, as two fools," they heard voices cry, and a man was carried into the lighted entrance hall.

"You ought to go up to him again; he's getting to be the general laughing-stock at the rate he's going on," said his wife, as Gottfried, breathing deeply, turned back to the room.

"Time enough to-morrow," answered Gottfried; "you women always think that to-morrow'll never come."

"If you want to take your sister's child home, I'm perfectly willing; the child will be ruined by living in such a disorderly way, and with her harsh step-mother."

"He doesn't let me keep her mother's money with a good will, and he won't let me have the child. My business is to take care that my niece doesn't come to poverty; other care of her must be trusted to God, and her dead mother will watch over" —

The quiet man's firm voice trembled a little as he uttered the last words; he passed his hand over his long, thin face, rose, and went with heavy steps to his bedroom.

Years before, Cyprian had married Gottfried's only sister, who had died, leaving one child, named Erdmutha, for the mother. Since Cyprian's second marriage, the brothers-in-law had lived on cool terms, and became more and more estranged as Cyprian gave himself up to a restless life, seeking amusement among people who were no fitting companions for a rich farmer, — often even playing ninepins the whole of a Sunday afternoon with half-grown boys, from whom there was more shame in winning money than in losing to them. If Gottfried met his brother-in-law in the market town of Leutershofen, at the corn market or the inn, they nodded to each other and exchanged some words, but it was plainly because people were observing them; they sat at different tables, each with his own set of acquaintances, and at home, in their own village, they avoided each other as if by mutual consent. It was said that this estrangement was the fault of Cyprian's wife, who could not bear to have Cyprian so dependent upon Gottfried that he could not buy a horse, nor indeed transact any kind of business, without his advice. But Cyprian hated his brother-in-law for his own reasons, and the hatred gained new strength from various causes. Formerly, Cyprian had been proud of being Gottfried's brother-in-law, but now he was angry that every one talked of Gottfried, and that no one in the village or neighborhood could gain any higher respect than just what Gottfried chose to grant him. The main cause of the hatred, however, was the fact that Gottfried grew constantly richer, while Cyprian, in spite of his hard work, almost always lost where he was hoping to make some extraordinary profit; in buying and selling he insisted on taking his own course, instead of following Gottfried's example, as others did, and his bargains generally turned out ill. With Gottfried's prosperity, Cyprian's hatred increased; and, as Gottfried might be called extremely economical, or even penurious, Cyprian charged him with being niggardly, avaricious, and extortionate, and there were good people enough who reported these accusations to their subject with various additions. The quiet, remote village, where every one lived absorbed in his own private affairs, as is the habit among well-to-do farmers, began to seem no true home to Cyprian; he often sat all day, with no apparent object, in the nearest county town, or in the market town on the boundary, and when he entered the inns, the attendants knew what he wanted to drink, and brought it unordered: one kind of red wine, in particular, which the host of the Sun had nicknamed "woman's anger," seemed to be grown especially for Cyprian's use. The story was told of his having once drunk and gamed away the price of a whole wagon-load of boards, and when he went home in the evening, he called out, "Open the great gates, a wagon-load of boards has got to go through." Another time he wasted, in the same way, the money he had received for a calf, and at every fresh pint of wine he lowed like a calf. Such stories spread the fame of his merry wit, but Cyprian was clear-sighted enough to know that he lost respect and position by such means. Often, for weeks at a time, he subjected himself to every sort of privation, worked incessantly, and spoke to no one, but the very violence of the restraint made him fall back at the first opportunity. At last he convinced himself that the loneliness and remoteness of the place drove him out of it, and that, if he had pleasant companionship close at hand, or were in a place where he should be considered as a leader, and not always as subject to Gottfried, — in short, if he had an inn of his own, — it would soon come about that he would regain his old standing, or rise still higher. For this reason he had bought the "Sun," and given himself up to an unrestrained carouse at the wine-sale, saying, "This shall be the last of my sprees; it's sad to take leave of them for ever, but it must be so: a host who goes about half tipsy all the time is good for nothing; one may just drink enough to quench thirst, but no more. So now for the last spree, the very last and final one." In the early morning Gottfried looked out of the window through the iron bars, for his house was one of the oldest in the village, and all the windows were furnished with strong iron gratings. He had often been advised to do away with this remnant of the old times of insecurity, but could never be persuaded; he not only thought the gratings an ornament to the house, but found in them something which harmonized with himself, and it might almost be said that they had stamped themselves on his character, there being something of hostility in his way of looking out upon the world; he was at all times prepared for attacks from robbers, and armed against them, and in this defence against a hostile world his eyes, though looking through no visible bars, seemed to be guarded by some inward armor. No one could boast of ever having completely got the better of him.

Gottfried saw Cyprian already at work, in his shirt-sleeves, putting his Berne wagon in order; turning the winch, he raised up the vehicle, took off one wheel after the other, greased the axles, then, with a light touch, gave the wheel a turn which long kept it spinning in the air. All his vigorous movements showed that he was resolved to begin a new life from that day forth. Cyprian was one of the handsomest men in all the country round, — tall, strongly built, with a full, round face, and dark eyes, full of a quiet fire, smooth white brow, and brown curling hair. When he smiled, and showed his white teeth, there was a subtle charm, half roguish, half good-natured, in his partly closed "hound's eyes," as old Gottfried called them.

"Blase!" called Gottfried from the window to his son Blasius, a youth hardly out of school, who was yoking the oxen in the yard; "Blase, go up to uncle Cyprian, and tell him I sent you to ask him if he would not come to me."

Blase fastened the strap, left the other half of the yoke empty, and went up the village. He was an unusually slender stripling, and, as he strode off in his leather breeches and high boots, he looked quite manly, though a little stiff. When he delivered his message to Cyprian, the latter answered, laughing, and tossing his head, —

"Tell your father that it's just as far from his house to mine as from mine to his."

Blase clenched his fist, and pressed his full lips together, as he came back down the village street. He gave his father the answer, adding, as he yoked the second ox, "It's the last time I'll carry any message to *him*."

Gottfried ordered that his Berne wagon should be got ready; he had wished to settle the business amicably with Cyprian, now it must be left to the law.

The dust was still whirling in the street behind the swift wheels of Cyprian's wagon, when Gottfried drove after him. Each had an empty seat beside him, but invisibly by each sat the brother-in-law transformed into an enemy, for each was cherishing angry thoughts of the other. Gottfried was ashamed of showing their discord in the villages through which they drove, and let Cyprian keep some distance in advance. They did not meet until they were on the court-house steps, which Cyprian was descending as Gottfried went up; they passed each other in silence, but Gottfried had gone only a few steps when he turned back, and said, in a gentle tone, —

"Cyprian, let me have a few friendly words with you."

"I've never been unfriendly."

"Come into the inn, there we can settle matters."

"What do you want?"

"Give me the child. Let me have Erdmutha."

"And do you want nothing else?"

"Nothing for myself."

"For whom, then?"

"For the child. Don't do her who is under ground the wrong of forcing me to compel you by law to give up her child's inheritance."

"So, then, you can compel me?"

"I don't want to."

"Let's see you do it."

"Do it of your own free will, it's a shame before God and men. You are going to move away; the child's legal domicile is with us" —

"You haven't the whole law in your head; a child belongs to the father."

"May be, but her mother's property must be secured

here; do it voluntarily, and I leave those doors closed yonder."

"You may open them for all I care."

"Cyprian," said Gottfried, with a tone of emotion, "these are my last words to you; consider them twice."

"You can go thrice to the devil for all me. What's mine you shan't get behind your iron bars," said Cyprian, scornfully.

"And you'll die yet a prisoner behind some different iron bars," growled Gottfried, full of wrath.

Cyprian went off laughing loudly. He did not look back, and Gottfried opened the court-room door.

Gottfried of Hollmaringen was a man who carried out unflinchingly what he had once resolved on. He succeeded in delaying Cyprian's removal, and the public auction of his house and land. Cyprian was especially enraged by the latter circumstance; he had intended to sell the fields with the standing harvest, which would have been no small advantage to him, now he had to reap and thresh and plough and sow, though he had meant to do nothing of it at all; and, beside, he had his inn and property at Leutershofen, the house stood empty, and he was cheated out of half the harvest. He had to be constantly on the road between the two places, and often before the court. To forget all these torments, Cyprian had to call in the help of wine, but, whether drinking or sober in the morning, he abused Gottfried, who was bringing him to ruin. Gottfried's fields bordered upon those of many a neighbor, he could boast that he had never had a quarrel with any of them; this year he had the most vexatious disputes where his land touched Cyprian's; the quarrel was of course taken up by the servants on both sides, and turned to account. So Cyprian, who had been at first only ill-humored and obstinate, grew into a bitter enemy.

Gottfried, however, went his own way quietly ; he forbade that Cyprian's bitter speeches should be repeated in his house, and took no notice when Cyprian once openly insulted him ; he wished to bring no further misfortune upon him ; he had done his duty, and waited quietly and composedly for whatever else might happen.

CHAPTER II.

THE CHILDREN OF THE ENEMIES, AND THE SISTER'S BRIDAL OUTFIT.

HERE is an old game, known under various names among children everywhere; a flat pebble is thrown horizontally over the surface of the water, which it just touches, as it skips on farther and farther, before it finally sinks. This is called, in our part of the country, "catching brides:" a name given, they say, because the pebble seems to symbolize the mischievous, merry, dancing bride who is not easily caught, but holds herself back coquettishly, till finally, yielding to the law of nature, she is overwhelmed by the stream of life. Whether this is what the name means or not, boys and girls have much amusement in the sport. Blase, who often played the game with the other children at the fish-pond by the hemp-brake, knew how to make the stone skip farther than any one else, and Cyprian's Erdmutha, whom the children called his little wife, often had to hear that she led him a long dance. Blase, in fact, treated his cousin with brotherly attention, and had no objection to hear her called his bride; but now that their fathers were on such bad terms, matters had changed between them.

It is a strange but often proved fact, that the children of relations who are at enmity take up the family quarrel in their own peculiar manner, and often make it felt on the play-ground. The ten-year old Erdmutha, a sturdy little brunette, with her father's dark eyes, had been strictly forbidden to go to the house of her uncle Gottfried, or to speak to any of the family; and every day she heard the most bitter words spoken of her uncle, understanding nothing but that he wanted to bring her father to the gallows.

An old servant in the family named Truda (Gertrude), who had lived with her dead mother, tried to explain to her how matters really stood; but the child only grasped the main fact of the existence of the enmity, and loved her father, who was always kind and affectionate, more than all the world beside; and now, without her noticing the beginning of the change, her mother treated her more mildly and gently, took great pains to dress her neatly, and often called her "dear little Erdie."

When Erdmutha passed her uncle's house, she kept her eyes bent on the ground, and shook her head angrily, as if saying: "I won't look at any of you." She often sat knitting for hours on the stone seat before her home, casting occasional angry glances at her uncle's house, and clenching her fist, while her whole manner said: "Why are you so wicked?" The house seemed to her as defiant, rigid, and dark as the iron gratings which looked so gloomily upon the street. A neighbor's son, Claus, a lame boy, who went on crutches, often sat by Erdmutha, and told her many stories of Blase's mischievous tricks; for, young as Claus was, his jealousy of Blase gave him many grown-up thoughts.

Blase passed Erdmutha as if she did not exist. He had once secretly sent her some cherries, but she threw them to the geese in the street. Blase or Erdmutha drew back from any game, if the other was seen to be taking any part in it. Blase hated Cyprian so bitterly that he carried a stone about with him for weeks, ready to throw it at his head if he should attempt to touch him.

Thus the family quarrel had taken a strong hold on the children.

With the falling leaves, there came into the village a great stamped document which brought the final decision in the lawsuit between Cyprian and Gottfried: it was in favor of the latter. The day for the auction was now fixed, but the people of Hollmaringen are proud, well-to-do farmers, who are not inclined to allow any stranger to get a footing among them by the purchase of property; they are glad, if any land is for sale in the village, to add it to their own or to settle a son or daughter upon it: so that outside purchasers are rare at Hollmaringen, and the few bidders whom Cyprian had collected could not effect much; some few articles were knocked off to them, people feeling sure that they would soon be obliged to sell them back again. The house and most of the other property were bought by Gottfried through a by-bidder, and Cyprian was freshly enraged when he discovered it. Although he knew the customs of the village, and, thanks to them, got a considerable price, he considered himself overreached, and gave vent to his wrath against the whole village, and Gottfried especially, over the wine which was drunk as the sale went on. He was allowed to scold as much as he liked; he was no longer on an equality with his neighbors, and his vexation at the fact was easily pardoned. A considerable portion of the price paid for the purchase remained as an irredeemable mortgage, to secure the inheritance Erdmutha had received from her mother. In order to annoy Gottfried, who had so resolutely carried out his determination, Cyprian announced that, on the following day, together with the household furniture, he should sell a complete bridal outfit, that of his deceased wife. Every one looked at Gottfried, and none but Cyprian's paid bidders waited to drink more of his wine; all the rest went silently home, without the customary glass of Johannisberger.

Next day, at the sale of the household furniture, Gottfried was almost the only man among the gathered women, and not till towards the end of the sale was the bridal outfit brought forward. Gottfried gave no sign of what was passing within him, as he bid off, at a high price, one article of dress after another. He made his bids always in the same quiet tone. It was an outfit already handed down through one generation of honorable farmers. The little round straw hat with its trimming of black watered ribbons adorned with red roses, the red hair-ribbons, the black satin jacket slashed at the back, the scarlet boddice with silver lacings and chains, the girdle wound with silver wire and velvet rolls, one dress which had been worn only on state occasions, a full blue petticoat with many colored trimmings, a fine white apron, red stockings and slippers,—all these Gottfried bought in turn, and laid them again in the well-worn folds, which the auctioneer had shaken out. He spoke no word beyond the offered price of each article; but when the sale of the furniture began, calling for silence, he asked the auctioneer·

"Isn't the necklace with seven rows of garnets and the Swedish ducats there too?"

"I've got the necklace," laughed Cyprian. "It has run down my throat."

Gottfried tied up all his purchases in a white cloth, and went his way with them.

Before the house, he found little Erdmutha sitting on the stone seat, crying.

"What's the matter? has anybody hurt you?" he said, laying his hand on the child's head; but she did not answer, and he went on:

"I dare say all this confusion frightens you; there's nobody to look after you. Have you had any dinner?" The child nodded, and Gottfried continued: "I wish I could do something else for you, but I can't. Only be patient and obedient and good, and when you are grown up and as good as your blessed mother, — see, there's her most beautiful dress for you! but you must be good, and remember that you've still got a protector in the world; you don't know what that means now, but you'll be sure to learn. Now don't cry any more, and don't let them forbid you, but come and see me once more before you go away. Now don't cry any more."

Gottfried quieted the child, but the tears ran from his own eyes in spite of all his efforts to repress them; he dried them with a corner of the apron which was hanging out of the bundle, and the wedding-dress of the departed drank up his tears. He quickly regained his composure, for Truda was coming out of the garden; she gave Erdmutha some plums, and so proved that promises of the future are of little avail with a child: the present plums did more than the future wedding-dress. Erdmutha was happy again, and Gottfried told Truda that she should have, every year, a Christmas present from him as long as she would stay with Cyprian and take care of the child. Truda promised to do it for the sake of the dead.

"I have had to give my child to my sister in Lichtenhardt," she added, "I will take Erdmutha for my own."

Truda was, properly speaking, Cyprian's sister-in-law, for, with her child, she was left on his hands by his brother, a notoriously dissipated fellow, who had been drowned after a wedding at Isenburg. The host had placed four glasses of mulled wine, which were left, on a table, and Cyprian's brother called out, "Here, they are all mine!" and as he went home, he missed his way and was drowned. When Gottfried's sister married Cyprian, she took Truda home, and there she had stayed, exercising a certain influence over him.

Cyprian strictly forbade Erdmutha's going to her uncle's house to say good-by: it was the only means left him of vexing Gottfried, and he chose to use it. Gottfried had spoiled all his pleasure in the removal, by the lawsuit and the losses he had incurred, and he forced himself to exaggerated merriment on his departure. But as he drove by Gottfried's house, and saw the wedding outfit hanging to air on the window-sills outside of the gratings, he became suddenly silent, and looked back at the children, who, with Erdmutha among them, were sitting behind him.

CHAPTER III.

THE SUN RISES AND STOPS ON THE MERIDIAN.

N the Sun at Leutershofen, Cyprian seemed to bloom and unfold for the first time. In spite of all the delay, he had made a good bargain; the large rooms of the house were pleasant to him, and the stirring life still more so. All the habits of the cheerful, busy place suited him, and he often said that here one could know that he was in the world; in a village like Hollmaringen, one felt half dead while his body was still alive. Here fresh bread could be had every day from several bakers. Every evening as the clock struck eight, and every morning, punctually at half-past six, the stage-coach rolled through the place, and on summer evenings, especially on Saturday, the postilion blew his horn from one end of the town to the other, for the children ran nimbly after him, and gave him no peace till the post-horn sounded, and then they shouted and capered about at the blasts, while their parents, who were resting from work before the houses, looked up well pleased. Leutershofen was not only a market town on the turnpike, with a trade in cattle of no little importance, it was also fortunately situated between two mountains; if the vehicles came up from the valley, they were obliged to get fresh horses here, so that there were almost always several canvas-covered wagons standing before the house, and

while the horses were feeding from the movable racks, and the sparrows stealing their corn, the blue-frocked carters sat in the inn and refreshed themselves with food and drink, and Cyprian pledged them; he never allowed the red "woman's anger" to be exhausted. Cyprian's wife proved herself an active hostess, and Truda was soon the most popular and talkative of all the attendants who could be found far and wide, to take the hats and whips of the carters and give a relish to the fare of the house by praising what was set upon the table. Coaches, too, with travellers of rank, sometimes stopped before the Sun, whose sign Cyprian had had newly gilded; and Cyprian knew how to bring forward the newspaper, with a few words which would easily lead the communicative into a conversation. The golden harvest of the week was gathered on the day of the corn-market; then there was even more noise and bustle in the great room of the inn than in the market-place itself, and if the prices rose high, the carouse went on far into the night, the simple native wine did not suffice, but hot wine of a stronger sort was brought out, sometimes even that from beyond the Rhine, and even champagne. Cyprian, of course, did not fail to play the disinterested host sometimes, and, before a year had gone by, his face was as broad as the sun on his sign. He laughed a great deal, especially when joked about his size, and he often said that it was not eating and drinking which made him grow fat, but not having the "Blackcap" — this was Gottfried's nickname — before his eyes all the time. Indeed, few Hollmaringen people, and none of Gottfried's friends, came to the Sun: most of them frequented the "Ox" instead. Cyprian had, most of the time, six horses on the road, furnishing relays to travellers, and for three years he undertook to furnish oats for the cavalry of two garrison towns, but must have found that there was no profit to be made from this, as he would have nothing more to do with it.

In all this busy life, Erdmutha was scarcely noticed as she outgrew her school-days ; Truda alone watched over her, and comforted her when she complained that her uncle Gottfried and Blase went by the house without nodding to her or taking the least notice of her ; she dared not approach them herself, for her father had threatened the severest punishment if she did so ; her father was her only reliance except Truda, and he gave her many a kind word in private. She had much scolding to bear, for she now helped in serving the guests, but she was shy and timid, blushing deeply at every word a stranger said to her, and still more deeply if told that the blush made her even prettier than she was before. In her fear of strangers and of her own family, she often let glasses and bottles fall from her hands, for which she was sharply reproved. Truda comforted her, when bedtime came, with many an old tale of children who had had to endure a great deal and then got a crown at last. Erdmutha had not the least idea where the crown was to come from, but the stories consoled her, their wonders exerted a nameless charm over her heart, and, like a little child, she often begged Truda at night for more of them. At last her father set her free from the service in the inn and the constant torment from her stern mother ; one Sunday, after Erdmutha had justified the name of "woman's anger," by spilling a bottle of the red wine over a lady's white dress, her father said, in the evening, in the family circle : "I see, Erdmutha, you take after Gottfried's family, and any one of that stamp can't get along among men, but only among cattle and in the field. From to-morrow morning you need have nothing more to do in the house, you can help the man and maid in the farm work. Do you like that?"

"Yes: thank you, father."

His wife did not like to agree to this new arrangement; she said that people would accuse her of setting Erdmutha below her own children; but Cyprian remained firm in his determination.

From this time forth Erdmutha was very happy, the farm servants said they had never known what a merry bird she was: she sang all day long, and at resting-time told them such wonderful stories that they seemed to be in a new world; and she turned off all kinds of work as easily as if she had been used to the hardest of it for years.

Erdmutha grew sunburnt, but tall and strong at the same time, having no resemblance to her father except in her brown eyes with their quiet light; in all other respects, she was like her mother. On market-days, when every thing was going merrily in the house, Erdmutha was almost always troubled. Some strange fate seemed to decree, that, if she went a step from the door, she should meet Blase, he always drove, rode, or walked by her, as if a spirit had told him that she was coming. They passed each other quickly without a word of greeting; at first, it was her father's strict command which held Erdmutha back, but soon a feeling of hostility took firm hold upon her and upon Blase also. In Hollmaringen, Blase would say, in the evening, to his married sister, who lived in Cyprian's house: "It's strange that Erdmutha, my only relation, should go by me as if I were a stick; but I'll just tell her next time that she's nothing to me, no relation to me any longer." Erdmutha would say almost the same thing to Truda, and when the latter prophesied love in the future from such talk, she contradicted her with all her might, and said she never would speak of Blase to her again; but she could not refrain from telling her, again and again, how she had that day looked at Blase so angrily that he had to cast down his eyes. Once she said that Blase had tried to speak to her, but she had run away, and had not even turned back to look at him.

Cyprian was often out of humor, he must have had many private vexations, but he spoke openly of only one; it vexed him that he had allowed his oldest child, of whom he was very fond, to be driven away from him, thus bringing many harsh remarks upon himself. He wanted Erdmutha to come back into the house, but she would not consent. Behind his bar, he tried to drink himself into forgetfulness of many things, but only brought new troubles upon himself; his vow that the drinking-bout on the sale of the house should be his very last, had been long broken and forgotten. Erdmutha saw the ruin which was coming on the family, and, though it pained her to leave her father alone, she was doubly glad to be busy in field and stable; and even in winter, she generally sat quietly in the spinning-room. Many wooers came for Erdmutha, but her father sent them all away, and if one of them approached the girl herself, her father managed to say so much that was bad of him that Erdmutha willingly did her part in rejecting him. Truda also helped Cyprian in this matter, for she constantly cherished the hope that Erdmutha would marry Blase and take her back with them to Hollmaringen.

CHAPTER IV.

THE SUN SETS.

FLOURISHING green tree, that is suddenly torn up from the banks of the brook which watered its roots, can give no utterance to its sufferings, and withers in silence ; but a man, even if bound to the soil, can lament and complain if he is pining away, and can even make an effort to gain a fresh footing.

The railroad, which was laid out through Suabia, occupied the minds of men all over the country; people scolded about it, and here and there resisted it, and the knowing ones laughed at the new fashion, which would soon be abandoned like many others. The railroad was built; all sorts of wonderful stories were told of it, and it soon appeared that it had drawn away much of the travel over the distant high-road which led through Leutershofen. Relays of horses were less often needed, but Cyprian hit upon a new plan ; he bought a stage-coach, which had never been seen in the place before, and sent it on regular trips twice a week to the capital, making sure in this way of constant business and a profitable custom in his inn ; but hardly had a year passed when a new misfortune came upon him. The art of road-building took a new form, through the experience won by the railroads: roads had formerly been laid out over the mountains, but now people were not afraid of making a wide circuit, if a level course for the road could thereby be gained. The new generation wants to ride at a trot, and not to crawl toilsomely over mountains. The century-old highway was deserted, and a new one opened in the valley and over causeways. All Leutershofen, the host of the Sun especially, felt the inevitable decay creeping on, and yet every thing must hold its ground, to give way suddenly at last. On the market-days, the new condition of affairs made itself felt most plainly in the provoking banter of the inhabitants of Bieringen, Isenberg, &c.; these were villages which had formerly never been spoken of except to be laughed at for their remoteness, but the people of the new age were not wanting in all sorts of boasting insults to the inhabitants of the villages which had been so proud of their position on the high-road.

Cyprian, trying to turn to some account the cause of his ill luck, made a contract to draw several hundred loads of stone for the new road, and set servants, horses, and carts at work; but it often seems as if, when Fortune has once shown herself hostile, she played her tricks on every occasion, and Cyprian's horses, carts, and servants met with so many accidents that he suffered serious losses. Next he began to think of selling his establishment and removing to the valley, but he could find no one to avail himself of the offered bargain. At last, he determined to devote himself to his farm, and went zealously to work, but he had grown too stout, as he had already often laughingly asserted; at the least hard work he lost his breath, and the perspiration poured off his forehead. Then he gave up, and let things take their own course.

The road though the valley was finished, and it became doubly dreary in the Sun, with its large rooms, ready for the reception of many guests. The proverb says that it is easy to quarrel over the empty crib, and this now proved itself true. But the host had many a comforter in the darkness under ground, which helped to shorten the time and make him forget his troubles. For hours, and even days, he lay at the open window, with his red pocket-book for a pillow, and looked dreamily out for the right customer, who, he thought, must come, for he had advertised in the newspapers that he would sell the place on easy terms. What he would then do, he left to the future to settle. How empty and desolate was the great open square before the house! Nothing was heard but the plashing of the never-failing spring; the movable racks, formerly kept constantly ready for the carters' use, lay as if worn out, and with many a broken leg, in a corner with the cracked bottles, and the whole village was as still as if sleeping at high noon. There was no market-day now, and no fresh-baked bread every morning; no post-horn sounded among the shouting and springing children in the streets.

Cyprian looked upon the ruin of his affairs with that stunned feeling of indifference, which a dim sense of unavoidable, coming misfortune so often produces. His wife, who had always been frivolous and thoughtless, made the most of the good days left her, and, when she found that scolding and complaining to her husband did no good, she made up her mind to enjoy what she could as long as any thing was left; the hoops were sprung from casks and tubs, and she used the staves which were at hand for her fire. Two acres of the land were sold, others mortgaged, and they lived on the money as long as it lasted. Cyprian assured himself that he would sell of his own free will, while every day brought him nearer the time when he would be turned out of his house and land. He did not give up his inn-keeper's license, even after his receipts were less than the tax demanded; he believed he must keep up the business, even if it were only in the smallest way, on account of the future sale of the place. Now and then he got a small cask of brandy, or of half-sour wine, at a high price on credit, but generally the cellar was empty; and if a travelling apprentice, coming up the village road, entered the Sun, Truda was sent off to the Ox to bring back, under her apron, what was called for, and Cyprian said to the waiting customer, as if scoffing at himself, "My cellar is at some little distance."

By degrees, Cyprian went farther, and sold what were not absolute fixtures in the house; one day they ate up some chairs, the next a table, and then glasses, pans, harnesses, &c. Truda, or more frequently Erdmutha, often had to go with Cyprian to the town, in the evening, to carry small articles of furniture or bedding. These were sad trips; her father complained all the way, and wished himself dead; and if, on the way home, after a visit to the tavern, he was more cheerful, the least accident would make him weep over his fate again, and it was very hard to quiet him.

Singularly enough, but not without reason, Erdmutha had really happy days after the ruin which had come upon the family; even her mother seldom scolded her, and was often affectionate. This woman was always cheerful when there was temporary abundance in the house. Erdmutha felt the money troubles bitterly, and it seemed sometimes as if the roof were ready to fall and crush her; but the consciousness of being lovingly cherished and considered as the chief person in the house, often made her forget all beside.

On the day when, by order of the magistrate, the golden sign was taken down and the auction announced, the whole household, great and small, wept, and avoided showing themselves on the street or at the windows; and Erdmutha learned, for the first time, that she was the sole dependence and hope of the family. In the evening, Truda explained to her what this meant, and warned her that she could not help the others without bringing herself to ruin.

Before the announcement of the auction, Erdmutha had to submit to carry by night many articles out of the house to dispose of them among acquaintances; now, after the public announcement, a genuine robbery of the house went on, as if it were that of a stranger and enemy. The authorities had indeed made an inventory of the property, but there were many things which could be got out of the way, and at last the floors were torn up in the loft and the boards sold. Cyprian had managed cunningly to have the legal proceedings protracted, and he seemed never to have lived more happily than now while his creditors had to support him; he was spending his principal, as it were, or living like an official on his salary; but this also came to an end, and, in the spring, when Erdmutha was twenty, she had to remove into a small house with her parents and brothers and sisters.

Cyprian wished to dismiss Truda, but retained her at

Erdmutha's request, declaring and showing plainly that he did every thing for her sake. Cyprian was advised to make his peace with Gottfried, and submit to him, on the ground that if a man wanted fire he must look among the ashes; but he would listen to no such proposal: he said that the next year he should emigrate to the new world.

Uncle Gottfried came once from Hollmaringen, and sent for Erdmutha to come to him at the inn. Cyprian told her she might go, if she chose to speak to a man who would not vouchsafe a word to her father, and who was to blame for his misfortunes, by increasing so much the loss he suffered in his removal. Erdmutha refused to go, and then Gottfried came to the house, and, looking about him, said to Erdmutha, without a word of greeting to Cyprian, that he had no secrets from her father, and only wished to ask her whether she would go home with him to take the place of his second daughter, who was about to be married. Erdmutha said that she should stay with her father, and when Gottfried invited her to come to his daughter's wedding, she declined again; she was bitterly angry with the man who could grudge a word to her father because he was now in poverty.

CHAPTER V.

ADORNED FOR THE SACRIFICE.

T seemed like a scene from one of the happy old fairy tales when Erdmutha awoke in her attic-room, on her twenty-first birthday, and saw glittering jewels suspended before her eyes, but it was no magician nor spirit that was holding them out to her, but her father, who fastened them about her neck, and then weeping, kissed her silently.

"What is it? what is it?" asked Erdmutha, still half dreaming. Her father sat down by her on the edge of the bed, and, breathing heavily, began:

"It is the necklace of your blessed mother. I have never parted with it in any strait; always determined that you should have it on this day. Twenty-one years ago to-day—" Lost in memories of the past, the strong man could not go on, but wept aloud.

"Didn't you sell my mother's wedding outfit? Wasn't Uncle Gottfried angry with you for that?" asked Erdmutha.

"I sold the clothes to vex the Blackcap; they were all falling to pieces, but I kept what was of real value. See, Erdmutha," and Cyprian grasped her hand, "you are my dear child, my own precious child, my own — you have grown into my heart like no one else — you know, without my telling you often — "

"Yes, yes, father, I know."

"See, then, you can do what you please for me; you can make me a beggar or a respectable man, or you can make me kill myself."

"What can I do?"

"Listen quietly, only listen. You see, you are of age to-day, and you can deserve a heaven on earth; if you'll take your property into your own hands, you shall keep it. I won't take a farthing of it more than we want for the voyage, and over yonder we can take a fresh start. Do you see? do you understand me?"

"Yes, yes, I'll do it with all my heart. Truda has foreseen this a long time, and wanted to persuade me not to do it, but I will; there's my hand on it. Only manage that no one need know any thing about it — "

"No, no, my child, that can't be. You must claim your property before the court; you can now — "

"Can't you do it for me?"

"No, you must do it yourself, and there's no danger; you needn't be afraid. Only you must be firm. You'll see that everybody will come to you and tell you that your father's a scamp who'll waste your money, and all that sort of thing. But you mustn't let them move you with good words or bad. Can you do that? You can if you choose, and if you think that you are saving your father and family from shame and starvation — "

"Yes, I can, you shall see I can; I'll put on the necklace and grasp it with my hand, and then no word will stick in my throat. Depend upon me."

"Swear to me, that, as your mother protects you in heaven, you will stand firm."

"I don't need to swear. Let me do it without that: it's easier. Don't you trust your child?"

Cyprian quickly covered his eyes with his hand, and said: "Yes, yes, entirely, dear good child." Then he told her that she must keep the necklace hidden, and let no one know any thing of it; he prided himself on seeming worse than he was.

When Cyprian went to his wife in the sitting-room, he said to her:

"There's a child for you; she's a real angel. I don't deserve to have such a daughter."

His wife laughed quietly to herself.

There was merriment and plenty in Cyprian's house that day, almost as in its best time, and Erdmutha was the central point of the festivity; even her brothers and sisters, who generally tormented her mischievously, were affectionate and grateful for the cakes which they got on her account.

The next day, her father himself accompanied Erdmutha to Hollmaringen; he said little, only impressing upon his daughter how she must conduct herself towards the enemies who would endeavor to turn her from him. He tried to induce Erdmutha to promise to say that the whole plan was her own, and that no one had put it into her head; but she said:

"That won't do, father; I can get on much better if I stick to the truth. Why should we lie and conceal? It is all right that a child should follow her father's wishes; no one can find fault with that."

While her father bent his eyes to the ground, and strode

on with gloomy countenance, Erdmutha cast frequent glances of compassion upon him, and felt fresh joy that it was in her power to restore him to prosperity; and, in the midst of her practical schemes, she remembered the story of the children who go out to find the life-giving plant for their sick father, and courageously withstand all sorts of dangers on the way.

When they came in sight of Hollmaringen in its wide plain, and the path turned aside from the old high-road to lead to the village, Cyprian stopped and said that he would turn back and wait for Erdmutha's return at Seebronn in the 'Horse' inn, the first house on the Hollmaringen side of the village. "You know all," said he; "go, and God be with you." He seated himself on the side of the road, and pressed his folded hands on the blackthorn stick between his knees. When he looked up, after a little time, he saw Erdmutha entering the village; she did not turn round, but walked quietly forward, and suddenly a great fear came over her father; there was his child going on an errand which was a question of life or death to him. If her relations should persuade the girl to stay with them, he was lost; she was of age, and free to decide for herself. With trembling steps, and stopping often to rest, Cyprian retraced his steps; the country wore the fresh green of spring, and was full of sunshine and the song of larks; but he who is oppressed by heavy troubles feels the world a prison. Care and anxiety cast their black lines across the landscape like the iron bars of a prison window.

Meanwhile, Erdmütha went on her way as if in a dream; the people in the fields and on the road she did not know; but every tree, every hedge, every ditch, greeted her with a thousand half-forgotten childish memories, and she looked around her with great wondering eyes, like a child just awakened from sleep; the larks carolled, the trees blossomed, the sun shone so bright, and in the maiden's heart, unacknowledged by herself, lay the happy thought that she was going to do a good deed, and her whole being was running over with joy. She went on, as if an invisible being was leading her by the hand, till suddenly she stopped, as a deep sadness stole into her heart that she could not remain here, where alone she was so thoroughly at home. "And here thou art to remain for ever," she said half aloud to herself, scarcely knowing whence the words came. Then she saw before her the burial-ground, shut in with its hedge of beeches, and she knew what had spoken so strangely within her; she went into the enclosure, read the inscriptions on many crosses, and grew bewildered by the countless deaths, of which every step here spoke to her. Then, struck with the deepest awe, she read on a half-sunken cross her own name: it was her mother's grave; she sank down, and lay long with her head buried in the fresh grass. At last she rose and gazed round her; she could not weep, though her whole heart was full of deep sorrow. She laid her hand on the grave as if she were grasping her mother's hand, and looked out into the wide world. The larks sang over her head, a chaffinch trilled his clear notes from a weeping-willow whose young leaves glanced in the sunshine; a gentle breeze swept through the solitary pine-trees, which were scattered here and there, and butterflies flew hither and thither. She gathered a few grass stems and some wild thyme from the grave, put them in her bosom, and walked firmly forward. She went through the village, without looking round her or speaking to any one. Noon was past, and the people were going back to their work in the fields; only before her old home did she stay her steps, and gaze long at the house and the stone seat before it, where, as a child, she had so often sat. Every thing was as it used to be, except that the neighbor's son, lame Claus, who was knitting a worsted jacket on the stone seat, had grown, in the ten years, into a tall fellow, and in the garden a new barn was built. Just as Erdmutha was about to speak to Claus, Blase came out of the house-door with a horse-collar over his shoulder; he recognized Erdmutha, in spite of the great white handkerchief in which she had almost buried her face, and said:

"What! are you here? Are you going to stay with us now?"

"No," answered Erdmutha, as she moved on; it wounded her that Blase would neither hold out his hand to her nor say a really friendly word. As she went up the steps of her uncle Gottfried's house, it seemed as if her limbs were failing her; but she composed herself, as she became conscious that her undertaking was not so easy as she had pictured it to herself. Uncle Gottfried, who sat reading some papers at a table, did not rise, but held out his hand to her in welcome, saying:

"That's good; you've come to show yourself again! You'll be as well taken care of here as with your father, and better too. You must be coming of age about this time. Stop — to-day is the twelfth of May; yesterday was your birthday; now you can do what you please with yourself."

"Yes, that's the reason I came, and I wanted to tell you —"

Erdmutha could not finish her sentence, for Gottfried's wife, who had just shaken hands with her, interrupted with the words:

"You can talk about that afterwards; you must have something to eat first. If you had only come half an hour sooner, you would have been in time for dinner. Rosa!" she called, and a slender girl came into the room, who gave Erdmutha a hearty welcome, on her mother's telling her who had come; but the good woman cut off any further talk by saying: "Rosa, warm up the calf's liver that was left from dinner; put in a spoonful more salt, and beat up a couple of eggs for your cousin as quick as you can."

Erdmutha tried to thank them, but they would not listen to her; and, in spite of her weariness and undeniable hunger, she was suddenly filled with such a satisfied feeling, that it seemed to her she must jump up and run away. This trusting, cordial treatment from people whom she had looked upon as ungracious enemies; this kindly greeting from those who she supposed had forgotten her; this feeling that she was among relations, who looked upon love and kindness towards her as a matter of course; and with these, the thought that she had come with a project which was adverse to them, — all this seemed to oppress her almost to suffocation.

Her uncle collected his papers, and said that he would be back in an hour, but must now go to the meeting of the town council. Erdmutha rose, and courtesied modestly as he went out; speak, she could not.

When Rosa, who, her mother said, was to be married in a week, brought in the food, Erdmutha did not want to touch it. There is an old saying that we must not take meat nor drink from spirits that would lead us astray, unless we would fall into their power. Erdmutha knew this saying, and she seemed to herself within a charmed circle; but these were good spirits, and she would take nothing only because it would make the unfriendliness she must soon show seem so ungrateful. But her aunt would not be refused, and repeatedly told her that she must get over her shyness, that she was among people who felt kindly towards her, and Erdmutha listened with surprise as she found how much was known of her life; and she heard, blushing, her own praise as a skilful farm-hand, who had not turned into a landlady unused to hard work. Erdmutha, who scarcely ever shed tears; wept freely; all which she had been through that day suddenly overwhelmed her. Her aunt tried to comfort her with the kindest words, and Rosa told her that she must be bridesmaid at her wedding. Erdmutha replied to them that she could tell no one but her uncle what it was that lay heavy on her heart.

When uncle Gottfried, who held in the town council the office of guardian of orphans, came back, he opened a chest, and took from it several stamped papers, saying: "You, probably, want to hear how your property stands; these are the mortgages, — three thousand four hundred florins was the amount at first, and so it has remained, for your father has drawn the interest every year, even while he was well off. If you get an honest husband, who has something of his own, this will be a good addition to help you set up house-keeping."

"I'm not thinking about that, uncle."

"Well, all in good time."

"No, listen kindly to me, uncle."

"Yes, yes ; say what you have to say."

"You see, uncle, I am — I ought — I want — yes, I must have my money."

"Ah, indeed! I can easily believe that your father wants to have it so."

"And I, too."

"But I don't."

Gottfried put the papers back into the chest, double-locked it, and tied the leather band, which held the keys, into the button-hole of his waistcoat again.

Erdmutha sat silent.

"What do you want to do with the money?" asked Gottfried.

"Help my father with it."

"That the good-for-nothing fellow may waste it all in eating and drinking."

Erdmutha rose; her hand closed tightly over the necklace in her pocket, as she said, firmly:

"Uncle, I will not bear such words. My father is as good as any one; and those who insult him are to blame for what is wrong in him."

"I see plain enough your father has spoiled you, too."

"And supposing that's true, whose fault is it? Not my father's only; it's yours, yours, too. You ought to have put aside your hard feelings, and taken care that your sister's child should not be spoiled; but to drive by in your great wagon with no more notice than if she were a dog; there isn't much to be proud of in that."

Gottfried was amazed; for the first time in his life he found his conduct called in question, and he could not silence a certain inward voice which acknowledged the justice of the charge, but he was angry with the person that brought it. He very nearly lost his calmness, but, quickly controlling himself, said, with a bitter laugh:

"Your father has put that into your head, too."

"No, no; I have silently thought over what I am saying a thousand times. But we will not reproach each other; I've been kindly treated in your house to-day, and I should like to carry pleasant memories of my relations with me when I go away."

"Where are you going?"

"To America, with my father and brothers and sisters. You say I might have a handsome property; I will not be rich while my father is a beggar —"

"And he'll be one again as soon as he has spent what belongs to you. I see that a man can talk sensibly with you, and you have a good heart that's worthy of your blessed mother; she believed in me; you feel differently, and I won't find fault with you; but consider, try to feel as if some one else was speaking to you: how can a man who has run through a good property in his best years, and who has met with no misfortune, whatever he chooses to say about it, — how can such a man become industrious and thrifty all at once? You are young, you have your life before you, and you ought not to bring misfortune upon it for the sake of a man who has almost ended his. Wait and think it over, at any rate for a year, or as long as you like; you can stay with us, or wherever else you please."

It was strange to see with what strength and firmness Erdmutha resisted all arguments; finally, Gottfried brought forward her mother's wedding outfit, and told her with trembling voice, how Cyprian had sold, and he had bought it to give to her on her wedding day; and when

Erdmutha insisted that her father had not sold the necklace, Gottfried stamped in anger at her obstinacy; but he composed himself again, and besought her, in the name of her dead mother, to follow his wishes instead of her father's. When he found that Erdmutha still held out steadily, his manner suddenly changed, and he cried out in a voice of anger:

"Well, go then, go! But I swear to you, if you cast me off, I'll disown you for ever, for ever! You shall be dead to me, and buried — with the grass growing over you. Go —"

His voice suddenly failed, he could not go on; his wife, who, with Blase and her two daughters, had heard him in the kitchen, came in, and said, with exclamations of fear, that the attack was like one which Gottfried had had before; he made a sign for Erdmutha to go, and she left the house. No one spoke to her, no one went with her. She walked through the village as if she were on the deck of a tossing vessel; she did not look round or stop until she reached the point where the road met the highway; there she seated herself by a guidepost, under a blossoming apple-tree. She sat with downcast eyes, and did not answer the greetings of the women who were coming with bundles of weeds out of the cornfields.

CHAPTER VI.

A TREE BLOSSOMS OUT AT THE PARTING OF THE ROADS.

"I'M glad I've caught you here," said a voice, suddenly. Erdmutha looked up: it was Blase, with a strange expression on his glowing face.

"Did your father send you with any message to me?" replied Erdmutha, trying to rise; a thrill passed through her, when Blase touched her for the first time, laying his hand on her arm with the words:

"Sit still, no one sent me, I came of my own accord, and I have something that I want to say to you out of my own head. Will you listen quietly and patiently to what I say?"

"You've no reason to think that I won't listen calmly to any thing that one can hear with calmness."

"You may be right, for all I know," said Blase, sitting down by her side. "Now, let's leave old matters; I've something else to talk to you about. Do you know I've wished a hundred times that I could get a chance to talk to you quietly, like this? I've thought a hundred times that our Lord God must be very good and merciful not to punish us for living so at sword's points with each other, when we are such near relations; a hundred times, when I've met you, I've wanted to stop you, but you've always been so scornful and proud —"

"I? proud?" interrupted Erdmutha, with a bitter laugh. Blase continued:

"You are my only relation on my father's side, and it has made my heart sink when I've seen you, and not dared to speak to you. And my father, too, he doesn't say much, but he is good at heart, you don't know him, and your father —"

"Don't say any thing about him; it's right that you should praise your father, and I'll believe all you say; but my father is my father too, and I won't hear any thing against him —"

"Hearing you say that, is just what gives me the more respect for you. But we haven't got to settle that now. Here we are sitting together as if we hadn't any parents, and we're all alone in the world, and it is the same to both of us —"

Blase stopped and wiped the perspiration from his forehead; looking down, Erdmutha said: "Why didn't you say a kind word to me when I came into the village?"

"Because I thought you were going to stay with us, and I should have chances enough, and I didn't want to be the first to come round. You've tormented me enough all your life long, and from the time you threw away my cherries I've wanted to pay you off —"

Resting her chin and underlip on her closed hand, Erdmutha looked up at Blase with a fleeting smile, and said:

"What has changed you now?"

"Because you're spoiling every thing again, by going off

in anger. It isn't right, it isn't good. I won't bear it. You belong to us, and not to those Leutershofen people, and you shall not say that we've cast you off — "

" I don't say it, it would be a lie."

" I don't mean that; you twist my words, interrupt me so, that I never know what I'm saying — "

" Well, I'll be quite still, you shall do all the talking."

Rubbing his hands, and trying to speak with great calmness, Blase began again:

" You ought to stay with us; I won't say any thing about your own people, but this much you must see, that we are very different, and you ought to be glad that you have such a dependence. Say, am I not right?"

" Yes; but if my father were in jail I wouldn't depend on anybody's pity: I would go out to service and maintain my own honor."

" That's all right, you get that pride from our family, it shows you belong to us; but you needn't go out to service, far from it. If one could only know whether — I love you with all my heart, and I will never let you go" — He threw his arms round her neck, and pressed a kiss on her lips, but she tore herself away from him.

" Don't you care for me, then? Why do you weep? Tell me why," asked Blase, with trembling voice.

" Oh, Blase!" began Erdmutha, at last, "this isn't right, it is a sin; we must part, part for ever; it cannot be."

" What cannot be?"

" I have never been willing to confess it to myself, and now I dare not; it's better you should think of me as dead long ago."

" But I will not. Tell me, truly, do you like me or not?"

"Oh, Blase! I can't tell you how dearly—" she put her arms around his neck, and they held each other in a long, close embrace; the whole world was forgotten, and they heard nothing but the beating of their own hearts, and saw only themselves reflected in each other's eyes. Blase was first able to speak again:

"Do you still wish to go back to your home?"

"I must, indeed I must."

"Perhaps it is better. My father is more angry with you than I ever saw him with any one, but it won't last. Didn't you have any presentiment as you came to us?"

"I don't know, as I came towards the village I felt as if the ground was holding me fast, and then I stopped up there, by my mother's grave, and when I came into your house every thing seemed so home-like, and all sorts of things ran through my head, but when I heard my father so harshly spoken of, all my pleasure was spoiled; I won't stay in any house where such things are said of him; he has the best heart in the world, it's true he's weak, but he has to suffer more from that than any one else, and nobody has the right to abuse him for it. Now, Blase, you must help me; I don't know where I am, nor what I ought to do."

With a proud consciousness of his own manliness, Blase told her that he had already settled it in his own mind. Erdmutha should give her father enough money for his passage, and come with the rest to Hollmaringen, then both parties would be benefited. Instead of praising this plan as a wise one, as Blase had expected, Erdmutha said:

"I would rather give him all of it, I don't want to have any thing more to do with money, I'm afraid of it; other girls don't have to trouble themselves about it, and I don't see why I should have the torment."

Blase thought his own plan the best, only half comprehending Erdmutha's feelings. He repeated to her that she was of age, and that it was a sin to waste the money on Cyprian. In the midst of the sunny light of love, a dark shadow seemed suddenly to hover over Erdmutha; she had for years heard much of Gottfried's avarice, and now it seemed to her that Blase was influenced by it. If it were not so, why was he not willing to give her father all, in order to free her? Blase gave a different interpretation to the change in her countenance and to her silence. He advised Erdmutha, if she felt afraid of settling the matter herself, to go back to his married sister in the village, and leave it all to him or his brother-in-law. To this Erdmutha would not and could not agree; she alone would know how to manage matters with her father, and she would not deceive his confidence in her coming back; he would lose all faith in the world if she, his last hope, should turn traitor to him. Or did she wish to prove to Blase that she possessed strength enough within herself?

Then again the overwhelming power of youthful love gained the victory, and she embraced Blase again with the exclamation: "There's no such thing as money in the world! hear how merry that finch is over our heads, and he hasn't a farthing in his sack;" and then they laughed merrily over a thousand reminiscences of old times, and they devised different kinds of kisses,—one for the cousin, one for the lover, and one for the bride. Then Blase had to rise, walk towards her, greet her, and begin a conversation as he ought to have done in the past time, and Erdmutha did the same, playing her part most amusingly. Then they sat down again with their arms round each other, saying, "Now a year has gone by;" again and again they went through their play, as the sun sank in the west, and Blase said:

"Seven and seventy years I would like to live so."

"And after that, I'd let you give me something," laughed Erdmutha. Blase lamented that he had nothing to give her for a keepsake; but he promised if she would come to Rosa's wedding that he would have a gold ring for her.

"Silver or gold, it's all the same to me," said Erdmutha, merrily.

"The promise holds," said Blase, and Erdmutha shrank back frightened at the words; had she not promised her father, too, to stand out resolutely? Should she dare to trust another's promise, or could any one rely on hers in future?

With the quietness which generally comes after great emotion, Blase and Erdmutha now held each other's hands, as they passed along the deserted high-road, Blase gladly walking on the sharp stones and leaving the smooth path to his companion. Erdmutha had told him that her father was waiting for her at Seebronn, and he wanted to go with her and give her his support, but she would not consent, and he had to promise her solemnly not to take any part in the affair, and not to send or come to Leutershofen; she feared that the interference of any of Gottfried's family would have the worst effect on her father, and chose to manage matters entirely by herself. On the other hand, she promised Blase not to come again to Hollmaringen on foot, but in a Berne wagon, as befitted her position. They did not part until they were very near the village, and then it seemed as if they could not tear themselves from each other: they constantly repeated their farewells, but still kept their hands firmly clasped. Blase appeared to have something more to say, which he could not utter; he would not let Erdmutha go, but as she heard her father's loud voice in the inn, which was the first house in the village, she insisted on his leaving her, and went on alone. Blase turned homeward, for he, too, had a father to fear.

CHAPTER VII.

AN ALL–SOULS' CANDLE.

AY after day passed, and nothing was heard of Erdmutha. On the evening before his sister's marriage, when the whole family were assembled in Gottfried's house, and that quiet mood prevailed when all hearts seem filled with silent happiness on the eve of some joyful event, Blase was not to be seen in the party; he had walked alone and thoughtful along the road to Seebronn, and was sitting by the guidepost under the apple-tree, whose blossoms were falling, and strewing the road and foot-path as if adorning it for the entrance of some joyful procession. Blase went on as far as Seebronn, holding in his hand the ring that he was to give to Erdmutha, but she did not come, though he had expected her to-day with such certainty; he would have wandered on and on to Leutershofen, drawn forward by a great longing, but he would not disturb the joy at home by his absence. He found all the relations collected, pleasing themselves with the prospect of the coming festivities as they did with the odor of the freshly cooked viands which pervaded the house, for both were to be fully enjoyed on the morrow. Blase did not answer a word when his sister reminded him that it was the last time she should put his Sunday suit in order for him, and told him

he would miss her, for she was to marry a wood-dealer in Enzthal. Blase felt as if under a spell, scanning all the people present, one after another, to make sure again that Erdmutha was not among them; and no one missed her except himself. When he was laughingly told that it was his turn to be married next, and that he must look about him, he said nothing, and many a maiden's beaming glance which had rested on him turned away unanswered.

Next morning, as wagon after wagon brought the bridegroom and his family, as well as the bride's more distant relations, Blase moved about as if in a dream, without greeting any one as he should. He forced himself to merriment when the dance began, but it was easy to see that it was not genuine, though no one except his married sister knew what was the matter with him. When Rosa went away, no one wept as he did.

When he was in the village, or at work in the fields, and heard a wagon roll by in the road, he ran with beating heart to meet it, always feeling that it must be Erdmutha who was coming; but it was always some stranger, who gazed with astonishment at the young man's quick retreat at sight of him. Over and over again Blase resolved not to trouble himself about any rattling carriage again; but the next time he heard the quick trot of horses, he could not keep himself quiet in his place, but felt that he must go just this once more before breaking himself finally of the habit.

One morning, the official newspaper, which Gottfried, as mayor, was obliged to take, brought disagreeable intelligence into the house, for a notice demanded that all Cyprian's creditors should present themselves, as he was about to emigrate to America; adding, however, that no one need hope for payment, since he emigrated at the expense of the child of his first marriage. While Gottfried was reading this in the house, Truda had gone to Blase in the barn to carry him Erdmutha's last message of farewell, as she had already gone with her father to the seaport, leaving the rest of the family to follow. Truda told him much of Erdmutha's sorrow at the departure, she had been her *confidante* through all; but she did not say what had brought her to consent to going with the family. Truda was now left alone, and begged Gottfried to take her into service, but he would have nothing to do with any one who reminded him of Erdmutha. She then went to her daughter at Lichtenhardt, to which place she had thought never to return, for the village was so poor and deserted, that every one shunned calling himself a native of it. After Erdmutha had gone, Truda had no place in the larger farming world which the Lichtenhardt people gazed upon in admiration.

Cyprian must have formed his plans long beforehand. Provided with a legal power-of-attorney signed by Erdmutha, he had sold the mortgages to a broker, who had paid cash for them, deducting a considerable commission for himself.

The day on which Gottfried had to give up the carefully guarded mortgages, was a sad one; a deep sorrow rested in his heart, not only for the loss of the money, but for the loss of his sister's child; he excited the wonder of all who saw him, by putting on crape for the departed one, and for weeks spoke only of Erdmutha as dead. Gottfried was a man of determined independence, who yielded to no outside influence: people blamed him for this strange, self-imposed badge of mourning, and warned him that it was tempting Providence to change his pretence into reality by inflicting a true loss by death upon him; he persisted, only declaring that a person must be either living or dead to him, and he did not choose to consider one as still in existence of whom he knew nothing. Erdmutha was dead to him, it made no difference whether she were still alive in America, she was dead to him, and no member of his family should speak otherwise of her.

Perhaps Gottfried had some other end in view, in showing this peculiar obstinacy.

After a few weeks, he laid aside the mourning, but a mood of depression lay over the family, which could not be banished. Rosa, who had been the light of the house, was gone, and Blase became every day more silent and reserved. He had put on no outward sign of mourning for Erdmutha, and had been more displeased than any one at his father's course, because he felt that it was intended to influence himself.

Gottfried had wished gradually to give up all the farm-work to his son's care, but Blase now asked him about every thing that was to be done, and seemed quite incapable of deciding and acting for himself. He seemed, in his own home, like a servant on the first day of work in a new situation. Formerly, he had made out most of the official papers for his father, who was pleased with his readiness; but now, every word had to be dictated to him, and, even then, he often made mistakes. His parents talked over the altered bearing of their son, who made no denial when he was charged with having sat by Erdmutha at the guide-post and kissed her. His father threatened him severely if he so much as thought of her, and even worked his own passion up to bitter curses against the "dead" girl, and it now appeared that he had put on mourning for her principally as an example to Blase. He even went farther, and on All-Souls' Day kindled two lights on his sister's grave. At last, having made up his mind as to the best means of extinguishing every spark of hope in Blase, he announced his resolution, and his son had to obey; he betrothed him to the pretty daughter of the church-warden of Seebronn. Blase had formerly shown some fancy for the girl, but Gottfried had had much higher views for him; now he urged on the betrothal himself, and every one spoke of the change in him in such a way that the praise seemed more like blame, since it showed what the opinion of his neighbors had formerly been.

There never was a less animated lover than Blase; he did every thing which his father and mother directed, but nothing more. He walked over the same road that he had trodden with Erdmutha to visit his bride, and when he reached her house, he always had to remind himself who he was and why he was there. The people shook their heads at his strange ways. Once when his bride had walked some distance towards home with him, and wanted to sit down under the apple-tree, by the guidepost, he cried with an expression of fear:

"No, no, not there, there's a spirit sitting there," and ran away from the spot.

The next day, the church-warden appeared, bringing back the betrothal presents, to break off the match on the plea that Blase was insane.

Gottfried had never experienced a deeper mortification than to have his son rejected on such a charge. From that time he said no more than was necessary to Blase, who took the breaking up of his marriage prospects as a matter which did not at all concern him, and remained always silent with a dreamy expression in his eyes. His brother-in-law was the only person to whom he attached himself; he liked better to work for him than at home, and when he went to the corn-market, which was now held in the town, he liked to go with him as his servant to take charge of the horses. He still looked fresh and young, only showing the strange peculiarity of not answering many things that were said to him, except by a quiet, sad smile.

So three years passed.

One day, at the beginning of haying, when Blase was watering his horses in the market-place of the town, Truda came towards him and beckoned; he saw her coming, but did not move, nor answer her greeting.

"God be praised that you are here," cried Truda. Blase saw that his horses were raising their dripping mouths from the water; he whistled to them, and then, seeing that they would drink no more, led them back towards the inn. Truda, too much out of breath to speak at once, walked by his side, and said at last:

"Blase, wake up; the time for sleep is over." He hardly looked at her, as he fastened his horses at their crib.

"Don't you hear me? I have some good news for you, which nobody dreams of. For God's sake, are you really out of your mind?" asked Truda, with growing anxiety, and shrinking back as Blase looked searchingly at her.

"What do you want of me? what is it?" he asked at last.

"Up there on the bridge behind the mill, a girl is waiting for you, and she sent me to find you. Tell me, don't you care when I tell you who it is? Tell me. It's a girl that brings you a message from Erdmutha."

Blase's face lighted up, as if the sun had suddenly risen upon it, and seizing Truda's arm so violently that she cried out, he asked:

"Where is the girl? Where?"

"Come with me."

He followed Truda with rapid steps, and as they crossed the bridge, he saw a female figure, wrapped in a cloak, with white handkerchief over her head and bundle on her back, like the women of the neighborhood when on a pilgrimage. The figure sat crouching under a willow-tree; she raised her head, a brown eye flashed, she rose, and Blase cried:

"Is it not you? Oh, holy God in Heaven, it is!"

A cry of joy rang out over the sound of the rushing mill-stream. Erdmutha and Blase lay in each other's arms

CHAPTER VIII.

BY THE ROARING WATERS.

"O not think me unmanly: I can't help crying; you don't know how many thousand tears have sunk back on my heart. I shall get rid of their weight now, — let me cry."

So Blase answered Erdmutha, as she tried to soothe his irrepressible emotion: "I'm so glad I knew you directly; you've changed very much, except your eyes, they're just the same. Now tell me, how is it possible? Is it really true that you are here? How has it all come about? Is it three years since you went away, or was it only yesterday?"

As often as Erdmutha tried to begin her story, it was broken in upon by exclamations of love and wonder; at last, she forbade any interruption, and began:

"Here on the very spot that we are sitting, my unhappiness began; here my father threatened to throw himself into the water if I would not go with him; and it's true that through all that had passed I had been his only joy, and as we went on, he thanked me constantly that I had not deserted him. Oh, Blase, believe me, and, for my sake, — I'll reward you for it all my life, — do not doubt that, in all that happened afterwards, he was as little to blame as you; this was the only wrong thing he did: he pictured what trouble it would bring if I went to you, and how your father would torment you to death — and so, for your sake — I hardly know now how it happened — I thought it would be easier for you, and my father had no one but me to give him a kind word, great and small turned against him if he spoke — and so I went, though it seemed to me as if all were not real, and I could come back the next day; but we travelled on and on, hundreds and hundreds of miles away, until we stopped by the great ocean, at a place they called Antwerp. We had to wait there a long time for the others to come; my father gave me an account of every penny he spent, and made me keep my money always about me; he would not let me lock it up in a chest, and he would not take it himself; there my thoughts were always running on you; I was so troubled that I could scarcely move about, and my heart grew heavier and heavier, and I was almost crazy with thinking why just I should have to bear it all, but I never could find the reason. I was frightened almost to death with the confusion of people and ships; and if it hadn't been a sin, I'd have jumped into the water, — all the more gladly, if I could have taken all the money in the world and let it sink with me. Money is the root of all the evil in the world."

Blase only shook his head doubtfully, and Erdmutha continued:

"When my father's wife and my brothers and sisters came, I had to put my money in my trunk, and one of them always stayed by to watch. Once, when I came in, I found my father in a hot quarrel with my step-mother; but when they saw me, both became suddenly silent; and, afterwards, when I was alone with my father, he held my hand fast for as much as an hour, crying and saying all sorts of kind and affectionate words. I did not think much about it at the time, but afterwards I was made to see what it all meant. On the morning of the day when the vessel was to sail, when we were all on board, my — my mother sent me back once more into the town to get a bag of peas which we had left at the inn. My father wanted to go, but she would not let him, and he, I am sorry to say, was not quite himself; going on board the ship had been a sad thing to him, and he had tried to drown his trouble in wine. As I left the vessel, some one jabbered something to me, but I could not understand him. I went into the town, but I couldn't find the bag, no one knew any thing about our having left it; I went back to the vessel — Blase, it seemed to me I must jump into the water — the ship was gone, and there I was alone, left behind, deserted and outcast. Can you imagine how I felt, Blase? The people saw what had happened to me, and they raised me from the ground where I had fallen; there was a German who comforted me, and promised to help me to get back to my home; I sat on the ground, not able to speak or move, while the people dropped silver and copper coins into my lap. Still, money, money! what did I want of it? I wanted to die. They led me into the town, and when I next came to myself they told me I had slept a long time. Truda has often told me stories of children sent out, into the wild wood, in the deep snow, by their cruel parents; but, certainly, I was worse off than any of them, deserted and helpless as a little child who can scarcely say what its father's name is. The German — he was a Jew, who helped send forward emigrants — tried in vain to make me go over the sea. I would not go, and I stayed as servant in his house for a year; he and his wife, who was a Swabian, were kind to me, but I left them and went to Cologne, where I was sick, and there I took service again in a farm-house, and now here I am. I thought you must have married long ago, Blase, and I wanted to be your servant, but I went first to Truda, who has had trouble, too; her daughter is dead, and we comforted each other as well as we could; she told me that you had taken my going away so much to heart that you were crazy, and then I wanted to care for you —"

"You have cured me, and I know now that I should have died if you hadn't come —"

"But tell me, Blase, what shall I do now?"

"You must go home with me."

"No, no, that won't do."

"You are right; I've thought of another plan that would be better. You used to understand field-work; can you still do it?"

"Yes, indeed, and I wanted to go out to service with Truda for the summer. Ah! I didn't think I should come back to you; and, yet, if I must say it —"

"Well, what would you say?"

"That Truda was right. I came home, and yet I had no home, so I went to Truda, and arrived just in time to comfort her for her daughter's death, and we could cry over each other's troubles. But that didn't give us any thing to eat; instead of that, crying made me a good deal more hungry —"

"Have you had any thing to eat to-day?"

"Oh yes, see; I still have some bread in my bag. You have a thoroughly good heart: I always knew it; but I thought you would have been married long ago. The very evening I parted from you I heard that you were to be betrothed to the daughter of the church-warden of Seebronn."

"Then, why did you come back?"

"I've said to myself a hundred times on the road: you'll only make yourself and him still more unhappy. But still I came on, and I wanted to do you some good, and to work for you, and for your father, too; he meant well by me —"

"Yes, that he did, and he put on mourning for you, and said that you were dead, and no one dared speak of you as alive."

Erdmutha wept aloud on hearing this; but Truda came up, blaming Blase for making the heart of the lonely girl heavier than before, and said that they must put an end to their talk, and Blase must show himself a man, and take some decided measures.

With a cheerful satisfaction in his proposal, which seemed more than the project deserved, Blase now explained:

"I don't believe any one in the place would know you, Erdmutha, especially with that handkerchief on; and you mustn't let any one recognize you. Truda, what was your daughter's name?"

"Regela" (Regina), answered Truda, with a deep sigh.

"Well, did any one in Hollmaringen know her?"

"No, she was never there; my sister adopted her because she had no child of her own. When I look at Erdmutha, I feel as if Regela were still alive; and people said in Lichtenhardt that they looked alike. Why shouldn't they? They were cousins."

"So much the better," said Blase; "Erdmutha, your name is Regela now, and you are Truda's daughter."

"I love her like my own child, and she has been more to me than my own," said Truda, wiping her eyes, and Blase went on:

"All right, I engage you as day-laborers, and you must let my father get used to you, Regela. Take care not to betray yourself in any way till the right time comes, — until I tell you that it will do; we shall find the time at last."

"Yes, every thing is found when we sweep up," said Erdmutha, jestingly, and Truda answered, sadly smiling:

"That's right; if you want to be my Regela you must be merry: no creature on earth was ever merrier."

"I think I can promise that," said Erdmutha, confidently. Blase told the two women that they must walk to Hollmaringen; he did not dare take them in the wagon lest he should betray himself. He whispered to Erdmutha:

"If you will dig a little under the apple-tree by the guidepost, on the side towards the field, you'll find something for yourself."

A peculiar, roguish expression flitted over his face as he bade 'Regela,' aloud, not to take it ill if he was sometimes rough and cross with her; and, as a Hollmaringen man passed just then, he began directly, and repeated in arbitrary tones, the conditions on which he engaged the servants, and left them.

CHAPTER IX.

THE RETURN OF THE VEILED ONE.

F Blase seemed changed by a miracle to his brother-in-law as they drove home together, he seemed not less so to himself, and the whole world with him. Was it possible, was it not a dream, that Erdmutha had come back? He trembled when he said the name to himself, as if he had betrayed his secret, and said "Regela" in a whisper.

The two women walked barefoot along the foot-path by the road-side, carrying their shoes tied on to their bundles; Blase pointed them out with his whip in the distance, and asked his brother-in-law:

"What do you think my father will say to my having hired them?"

"He'll be glad that you've cheered up enough to have the courage to do something of your own accord."

Blase cracked his whip as he drove by the two women, who courtesied silently to him; he went on cracking it again and again on every side; it was the only sign of joy that he could give, and intelligible only to them; Erdmutha understood the hidden music which sounded in the unmelodious noise. She went on silently for hours with Truda, only occasionally complaining over the difficulty she had in walking.

"I have been half over the world," she said, "but now it seems as if my knees would break under me at every step."

She had been through too much that day, to feel her usual strength. Truda was inclined to complain of Blase for not taking them in the wagon, but the arguments of her companion soon silenced her.

As they approached the guidepost by the apple-tree, Erdmutha ran on before Truda, dug up the earth in the place that Blase had indicated, and found a silver ring of the kind that young men give their betrothed brides. She put it on her finger and kissed it, and Truda was the first to wish her joy; she had doubted Blase a little till now, but now she was convinced. Erdmutha told her, with pure joy, how she had once sat there with Blase, and now when she rose to go on she was filled with fresh strength, and felt as if she had wings. But once more she was overcome by sadness, as she looked over the beechen hedge at the black crosses, and remembered that she could no longer throw herself down there: she was a different person and a beggar, walking barefoot to her home. She wanted to put on her shoes before entering the village, but Truda told her that it would not befit a field laborer, and would be set down against her. She hardly looked up as she passed through the street, and turned her head resolutely aside as she passed her parents' house. Lame Claus was sitting, knitting again on the stone seat; he stared at her, and dropped the ball from under his arm; he did not recognize her, but Erdmutha would have been glad if he had done so, for she trembled at the prospect of all the dissimulation before her; she must approach the only people who were left her on earth, without holding out a hand to them, or speaking a word of love.

The mayor's wife bade Truda and her daughter welcome, and gave them something to eat in the entrance hall; they heard Gottfried's loud voice in the sitting-room, as he tried to settle a quarrel between two men.

Blase passed the two women as they were eating from the plates held in their laps, and said:

"God bless the food, Truda, I think your daughter is a bit dainty: tell her to eat, you won't have any thing more till evening; when you've done, you can go with me and help get in the hay."

Erdmutha ate with good appetite, and the mayor's wife gave her high praise afterwards, because she seemed so soon at home in the house, washed up the dishes and put them in their places before any one gave her directions.

Blase stood in the wagon, and Truda and Erdmutha drove with him to the meadow; he found fault with Erdmutha's slowness at her work, and said: "Your name ought to be 'Lahmele' (lazy-bones) not Regela." He played his part better than Erdmutha; indeed, it was an easier one.

The hay was brought in crisp and dry, and then, as two of the mowers had been suddenly taken sick, Erdmutha enjoyed a special triumph; she mowed with Blase and the farm servant, keeping in line with them, and never falling behind. Gottfried, who, as his son-in-law had predicted, was much pleased with Blase's new resolution and energy, allowed the new hand to profit by a portion of this satisfaction, and warned Blase not to be too hard with her. He laughed when his wife said she knew that Blase was not indifferent to Truda's daughter, just because he found so much fault with her; he knew his proud son better. There was no pause or rest through the whole week, not even on Sunday, so hurried were they by the threatening weather, and even while they were eating in the fields not many words were exchanged. The farm-servant said, one day:

"The cattle have the best of it; people look out for their food first, and then see to their own."

"That's all as it should be," said Erdmutha; "if a man takes care of others first, he feels the benefit of it himself: the cows and oxen eat the hay for us, we get it afterwards in milk and butter and meat."

"And the horses?" said Blase.

"They are our poor people: they have to drag the plough and the wagon for us."

"Your tongue doesn't need any whetstone," laughed the servant, and Blase gave Erdmutha a silent nod.

On the second Sunday, Gottfried spoke to her for the first time:

"I heard your voice in church to-day, my girl, above all the others; there's something peculiar about it, I can't tell what."

Erdmutha gazed at him; was it her mother's voice speaking through her to her uncle? How gladly would she have laid aside all disguise, but she dared not, and constantly had to remind herself that this man had worn mourning for her as for one dead; she had already brought him once to the brink of the grave by rousing his passion, and she dared not run the risk again.

That evening, in the twilight, Erdmutha went through the village with Truda, who knew and talked with every one, and she stood by, feeling desolate and cut to the heart as she heard herself called Truda's daughter. Was she disowning her mother? She seemed to herself like a thief, and spoke but little, as she cast stolen glances on the play-grounds of her childhood. Blase had laid a heavy task upon her, but she trusted him, and would endure it. In her old home she stood long by Blase's sister, and could hardly restrain herself from calling her cousin.

Was not all this mummery unnecessary and cruel? But Blase should see that she could obey him without question. The young men and girls walked singing through the village, and Blase's sister told them with delight that it was the first time for years that he had been seen with them. Erdmutha sighed sadly, and again came the question why the heavy lot must fall on her alone. The village watchman rang his bell, and gave notice that next day the harvest would begin, and that, first of all, every man must cut paths through his fields so that his neighbor could get in his grain without injury to others.

The village was soon asleep, for all must be early awake the next morning.

"We ought not to grow fond of anybody," said Erdmutha to Truda, before they went to sleep, "for we see how people live on, when we are away, without ever thinking that we were once with them."

"You can't say that of your Blase."

"No, thank God; but don't speak so loud. Good-night."

Erdmutha was up before any one else in the house, and moved about as silently as a spirit, setting every thing in order, and, for the first time since she had been in the house, Blase surprised her at the well as she was drawing water. She complained to him a little of the pain it gave her to deny her name and former life, but he comforted her, saying it was the only way to win over his father, who had driven her for ever from his heart; if every thing else were atoned for, it would be excessively difficult to make him pardon her for wasting her mother's property; even now he would burst into a violent passion on coming to a field now in the hands of strangers, which ought to have belonged to Erdmutha. Erdmutha just ventured to utter a word against this hard avarice, but Blase laid a heavy hand upon her, and said that he would never remember the careless extravagance of her father, and she must cherish no ill-will against his, but rather respect and honor him. Erdmutha promised willingly, and only begged that she might make herself known to his mother or sister, it lay so heavy on her heart to be able to talk about herself to no one. But Blase insisted that she ought to rest content with his knowing who she was, and feel the need of no one else; and, with the submission of true love, Erdmutha said that she was willing to do penance for having left him, that she belonged to him alone, and would not ask for any thing again until he thought that the right time had come.

The two lovers stood locked in a silent embrace, till the morning star grew pale in the heavens.

CHAPTER X.

THE NEW RUTH.

ARMING brings a constant succession of different kinds of labor, going on in uniform course through the whole year, till in the haying time, and still more at harvest, the work grows into a passion, a feverish excitement; every moment, every strength, and every means are brought into use; the clattering wagon is driven at a gallop along the street, turns towards the field where the wheels roll noiselessly, and then comes back creaking under its load, to hurry out again for the sheaves which are waiting for it ready bound. Even the meal-times, which, at other seasons are scrupulously observed as a period of rest, are not free from hurry in the field, however much the workers are resolved not to yield to it.

It is a beautiful trait of human nature, that the heart beats the more joyfully in the midst of labor, that a kind and cheerful word never falls more refreshingly on the soul, that a mouthful of food never tastes better than during such ceaseless activity, nor do people ever feel more inclined to cordial relations with their fellow-men, even though the ties must soon be broken. All the virtues and joys of life grow up in labor, and the ancient curse is changed to a blessing ; only through labor does a human being become truly a man.

Like the dew which lay fresh and cool on every bush and blade of grass, a feeling of refreshment rested in the hearts of all who went with their sickles towards the fields from Gottfried's house. Blase walked in front with the men, the women coming behind with baskets and jugs in their hands. For a time they went on in silence, then a jest of Truda's set them all laughing ; she said : "When are farmers the strongest ?" No one could tell, and she answered : "Before the harvest, when they can carry all their grain to mill on their backs." This slight impulse only was needed to bring out all the latent merriment of the party. Others joined the group after they had gone a short distance, and the laughs and jokes rang out over the broad fields ripe for the harvest. When Gottfried's laborers came near the field of barley which was first to be cut, the farm-servant began to complain of the neighbor, lame Claus's father, who had made no path for them through his field.

"We'll let daylight in," said Erdmutha, plying her sickle among the ears, and Blase added :

"She's right, it brings a blessing to work first for other people."

Blase could have spoken no words of love more welcome to her than this application of what Erdmutha had once said. Only walking now a little more slowly, they laid open a broad path through the neighbor's field to their own. The women cut the smaller bent stalks which the men left standing between them, as, with their greater strength, they made broad sweeps with their sickles. Erdmutha, who was between Blase and the servant-man, laid down the ears so skilfully and quickly that it seemed as if she wielded a magic sickle; she went in advance of the others, finished her work first, and, raising her sickle above her head, gave a "Hurrah" which echoed far, and was repeated from the neighboring fields. Truda stood upright also, and said: "That's done! as the parson said, when he forgot the Amen." All laughed, as they turned back, and whenever they came to the end of a row the reaping went on the faster, because they all moved together; the work went on as if they were pillaging the field, and the talk between the companions, separated by no barrier, took a fresh start, until it gradually ceased again, and nothing was heard but the whetting of the sickles or an occasional sigh over aching backs.

They laughed at Erdmutha for leaving the stubble standing higher than the others, but she answered:

"If the stalks are not cut too close, the field is half dressed, and bears so much the more next time."

Gottfried, who was passing by unheard, listened to these words, and looked vexed; did they mean to imply a reflection on his parsimony?

They sat down to the morning lunch, which a maid had brought. Truda could not resist making a scornful remark on the badly baked bread: "There are miserable people who spoil God's gifts, by baking bad bread to lie in the stomach like stones."

They were all silent, till Erdmutha, cutting for herself a large bit of bread, said, half-singing:

"Little loaf, little beet must be called;
Little beet must be eaten all up."

Gottfried looked carefully at the slits in the ears in the neighboring cornfield, for there is an old rule that the more breaks there are in the outer husk the higher will be the price of corn. He gave a nod of satisfaction.

A stork flew over the heads of the reapers, and Erdmutha said, leaning back and looking up into the sky:

"I should like to know what the birds think as they look on all the stir among us down here; it must seem to them as it does to us when we look at an ant-hill."

Gottfried went off muttering to himself; he seldom came into the fields, as he was busy with his official business, but left the superintendence of the work to Blase, and the young people were doubly merry when he left them. At noon, came the well-filled basket. They sat on the edge of the field, and Erdmutha was kept busy pouring the new cider into the tin cups, which were passed from hand to hand.

They did not go back to the village through the whole day, and worked diligently till the dew was falling on the fields; only the yellow-hammer was whistling from the fruit-trees, and the starlings were flying home in flocks. The full moon rose red behind the mountains, and, on the way home, Erdmutha said:

"It's always so strange to me that we hear nothing when the moon comes up, she's there before us all at once so silently."

There was a bright activity of mind about the maiden peculiarly her own, and Blase secretly congratulated himself on his good fortune in having her restored to him so wonderfully.

Day after day went by, and the cheerful life continued with the pleasant weather. In the evening, nothing was heard in the village but the cutting of fodder and the sharpening of sickles. Erdmutha helped take care of the cattle, of which double care must now be taken, and was equally active in the kitchen and the sitting-room. Gottfried often looked at her with a friendly glance, and once he even said to her:

" When my Blase is married, you can stay with us as maid-servant: you are a handy girl."

Erdmutha made no answer.

When the time for bringing in the harvest came, Gottfried was constantly in the field, and could always judge correctly, by looking at the gathered sheaves, how many wagons should be taken in order to lose no time.

The girls gathered the ears into bundles for the men to bind; Erdmutha had the truest eye: she never needed to reduce or add to her sheaves, which lay in even rows as if they had been exactly measured. She looked beautiful, as she raised the grain in both arms, so that the ears waved high above her head. Her head was always covered; she wore a tight-fitting red jacket, buttoned closely to the neck, which yielded easily to the movements of her graceful figure. She was not unobserved by old Gottfried, who, in spite of his age, easily lifted the sheaves upon the wagons; it was only in raising them from the ground that he showed any fatigue, for after the sheaf was once raised, he carried it easily. But when Blase took up the bundles, it seemed as if they rose of their own accord before him.

This life in the fields was worth living. It seemed as if the countless wagons sprang out of the ground; the girls glowed with exercise, the young men cracked their whips; bands were passed from hand to hand, people called out to each other as they drove in and out of the village, and praised, giving thanks to God, the abundance of the harvest, as they drank each other's health.

In such a season, all trouble and care are forgotten for a time, and men are like brothers in their mother's lap.

The possessor of wide lands and the day laborer who earns only a mean pittance from them are, for a while, on a level, for labor makes all equal; and the food eaten on the ground and the draught from the common cup become a communion feast, sacred in and by itself. Old Gottfried did a kind turn to many of his workmen ; he sat with them, talked to them, and forgot his pride. He even jested with Truda about old times when they were both young, and Truda was often on the point of telling him all, but she did not wish to forestall Blase, whom she often pressed in the evening to bring this dangerous game to an end, now while Gottfried was in a yielding mood of good-natured satisfaction ; but Blase was much opposed to causing such an excitement in the midst of the harvest, and so she had to wait patiently.

Blase was exactly like a person, who, with violent exertion has broken open a door, and then stands irresolute, not knowing what to do next. He chose to wait quietly, and he was helped to do it by his farmer's habit of waiting without hurry or excitement for things to grow and ripen.

There came rainy days, when they threshed in the barns, with the poultry clucking about them, and stealing many a kernel of grain. Blase always threshed in the same party with Erdmutha. Then came days and nights of anxiety, when they heard of hail-storms in the lowlands, and a drizzling rain fell constantly, increasing only now and then to a hard shower. There was much grain cut which had not been brought in, and fear was felt that it would sprout ; and even when the sun came out again that it would not dry as easily as what was standing. Gottfried went about grumbling, and Blase was anxious ; Erdmutha tried to cheer him by jests, but he reproved her for it, and cut her to the heart by saying: " It seems that you don't know how bad it is to have every thing going to rack and ruin out-doors." Did Blase think she was extravagant, and must she always suffer for having come of a ruined family? She would not bear it, she would rather give up all once more.

Beautiful is a summer morning after rainy days ; a light, warm mist rises from the thoroughly soaked ground ; the mountains, long hidden, rise in the blue air, the birds sing joyously, the sun shows anew his never-failing power, and men breathe freely again.

Trouble vanished, the cheerful, active labor went on again, and it appeared that the anxiety had been unnecessary. Once when Erdmutha was helping Blase to bind the sheaves, apart from the others, she said:

"I can't keep any thing back long; I must tell you, that I'm angry with you still about what you said to me at the threshing."

" I know it, but you ought not to take it ill, you must be a little more considerate ; you're a bit thoughtless, you can't help it — you are used — "

" I'm not used to be found fault with so. I won't deny that I don't take enough care upon myself, I'm willing to grant that, but you take too much ; don't you see now things are not so bad ? I'll willingly learn of you, but you must learn of me too, you may be sure, you need to."

"Give me another armful, this band will hold it," said Blase, and peace was made. As they went on working silently, Blase, at first, tried to deny the truth of Erdmutha's admonition, but he was too honest not to see that she was right, and it was a pleasure to him to acknowledge it.

After the rainy days, the activity and cheerfulness in the field were redoubled. Even the usually stern Gottfried told his wife that they had never had so merry a summer, and charged her to spare nothing at the harvest feast.

With the completion of the harvest, the pressure of work did not cease. New plantings had to be made in the just cleared fields. Men and women busied themselves in various kinds of work: some pulled the hemp, beat out the seed, spread and soaked it in the pond, while others stored the grain, got in the potatoes and turnips, and attended to the hundred kinds of less laborious work which belong to a large farm. Blase had most to do with the planting, and came home weary, for sowing is one of the hardest kinds of work, — to carry from one to two bushels of seed before one, and to move with measured steps and in a straight line through ground so heavy that one can scarcely lift his feet, and at the same time to cast the seed in equal handfuls — Blase was asleep soon after he came home, and there was no telling when the concealment about Erdmutha was to end.

The leaves on the trees were beginning to turn, cloud-wreaths hung over the mountains, and a light autumn mist lay upon the fields, when, one day, Gottfried came with a strange gentleman to the harvesters in the field where they were reaping the late oats on the Hubelberg. Erdmutha was chosen, by her companions' wish, to "catch him in the wisp," according to the old custom. She took a handful of ears, wound them about the stranger's arm, laid her sickle on his shoulder, and said:

"With the reapers I go
To the end of the row;
And a blessing is said
When the man's pledge is paid."

"If you catch me in the wisp, you'll get something for it," said Gottfried, with unusual affability. As Erdmutha laid her hand on his shoulder, a thrill ran through him; did he feel something of their blood-relationship? He was, at any rate, so embarrassed that he could give the county-commissioner — for such was the stranger — only a confused statement of the way in which the land now cut up into small parcels might, by exchange, &c., be laid out so as to give large fields to the different owners.

That evening the harvest-supper was held, and Gottfried told Blase that he should pay the outside hands, and dismiss them; but Blase objected that the people from Lichtenhardt ought to be retained.

"Have you got a fancy for the girl into your head?" asked his father.

"I give you my word of honor, I care nothing about Truda's daughter," answered Blase, and his father yielded readily to his wish, rejoiced to have his son's clouded spirits restored to such cheerful brightness.

CHAPTER XI.

CATCHING A BRIDE AND ALL-SOULS' DAY.

HY did Blase still put off revealing the secret? He was still afraid, for he knew the iron hardness of his father, and had hoped for some favorable opportunity which did not present itself; and, while matters were going on thus, a new thought arose within him.

Men often pride themselves on events and plans which have grown up gradually with the course of time, and they convince themselves and others that all has come about exactly according to their original idea. In this way, Blase now told himself that he had projected this long concealment in order to try and to strengthen Erdmutha's prudence and frugality; for deep and true as was his love for Erdmutha, he had enough of Gottfried's character in him to fear wanton extravagance, or even simple carelessness, as the worst of evils; and no one could tell how much of the habits of her father's house still clung to Erdmutha.

Erdmutha had never begged him to make known the secret since the morning before the harvest, but had waited in silence and patience. Truda was so much the more urgent; she pointed out the danger of some one's coming from Lichtenhardt, who would say that her daughter was dead; she painted her trials and Erdmutha's in the most vivid colors, and would see no reason for delay. For some weeks the anxiety, lest the secret, which had been long so strangely kept, should come out through some outside channel, had been growing upon them; lame Claus must have half recognized Erdmutha, for he often watched her, hurried after her on his crutches, and asked her if she knew nothing of Erdmutha; she answered him sharply, but wept over it in secret. The unfortunate know each other, only Claus had recognized her, and now she had to keep him at a distance and hide from him, but he did not cease to follow her till Truda begged him to leave her child in peace.

The harvest supper passed off merrily. After Gottfried had paid off the extra hands for their work up to that time, and had made a special present to Erdmutha as the "Wisptaker," Truda went to Blase with renewed urgency, but he sought out Erdmutha, who was slicing cabbage in the cellar, and asked her what she had done with her money.

"I've given it to Truda, except two florins," she replied, and Blase broke out into angry fault-finding with extravagance and bad habits. Erdmutha let him storm, then she declared to him that she did not care whether she were poor or rich, and cared for wealth only that she might do good to others without spending all she had; if she could not do that, and if Blase did not trust her prudence, she would rather leave the house that hour, and wander out into the wide world without telling any one who she was. Then came a fresh and thorough discussion of the value which each put upon money, and Blase, who had meant to convert Erdmutha, was obliged to confess that, with the anxiety and care which constantly reigned in his father's house, a man did not really possess property, but was possessed by it, and that a day-laborer was better off than a rich man who always had a gold key tied to his heart. Blase well understood this last turn, and only begged Erdmutha not to let his father see that they held different opinions. Erdmutha promised joyfully, and appeased him at last, completely, by saying:

"I'll just confess now that I have my money still, and only gave Truda two florins; I told you just the contrary because you asked me so distrustfully; you must believe in me, unquestioned, as I do in you: I think I've proved that I trust you."

"Yes, and now all's well, and on All-Souls' Day every thing will come out right; I've taken the precaution to tell my sister, and you shall go to her this evening. Matters are going on, — be prepared."

In her father's old house, Erdmutha found herself for the first time recognized and at home, and Blase's sister gave her the highest praise that could come from one of Gottfried's family, in saying:

"You are a greater treasure to my brother than double or treble your old property would be."

Next day, Erdmutha was beating hemp at the pond with many other women, when Blase came up and gladly paid the usual fine which is exacted from a man who finds women busy at this work. A number of boys were near by, braiding whip-lashes, and skipping stones on the pond; Blase entered into the sport as if he were still a child, and they were all astonished and delighted at his skill. Made bold by his happy secret, and with a rash desire to betray it, he cried:

"I played that many years ago with Erdmutha; she danced on the water a long time, but at last she plumped under."

No one but Erdmutha and his sister understood him; the others looked at each other in astonishment, and their glances said: People think he's cured, but he evidently isn't right in his mind.

A quiet, sunless day dawned; the sky was pale gray, and the earth too, for a hoar-frost lay on grass and clod, and on the heads of the winter grain. Within that beechen hedge outside of the village burned hundreds of lights on the black crosses, no breath of wind blew, and the lights burned steadily; on one cross there flamed two tapers, and under them stood the name: Erdmutha. The living moved about among the graves of the departed, not speaking a word aloud, only murmuring low prayers; they looked themselves like wandering spirits, and many a one must have thought that the next year might find him lying under the frosty ground with a light burning over his head. Gottfried wandered here and there, he had graves of parents and children and sister here. As he approached the last, there lay stretched upon it a woman's form shaken by violent sobs; was it not Truda's daughter, bareheaded for the first time?

"What's the matter with you? What is this grave to you?" asked Gottfried. Did the face of the dead rise from the earth? With white lips, Gottfried asked again:

"You are —?"

"Yes, I am Erdmutha, your sister's —"

Without uttering a sound Gottfried sank down: people hurried to the spot and he was borne away insensible, — a corpse carried out of the church-yard.

Erdmutha followed, weeping; Blase and his sister came to meet her, and saw with terror what had happened. Blase had intended to tell his father every thing that day in the church-yard, thinking that only in that way could he soften him; the plan was for Erdmutha to work in the potato-field by the guidepost, and to wait until she was summoned, but she could not bear it; she hurried to the graveyard before the time, and so brought about the results that we have described.

In the midst of the lamentations over Gottfried, whom every one now praised, people became aware that she, who had passed for Truda's daughter, was Cyprian's Erdmutha, who was almost forgotten; they would not believe that she had been in the village all through the summer, it seemed so impossible. The curious and sympathetic groups vibrated between Gottfried's house and Cyprian's, to which her cousin had taken Erdmutha and put her into a quiet room by herself.

After an hour, during which Erdmutha experienced the greatest suffering of her life, her cousin came to her, saying that her father had been restored to life, but that he could not yet speak. Soon afterwards, came Blase with the news that his father had spoken, but only to say that he must be about to die, because his sister had appeared to him. Erdmutha was inconsolable because she could not stir out of the house, nor do any thing to cure the great sorrow which she had brought upon the family; but Blase comforted her, saying:

"We have done wrong, I especially; it was a sin to hold you back so long. Don't lay any blame upon yourself, and nobody else shall blame you."

His sister went back to her father's house, and the

mayor's wife soon came in her place, embraced Erdmutha tenderly, and showed the kindness of her heart, as she blamed her for not making herself known long before; she could not forgive herself for having treated her as a common servant.

The first person who recovered her cheerfulness, looked upon Gottfried's attack as over and rejoiced in the importance of its probable consequences, was Truda, who kept repeating that her heart was as light as if a heavy burden had been lifted from it. Lame Claus sat on the stone bench in front of his house, lauding his own sharpness in having been the only person to recognize Erdmutha. He complained bitterly that no one was ready to acknowledge how much brighter he was than any one else in the village; but when the first fright was over, they jested and laughed at him about his wisdom. Erdmutha, however, sent for him first of all, and shook hands with him, so that he had his reward.

It was difficult to make old Gottfried understand that he had seen the living Erdmutha; he constantly shook his head, but at last he seemed to grasp the idea, for he said:

"I could have sooner believed that the dead would rise, than that she'd come back from America."

He desired to see Erdmutha, but they would not allow it till the next day, when he ordered the old wedding-dress to be brought, that she might come to him in it. The whole village assembled to see Erdmutha pass to her uncle's house, wearing her mother's wedding-dress and the necklace, which she had always faithfully kept. She kissed the trembling hand of Gottfried, who could not speak for a long time, but said at last, pointing to the garnet necklace with the Swedish ducats:

"Who gave you that?"

"My father."

"Have you saved any thing else of your mother's property?"

"No."

Gottfried closed his eyes, and was silent; Blase stepped forward, saying:

"She needs nothing else; she has father and mother still living, nothing more is wanting—"

"Except a husband," Truda added.

"And that she has too," Blase went on: "that ring on her hand I gave her; that is risen from the grave also."

He told them how he had buried the ring; Gottfried nodded silently. . . .

As soon as the license could be obtained before Lent, the marriage of Blase and Erdmutha was celebrated; and Gottfried, who had to stay much at home, was happiest when Erdmutha was with him: he said little, but her presence gave him pleasure.

In the spring, the house was newly fitted up, and at least one of the iron gratings taken down; Gottfried agreed with Erdmutha that he could look out on the street better without it.

A letter to Gottfried from Cyprian in the New World completed the atonement during the next summer. Cyprian mourned bitterly for his lost child, declared himself innocent, standing now face to face with death, as he often repeated. He must have been thoroughly broken down, for he begged Gottfried's forgiveness for all the injustice he had done him, and spoke constantly of his approaching death. Gottfried himself added a few words to the letter, in which Erdmutha related all that had happened; but they never knew whether the letter reached Cyprian before his death.

By the guidepost under the apple-tree, Blase placed a stone seat, and had the name of Erdmutha carved upon it; and the laughing and singing of merry young people were always to be heard there on Sunday afternoons in summer.

Cambridge: Press of John Wilson and Son.

www.ingramcontent.com/pod-product-compliance
Lightning Source LLC
LaVergne TN
LVHW010146110826
845151LV00002B/441

* 9 7 8 1 4 2 5 5 3 8 3 0 9 *